Carol Wensby-Scott was born and educated in Brighton, Sussex. Before becoming a full-time writer she ran an antiquarian bookshop. Her first novel, *Proud Conquest*, was published in 1979 and she then began work on her trilogy about the Percy family, at the same time moving to Northumberland, the home of the Percys.

By Carol Wensby-Scott

The Percy trilogy
LION OF ALNWICK
LION DORMANT
LION INVINCIBLE

★

PROUD CONQUEST
COAL BARON

CAROL WENSBY-SCOTT

Lion Dormant

Volume two of the Percy trilogy

Futura

A Futura Book

First published in Great Britain in 1983
by Michael Joseph Ltd

This edition published in 1983
by Futura Publications, a Division of
Macdonald & Co (Publishers) Ltd
London & Sydney
Reprinted 1989

ISBN 0 7088 2382 3

Reproduced, printed and bound in Great Britain by
Hazell Watson & Viney Limited
Member of BPCC plc
Aylesbury, Bucks, England

Futura Publications
A Division of
Macdonald & Co (Publishers) Ltd
66–73 Shoe Lane
London EC4P 4AB
A member of Maxwell Pergamon Publishing Corporation plc

For the people of Alnham, Scrainwood, Unthank and Prendwick with my thanks for their kindness and unfailing sources of inspiration.

PERCY, NEVILLE AND MORTIMER

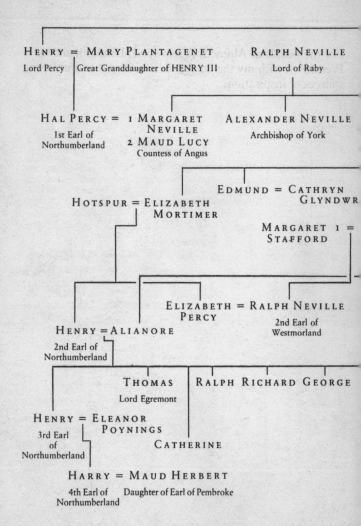

HENRY = **MARY PLANTAGENET**
Lord Percy | Great Granddaughter of HENRY III

RALPH NEVILLE
Lord of Raby

HAL PERCY = **1 MARGARET NEVILLE**
1st Earl of Northumberland | **2 MAUD LUCY** Countess of Angus

ALEXANDER NEVILLE
Archbishop of York

EDMUND = **CATHRYN GLYNDWR**

HOTSPUR = **ELIZABETH MORTIMER**

MARGARET 1 = **STAFFORD**

ELIZABETH PERCY = **RALPH NEVILLE**
2nd Earl of Westmorland

HENRY = **ALIANORE**
2nd Earl of Northumberland

THOMAS
Lord Egremont

RALPH RICHARD GEORGE

HENRY = **ELEANOR POYNINGS**
3rd Earl of Northumberland

CATHERINE

HARRY = **MAUD HERBERT**
4th Earl of Northumberland | Daughter of Earl of Pembroke

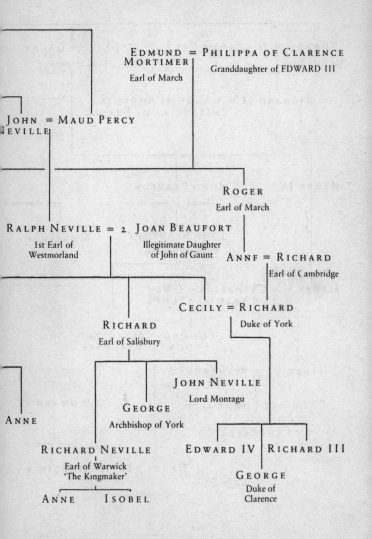

EDMUND = PHILIPPA OF CLARENCE
MORTIMER   Granddaughter of EDWARD III
Earl of March

JOHN = MAUD PERCY
NEVILLE

ROGER
Earl of March

RALPH NEVILLE = 2 JOAN BEAUFORT
1st Earl of   Illegitimate Daughter
Westmorland   of John of Gaunt

ANNE = RICHARD
Earl of Cambridge

CECILY = RICHARD
Duke of York

RICHARD
Earl of Salisbury

JOHN NEVILLE
Lord Montagu

GEORGE
Archbishop of York

ANNE

RICHARD NEVILLE
Earl of Warwick
'The Kingmaker'

EDWARD IV   RICHARD III

GEORGE
Duke of
Clarence

ANNE   ISOBEL

LANCASTER ·AND YORK·

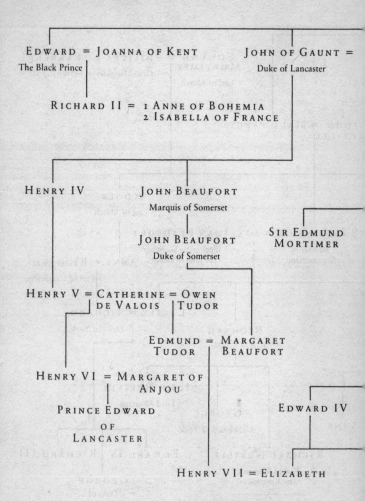

EDWARD = JOANNA OF KENT
The Black Prince

JOHN OF GAUNT =
Duke of Lancaster

RICHARD II = 1 ANNE OF BOHEMIA
2 ISABELLA OF FRANCE

HENRY IV

JOHN BEAUFORT
Marquis of Somerset

SIR EDMUND
MORTIMER

JOHN BEAUFORT
Duke of Somerset

HENRY V = CATHERINE = OWEN
DE VALOIS   TUDOR

EDMUND = MARGARET
TUDOR   BEAUFORT

HENRY VI = MARGARET OF
ANJOU

PRINCE EDWARD
OF
LANCASTER

EDWARD IV

HENRY VII = ELIZABETH

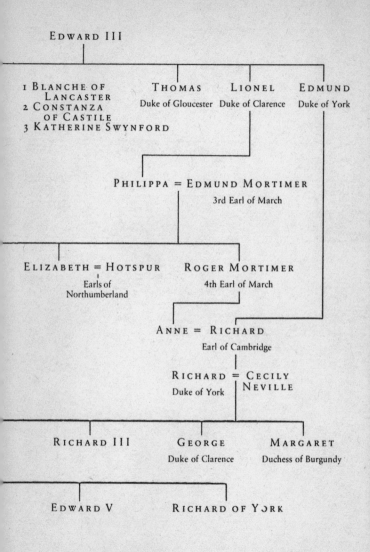

BLACK PRINCE		LIONEL	JOHN OF GAUNT	Thomas

PHILIPPA = EDMUND MORTIMER

ELIZABETH =	ROGER MORTIMER

ANNE MORTIMER

RICHARD = Cicely

EDWARD IV	GEORGE	MARGARET

RICHARD OF YORK

1414–1425

I saw the rose whanne I was nigh
Was greater waxen and more high
Fresshe, rody and faire of hewe
Of colour ever ilyche newe.

— Chaucer

Ralph Neville, Earl of Westmorland and tentative master of the north, regarded his wife with carefully veiled antagonism and perhaps if he were honest, even a little distaste. The stain of sweat shadowing her armpits dilated his fastidious nostrils. And her great belly, straining at the pink silk gown like a huge pustule about to burst. How many children was it now that she had borne him? He thought that perhaps this was the tenth. It was hard to believe that once she had been beautiful, as pink and fresh as a young rose, the Lancastrian rose that he'd so coveted: soft and round and biddable. He almost smiled. That was error. There had never been anything remotely biddable about Joan. She always had her way, in the beginning because he had cared for her, in later years through a tenacious persistence that would have worn down a stone. Now she was fat and coarse and hard. His one consolation was her influence. She was still close kin to the young king.

Joan said again, 'I cannot see your objection, Ralph. Alianore is our eldest daughter and without a husband since that fool Despenser had the discourtesy to die on us. Jesu, man, she's still virgin. Richard Despenser was only ten. What better, then, than she wed the exiled Percy? He's young and bound to be grateful.'

Neville winced. He could not in all his wildest dreams imagine a Percy being grateful. The very name was anathema to him, dragging up a host of forgotten fears and jealousies. 'You think he will be grateful to the man who was responsible for his exile, to the man who killed his grandfather?'

Joan waved a plump hand, dismissing the blood and carnage of years in a careless gesture. 'That's past. Forgotten,' she said. 'It's now that counts and I tell you that King Henry is set on a policy of internal peace and restoration. He's released Edmund Mortimer. Scrope has his lands back and Mowbray is Earl Marshal again.'

'The least Henry could do to compensate for the hacking off of his brother's head without trial,' Neville commented dryly.

Joan's small blue eyes narrowed at the criticism. 'You're not exactly without blame in that quarter yourself, my lord. Have you forgotten that it was you who tricked Archbishop Scrope into surrender and talked him all the way to the block?'

Neville did not reply. He had not forgotten, though the memories were not ones he cared to recall: the one flaw in the careful well-laid pattern of his life, the stain on the rich and otherwise perfect tapestry. He was a man who preferred cunning and guile to violence and in the long term he found it served him better. All his wealth and power had been accumulated in such a way; sound and advantageous marriages for himself and his sons, an eye always to the main chance, his finger on the pulse of events, scenting change and innovation like a well-trained hound. It had kept him on the winning side for thirty years and if his honour had become a little tarnished on the way, well, what of it? A man could not plough a field without the odd worm being crushed beneath his heel. Yet somehow today the thought did not soothe his conscience as well as it had always done. Scrope, Northumberland, his son Harry Hotspur: the memories sprang up again like persistent weeds. He had not forgotten. At the back of his devious and accomplished mind every detail was still bright and memorable, down to that last day when he had faced the man he had feared all his life on Bramham Moor. An old, blind man, his conscience reminded him. How had he thought that there was triumph in that?

'There's no point in raking all that up again,' Joan said, anxious lest he fall into one of those cold steely silences from which even her acid tongue could not prise him. 'As I said, it's past now and I might remind you that we've much at stake in Northumberland. Land, money, years of influence and effort, all lost if the Percy is reinstated and allies himself elsewhere. If we want to salvage any of it we must bind him to us. I might also remind you that you are not so well loved that some other will not leap at the chance to make his daughter Countess of Northumberland. For heaven's sake, Ralph. You're making too much of it. Your own mother was a Percy.'

Neville smiled. Could she have said anything worse to turn him against the match? The memory of that drab, witless, ineffectual woman only added to his hatred.

Joan came and stood close to him and he smelt the strange dry smell of her perfumed and unwashed flesh. 'I could convince Henry to make it a condition of his release,' she said persuasively. 'Marriage to Alianore and perhaps a year in our wardship before he entered into full possession of his lands. It would give us a little time, a breathing space.'

Neville stared blankly from the high window. It was the thought of King Henry that swayed him more than his wife's persistent argument. Henry was young, devout and suffering from that most fearful of diseases, an uneasy conscience. It was not so long ago that his father Bolingbroke had been branded usurper. The epithet clung as closely to him, and his veneration of the murdered King Richard's tomb was as unhealthy as this orgy of reconciliation. Mortimer, Scrope, Mowbray and now Percy – all the rats let out of their traps. Joan was right. If and when Henry brought the Percy out of Scotland, where would he be with his share of Northumberland's sequestered lands and those which he had wheedled, bribed and sometimes flagrantly stolen since? Yet if he turned the stone, only God knew what manner of unspeakable filth would crawl out. And Alianore. He wished it did not have to be Alianore. He looked across the pleasance to where his plethora of sons and daughters romped and shrieked and terrorised their nurses and preceptors. All fair and rosy, all Beaufort, all Joan. Except Alianore. She was purely Neville, tall and dark. His first-born child by Joan, conceived and raised in what he had thought of then as love, before disillusionment had finally hardened into open dislike, before she had deluged him

3

with pale plump replicas of herself. He looked down into her pink, bovine face. Lusty breeders both of them. He had heard it said: '*the Neville bull serving the Beaufort cow.*' Not that he could complain. He had used his children well to increase his wealth and standing. Betrothed at birth, married at puberty, they had bound him to every major family in England – except one. Joan smiled at him and the smile touched the dark and dishonourable little part of him that only she knew was there. He thought of all his lands, his wealth, amassed at a terrifying pace, built on the fall of countless dead and disinherited men. He thought of Northumberland, of his complete and utter control of the Marches, of the Percy manors of Cockermouth and Langley whose revenues had somehow found their way into his pocket, of the jewels and ornament that he had appropriated and a large part of which adorned his wife's quivering bulk at this moment. He thought of the old man, those golden tiercel eyes, that proud glorious head upraised to meet his descending sword. He shivered and said bleakly, 'I only hope, madam, you know what manner of mischief you have begun.'

Scotland

Hal watched the white falcon sweep in wide lazy circles above the meadow, drifting effortlessly on the wind then rising sharply on a current of air to a vantage point high in the clear April sky. She waited on, motionless except for an imperceptible trembling of her wings. Then her round golden eye caught a streak of movement, her ears the soft panic-stricken beating of wings. She stiffened, the bells on her legs tinkling softly as she flexed her talons. She dropped like a stone, her wings arched above her back, skimming the spiked hawthorn bushes and the flattened grass till the spread claws were within inches of her quarry. Then the vicious talons sank like knives into the soft feathered back and her screech of triumph drowned its pitiful cry. Abruptly, she soared skywards again over the pale upturned face of the man below her. She circled once, then dropped obediently to the whine of the lure calling her home.

The falcon alighted in a rush of air on Hal's outstretched wrist and gulped greedily at the raw and pungent meat. He smiled and stroked her ruffled breast, murmuring soft praise before he slipped the velvet hood over her sleek and vicious head. They had much in common, enjoying a similar freedom; free to come and go as long as it suited their keepers. But the leash only extended so far. They always came back to the lure. For him at least there was nowhere else to go.

He turned and rode his horse toward the tall, still leafless, trees that edged the stream. It was a privilege, to ride alone without the accompanying drum of hoofbeats at his back, to set his own pace and course, to lead instead of follow. It was only a pretence of freedom. Like the falcon he would have to go back.

He urged the ancient horse to a gallop. The mare was long past her best, like everything else he owned. Serviceable enough to maintain respectability but shabby enough to remind him of who and what he was. Sometimes he needed reminding. It was easy enough to sink into obscurity here, to become another of the faceless forgotten knights who waited for a ransom that never came. For the first few years he had made a ritual of it. When he rose in the morning, before he slept at night. He had said the words aloud: 'I am Henry Percy, Earl of Northumberland. I am Henry Percy, Earl of Northumberland.' He had been a child then and had only realised the futility of it when he became a man. He was Henry Percy, prisoner and outlaw, lord of nothing save his own bitterness and loneliness. He had almost accepted it now. Only on days like this did he feel the real pain of it.

The old horse began to flag as it struck the base of the hill and Hal eased the bit from its mouth and spoke to it softly. He had discovered long ago that with horseflesh, his voice worked better than his spurs. On the summit he dismounted and turned the tired horse loose to crop the wind-burnt grass. The wind was colder here and tore relentlessly at his hair, numbing his face and hands. But he could see for miles, clear across into England. It was the reason he had come. It was less than half a day's ride to Northumberland. He could see the dark slick of the Tweed where it emerged from the black impenetrable wall of Ettrick Forest and wound across the valley floor toward the dark rounded cones of the Cheviots. He knew all of their names, the familiar names of his childhood: Hedgehope, Yeavering Bell, Comb Fell and the Shill, the high dominating peak of the Cheviot sloping down to Homildon Hill where his father and grandfather had given the Douglas' the thrashing of their lives – a long time ago, before Bolingbroke had slain his father on Shrewsbury field and torn his shattered body from its grave to butcher and dishonour it; before his grandfather had been slaughtered like a dog on Bramham Moor. It was strange that he had so few memories of his father. The magical name of Hotspur had become so clouded with legend that it was hard to remember the reality of the man. He could recall the clear grey eyes and the dark tousled hair and ridiculously, the hard lean hands that had sometimes unknowingly gripped him with such incredible strength that he had cried out. So little to know of a man that half England had adored and still mourned. He accepted that. Hotspur had always belonged to the people. He was content to let him go. It was the old man's image that had stayed fresh and clear all these years. The tall cadaverous body crowned by the mane of silver-gilt hair; at nearly seventy he had been a sight to turn men's eyes. Kings had feared him, and with good cause. He had broken one and made another with ease. It was that which had brought him down in the end. Too much power, too much fear and envy set against him. But even then they'd had to wait till he was an old blind man with none but a small boy by him. He'd given them a run, though, even to that last day when he had ridden down into England for the last time. It had been hard to forgive him for that, for leaving him alone, even though it had been done for his sake. His grandfather had known that there would be no forgiveness for Hal whilst he lived. It was the last time he had ever cried. He had been twelve years old then.

It was colder still now with the sun gone and the wind sharpening from the east, but still he sat motionless and staring at the distant shadow of Northumberland. It seemed so close. He could have reached Alnwick by nightfall. The temptation passed as it always did. There was nothing for him there except a price on his head. He would only exchange one prison for another.

Stiffly he rose and called the horse from its grazing. He threw one last useless look toward England and fought harder than he ever had against the crushing weight of despair that threatened to overwhelm him. It was a long ride back with nothing but emptiness at the end of it.

In the great hall at Dalkeith less than fifty men sat beneath the dark hammer-beamed roof, though the vast chamber could have housed ten times that number with ease. But then Robert Stewart, Duke of Albany and Regent of Scotland, was not famed for his hospitality. His table was reputedly poor and his temper worse. He encouraged neither hangers-on nor courtiers and he let it be well known that any who sat beneath his roof did so for one reason only – because they were or could be of use to Robert Stewart.

Only a few men looked up as Hal entered. Albany was one, his mouth pursed in quiet speculation. The Earl of Douglas was another, his one eye narrowing at the sight of him and his hand instinctively straying to the eye-patch that covered the red raw socket that was his legacy from Homildon Hill. He never forgot that he owed the loss of it to a Percy. Albany continued to watch him, and the old man felt a twinge of envy at the boy's fair good looks. Even the sight made his bones creak. Growing old was the curse of all men yet the Percys seemed to cheat the years better than most. Albany had known Hal's father well, his grandfather even better. Till the day he died Northumberland had not looked a day past fifty and the boy was enough like him to take Albany back thirty years. He had the same sharp arrogance of bone, the same remarkable silver-gilt hair. But there the resemblance ended. Northumberland had had a glitter and malice about him that had kept men in dread long after there was cause. He doubted if the boy would ever match that. Involuntarily his mouth tightened. He'd hated the old man even though he had sheltered him when Bolingbroke hounded him out of England. That had been for Scotland's sake. One always gave succour to the enemy's enemy and besides, it would have more than pleased him a little to see the old fox humbled. Not that he'd been gratified in that. Half blind and penniless, Northumberland had still walked like a king.

He drank sparingly of the pale Rhenish that had lain in his

cellar six months too long and was sour in consequence. He counted up the years of his fruitless stewardship. It was eight years since Northumberland had been slain and for three years before that, off and on, he'd sheltered the two of them. And not a penny piece for his trouble in all that time. Albany gnawed at his lower lip. He could not let Hal go for all that. Dead weight he might be now but fortunes changed, men rose and fell with the unpredictability of the wind. And besides, Percy was all he had to bargain with for the release of his own son Murdac still languishing in the Tower since the Scots' defeat at Homildon. And then there was Scotland's own king, James, England's hostage for the past nine years. Not that he'd ever exerted himself over Jamie's release. He'd grown too used to the power of kingship to give it up to a raw boy who'd not laid eyes on Scotland since he was eleven years old. He smiled unpleasantly to himself. No, he'd not fret overmuch if Jamie was held in ward for a few more years. But Hal Percy? Again Albany's pale eyes sought him out. He prided himself on being a good judge of men, especially young ones. Youth was always so predictable, so transparent – but not this one. Hal Percy was a hard man to know, an even harder one to like. He said little and smiled less and of late he'd been particularly out of temper, picking quarrels where there were none. It was hard to judge a beast when it was caged. Albany thought that perhaps he was like the Rhenish, sour and bitter for lying idle too long. Then he thought musingly on the Englishman who had taken an hour of his time that morning. A bargain on the surface: his son Murdac and Berwick in return for this sour young man's freedom and five thousand men to help him win it. That had galled him a little. He would have preferred something sounder and above board. It was not the straight, uncomplicated exchange he had hoped for when the usurper Bolingbroke had died. There had been much talk of pardons and reconciliations then. The new king Henry of Monmouth suffered from conscience, it seemed. No man who'd suffered because of his father would suffer because of him. All the debts were to be paid, all the grievances redressed. Noble sentiments but hardly practical, Albany thought cynically. But then conscience did strange things to men. Fortunately, he had never suffered from it himself. No word had come regarding Hal Percy though King Henry, it seemed, had been foolish enough to release Edmund Mortimer. His visitor today had endorsed his cynical view of Henry's leniency. How typical of the English. An overmighty land full of overmighty subjects. King Henry must be touched if he thought that forgiveness was the way to the hearts of men like that. Albany thought again of how this new discontent might be of use to him. It was a risk, a gamble, but then what did he have to lose? His worthless and cumbersome hostage and a few thousand common men, for any troops he did supply to the English would be of the lowest and most dispensable kind. Perhaps not so much of a gamble after all. Little to lose and Murdac and Berwick to gain. The only question now was whether Hal Percy himself had the stomach for it. Albany wiped his mouth delicately on a linen square. He supposed there was nothing else for it but to ask him.

Albany did not look up immediately when Hal entered his private chamber; neither did he bid him be seated. Hal watched him as he continued to set the rolls of parchment in order on the ornate and polished desk – a gift from the king of France as Albany had told him a hundred times. The Regent was always inordinately pleased at that which cost him nothing. He was a small man, thin to the point of emaciation though the slack skin at his throat suggested that he had carried more flesh in his youth. His grey hair was combed flat and sleek to his cheeks. His eyes were pale as ice and held as little warmth. He raised them now, smiling the little predatory smile that showed his broken and discoloured teeth.

'Well then.' He had a soft, deceptive voice like the purr of a cat. 'Good news – perhaps. If you have the nerve for it.' Albany tilted his chair back and regarded Hal down the length of his nose. 'No doubt you are aware that I had a visitor today. You might even have seen him if you had not preferred to cavort in fields and hayricks – without my consent, I might add.'

'I had Douglas' consent,' Hal answered defiantly.

'The Lord Douglas is not your keeper. I am,' Albany snapped. Then he smiled again with that effortless change of face that had broken the nerve of better men than Hal. 'But that is by the by,' he

9

went on amiably. 'It is of our visitor that we were speaking. Sir Thomas Grey of Heton. Heton is in Northumberland in case you had forgotten,' he added mockingly.

'I had not forgotten,' Hal's voice was as expressionless as his face. He had not forgotten Tom Grey either. He had been his father's squire and no more than eighteen when Hal had last seen him. 'What did he want?'

'You.' Albany rose and paced a step or two behind the monstrous desk. 'It seems that the English, true to form, are not too happy with their new king. Some are seeking a change.' He halted in his pacing and stared hard at Hal. 'Namely your cousin, Edmund Mortimer, Earl of March.'

He smiled as he saw the colour drain from Hal's face. 'Why so shocked, my dear Hal? Was it not what your father and grand-father strove for in the end, to replace Bolingbroke with Edmund Mortimer's father? Are you not half a Mortimer yourself?' He turned away and poured two grudging measures of the special Burgundy he kept for himself. 'By the way,' he asked over his shoulder, 'is your mother still alive?'

'Yes. She is still alive.' Hal had not heard from her in ten years but he knew she was still alive. Women like Elizabeth Mortimer did not die easily.

He swallowed hard to ease the dryness of his throat, glad of the respite from Albany's probing stare. Whatever he had expected it was not this. Rebellion; the old cause which had already cost his father and grandfather their lives. It was the very reason he was here at all. 'I thought Edmund Mortimer was confined at Wind-sor,' he said at last.

'He was,' Albany handed him the half-full cup of wine. 'It seems that your King Henry is full of good intentions. A new broom sweeps clean, as they say. Unfortunately, his largesse of mercy does not extend quite so far as yourself. Wisely, he thinks to keep you well out of harm's way.' He paused and his gaze rested measuringly on Hal's face. 'So there is your choice. Take what is yours by force; or wait, bearing in mind that you might wait for ever. Sir Thomas Grey will be at Etal till the end of the month. I shall allow you three days to get there and back and discuss your business.' He drew a number of silver coins from the purse he carried at his belt and laid them grudgingly on the desk. 'This should suffice for your journey,' he said. 'No doubt they will feast you well at Etal.'

Hal stared at the small pile of coins. Barely enough to cover a night's, decent lodging but he supposed that for Albany this was generous. He said so and saw Albany stiffen at the light mockery of his voice.

'You mistake me,' he said sharply. 'Generosity was not my intent. Merely some small return for the years I have fed and clothed you without reward. How many years is it now? Nine or ten; and three years before that I gave you and Northumberland shelter when no other man would.' The mean rat-trap mouth curved in the parody of a smile. 'Understand me well, Hal. I have kept you here from no love of charity but because I hoped to make use of you. But while you have nothing and are nothing you are no use to me or any man. I give you leave to go to Etal in the hope that you can rectify that.'

Hal returned his look of cold dislike. 'How foolish of me,' he said acidly. 'And I had thought all done out of kindness.'

'Kindness? What kindness should I feel for the kin of Northumberland? Perhaps your long captivity has made you forget who you are. Shall I remind you? Outlaw, fugitive and my prisoner till I decree otherwise. All your family are attainted rebels . . .'

'Not rebels,' Hal broke in hotly. 'Loyalists. Loyal to King Richard against the usurper Bolingbroke.'

'Might I remind you that it was Northumberland who made Henry Bolingbroke king, and murdered another to do it?'

'Bolingbroke murdered Richard and well you know it,' Hal retorted grimly. 'He starved him to death in Pontefract castle.'

Albany raised a cynical brow. 'You are well rehearsed in your defence. Who taught you to say that? Your grandfather?'

'He taught me the truth and had no reason to lie to me.' It was the small boy in him talking now, defending the old man with a ferocity with which he would never have defended himself. He looked away from Albany's sneering gaze. Let him believe what he liked. He knew the truth. He had asked his grandfather outright one day. He remembered his high childish voice asking the question no other would have dared.

'Why do they say we murdered King Richard?'

Northumberland had smiled his wry oblique smile. 'I did not know that they did, Hal. If they say it, it is because it was your father and I put the tools in Bolingbroke's hand so that he could do it. Once he was king he could not afford to let Richard live. So Richard died, through lack of judgement and foresight. In a way, through me.'

Hal could still recall the sense of shock the admission had given him. Until then he had believed his grandfather all but perfect. Uncertainly he had said, 'But Richard was mad. He was not fit to be king.'

'No,' Northumberland had said wearily. 'Richard was not fit to be king. But he *was* king. Crowned, anointed, hallowed. No man had the right to take it from him.'

Hal glanced at Albany and allowed a little of his hatred to creep into his eyes. 'And anyway, how much better are you who keep your own king a prisoner because it suits you to wield his power?' he said.

Only the minutest flicker of the Regent's hooded lids showed that the thrust had found its mark. His voice when he spoke was quite calm. 'We have taught you much here,' he said lightly. 'Latin and Greek and I understand from the Bishop of St Andrew's that you speak French like a native.' He paused and smiled his unpleasant smile. 'A wise and civil tongue is something that only life can teach you. Learn quickly, young man, or it will cost you dearly.'

Hal lay quietly in the half-darkness listening to the sighs and whispers of the room: the splutter of the single cresset that burnt feebly against the far wall; the creak of the unyielding straw mattress beneath his back; and outside the door, the heavy, undisturbed breathing of the guard who always slept there. The room was small and bare as a monk's cell. It contained nothing except the low truckle bed on which he slept and a small iron-bound trunk. On a pole by the bed were the few garments he possessed, a change of shirt and doublet and four pairs of dark serviceable hose, all well used and well darned, all secondhand.

He slid his hand beneath the bolster and felt for the coins that Albany had given him. It was strange that the Regent had never doubted that he would go but then would he have ever doubted it himself before the reality of it had been placed before him? He drew his knees up to his chest to ease the gnawing ache in his belly. Fear. Cold, hard, sickening fear, and the shame of it was an even greater pain. *Coward*. The thought set him writhing in agony. All those years of waiting and dreaming of freedom and now the chance of it was here, he baulked at it. But Edmund Mortimer for king? Could he fight for that with any conviction? Did he even care? That's where all the doubts began. He should have cared. He had been bred to it, learning his hatreds early from his mother's knee. *Mortimer for king above the usurper Lancaster*. His child's mind had accepted it unquestioningly. But that had been ten years ago when Bolingbroke tottered on his throne and the memory of Richard was still fresh in men's hearts. He had known neither man well, nor did he know Henry of Monmouth, now king in his father's stead. They were only names to him, names without faces, names he'd heard from old men like Albany and his grandfather. There were other names, names that dripped blood, an army of dead names and not one of them had ever managed to dislodge Bolingbroke. He saw his father's head on Micklegate Bar, his limbs hacked and quartered like butcher's meat; his grandfather's on London Bridge, still there, a white bleached skull rattling on its spike. And he would begin it all again. All the old names, all the old hatreds. Abruptly he sat up and wiped the sweat from his face. It was all so futile and useless. What could they do now after all these years? He did not want to die before he had ever lived.

He sank his teeth hard into his lip to stop himself from trembling. Dear God, he had never been afraid like this before, not even that last time when his grandfather had left him. The thought of the old man eased him. If he closed his eyes he could conjure up the image of his face, the gaunt splendour of bronzed and polished flesh, those dreadful golden eyes that had lost none of their brilliance even when all they looked upon was darkness. He could remember the soft reassuring voice in his ear, the steady beat of the great and generous heart. It was the last time he had held him close, the last bright colours before the dark void of the next nine years. He felt the numbing fear recede. The old man had once told him that only lackwits and martyrs were never afraid. *Fear will keep you alive.* And it had, except that it had made him wary and distrustful of all men and their motives. The only real truth was Northumberland itself.

'Northumberland.' He whispered the name softly, and heard it fall into the silence of the room. The one word encompassed all he had ever loved. Not just a dream, a distant view from a hilltop, an unfulfilled ache in his heart, but the reality. His by right. Earl of Northumberland as his grandfather had been, as his father should have been.

Slowly he rose from the bed and went to kneel by the chest that stood by the window. He raised the lid and stared down at the meagre contents. The few treasured books that had been the gift of Bishop Thomas, a half dozen stumps of candle scrounged from the pantler to read them by. And the ring, his grandfather's ring, nestling in its scrap of velvet. He slid it tentatively on to his finger and traced the lion rampant gouged deep into the gold. Then he laid it carefully back in its place. The lion was dead. He was not fit to take his place yet.

It was dusk before he reached Berwick and it had begun to rain. The pale half-darkness of the summer evening merged the turrets and walls into a blur of shadowy softness that hid the labyrinth of stinking streets and the squat lime-washed houses climbing their sides like steps. It was hot and damp. The town sweated and was still.

Hal kept to the shadows, riding close beneath the jutting eaves that sheltered clouds of somnolent flies replete from the runnels that gleamed wet with slops. A sudden shaft of light from an opened shutter fell across his path and he averted his face instinctively. Then he smiled wryly. Who would know him here? It was twelve years since he had set foot in Berwick.

He pricked his horse to a trot, past the closed and shuttered shops and the stink of the fish market. There was a tailor's shop near here with a damp rat-infested cellar that had once been his home for more than a week. He couldn't remember quite where, though he remembered the tailor, a fat, kindly man who had carried him like a baby down to the waiting boat and wept like a child himself to see him go. Neville's men had hung him afterwards and burnt his corpse in the market square – a warning to any who thought to aid the traitor Northumberland.

He halted uncertainly where the street broadened into the market place. It was almost deserted. A handful of men lounged outside an open alehouse door, soldiers mostly from the massive fortress that menaced the town from the rock above Tweedmouth. He glanced up at the square keep, hard and black against the sky. Both his father and grandfather had been governors there once. Then the sound of hooves striking hard and sharp behind him swung him round. A dozen horsemen rode flank to flank down the narrow street. They carried torches, tongues of spasmodic flame that left all but their faces in shadow. Quite clearly Hal recognised the man riding in the lead. He did not need to see the device of the bull ramped on the sleeves of the men at his back. Even after twelve years he would have known Ralph Neville anywhere.

He drew back into the shadows, smoothing the mare's flattened ears to keep her steady. The horsemen passed almost close enough for him to touch and he waited nervously till they had crossed the square and mounted the castle ramp before he moved away.

The soldiers outside the tavern glanced up indifferently as he dismounted, then buried their faces in their ale pots again. There was a yard at the back with a ramshackle shed that passed as a stable and a squat, surly little man in a soiled leather jerkin sprawled on a bale of hay. He heaved himself up, scratched his groin and gave the old mare a disparaging look.

'Ha'penny the night. Penny with hay,' he said in the toneless voice of a man who has already said the same thing a hundred times that day.

Hal relinquished both the penny and the reins into the ostler's grubby outstretched hand. Then he picked his way through the piles of dung that littered the yard. The inn itself smelt no better and he hesitated a moment outside the open door breathing stale beer and sweat. He reminded himself that he'd known a great deal worse.

The single windowless room was hot and hazy with sweat. A dozen men in various stages of drunkenness sprawled on narrow benches, belching, laughing, banging their pots on the swimming tables. One had slid down to the floor and snored happily, his head pillowed on a heap of filthy rushes scraped up from the floor. In a corner an old woman crooned and dribbled into her beer, occasionally bursting into a shrill cracked parody of a love song. All this was watched soberly by a large dour man in a leather apron who advanced purposefully toward Hal who had chosen a table where at least the occupants were upright. Opposite him a man-at-arms in Neville's livery sat fingering his empty pot. He was tall and broad with a ready smile that revealed large white teeth. His dark eyes measured Hal at a glance and assessed him to be worth a quart of free ale at least. He smiled hopefully at Hal.

'Don't touch the beef if you've a mind to eat,' he said by way of introduction. 'It's crawling.'

The innkeeper came to stand at Hal's elbow with a creak of well soaped leather. 'Meat and bread a ha'penny. The same for stew. Fresh straw a farthing if you're wanting a bed,' he recited like a parrot.

Hal glanced at the man-at-arms and received a knowing wink. 'I'll take the stew,' he said and felt a wild desire to laugh, remembering that last night he'd supped on venison with half the nobility of Scotland.

'Very wise.' The soldier leant forward and grinned. 'The stew's no better but at least the maggots are cooked. Like as not it's all the meat you'll find in the slop that's served up here.' He elbowed awake the faded middle-aged man who sat beside him. 'You tell him, Wat.'

Wat blinked and smiled weakly at Hal then turned to ward off a second blow from his companion.

'I was just telling the young gentleman, Wat,' said the man-at-arms, who had by now confided that his name was Jack Allbright. 'You've got to be careful of the muck they give you here unless you want to leave your guts in the privy overnight.' He nodded sagely at Hal then looked expectantly to Wat for confirmation.

Wat inspected Hal with a bloodshot eye and nodded obediently as Jack's elbow hovered against his ribs. 'Filth,' he said. 'I'd rather eat my own mother than what you've got in that bowl there.' He nodded again, then sunk his head on his chest, snoring gently.

Hal stared down at the greasy dish that the innkeeper had slammed in front of him. What little appetite he'd had was gone as he pushed the food away without tasting it.

Jack Allbright stared wistfully at the steaming bowl. 'Seems a pity to waste it as you've paid for it,' he said. 'That old skinflint'll only tip it back in the pot.'

Hal laughed outright at the sheer blatancy of it. He knew Jack Allbright's sort well enough; a born scrounger who could sit in an alehouse all day and drink for nothing. But for some reason he rather liked him and it also pleased him to think of Albany's face if he'd known that his money was being poured down the throat of a common soldier and an Englishman at that. He pushed the bowl over towards Jack, who beamed at him. 'Well, that's right kind of you, friend.' He peered with one eye into his empty pot. 'I'd drink your health if I had aught to drink it with.'

Hal filled both men's cups. The ale at least was good, strong and surprisingly cool. He drank in silence and watched with amusement as Jack shovelled the greasy stew noisily down his throat. He used the last of the bread to clean the bowl, licked the spoon and belched loudly. Then he leant his arms on the table and grinned across at Hal.

By God, lad. I saved you from something there. Blown a hole in a tender belly like yours it would.' He patted his own. 'Cast iron this is. And I've eaten worse on campaign. Worms and beetles, even horse dung once.' He took a long swig of ale and belched again. 'And you, friend?' he resumed with open curiosity. 'What brings a fine young gentleman to a flea-bitten hole like this?'

'The need for a bed,' Hal answered evasively. 'I've ridden a long way.' He did not say from where.

'Seeking your fortune, eh, lad?' Jack nodded with understanding and helped himself to another draught of ale. 'Well, I hope you have better luck than I've had. Six years I've served that bastard Neville and nothing to show for it but a hole in my leg you could drive a cart through. Fourpence a day and livery's all very well in war time. There's pickings then to make it stretch but it doesn't go far when there's nothing better to do than kick your heels in an alehouse all day. What I need is a bloody good war.' He rolled his eyes ecstatically. 'Sixpence a day and pillage, as much as a man can carry off the field.' He stabbed the air with a long grubby forefinger. 'A good soldier wants for nothing then. He's somebody then, not just some liveried skivvy running errands between guard duty. And what's there to guard against here anyway?' he demanded in disgust. 'A few cattle thieves who come and go at night like the cowardly bloody heathens they are. We've those Scots bastards hamstrung while we've got their King Jamie under lock and key, and that's likely to be forever. That old skinflint Albany won't go on short commons to raise his ransom.'

'Albany's own son, the Earl of Fife, is also held prisoner in England,' Hal reminded him.

'And what does that mean? Don't think these high and mighty lords are above sacrificing their own kin if it suits them. A man can always have more sons. Look at Neville. I've never seen his wife out of pod. Twenty-three at the last count if you include those by his first wife. There's some bargaining power there, lad. I've never seen the fair Joan without a belly the size of a ship's hull. Still, that's the way to do it. Keep 'em breeding so they've no time for meddling.' He picked his large white teeth thoughtfully. 'No. It's France we'll have to look to for war.' He sighed loudly. 'Let's hope our Harry doesn't let those Frenchies buy him off as his father did. There'll be no better time than now, you mark my words. The French king's a loony and those fancy kinsmen of his are too busy fighting over a slice of the cake to see the rats nibbling it away. If any man can do it, it'll be our Harry. He's got the guts for it if those mealy-mouthed ministers would let him get on with it.' He chuckled and leant back against the wall. 'Man after my own heart, Harry is. I saw him once in London. Hardly stand for drink he couldn't. Been out raising hell all night with those brothers of his. 'Course he wasn't king *then*.' His mouth turned down mournfully. 'Gone all holy now, he has. Mass three

times a day and all that. Wearin' out his knees in chapel prayin'
for guidance. If you ask me all he needs to do is guide his boot
firmly up that French king's arse and kick him out of it. That
sanctimonious old bag of bones Arundel did that to him. Always
screechin' about heresy and never happy unless he's roastin'
some poor bastard on a pile of faggots. Dragged a dozen of 'em
out to St Giles three months ago and burnt the lot. And what
about that poor sod Badby or whatever his name was? Burnt him
in irons and then halfway through, Harry orders the flames to be
doused and goes on his knees to this Badby to recant. Offered him
a pension of threepence a day for life, he did. Christ's Blood, I'd
say anything for that.' He grinned. 'Be worth getting the soles of
your feet singed a bit for a royal pension, wouldn't it?' He shook
his head and drained the last of the ale. 'But this Badby didn't
think so. Kept saying that bread was bread and the priest only a
man. He wouldn't back down, not even for the king. So they piled
the faggots back on and lights them again.' He crossed himself
devoutly. 'Poor bastard. He must have died in agony.'

'He died for what he believed in, I suppose,' Hal observed, glad
to be able to contribute something to this one-sided conversation.

'I believe in staying alive,' Jack said firmly. 'And if you've got to
die then let it be quick and clean. Not for God, king or country
would I suffer a death like that if I had a choice. Not that I would
have a choice,' he added glumly. 'When you're like Wat and me
you does as you're told and like it, see. There's no pickin' and
choosin' for the likes of us.' He launched a sudden attack with his
elbow on the sleeping Wat. 'Common stock, eh, Wat? Common
as pigs, born in a trough and no hope of ever climbing out of it.
No reason to trouble about justice and fair play for the likes of us,
'cos as soon as we're down there'll be another poor hungry sod
ready to step into our boots before we're even half cold. Now this
Badby, he was common stock. Tailor or something, but nobody
that anyone's going to fret themselves over. So he's got himself
mixed up in this Lollard business and before he knows where he
is, he's getting his backside roasted. But what about Oldcastle,
eh? He's a Lollard. Admits it even. Where's the difference, eh?
Except of course that Sir John high and mighty bloody Oldcastle
is a friend of the king.'

'Who's Oldcastle?' asked Hal and immediately regretted it.

'Who's Oldcastle?' Jack yelled. 'Ye gods, boy. Where have you been, in a convent? Sir John Oldcastle. Fought with the king in Wales. Mind you, he was plain John Oldcastle then. Only raised himself up 'cos he toadied to the king's brother Gloucester. But then he's discovered with these pamphlets. Seditious, Arundel called them. Anyway they were hot stuff, preachin' about the wealth of the clergy and all that. Mind you,' he dropped his voice to a conspiratorial whisper. 'You can't help agreeing with that, can you? Have you seen that leech Beaufort lately? Always crawling round the king's backside and so swelled up with money that he'd burst if he swallowed a ha'penny. Bishop of Winchester he is now and with his eye on a cardinal's hat for all he's bastard stock.' He paused, distracted by a drab-looking girl who emerged from a back room and came toward them. He winked lecherously at Hal. 'I've had her,' he grinned. 'Not that that's anything to boast about. So has half the garrison. But she's clean and obliging if you've a fancy for it. She'll keep the draught from your back for a shilling; maybe less, seeing as you're a nice young gentleman.'

He slid his hand surreptitiously over the girl's rump as she laid a pitcher on the table next to them. She slapped him sharply and swore at him, then disappeared into the back of the inn again.

Jack rubbed his cheek ruefully. 'Just like a woman, that is,' he exclaimed. 'Lay on their back for you one night then slap you down because you pinch their arse the next.' He solaced himself with a long pull of ale. 'Now where was I? Beaufort? No, Oldcastle. Well, Archbishop Arundel's given him what for over these pamphlets and Oldcastle's admitted it and called Arundel a few choice names into the bargain. Then the king's intervened and given Oldcastle forty days' respite to change his mind.' He tapped his finger significantly on the table. 'Forty days, mind. Didn't give poor old Badby forty days, did they?' He let the significance of this sink in, then said, 'Didn't do them any good, though. Put him in the Tower after that, they did, and strike me if Oldcastle hadn't escaped within a week. From the *Tower*, mind.' He folded his arms emphatically across his massive chest. 'You're not telling me but something don't smell right there, lad. Still on the loose, he is. Causin' trouble. There's talk he's here in the north.'

Wat suddenly stirred himself and looked uncomfortably sober, a condition he immediately remedied with a long, noisy gulp. He belched, wiped his mouth and said, 'You'll talk yourself into the Tower one of these days.'

Jack looked outraged. 'Because I've got something between my ears but Newcastle mud?' His glazed stare fastened possessively on Hal's face again. 'I can read, you know. Write a bit as well. Nothing fancy. Just plain English and a bit of French though in my book there's nothing better than a sharp blade at a man's throat to make yourself understood.' He cackled with laughter. 'They all know what that means.'

He swilled the last of the ale from the pitcher and swallowed it down. 'Don't talk much, do you?' he said almost belligerently to Hal. 'Or drink much either,' he added, staring at Hal's full tankard. 'Still, perhaps that's a blessing. Got to keep your wits about you these days. Can you fight?'

'A bit,' Hal admitted, smiling. 'Enough to stay alive.'

'Well, that's more than enough,' Jack said generously. He nodded and yawned, worn out by the flux of words. He pillowed his head happily in his arms. 'Staying alive, that's the thing. I'd drink to that if I had one.' He nudged Wat. 'Your turn, Wat. You're surely not going to swill this lad's good ale all night and not return the compliment.' He lifted his head and smiled drunkenly. 'Wat's the rich one. Sixpence a day and all found. He's an armourer.'

'And a good one, if I say it myself.' Wat surveyed Hal blearily over the rim of his pot. 'I've served some of the best in my time. Three years under Allbright Mailmaker, the king's armourer. Five years before that with Warwick. I served Northumberland himself once for two years. Now there was a man for you. He stood over six foot two, you know. And by Christ, he knew how to wear armour. Specially made for him in Cologne, it was. The finest steel inlaid with silver, gold sometimes. Even the rivets were engraved with his crest.' He sighed regretfully. 'He knew what being a lord was all about. It's all mend and make do with Neville. Patchin'. Knocking out dents.' He shook his head.

'Man can't take a pride in work like that. Northumberland, now. He knew what pride really meant. You'd have liked him, Jack. He understood men like you and me.'

'Perhaps I would,' said Jack drunkenly. 'Perhaps I wouldn't.'

'I was with Northumberland that last time when he rode down to York. By God, you had to admire his courage. He couldn't have had more than two hundred men at his back when he crossed the Border though by the time he reached York it was more like two thousand. He never asked them. They just came. Just upped and left what they were doing and followed him.' He blinked emotionally. 'It was a rare sight, lad. A rare sight. And even when he knew that he had been tricked and that it was Neville waiting for him instead of Rokeby, he told the men to disperse and go home. He would have given himself to save them, you see.' He shook his head. 'But none left. They stayed with him to the end.' He sighed again. 'It was the only time in my life I regretted being on the winning side.'

There was a silence broken by Jack's gentle snoring. Hal stared down at his hands. So many things he wanted to ask and dare not.

Then the sharp impatient clang of the curfew bell sounded from the castle. Wat prodded the somnolent Jack and looked glumly at Hal. 'Talks himself into a stupor, he does.'

He rose precariously and hauled at Jack who grudgingly opened his eyes. They took at least a minute to focus on Hal. Then he grinned. 'Good luck to you, lad.' He hiccoughed and pushed his massive bulk ponderously from the bench. 'And if you ever need a stout man by you, Jack Allbright's the name. Don't forget now. Jack Allbright's the name.'

Hal watched the two men weave their way unsteadily to the door. He heard Jack's strident voice bawling across the market square, 'Don't forget now. Jack Allbright's the name.' He smiled. No. He would not forget.

He stopped on the last rise of ground before it fell away to the sea coast plain that ran flat and green down to Alnwick. He could just see Bamburgh on its rock and further south the tiny speck of Holy Island with the sea rolled back from its causeway as if by the hand of God. Beneath him the moor dropped gently away to the valley where the stubbled fields lay beneath a golden haze of corn dust and the dark languid river flowed silently in its cleft of sandstone. Beyond there was nothing but the moor, its harshness softened by summer green and clumps of yellow gorse. Mile after mile of unbroken space and silence rising abruptly to the bleak misted dome of the Cheviot, plunging again to the dark wolf-ridden heart of Redesdale Forest. Hal looked across the rim of the moorland where the stunted trees stood bent as drawn bows against the wind. The vast engulfing silence seemed to smother all life, every sound distorted and diminished by the wind. There was always wind, a perpetual whine in his ears, sometimes gusting down from the heights of Cheviot with such force that a man could hardly keep upright in the saddle. He lifted his head like a dog and breathed its scent; peat and heather and summer grass. He smiled up into the sun. He was home, albeit for only a day, but he was home.

He followed the line of the river, riding through fields knee-high with meadowsweet, past the ramshackle huts of the salmon fishers that lined the banks. The air had a heavy somnolent quality here. It was warmer and the wind not so fierce, carrying the drone of grazing sheep from their drystone pens; the monotonous clack of a millwheel from downstream. A man sat by the river cutting withies to patch the roof of his hut. He raised his hand and called a greeting as Hal passed. It was the sound of his voice more than anything, the soft lilting burr of the Border, the sound of his childhood, came rushing back to fill up the void of the past ten years. He saw himself on the saddle-bow of his father's horse riding to the fair at Wooler; he had eaten cinnamon cake till he was sick that day. He remembered his great-uncle Thomas teaching him with heavy patience to fly his first hawk in the flat green fields by the Aln; his father's brothers Ralph and Tom, teasing him and carrying him shoulder high down to the hall at night. Tom had gone off to the war in Spain and never came back. Ralph had died. He could not remember when. All dead. His world was full of the dead. He had almost forgotten the art of living himself.

He was within sight of Etal, the small perfect castle above the river that mirrored its white walls and the cluster of houses at its feet. Outside the barbican a single guard yawned, swatted flies and scratched himself. He looked up as Hal approached and reached reluctantly for the halberd propped against the wall. The doubts came crowding in then. It was not too late, he could still turn back. Back to Albany? Back to his world of dead memories?

He breathed deeply as the guard came out to challenge him.

'Lord Grey,' he said hoarsely. 'I wish to see Lord Grey.'

The guard squinted up at him, shading his eyes from the sun at Hal's back and taking in the shabby horse and clothes and a day's growth of beard.

'Who wants him?' he asked disrespectfully.

'Just tell him,' Hal snapped with nervous anger. 'And quickly.' There was at least enough authority in his voice to send the guard lumbering back through the gate. Hal followed him and waited in the small outer ward with nerves stretched like steel. Mercifully he did not have to wait long. A tall man appeared in a doorway, stared at him a moment, then beckoned.

In the shadow of the doorway Tom Grey clasped his hand.

'So you came, then,' he said softly. 'I did not know whether you would.' He smiled. 'It's been a long time, Hal, for all of us.'

They looked each other over, each aware of the change the years had made. The last time Hal had seen Tom Grey had been the day his father had ridden down to Shrewsbury field. Mounted and fully armed, Hotspur had bent to kiss his son, his warmth and vibrance encased in cold steel. He would always remember his father like that, cold, shining and untouchable. He had never seen him again.

Grey touched his arm. 'Will it irk you to wait in your chamber till nightfall? There are a few that I'd rather not let see you yet.' He smiled his wide disarming smile. 'You're very like him, you know. The old man, I mean.'

Hal nodded. Yes, he was like him, but only outwardly. Northumberland would not have quailed like a maid at the thought of rebellion.

Grey's steward led him up to the high tower room and he stood for a long time with his back against the closed door listening to the footsteps retreating down the stairs. The room was high and light, with soft muted tapestries lining the walls. There was a flagon of wine on a low chest by the window and he poured himself a full measure and drank it down in one, feeling the warmth burn down into his belly. He drew a deep breath. It was done. He was here; rebel and conspirator. It was too late to turn back now even if he'd had a mind to. And he hadn't now.

He stared down blindly at the shimmer of water and reflected sky. A pair of swans preened themselves on cushions of tall reeds; then as if aware of his gaze, slid quietly into the water. He watched them struggle against the slow but relentless current. He knew the river's course, down to Ford and Wooler, then curving back upon itself by Cushat Law to its source high in the Cheviot. And down river, the way he had come; back to the Tweed, back to Scotland. And what was there to take him back? Only honour, the fact that he had given his word to Albany to return, come what may. The wild thought of freedom died before it was born. Honour was all he had left. Albany would never have let him go if he had not believed that.

He swung round, startled by the opening of the door. He saw the lambent gleam of red-gold hair, the pale triangle of a high boned face and his heart turned suddenly cold till he saw that the face was young and the eyes that watched him calm and grey. He had thought for a moment that it was his mother.

'Bess?' Then surer as she came from shadow into light. 'Oh Bess. Dear God. It *is* you, Bess.'

His sister came wordlessly into his arms. He held her close. His own flesh, his own blood. It was so long since he had felt warmth or love, a long time since he had held any woman save a whore.

She was weeping. 'Oh, Hal.' She leant back and looked up into his face. 'I'd almost forgotten that you'd be a man, now.'

'And I that you'd be a woman.' He stared down into her face, their mother's face except for the eyes. Gently he brushed the tears from her cheeks. She had been weeping the last time he had seen her, the day their father had been killed and Bolingbroke's men had come and dragged them from sanctuary to the Tower.

'What happened to you?' he asked quietly. 'Grandfather never told me, except that you were safe.'

She moved away from him and he saw how thin and frail she was.

'They took us to Bermondsey Abbey and then after a little while some men came and took Elizabeth away. I never knew where. I stayed alone for the rest of the time that grandfather was in prison. Then after his trial and release I was wed to John Clifford.' She shrugged her shoulders and smiled faintly. 'I have been married to John ever since.'

'Happily?'

'Yes. I think so. John was only ten years old when I married him. I was sixteen. He was more like a brother to me then.' She smiled. 'I'm happier now. Our son Thomas was born a year ago. I look for nothing else.'

'And Elizabeth?' They never spoke of their mother as anything else but that. She would always be Elizabeth. 'Have you seen her?'

'No.' Bess' eyes clouded with pain and fear. She had been almost glad when Bolingbroke's men had come to take her. Her mother's strange and utter stillness had frightened her more than the rough, brutal nuns ever had. 'Bolingbroke married her to one of his henchmen,' she said. 'She is Lady Camoys now. I've never seen or heard from her since, nor wanted to. I think she must be quite mad by now, Hal. If our father's death did not turn her mind, then those months in Bermondsey did. She was far more persecuted than I ever was. Sometimes she would not move or speak for days. She just sat there, staring, in a world of her own. The nuns would come and slap her and she would sit for a while rocking from side to side under the blows. Then suddenly she would raise her head and look at them and they would leave her be. They were afraid of her, too.' She shivered, blown by the chill wind of remembrance. 'But they could not break her. Though they starved and beat her and shut her up alone for days, they could not break her. When the king's men came for her she went smiling.'

Hal's mouth tightened in anguish. For all that he had never really loved her, she was still his mother. 'Poor Elizabeth.'

'Don't pity her, Hal.' Bess swung round to face him and her eyes were hard as flint. 'She brought it on herself. She's evil. You know she's evil. If she hadn't meddled, if she hadn't tried so hard to put that idiot brother of hers on the throne, it might never have happened.' She came to stand close to him and clasped his hands. 'Oh, Hal. I know why you're here and I beg you to leave well alone. It's her doing. She's still at the heart of it, like a spider spinning the threads of her web. You're still doing her will whether you know it or not. *Mortimer for king!* Did we ever hear anything else? Father and grandfather died for it. Will you die for it, Hal? Because you'll never win. You'll never bring Lancaster down now.'

'Tom Grey seems to think we will.'

His sister smiled wearily. 'Tom's a dreamer. You're all dreamers. If any man could have brought Lancaster down it was grandfather. What makes you think that you can achieve what he could not?'

He stared at her and said nothing. She was saying all that he had already thought.

'I know these men you have come to meet. I know their motives and their greed. At least you are an open adversary of the king. These others purport to be his friends: Cambridge, Mortimer – Henry Scrope even boasts that he shares the king's bed.' She smiled scornfully. 'Do *you* know them, Hal? Will you put your trust in strangers, men that you have never met?'

'Christ, Bess, I may never have met them but they're hardly strangers. They're all tied to us by blood or marriage.'

'Yes,' Bess smiled wearily. 'Yes, I suppose it all seems possible to your starved exile's eyes. But it's finished, Hal. All finished. Henry of Monmouth is king now and he's a better king than Edmund Mortimer will ever be.'

'I'm not fighting for Mortimer. I'm fighting for Northumberland.'

'And you think these men will give it to you?' Bess threw back. 'They're using you, Hal, for their own ends. It's the old futile plot. Glyn Dwr and his magical army from Wales, a Percy to bring out the North. It's all been tried before and failed.' She caught at his hands. 'Leave it be, Hal,' she pleaded. 'There's been too much of our blood shed already.'

He pulled away from her. 'And for nothing. All for nothing if you have your way.'

'Better to accept our losses than add to them. It was grandfather's quarrel, Hal, grandfather's and Bolingbroke's. They're dead now. For pity's sake let it die with them. Revenge is always the poorest of motives.'

He stared at her with cold, alien eyes. 'I can't believe this of you, Bess. Can you forget so easily? You know what Bolingbroke did to our father; tore him out of the grave that even our worst enemy did not grudge him and hacked him limb from limb. Grandfather's head is *still* on London Bridge and the rest of him God knows where. Have you seen it, Bess? Do you look up when you pass and say, "what's done is done"?'

'Yes, I've seen it,' she cried. 'I saw it when there was still flesh on it, when it still had eyes.' She turned away and swayed against the wall. 'I don't want to see your head beside it, Hal. Is that so wrong? You're all that's left now.'

'Oh, Bess.' He went to her and drew her against him. 'Twelve years apart and we're quarrelling.'

She touched his cheek. 'Be patient a while longer, Hal, that's all I ask. It'll come in time, the right way, without the taste of treachery in your mouth. Grandfather would have wanted it so.'

'I can't wait much longer, Bess. Every day is a lost opportunity. If I give up this chance there might never be another.'

'It will come. I know it as surely as I know you'll fail if you do it this way. Bolingbroke's son he might be but he's not like his father. He's a just man. It's a new beginning for all of us if you can just be patient a while longer.'

'How long, Bess? How much longer? He's pardoned all the others, months, years ago. Why not me?'

'I suppose you are different, Hal. You're Albany's prisoner and your freedom won't come cheaply. Henry's a cautious man. And well he might be. So far his mercy has only been rewarded with treachery. But if you knew him, knew the real man, you would accept him.' She flushed under his critical gaze. 'You think me disloyal, don't you? Well, don't judge me till you have met him. He's good for England, Hal. He could make her strong again if he was given the chance.'

Hal turned away from her almost angrily and sat heavily on the great bed. He could feel his resolve weakening. There was just one certainty to cling to. He lifted his head and said slowly, 'All I want is Northumberland back. And I don't care who gives it or what I have to do to get it.'

She smiled sadly. 'Then you're a fool, Hal. There is no parcel of land on earth worth the murder of a king. Grandfather would have told you that.'

In the dimly lit hall the four men watched him, four men of trust and standing at the court of King Henry V, four men inextricably linked by blood and marriage, four would-be murderers. Richard, Earl of Cambridge, was the ring-leader, half smiling as he turned the tall goblet between his long, ringed fingers. Of all of them he had the most cause for rebellion; the most to lose, the most to gain. He was Edward of York's son and his blood was as good as his cousin the king's. His first wife had been a Mortimer, the child of Elizabeth's brother. He was wed to a Clifford now and his daughter Isobel to Tom Grey's eldest son.

Opposite him sat Henry Scrope, less assured, distrust turning down the corners of his womanly mouth. The nephew of the murdered Archbishop Scrope, his allegiance was more for gain than revenge, the same motive that had led him to wed Cambridge's elderly stepmother, the dowager Duchess of York, two years before. And between them, as out of place as a monk in an alehouse, sat Tom Grey, his ready smile tinged with nervousness. Perhaps of all of them only Tom could be forgiven. He had loved Hal's father well. There was another, come late when all but the four of them were in their beds: Edmund Mortimer, Earl of March. He was only a little older than Hal, with a weak mouth and pale irresolute eyes that never dwelt on anything for long. Hal liked and trusted him even less than the others.

Cambridge spoke softly to Hal. 'Well then, my lord? Are you with us?'

Hal hesitated. It seemed so easy. 'All you have to do is bring us the north,' Cambridge had said. 'They will follow you because of your father. All you have to do is show them your face.'

'Have I a choice?' Hal asked and saw Cambridge's mouth tighten. It was not the answer he had expected.

'Not if you want your freedom,' he answered coldly.

Hal inclined his head. 'Then I am with you.' They could tell nothing from his face, nothing of what it had cost him to say that. *All he had to do was bring them the north*. And trade on his father's name who had never done a shameful deed in all his short life. The label of traitor did not sit easily round his neck.

'We are agreed then?' Cambridge looked round the circle of faces. 'By the end of the year, before the king leaves for Southampton?'

'I'd rather it were sooner,' Scrope said without lifting his eyes from the cabochon diamond that adorned his thumb. 'If he thought it gave him advantage Henry might leave for France earlier than planned.'

'He cannot leave before all the men are mustered and it would take a miracle to do that before the end of the year. It'll be winter then and he'll not risk a winter campaign.'

Scrope smiled quietly to himself. 'Then you don't know Henry. He's capable of miracles where France is concerned. He eats and breathes nothing else. His chance is now and only now and he knows it.'

'I am well aware of the king's capabilities,' Cambridge said coldly. 'That is why I say he must not be allowed to leave for France. At the moment he is nothing. He's unsure of himself and the people are unsure of him. He has yet to prove himself. All he has to his credit so far is the persecution of a few wretched heretics. He's not popular with the commons, either. Wars cost money and only last month he had to go cap in hand again for another subsidy. His crown's in pawn to Beaufort and he's drained the London merchants dry.' He paused and tapped his long fingers on the rough, pitted surface of the table. 'But give him a victory in France and it will be another story.'

'He might lose,' Tom Grey ventured quietly.

'Henry won't lose. Not outright anyway,' Scrope said. 'He's laid his plans too well for that; every detail planned down to the last sack of grain. As I said, his chance is now, with the Duke of Burgundy backing him, though God knows for how long.'

'But Harfleur? It's nigh on impregnable.'

'Not against cannon. There's no fortress on earth that can stand against cannon. Henry treats them as if they were his children.' He laughed suddenly. 'He even has names for them: the

King's Daughter, the *London*, the *Messenger*. No. Henry will not lose. It's more than conquest to him. It's something of his own to bolster the title of king that even he's not sure he's entitled to. He's a man plagued by conscience and doubt not he'll win simply because he dare not lose.'

'And neither dare we,' Grey said grimly. 'Let us hope our campaign is planned as well as the king's.'

'It is,' said Cambridge, 'and will succeed for being the simpler. It takes little strategy to slip a blade between the shoulders of a sleeping man. Time and opportunity are all that are needed.' He smiled unpleasantly. 'And my lord Scrope has both in plenty.'

Conscience sharpened Scrope's tongue. 'It needs more than that. Just because Henry is dead doesn't mean to say that all England will come begging us to put Mortimer in his place. We need to consolidate, take the power into our own hands before Henry's party has time to recover.'

'Gently, gently,' Cambridge said mockingly as a note of panic crept into Scrope's voice. 'I am no less capable of strategy than our royal cousin. We can take our time. We have almost a year before Henry can be ready to move against France. There must be no mistakes, no bungling. We can sit back and let Henry do the work for us. Let him gather his army: ships and supplies, siege engines, cannon, weapons.' He laughed deep in his throat. 'A ready-made army, and once Henry is dead, ours for the taking.'

'And what makes you think they will follow you as readily?' Hal objected.

'Most armies follow the man that pays their wages and do not care too much who it is. The rest can be bought or bribed. Those that can't . . .' He smiled threateningly. 'Well, we have no need of those. It's all been planned. Oldcastle has two thousand men waiting in the west, the Duke of Albany is with us and we have the promise of five thousand men at least from Glyn Dwr of Wales.'

'I hope he keeps this pledge better than he did the last,' Hal interrupted. It was Glyn Dwr's failure to come up that had lost his father the fight at Shrewsbury.

Cambridge looked at him sharply. 'He will. He has better cause this time. Henry holds his son Gryffyd hostage.'

31

'And the Duke of Albany?' Hal enquired dryly. 'What has he promised?'

'Your freedom for one thing and five thousand men to hold the north.'

'In exchange for what?'

Cambridge paused, then said, 'The release of his son, the Earl of Fife – and Berwick.'

'Berwick?' Hal rose angrily to his feet. 'Berwick is Northumberland's. My father and grandfather nearly lost their lives keeping hold of Berwick.'

'Your father and grandfather are dead,' Cambridge reminded him coldly, 'And it is only by sheer good fortune that you are not also. If you want Northumberland back you cannot squeal over yielding a piece of it to the Scots. We have made similar concessions to Glyn Dwr of Wales. The Earl of March has had to yield some of his territories.'

'Perhaps that does not matter so much to a man when he is to be the next King of England,' Hal snapped.

Mortimer flushed. 'It's not that,' he protested. 'I don't care about being king . . .' His thin voice trailed away under Cambridge's freezing stare and Hal saw the look of unease that passed between the others. So they were not sure of Mortimer either.

'Perhaps it is my lord Mortimer's adherence we should question rather than my own,' Hal said coldly. 'He seems to lack the spirit one would expect from a man about to become king.'

'We'll question nothing,' Cambridge said testily. 'Our plans are laid, and they will succeed only if we keep our sense of purpose.' He drew his thin lips across his teeth and smiled down the table at Mortimer. 'No man *wishes* to be king, Edmund. It is a responsibility thrust upon him by birth and heritage. You will be king as your father wished you to be king, as King Richard of blessed memory wished *him* to be king.'

Mortimer said nothing and drained his cup to dull the threat in Cambridge's voice. *Murder.* The word brought sweat to the palms of his hands. Next year he would be a murderer and the man he called cousin and friend would be dead. The king's pale arrogant face floated before him, but bloody now, eyes dead and staring, staring at him, accusing him – murderer! His hand shook visibly as he held his cup out for more wine. Then slowly the courage came trickling back as it always did. He had the right. He was Edmund, Earl of March and Ulster. His father had been King Richard's designated heir, descended from the third son of old King Edward. Whereas Henry's was only from the fourth. No taint there. His blood was pure, purer than the usurper Lancaster's. He started as he felt Cambridge's hand familiarly on his arm. The pale insidious eyes held his for a moment, then Cambridge said, 'We are agreed then, Edmund? By the end of the year?'

The fear leapt and quietened again. Mortimer nodded and his voice rasped in his throat as if his mouth were full of sand. 'Yes,' he said, 'Let it be then.'

Hal watched him uneasily. There was the flaw, the weak link in the chain that would string them all up if Mortimer failed them. And he would in the end. He was not the stuff of which kings were made. *And he's a better king than Edmund Mortimer will ever be.* He looked round at the ring of faces, at Cambridge with his mean and crafty mouth, at Scrope with his pale hooded eyes and Mortimer's, dark with fear. At Tom Grey he could not look at all. He felt sick with shame. They were all that Bess had said and more and now he was one of them: traitor, rebel murderer. He swallowed hard on his disgust. Bess had been right. What need had the king of enemies with friends such as these?

It took the two days of his return journey for the cold realisation of what he had done to dawn on him. And strangely, it was not of himself or Northumberland that he thought but of the man that he conspired against. He could form no clear picture of Henry from the complexity of rumour and hearsay: lecher and drunkard, monk and priest, soldier and general, all these were Henry the king. Hal knew of him better as the young prince who had been his father's pupil in the war against Wales. Hotspur had been both his friend and mentor then, as close as brothers till the rift with Bolingbroke. Hal wondered if Henry had felt guilt or grief when he had ridden against him at Shrewsbury. He doubted it. From what he knew of Henry he was above such feelings. But *he* was not and they ate the heart out of him mile after mile. He remembered his grandfather, crushed beneath the weight of such a guilt. '*But he was king. Crowned, annointed and hallowed. No man had the right to take that from him.*'

Could he live with it? Not just the stain of murder but the shameful bargain of ceding Berwick, of seeing Albany's men looting his fair Northumberland before they handed the burnt empty shell of it back to him? There would be blood shed, English blood, northern blood. Even with Henry dead there would be resistance: the king's brothers, Clarence, Gloucester and Bedford; his Beaufort half brothers, Somerset and Exeter. All Henry's loyal partisans who would rather die themselves than see the puppet Mortimer raised to the throne. And all he had to do was bring out the North? Bess was right. It was only a dream. He was tired of dreams.

Albany's smug complacent smile was the final straw. Hal faced him again across the vast ornate desk.

'Berwick,' he said coldly. 'You said nothing of Berwick.'

Albany raised his sparse brows. 'I was not aware that I had to. The negotiations for your release were between the Earl of Cambridge and myself and none other. Berwick is not yours yet to yield. How then should it concern you?'

'And it's not Cambridge's either, or Scrope's or Mortimer's or any of that treacherous little crew of malcontents that you sent me to treat with.'

'For a man who owns nothing but the clothes he stands up in, you are more than a little demanding,' Albany said stiffly. 'With all the rest of Northumberland and the Yorkshire lands, you'll not miss Berwick.'

'I'd rather have none of it than yield the half of it to you for the privilege,' Hal shouted.

'Berwick is hardly half,' Albany countered.

'But it's the key to England,' Hal threw back. 'Once in control of Berwick you'd have Northumberland under your heel.' He glared at Albany with open dislike. 'I'll have all or nothing.'

'Then it might have to be nothing.'

They stared at each other for a while in hostile silence. Then Hal said bluntly, 'Then I am well content. I have not relished the thought of leading countless men to their deaths to place a crown on that idiot Mortimer's head.'

Albany chewed thoughtfully at his lip. 'Are you so certain of failure, then?'

'Yes.' Hal moved out of the line of Albany's intent gaze. 'For all Edmund Mortimer is my kin, he'll never make a king. He's no heart for this without Cambridge prodding and pushing him. He's as nervous as a rabbit. If any leaned on him heavily enough he would betray us all.'

Albany arranged a fold in his robe with meticulous care. 'What else?'

'There's no substance to it. It's all promises. Five thousand men from yourself, the same from Glyn Dwr, and the rebel Oldcastle says he has two thousand Lollards waiting in the West. Scots, Welsh, religious fanatics. Where are the English? Cambridge is relying too heavily on Henry's death to turn the tide for him, hoping that without Henry all England will acclaim Mortimer for king.' Hal shook his head. 'I doubt it can be done so easily.'

'Northumberland did it,' Albany said with a malicious smile. 'Henry Bolingbroke had only twelve men at his back when he landed. In six months Northumberland had made him master of England.'

'But Cambridge is not Northumberland, nor Edmund Mortimer, Bolingbroke. And Henry of Lancaster is no madman to yield without a murmur as Richard did!'

'Well, it seems that we have taught you a little Scots caution if nothing else.' Albany stroked his thin beard. 'So what now?'

Hal drew a deep breath. 'I'll not do it.'

Albany rose slowly to his feet. 'Did you tell Cambridge that?'

'No. I did not know it then. I thought that Northumberland would be worth any price.' He met Albany's hard, calculating stare. 'It isn't.'

'Did you swear an oath?'

'Only one of secrecy. I said I would not betray them.'

'Well, that's something, anyway. At least you'll not be forsworn.' He felt almost relieved. The cost of having to provide five thousand men had almost overlaid the joy of gaining Berwick, and for a hopeless cause at that if the boy was to be believed. He had another card yet to play, not so profitable to himself but with less risk involved: a straight exchange for his son Murdac plus a ransom of ten thousand pounds for Hal Percy. And Neville's way was the more certain, though of course, he'd lose the pledge of Berwick. He reminded himself again that it was indeed only a pledge. Dead men paid nothing.

'There is another way,' he began softly. He paused and chose his next few words carefully. 'Whilst you were away I received envoys from the Earl of Westmorland.' He cleared his throat loudly. 'It seems that you still have friends at court. The matter of your restoration has been broached to the king and received favourably.' He saw the sudden joyful widening of Hal's eyes and smiled. So far so good.

'There are conditions, of course,' he went on smoothly. 'But nothing so irksome as rebellion.' The sudden sideways shift of his eyes betrayed him.

'Such as?' Hal demanded sharply.

Albany drew a deep breath. There was nothing for it but to plunge straight in. 'Marriage to a daughter of Ralph Neville and to remain in his ward for a year.'

Hal heard the sound of his own breathing, loud and harsh in the heavy silence. Then stupidly, like a child, he said, 'Ralph Neville killed my grandfather.'

'I know it,' Albany said briefly. 'But there's your choice. Cambridge or Neville. Henry or Mortimer. And let us hope that you still have a choice. If Neville even got a sniff that you'd set foot in Etal, you'd never see Northumberland again. Christ, man, you cannot have it all,' he added irritably. 'There must be loss, be it of pride or liberty or conscience. It is up to you to choose which. And you could do worse. At least the wench'll not be more than twenty and the blood's good – royal blood at that.'

'Bastard blood,' Hal said scathingly. 'Joan Beaufort's only one of old Gaunt's bastards.'.

'Well, we've all a touch of that somewhere along the line,' Albany said. 'Are you telling me you're too proud to mix it with yours?'

Hal turned his face away. 'You don't understand,' he said stonily. 'It's more than that.'

'I understand hatred, if that's what you mean, and it's a virulent dangerous thing unless it's given purpose and direction. Like a woman it can bring you all or nothing. I detested your grandfather, yet in the end it was I who gave him protection and shelter when no other man would. I could have let Bolingbroke have him, or Neville. Both would have paid handsomely for him, dead or alive.'

'Then why didn't you?'

Albany shrugged. 'I really don't know,' he said. 'Perhaps because I hated the English more than I did him and thought that there was more profit to Scotland in keeping Bolingbroke unsteady on his throne, as he always would have been while Northumberland lived.' He smiled his small spiteful smile. 'Or perhaps it was because it gave me greater satisfaction to see him humbled and aware that every morsel of food that he put into his mouth came from me, that without me he'd be no more than one of the beggars queuing outside the gates for charity.' He raised his malevolent eyes to Hal's face. 'And how much better are you? Forever content to live on my generosity. Do you love us so well that you cannot bear to leave? Do you hate *me* any less than you do Neville?'

The calculated insult drained the colour from Hal's face but he kept his voice and eyes steady. He was used to Albany baiting him by now.

'Only a little, your Grace,' he said quietly. 'And that only because you are Scots and I English and that is cause enough for vengeance. But Neville had no cause except that Northumberland was greater than he was. He hounded him even when he was old and blind and dying.'

'Because he was afraid of him.' Albany smiled faintly. 'We were all afraid of him. He was a fearsome man, you know; even old and blind and dying.' He paused and met the impassive green eyes gravely. 'If it's revenge you're after you'll not get it here,' he said. 'You need wealth and power and position for that. Northumberland would have seen that, and he'd have allied himself to the Devil if it had given him what he wanted. And he'd have done

37

it smilingly, generously, as if it were the thing he wanted most in the world till none were sure who'd had the victory out of it.' He nodded slowly. 'Think on it, boy. I shall need your answer by morning.'

Was it such a betrayal? Perhaps only the ghosts of his mind thought so. Would the old man even have cared? He had married a Neville himself once by choice and scorned power and privilege to do it. But that was a long time ago, the small inner voice reminded him. There had been a wealth of Percy blood shed since then.

Hal paced out the confines of the narrow room. It looked shabbier and smaller since his visit to Etal. He could hardly breathe for the stifling heat and he thought longingly of Alnwick with its lofty rooms and jewel-hung walls. The air was always sweet there, cool and damp with the smell of river moss and heather on its breath. And it could all be his again; Alnwick and Warkworth, Prudhoe, Langley and Cockermouth, all the Lucy inheritance and the Yorkshire lands, almost all of the north from the Humber to the Tweed. So much for so little and all he had to do was marry Ralph Neville's daughter.

He sat heavily on the hard narrow bed. Even the thought of it turned him sick. He could feel his heart pounding against his ribs, beating up the old hatred like a war drum. The ugly memories came crowding back: Ralph Neville on Bramham Moor slitting his grandfather's throat like a dog; at York, smiling his cold complacent smile whilst Northumberland's lands were given away piecemeal. He'd had his share: all of Redesdale; Wressil in Yorkshire; and a dozen or more manors in Cumberland – the reward for the dog who had hounded his father and grandfather to their deaths. He stumbled to his feet. He was sweating, a cold nervous sweat that chilled him to the bone despite the heat. He had forgotten how much pain and hatred there was inside him. It lay heavy as lead in the pit of his stomach like a bellyful of sour wine.

'Think on it,' Albany had said, and he had done little else. There was some relief in the thought of vengeance. Every debt paid and with interest: his father, his grandfather – his mother, shut up like a nun these past ten years. The hatred uncoiled itself like a sleeping serpent and filled up the emptiness of him. He was surprised how warm and alive it made him feel. But Albany was right. He was nothing, had nothing and never would have while he was rebel and exile. He needed power and the promise of more. He needed Northumberland back. What did it matter if Ralph Neville was the man who brought it to him? That would have amused the old man. He had told him once, that last night they'd been together, the old man and the boy curled under the warmth of fur, 'Never forget that Northumberland is yours. Take it if it is offered you, no matter from whose hand.' Could he have dreamt then that it might be Ralph Neville? Hal smiled softly to himself. If there was anything of the old man in him they would see it now. What was it Albany had said? 'He'd have allied himself to the Devil if it could have given him Northumberland back.' Well, he would do no less. He'd wed his Neville wife, smilingly, generously as if it were the thing he wanted most in all the world. He'd breed sons from her, an army of sons to use against the very blood they had been born of. He'd spend every waking hour of his life bringing Neville and his house as low as they had once brought him. He sat very still, his breathing shallow and steady while the dark ugly thing took shape inside him. The last of the sun slanted in at the high window and dappled his face redly. From a distance he thought he could hear the sound of a woman's laughter. Sometimes he forgot that he was Elizabeth Mortimer's son.

Albany received his answer as if he had expected no other. 'Then you wish me to inform the Earl of Cambridge that you have withdrawn.'

'Yes,' answered Hal firmly. 'That is what I wish.'

Albany stroked his beard. 'He'll not be well pleased.'

Hal shrugged. 'I'm not afraid of Cambridge. There's nothing he can do to me without hurt to himself.'

'Unless he succeeds.' Albany grinned maliciously. 'What then, boy? What if you saddle yourself with a Neville wife and then find that the king you've to bend the knee to is Mortimer?' His laughter was like the cracking of dry twigs. 'You might find yourself back here before you know it, Neville wife and all.'

'I'll risk it,' Hal said grimly. 'If they do succeed then I'll have Henry's death on my conscience whether I was party to it or not. I could stop it, you know, if I had a mind to.'

'And find your head on the block before you knew where you were,' Albany cut him off swiftly. 'Don't be a fool. There's nothing to be done now and who would take your word for it anyway? An exile trying to worm his way into the king's good books with tales of imaginary plots. It's been tried before, you know.' He rose from the desk and poured them both an unusually generous measure of his spiced malmsey. 'It'll not come to that. Henry can look after himself. He's survived more rebellions than ever his father did. It's bred in him by now.' He handed Hal the fuller of the finely chased goblets. 'There. Let's not be thinking what might be. We've business to attend to.'

He sifted the sheaves of parchment that littered his desk, selected one and smoothed it out with his long pale fingers. 'My lord Neville requires that the marriage take place as soon as possible as a sign of good faith on our behalf,' he began briskly. 'He suggests October – at Berwick.' He glanced up at Hal. 'Does that suit you?' he asked drily.

'Does it matter?' Hal nodded toward the paper beneath Albany's spread palm. 'What else?'

'You will then return to Scotland while the negotiations for the release of my son, the Earl of Fife, are concluded. When these are complete,' he paused and sipped his wine slowly, 'then you are free to go.'

'Are you telling me that I'm still to be a prisoner even after the marriage?' Hal demanded hotly.

'Just so,' Albany answered him. 'That is *my* stipulation, not Neville's. Nothing is certain yet. The negotiations might fail. Parliament might refuse the exchange. Who knows? A man cannot be too careful.'

'And if that happens then I will have made the marriage for nothing,' Hal cried.

Albany lowered his eyes. 'In that case it will be of no consequence, for I shall not let you go.' He gave his small spiteful smile. 'You will not see Northumberland again till my son is home.'

'You're a treacherous bastard, Albany.'

The Regent raised his brows. 'I see that we failed to teach you manners also.' He leant forward and laid his arms on the desk. 'Let me give you a small word of advice, boy. Never see things as other than they are. The ifs and buts and maybes are for dreamers, men like Cambridge and his like. That's why they will fail and King Henry will succeed. He's a practical man like me. A survivor – like you.' For once there was warmth in the smile he gave Hal. 'Oh, yes. You're a born survivor. I've watched you grow – and not always liked what I saw, mind. Perhaps even to a degree you could say that I raised you.' He gave a sad little smile that sat oddly on a face accustomed only to harshness. 'Oh, I know that there's been little joy in it for you but there's been none for me either. My eldest son's been captive in England for longer than you have here. Twelve years, ever since your father took him at Homildon Hill.' Suddenly he looked all of his seventy years. 'That's a long time for a man to be without his heir. You're the only hope I've ever had of getting him back, all I've ever had to bargain with. Do you blame me for driving the bargain so hard?' He stared down into his wine. 'I'm an old man now. I'd like to have seen Murdac again before I died.'

Hal turned his goblet awkwardly between his fingers. There was nothing to say and it was too late to feel pity for a man who had soured half of his life. Yet perhaps at the heart of him he did. Albany was the same age that his grandfather would have been had he lived.

Then Albany looked up, his eyes bright and malicious again. 'I've no love for you or any of your house but if you're half the man that your grandsire was I'll not be ashamed to own you.'

Hal smiled drily and raised his cup. 'Then let us drink to the end of your stewardship, your Grace. And the homecoming of the Earl of Fife.'

For the second time in as many months he rode into Berwick. This time he wore new velvet and had fifty of Albany's men at his back. It was October, a dull overcast day of grey metallic light that plunged the narrow overhung streets into near darkness. There was a mist out on the river that blew in a fine insidious cloud up toward the town. It gave the day a luminous unreal quality.

They rode at walking pace behind creaking high-topped wains piled with impossible loads, past the moneychangers on the bridge crouched like jackdaws over shining piles of coin, past the fishmarket where the cobbles gleamed dangerously with the scales and entrails of gutted fish. The streets were full of harsh alien sounds, the grind of steel-rimmed wheels, the clack of wooden shoes, the raucous cries of merchants thumping their trestles to drum up trade. In the market square they could hardly move at all and Albany sent his herald on ahead to clear the way.

Hal glanced at the Regent's face and saw the pale acquisitive eyes taking stock of the wealth and trade that could have been Scotland's. On the wharves great vats of Burgundy were being stacked like siege towers. The flimsy wooden cranes jerked back and forth between ship and quay: bales of silk trussed in oilskin; drums of pepper and spice; the round unmistakable shapes of Flemish cheeses. Hal could understand Albany jumping at the chance of regaining Berwick. He wondered if the Regent was regretting that he had not become Cambridge's man after all.

They struggled on through the crowd, past stalls piled high with richness: the soft grey gleam of vair, the deeper sheen of sable. There was a booth that sold nothing but Burgundy velvet and he remembered that Burgundy was in favour now since the alliance with King Henry against the French. He glanced down at his own faultless doublet, the first he could ever remember that was not too short in the sleeves or straining at the seams. It was made in his own colours, azure velvet slashed with cloth of gold. Ralph Neville had paid for it, that and the horse he sat on with its silk housing and harness of red Spanish leather. He had accepted it as no more than his due. It was only the first of many debts that Neville was to repay him.

The crowds were thinning, falling back before Albany's herald, glancing first at the lion rampant on his coat, then staring at Albany, staring harder at Hal and the silver crescents worked on the housings of his horse. He heard the whisper of his name grow into a shout.

'Northumberland. It's Northumberland.'

Then the shout became a roar; hands were reaching out for

him, touching him. He stared disbelievingly at the sea of avid smiling faces. Their lips moved in the deafening repetition of his name. An old man reached up for his hand. He was weeping unashamedly. 'Welcome home, Lord. Oh, my dear lord, welcome home.'

Tears pricked at his own eyes and he raised his hand in tentative acknowledgement. The crowd surged toward him and he was in danger of being pulled from his horse till Albany grabbed his bridle and pulled him clear. He shouted to his men.

'For God's sake, clear this rabble.' He looked at Hal and saw the angry line of his mouth. 'Patience, lad,' he said mockingly. 'There'll be time for glory later. And besides you're not Northumberland yet, not till I and King Henry say so.'

Hal threw a last agonised look over his shoulder before a dozen burly Scotsmen closed in at his back. He saw Albany's men riding into the crowd and a woman screamed as a stall overturned and spilled bales of bright cloth into the crowd. On the edge of it he saw the pale incredulous face of Jack Allbright.

That sobered him more than all of Albany's sharpness . . . He'd almost forgotten Jack; Jack and Wat and that hot September night in Berwick when they had all drunk more than they should. He glanced up uneasily to the castle gates looming ahead. If Neville should discover that he'd been in Berwick that night . . . He felt suddenly cold, knowing how far from freedom he still was.

He waited alone in the empty hall. In the vault of the roof the dusty banners swung in ghostly silence; the crests and arms of all those who had held Berwick. Strangely enough Northumberland's was still there, the azure lion on its golden field quartered with the silver pike of the Lucys. The colours were faded, the gold-work dull, but it was still there. He was surprised that Neville had not had it taken down.

He paced the worn and polished tiles. It was more than twelve years since he had set foot in this room. He remembered nothing of it save that his father had been there, his long body sprawled on the couch by the door. That was all. His father's presence had always made all else seem forgettable. He mounted the steps of the dais and stared from the tall oriel window. He could see the mast-tips of the ships that choked the mouth of the Tweed. The tide was out and showed the pale luminous sands curving down to Lindisfarne and Bamburgh. Irrelevantly he remembered that it was a monk from Lindisfarne who had taught him Greek.

He did not turn immediately when the door opened. He waited till the solitary footsteps had advanced well down the hall. You could tell a lot from a man's footsteps and these were strong and purposeful. He knew instinctively that they belonged to Ralph Neville. He turned then, the light at his back, and heard the footsteps check in their long stride. There was a pause, the sound of a sharp intake of breath, then they came on toward him as firm and as sure as ever.

Ralph Neville stared at him for a moment in silence, the ghost exorcised from his mind by the sight of the firm young flesh and expressionless eyes. For a moment there, he had thought . . . He dropped his eyes and seated himself behind the long table, his square capable hands sifting the papers he had brought. He motioned Hal to be seated, then glanced up in mild surprise when he remained standing.

'I would rather stand,' said Hal quietly. 'I have been sitting idle ten years too long as it is.'

'As you please.' Neville bent his head to the parchments again. 'I believe that his grace of Albany has explained all to you.' He had a curious voice, each word carefully and sharply articulated as if he begrudged the breath for them. 'After the marriage to my daughter . . .'

Hal interrupted him. It had suddenly occurred to him that he did not even know her name.

Neville looked at him as if it was the last thing he should want to know. 'Alianore,' he said briefly. 'She is my eldest daughter and was recently wed to the eldest son of the Earl of Gloucester until his unfortunate and untimely death.' The tone of his voice implied quite clearly that he was second choice. He went on to speak of dowry, the least that could be given without loss of honour or prestige. 'In the meantime,' he ended, 'I shall endeavour to see that your petition is presented to Parliament and the king as soon as possible.'

'How soon?'

'As soon as possible,' Neville repeated. 'The king has weightier matters to deal with, delicate negotiations with the Dukes of Burgundy and Orleans, which cannot wait. There is talk of war,' he said, more to himself than to Hal.

'And naturally the king wishes to leave nothing but friends behind him,' Hal said cynically. 'Is that the reason I am suddenly being brought into favour?'

Irritation narrowed the corners of Neville's eyes. 'The king is anxious to forgive and forget past grievances,' he began.

'And if I am not?'

Slowly Neville laid his quill down. 'If you are not then you had better mount your horse and ride back the way you came. The king has no time for disloyalty.'

'It was not of the king that I spoke,' Hal said. 'King Henry himself has done me no harm.'

Neville let his breath out in a long elaborate sigh as if the cost of civility was becoming too much for him.

'Of whom did you speak, then?' he asked.

'Of you, my lord. Who else?'

Neville frowned. He had warned Henry. You could not keep a man in exile for ten years, then trot him out meek as a lamb. Especially a Percy you couldn't.

When he looked up he was smiling faintly. 'Well, at least we understand one another.'

'I thought that we should,' said Hal quietly.

Neville pursed his lips and swept him with a disdainful glance. 'I doubt if you'll be such a worthy adversary as he was.'

'But better than most. I promise you that at least.'

'Then why this? Why did you agree to this marriage if your bride's family is so obviously little to your taste?'

'For the same reason as you did, my lord. Gain. I did it to get Northumberland back and you, because it was the only way you could keep a hold on Northumberland and a watchful eye on me.'

'And you think I would sacrifice a daughter of mine to such a mercenary cause?' Neville was mocking him now, and openly too.

'With such a flock as you have, my lord, I doubt if you'll miss the one. And I hear that the Countess Joan is with child again.' Hal smiled insultingly. 'It is a wise merchant that never lets his stocks run low.'

In spite of himself Neville was amused. He was reminded of himself at that age, pitting himself against Northumberland's inexorable tongue in defence of his own father. He did not doubt that Hal hated him as much as he had hated Northumberland then. He could afford to smile. He was immune to hatred now.

'Well then, young Henry.' The quick dark eyes met his. 'Or do they call you Hal as they did your grandfather?'

'Only those that are close to me.'

'Well, I shall be close to you, shall I not? Your father-in-law,' he reminded him mockingly. 'I also shall call you Hal.'

He rose from the table and crossed to a tall coffer by the window. 'I have a gift for you,' he said over his shoulder.

Hal watched as he took an object wrapped in velvet from the cupboard. He laid it almost reverently on the table between them. 'Your wedding gift,' he said softly. He drew back the velvet. It was a sword, the hilt twined with the threshing body of a lion. On the blade was the one word, 'Esperaunce'.

'It was his,' the careful voice said quietly. 'I took it from him on the field at Bramham Moor.'

Hal stretched out a trembling hand and touched the cold steel. 'Before or after you killed him?' he asked savagely.

'Oh, afterwards,' Neville grinned maliciously. 'I would not strike down an unarmed man.'

It took all the effort of Hal's will to keep his voice and eyes steady. He grasped the hilt and felt the weight of the steel in his hand. Neville's voice continued to taunt him. 'Are you tempted, boy? Are you tempted to strike off my head as I did his? I sent it to Bolingbroke and he had it raised on London Bridge the same day. It's still there. What's left of it.'

Hal said nothing, felt nothing except the coldness of the sword in his hand.

'He wasn't dead, you know. Almost but not quite. He had such a defiant grip on life even though he was only half a man by then. He was in dreadful pain. To kill him was the only kindness I ever did him.'

Hal laid down the sword and looked up, his eyes bright and grim. This particular kind of baiting left no mark on him. He'd had years of it from Albany. 'It's a fine gift, my lord,' he said lightly as if he had heard none of it. 'I'm surprised that you kept it so long.' He touched the scarlet velvet. 'And with such reverence. Did you need such a constant reminder that he was dead?'

Neville did not answer him. But his eyes were suddenly bleak. He thought uneasily that he was no longer so sure that he was.

It was done almost furtively with no more ceremony than need be. He walked into the chapel between Albany and Douglas. Both were uneasy, anxious to get it done and be on their way and Albany had only entered Berwick at all after an elaborate exchange of hostages and a written safe conduct from King Henry himself.

Neville was already there with a short stocky young man whose dark hair was cropped almost to the crown. Douglas nudged him and whispered. 'That's Bedford, the king's brother.'

Hal walked on alone to where the chaplain fidgeted with his missal. Neville nodded formally to him and John of Bedford turned dark melancholy eyes upon him and smiled. A choir of a dozen boys had begun to sing, a high strained sound that grated on his nerves till they gathered strength and found pitch and resonance. Then he heard the brisk rustle of stiff brocade behind him. A plump bejewelled figure drifted into the periphery of his vision, her swollen belly stuck forward like the prow of a ship. He caught the shrewd blue eyes appraising him like a side of beef and inclined his head courteously. This was Joan Beaufort, Neville's wife and half-sister to the king.

When the girl was brought to stand beside him he did not turn his head. He sensed that she was tall, almost as tall as he was. And that her hair was dark. He caught the sharp distinct scent of vervain as she laid her hand on his for their joining. He was surprised to see that his own was trembling.

He knelt and stood and knelt again. From the corner of his eye he could see Douglas fidgeting with his eye-patch and rubbing the red raw socket it concealed. The priest droned on. He heard his own voice tight with strain, then hers, light and firm with no tremor or uncertainty. Then Albany gave the betrothal ring into his hand. It was an emerald, as green as his eyes. He slid it awkwardly onto her outstretched finger. The chaplain murmured the final blessing; the choir soared to the last note of the anthem and the fragile sound hung trembling in the vault of the roof. Then it was done. They were man and wife. For good or ill he had married Alianore Neville.

He turned for the first time and looked into her face. Her eyes were dark and flecked with little points of amber light. Her mouth was wide and generous, too wide for true beauty, but her teeth when she smiled were white and even. He kissed her clumsily and searched his mind frantically for something to say. There was no need. The Countess Joan had sailed between them. She nodded to him and said something he did not hear; then with her hand firmly beneath her daughter's elbow she led her from the room.

He saw her once more, at the grudging and hasty banquet that Neville had provided. The minstrels played fortissimo to cover the frequent lulls in the conversation which at the best of times was stilted and fraught with innuendo and veiled insults. Inevitably it turned to war.

Albany said in his patronising voice, 'Is it true that King Henry is preparing for war?' He cast a sly look at John of Bedford. 'I would have thought that he'd make sure his own realm was safely in his pocket before he cast about for others.'

Bedford answered him coolly. 'It is no secret that the king is negotiating with France for the restoration of certain territories and the recognition of his claim.'

'Claim!' Albany's voice was high with derision. 'What claim is this? Like the claim he makes to the overlordship of Scotland?'

'It's a just claim,' Bedford said defensively. 'My brother is rightful King of France by virtue of the third Edward's mother, Isabella of France. Through our grandfather John of Gaunt, the king's descent is direct from Philip the Fourth of France. King Charles' claim is only through that of King Philip's brother, Charles of Valois.'

There was a pause. Then Albany said, 'Then if you allow such a claim through the female line, I could point out that it is Edmund

Mortimer who should be sitting on England's throne, not your brother.'

'That's treason,' Neville snapped.

'Not for me it is not. I owe no allegiance to Henry,' Albany reminded him tartly. 'If I owe any it is to Charles of France. Scotland has always allied with France in time of war.'

'Only because they pay more,' Neville muttered.

'That surely would be for King James to decide if he were free,' Bedford said.

'Well, he's not free and never likely to be unless Henry drops his extortionate demands for ransom and homage.' Albany smiled disparagingly. 'We are a poor country. A sum such as you name is impossible to find.'

'I'll warrant you've more than that stuffed beneath your mattress,' Neville said insultingly. 'If it were King Henry held hostage there's not a man among us who would not beggar himself to set him free.'

'You think so?' Albany said. 'Well, that would be your privilege as it is mine not to do so. And besides, I doubt if Henry would let him go even if the ransom were paid. He's keeping James prisoner for a better reason than money. I believe he thinks it keeps us passive.'

'And does it not?'

'Only while it suits us.' Albany smiled. 'Perhaps when Henry turns his back on us and sails in pursuit of his imaginary French crown it will not suit us so well.'

'Is that a threat, Albany?' Bedford demanded, his heavy face stained with ugly colour.

'You may take it whichever way you please. If Henry chooses to take advantage of a mad king then he cannot complain if we do so of an absent one.' He smiled spitefully. 'The trouble with you English is that you never know when you are beaten.'

'Perhaps that is because we rarely are,' Neville said sharply. 'Unlike yourselves, who were weaned on defeat.'

Albany's face grew pale but he kept his composure. 'That is because we do not fight with the same weapons, my lord,' he said. 'Treachery, deceit and broken oaths such as you English are accustomed to use can be as lethal as the barb of an arrow.'

The conversation ground into a hostile silence that even the Countess Joan's bright chatter could not salvage and for the rest of the meal Albany kept frigid silence and Douglas sat hunched in his chair, gruff and monosyllabic, plunging his knife into capon as if he wished it was Neville's throat.

The countess smiled her bright birdlike smile. Her plump heavy face was filmed with sweat and flushed with too much wine. She sat between Hal and Alianore, a mountain of perfumed and jewelled flesh, and never once allowed the talk to rise above the level of commonplace. Not that Hal would have had anything to say if she had. He spoke directly to his wife only once. They'd exchanged the usual pleasantries. He'd enquired if her journey to Berwick had been comfortable and she in turn had asked after his, as if he were an unimportant knight in her father's hall. Her poise and total acceptance of her father's wishes irritated him. It occurred to him that if he'd been old and ugly and palsied she still would have married him.

The meal ground on to a strained and hostile conclusion and their brief stilted farewells were made with relief. Albany and Neville closeted themselves in the little room behind the dais. Douglas nodded curtly to all that he need to and stumped off down the hall. Smilingly Hal bent low over the Countess Joan's plump hand and bruised his lips on sapphires and seed pearls. Then he turned to his bride who waited quietly beside him. He lifted her outstretched hand to his mouth. The emerald shot a sliver of green light into his eyes. The colour of envy and greed and hatred.

'My lady,' was all he said. If she had expected more she did not show it. She smiled politely as he released her hand, and sank in a low formal curtsey. Then she followed the immense glittering figure of her mother from the hall. She did not look back even once.

He turned to find John of Bedford's dark eyes upon him.

'Your Grace,' he said and bowed.

Bedford smiled. It was only the smile which saved his face from complete ugliness. His features were heavy and blunt and his cropped hair did little to disguise them.

'Well, Northumberland,' he said, 'that's the worst of it done.'

Hal fell in beside him as he walked from the hall. 'I'm not Northumberland yet, your Grace,' he said, remembering Albany's warning. 'Not till King Henry says so. He might change his mind.'

'Henry never changes his mind. Once he's set on a course nothing can turn him. That's the good thing about Henry. The rules never change. You always know where you stand.' He glanced at Hal. 'You've never met him, have you?'

'No, I never have.' But he'd heard enough of him for there to be the spark of a reluctant admiration.

Bedford's eyes darkened with adoration. 'You'll like him. He'll ask only one thing of you and that's loyalty. If you give him that, then all else is forgivable to Henry.'

All else. Hal thought suddenly of that night at Etal, of Cambridge and Scrope, of silly Edmund . . .

Bedford leant his arms on the weathered merlons of the roof and stared out toward Scotland. 'Well, I shan't be sorry to give this into your hands,' he said pensively. 'They're a hard and stubborn people up here and they don't take to a change of master easily.'

Hal said nothing. He had forgotten that as Lord Warden of the Marches, his own restoration would mean considerable loss of land and revenue to Bedford.

'I hear there was near riot in the market place when you rode in.' Bedford shot him an almost envious glance. 'I would like to think that one day I could inspire that kind of loyalty.'

'It's not loyalty to me,' Hal said. 'It's loyalty to what I stand for. Northerners have long memories.'

Bedford nodded. 'Henry can,' he said fervently. 'Inspire loyalty, I mean. He cares, you see. He cares about little men and they know it. I sometimes think he'd starve himself rather than see any of his men go without.'

Hal nodded with understanding. His own father had been like that. Perhaps it was from him that King Henry had learnt to care. He felt a sudden stirring of conscience. If Cambridge's plot succeeded and he had done nothing; if Henry died . . . He glanced covertly at the man beside him. Did he dare to trust Bedford? Could he break the oath that he had so solemnly sworn? He had believed in it then. He too had wanted Henry of Lancaster dead.

Cautiously he said, 'All men have enemies, your Grace. Especially kings. I think there are some close to him who do not love him as well as they should.'

Bedford straightened slowly and turned to face him. 'You think, or you know?'

'I cannot say more, your Grace, without great loss of honour,' Hal answered him desperately. 'All I ask is that you stay close to the king. Watch him and trust none.'

Bedford's eyes narrowed. 'I don't think you need to say more. I've had my own thoughts about some of Henry's so-called friends for some time.' He picked idly at the lichens growing between the stones. 'Thank you for telling me,' he said and smiled his rare and brilliant smile. 'I can see that we shall do very well together.'

Hal returned the smile but said nothing. He hoped so, dear God, he hoped so. Both he and the king might be in sore need of a man like John of Bedford soon.

They were back across the Border by nightfall. Before they were a mile into Scotland it had begun to rain, a sharp stinging wintry rain that had them hunched and shivering in their saddles. At Melrose they halted for the night and after Albany had unceremoniously turfed the grumbling Abbot from his lodgings, they sat down to a frugal meal of cold mutton and ale.

Despite his hunger, Hal ate little. He felt subtly changed, as if the last few hours had alienated him from all that had been heart and home to him these last ten years. He looked at Albany, wiping his mouth fastidiously on his kerchief. Still well hated, but even the edges of that had been blunted by familiarity. It was more the hatred of captor and captive than hatred of the man. In truth, he could not say that Albany had done so badly by him. Even with Douglas, rough and overbearing and totally faithless as he was, there was always the thought that he had been beside his father when he died. It had almost formed a tenuous bond between them, not friendship but more the enforced and reluctant amity of long acquaintance. But all that was changing. They would soon be open enemies. He would be English and they Scots and the Border would lie between them. It was a strange and unfamiliar feeling, as if the years of exile had blurred his sense of nationality. In all that time he had felt no loyalty to any but himself, and Northumberland had been all of England to him. Now he felt the pull of a loyalty beyond that, to a country he hardly knew, to a king he did not know at all. He thought again of Bedford and glanced almost guiltily at Albany. The Regent would have torn him limb from limb if he had known that he had gambled all on a prick of conscience. Away from Bedford's stolidity he felt the hollow doubt. Could he trust a man he'd met only once? For all he knew Bedford might be shouting rebellion from the rooftops and once the king knew, he was not the kind of man to let it lie. Henry would want names and even if Scrope and Cambridge did not betray him he felt that Mortimer would. It would all have been for nothing. Northumberland would be out of his reach for ever and all would be as before. No, not all. He remembered he had a wife now, a Neville wife.

Then Douglas peered at his untouched plate. 'You've not eaten,' he observed brusquely. 'Are you sick?'

'Lovesick?' Albany mocked. 'Are you thinking of your bride, Hal?'

'It'll do him no good thinking, with her twenty miles away in Berwick,' Douglas said as he tipped the contents of Hal's plate onto his own. 'You'd have thought that at least they'd have let him bed the wench.'

'Not Neville. He's too shrewd for that.' Albany squinted slyly at Hal. 'He'd not take the chance of you fathering a brat on her before the bargain was fully struck. Still,' he smiled with rare humour, 'it must make you almost unique. You're the only man I know who spent his wedding night in a monastery.'

Hal smiled indulgently at the jest. *His wife.* He was surprised at how much pleasure the thought gave him. Alianore. He shaped her name softly in his mind and recalled her eyes, the warm smiling mouth, her body soft and rounded beneath the heavy silk gown. He raised his cup abruptly and drank. She was still a Neville and Neville was the enemy. She was no more to him than a means to an end. That end was Northumberland and freedom and she was the price.

He dragged the pitcher of ale from Douglas' grasp. Tonight he would get gloriously and uproariously drunk.

There was nothing to do but wait; all through the winter and the long slow thaw. By spring there was still no news save that King Henry prepared in earnest for war.

Albany's spies were thorough and well paid by the French for it. As Henry gave out his orders, so Albany had them before him in Dalkeith within the week.

King Henry still kept the French on tenterhooks, sending the Bishop of Paris scuttling back and forth across the Channel with fresh but equally impossible terms. The French tried desperately to sue for peace, at the same time trying to whittle down Henry's exhorbitant demands. And they were exhorbitant: all of Aquitaine and half of Provence; Normandy, Maine, Anjou and Touraine; the lordships of Beaumont and Nogent; and the hand of King Charles' daughter Katherine with a dowry of eight million crowns.

The French Count of Armagnac sent desperate messages to Albany. Could he count on the Scots for support? How many men could King Henry put in the field if it came to it? Had they cannon? When would he sail? Where would he land?

Hal watched the furtive comings and goings gloomily and noticed that Albany was careful he did not see too much. There was talk of nothing but war and it increased his frustration to know that he would have no part in it.

In May they moved to Stirling and on again to Edinburgh. Hal took the chance to ride over to St Andrews. It might be the last chance he had to see the man who had once provided all the kindness and affection he had known.

Thomas Wardlaw received him in the small cluttered room where he both worked and slept. Both table and floor were littered with books and parchments and the scrap of Turkey rug that took the chill from the flags was crusted with dust from the feet of the masons who tramped the fifty-three steps of the tower daily to report their progress.

Bishop Thomas flung his thin arm round Hal's shoulders, and drew him to the window. 'See? It grows.' He spoke proudly, his thin mobile face alight but it was not the pride of self but of achievement in a Holy cause.

Hal looked down to the confusion of half finished walls and piles of stone that had risen in the place of the wooden hall where he had struggled with Latin and Greek.

'It's a fair sight, is it not? The first seat of learning in Scotland. The University of St Andrews.'

Hal nodded. 'A fair sight, my lord. And your achievement.'

'Not mine, but God's,' the bishop disclaimed. 'Nothing is ever achieved without His help. All I pray now is that He gives me time and strength to see it done.' He turned and regarded Hal critically. 'Now you, you are my achievement.' He tilted his head on one side like a small inquisitive bird. 'You've grown,' he said. 'Almost as tall as your grandsire.'

'Did you expect me to stay the small puny child that you beat unmercifully for fumbling his verbs?'

'I doubt it did you harm.' The bishop swept a pile of books from a stool so that Hal could be seated. 'And besides I only did it the once and that was when you pushed poor Jamie from his bench.'

Hal saw the look of pain that touched the sensitive mouth when he spoke the king's name.

'There's no better news of Jamie then?'

'No better. No worse.' The bishop sighed. 'Though I fear it's James himself who is the stumbling block now. He still refuses to swear fealty to King Henry for Scotland.'

'Would you expect him to?' His stubbornness was one of the things Hal remembered best about James Stewart, that and the fact that his round chubby face would turn red as a turkey cock when he was bested. And he often was in those days. As the king's son he did not have to prove himself. Hal did. They had been friends then, too young to be set apart by race or privilege. They had eaten and slept together, cribbed sums from each other behind the bishop's back, stolen hams from the kitchen when their young bellies had rumbled with hunger on punishment days. And there had been enough of those for both of them. The bishop had never shown preference, king's son or no, James Stewart learnt his lessons or had a lean day for it. Hal was never

55

really sure whether they had outgrown the friendship or it had outgrown them. James had returned to his father's Court and Hal had seen less of him. The gap had widened and become unbreachable. Suddenly they were no longer boys growing up under the benign eye of Bishop Wardlaw. They were captor and captive, Scots and English with three hundred years of hatred between them. Overnight, without a word, they were enemies. Then James had been sent to France, though he had never even reached the Channel. His ship had foundered off Flamborough Head and within a week Bolingbroke had him lodged in the Tower. He had been there ever since. Hal thought that he would be much changed now. A man, the same age as Hal himself and captive too. At least they had that in common.

The bishop answered his question. 'No. I do not expect him to. Though sometimes I wish he were not so obdurate. Scotland needs a king. Albany's old and that pack of sons of his are not fit to have charge of an alehouse, let alone a kingdom.' He shrugged. 'So James swears fealty to Henry of England. Kings of Scotland have done it before and it's done England no good and Scotland no harm. It'll do her more harm to be without him, for him to be cooped up in the Tower for the rest of his life. There's always a middle road.' He smiled his gentle smile. 'You've found it, my son. I doubt if it was any easier to ally yourself to the house of Neville than it would be for James to acknowledge Henry as his overlord.'

Hal flushed. Why should he feel so guilty?

'Don't look so shamefaced. You only did what you had to.'

'I didn't *have* to,' said Hal.

'In your own mind you did. What else, my son? To stay in ward for the rest of your life out of pride and spleen like Jamie? Pride without liberty is a useless thing.'

'But better than none at all.'

'But not better than a king's blood on your hands. Oh, I know that too and I thanked God with all my heart that He had kept you from it. Your grandsire suffered long enough for it. He would not have wanted the same for you.'

Hal rose to his feet and went to stare from the high window.

'What would he have wanted, Father?' he asked quietly.

'For you to forget, to begin anew. There's no virtue in hatred. It's corrosive, destructive. It destroyed both him and your father. Oh, I can feel it's there, Hal. I know you too well not to know what's in your heart. You've been a prisoner too long, always looking back, never forward. He would not have wanted that for you. Believe me, you've not broken faith. He'd have done no less himself.'

'Would he not?' said Hal softly and covered his disbelief with a smile. He knew better. For all he loved the old bishop he was still a priest and priests knew nothing of hatred.

'Anyway,' he said lightly, 'I'm not free yet. There's been no word from England. Henry might well have changed his mind. He's set on invading France this year and he might feel that I'm better left where I am.'

'Don't worry. It'll come.' Bishop Thomas rose and took his arm. 'It'll come in God's good time.'

It came at the end of July, on a hot sweltering day like the day he had ridden down to Berwick almost a year before. He was eating supper, week-old mutton doused with vinegar sauce to keep off the flies, and listening with half an ear to Douglas' loud and belligerent discourse on the treachery of Burgundy. War again, with Henry of England riding the crest of the diplomatic wave. Surprisingly the precarious amity with John of Burgundy still held and Henry had wined and dined the German Emperor Sigismund into fervent alliance. It seemed that there was nothing to stop him now.

Hal sipped his ale thoughtfully. It was warm and bitter but the heat had turned the wine to vinegar weeks ago and it was all they had. It was better than nothing and enough of it could dull the nagging ache of frustration that grew worse each day.

How much longer? he thought desperately. The uncertainty was killing. Albany was evasive and more concerned with pleasing his French paymasters. The dreadful thought came into his mind: if he were not freed before the war then he might never be. If Henry of England lost, were taken prisoner?

Then the loud intrusive grind of the portcullis chain cut harshly into his thoughts. The bridge was down. He glanced at Albany and saw him stiffen. At this hour?

The knights at the lower tables had already risen and stood with hands poised on their swords. Albany laid his goblet down carefully and stared at the door.

Then the room seemed full of men and out of their midst came Ralph Neville. He came toward them with his long unfaltering stride. He looked once at Albany and then directly at Hal.

'You fool,' he said. 'You bloody, stupid fool.'

There was a wind blowing hard from the sea, sharp and clean and laden with salt that crusted the thick panes of the dark little room where he was kept. He had been asleep and it took the first few minutes of waking for him to remember where he was: Portchester, the royal castle of Portchester. He was waiting to be brought before the king, charged with high treason.

He sat up and winced as the iron manacle clamping his wrist dragged him back against the wall. *Treason*. The word had lost none of its dreadful implication in the three weeks it had taken for him to come south, three weeks in which Cambridge and Grey had already lost their heads. For Scrope, the beloved, had been reserved all of the king's spleen. He had been hung like a felon and his bowels burnt before his eyes. His body still swung, what was left of it, from the gibbet on the Southampton road.

It was Mortimer who had cracked, as cleanly and loudly as a year-old twig. And of his own free will, not, as Hal had first thought, because Bedford had brought pressure to bear. Like him, his cousin Mortimer had balked at outright murder. It was Cambridge who had implicated Hal, out of spite or necessity he would never know. Tom Grey had confessed, but only to his own guilt. Henry Scrope had said nothing at all, even to the very hour they had hanged him. He swallowed hard to ease the knot of fear in his throat. Was this how it was going to end? Ignominious death and his head on Bargate like Tom Grey's? He had passed directly beneath it as he had entered Southampton. The stump of the neck was already baked black by the sun. The eyes were turned up, white glassy pebbles sunk deep in the red blistering skin. The mouth hung open as if in horror, filled with black feasting flies. Dear Tom. Dear faithful Tom. The thought had crossed his mind: had his father's head looked like that on Micklegate? Like father, like son? And the irony of it was that he need not have come at all. Neville could never have brought him out of Scotland by force. Albany's protection had still held and he had been prepared to risk bloodshed to enforce it. Neville had not. But he had come, because the thought of perpetual exile had been worse than death. Now, after three days in this stinking cell, he would gladly have gone back. He had never felt death so close.

He dragged himself to his feet and walked the length of his chain. It barely reached the small leaded window and the iron cuff bit hard into his wrist as he leant to watch the guard pacing the walk below him. There was nothing else to see but water and ships, fifteen hundred of them in all, crowding the broad smooth sheet of the Solent and every inlet and creek along the coast that could afford them shelter. Outside the harbour, by Spithead, the royal ships rode the light swell. He knew their names. The jailer who brought him his food and the scraps of news that he devoured more eagerly than the bowl of greasy soup that was his sole diet had pointed them out to him: the *Katherine de la Toure*, the *Petite Trinité*, the *Coq de la Toure*, and a little way apart, dwarfing them all in size and brilliance, Henry's flagship, the *Trinité Royale*. At her masthead, streaking the sky with scarlet and blue, the banners of the Trinity and the arms of St Edward, St George and England streamed stiffly seaward. From the topcastle a gilded crown glinted in the sun, throwing back a hundred points of light. Her broad hull writhed with painted serpents; her sails were alive with embroidered birds: falcons with long silvered wings; griffons with tearing beaks and gilded claws; a phoenix on a nest of vermilion flame. From the prow a crowned and gilded leopard strained eagerly toward France.

Hal turned back into the dim little room, twice as dark now after the sunlight. Today. It would be today. The jailer had brought him a clean shirt and hose that morning and the news that the fleet would sail on the following day. He thought that Neville might have come but perhaps his father-in-law had considered his duty done with the brief visit of yesterday. He had primed Hal well: what to say at his trial and when; the manner in which to say it. Humility without obsequiousness. He doubted if Ralph Neville had knowledge of either. But it was the nearest Hal had come to laughter for a long time, to see Ralph Neville fretting for his welfare, if only because the smell of treason clung to a man's kin. And whether Neville liked it or not he was kin. He himself sometimes forgot that he was married to Neville's daughter. He thought of her now. Did she know? Did she care? He shrugged and moved back to the low truckle bed. It did not matter now. He doubted if he would ever see her again.

He lay down upon his back and closed his eyes. The clock on the harbour church struck the hour. Four o'clock. It must be almost time.

Yet when the footsteps came he did not hear them. It was the grind of the key in the lock that woke him. Ralph Neville filled the narrow doorway, waiting while the jailer struck off his chains. 'Come then,' he said in his clipped grudging voice. 'The king must not be kept waiting.'

The bright sunlight of the hall brought stinging tears to Hal's eyes and he blinked them away fiercely lest any thought that he wept. Neville walked beside him, matching him stride for stride like a shadow and for once he was glad of his proximity among the throng of alien faces. He could feel the hostility, as tangible as heat or cold. Cambridge and Scrope had set the mood before him. They were traitors, and he was another. He was adjudged guilty before he had uttered a word.

Then Neville was gone to his place and he was alone, the focal point of a hundred pairs of eyes. There was not a face he knew or could put a name to till a steward's deferential whisper proclaimed a tall, elderly man as my lord of Warwick. Hal flinched inwardly. Richard Beauchamp, Earl of Warwick, his father's greatest adversary at Shrewsbury. He could expect no mercy there. On the edge of the crowd a thin dark-haired young man smiled at him encouragingly. Hal thought that it might be his sister Bess' husband, John Clifford. He swallowed hard. He prayed to God that Bess was not here. She'd had enough griefs.

The shrill of the trumpets at his back tore the last of his nerves to shreds. Lancaster Herald came down the steps of the dais and laid a jewelled shoe on the polished jasper tiles.

'Henry, by the Grace of God, King of England and France, Lord of Ireland, enters here . . .'

Hal kept his eyes fixed on the herald's face till the king was seated on the small gilded throne and but for that he would never have known that he *was* king, flanked as he was by the jewelled magnificence of his brothers, Clarence and Gloucester. Henry himself wore plain, clerkly black, his only adornment a gold Lancastrian collar. He looked more the priest than the mitred bishop who stood obsequiously at his elbow. There was no doubt who he was; sleek and eager as a questing hound, this must be Henry Beaufort, Bishop of Winchester. John of Bedford was there too, deferential and almost as plainly attired as the king. He smiled encouragingly as the herald began to read the charge.

Hal looked up into the king's face, an old face though there could have been no more than a few years or so between them, almost a holy face with that pale glowing skin and the smooth dark hair cropped so short above his ears. Only the red voluptuous mouth dispelled the priestly image. His eyes were large and grey and cold as winter. They stared at Hal as though his head were already fixed on Southampton gate.

The herald had finished reading the charge and demanded in a high querulous voice, 'Are you guilty or not?'

Was he guilty? Yes, in thought if not in deed. Would Henry care about the difference?

Slowly he said, 'I do not deny that I met with the lords Scrope and Cambridge at Etal and agreed to support them in a rebellion against the king. I later withdrew that support through the offices of the Duke of Albany.'

Henry spoke for the first time. 'Why did you so withdraw?'

Again Hal met the cold lambent stare. From the corner of his eye he could see Neville prompting him. Now, now was the time – because he could not bring himself to make war on his lawful king, because he feared God and Henry more than exile, because he trusted in Henry to right all his wrongs. Humility but not obseqiousness. Perhaps it was ten years of just that that made the words stick in his throat or perhaps it was the small malevolent voice inside him that whispered, 'Remember who he is. This is Lancaster, the son of the man who persecuted your father and

grandfather because they raised him up to be better than he was.'
He glanced around him. The smug, arrogant faces fenced him in
on all sides, all waiting for the expected plea for mercy. Mortimer
was there, all fearful eyes and trembling mouth. Hal's own
mouth tightened in disgust. He'd not grovel for his life as *he* had
done. If he was going to die, then at least let him go to it with
honour. It was all he had left now.

Loudly he said, 'I withdrew because I thought the plot too
weak to succeed.' He waited till Henry's eyes were full upon him.
'And because I thought that Edmund Mortimer would make an
even worse king than you.'

The king continued to regard him without expression. 'You
have nerve,' he said, 'for the son of a rebel and traitor.'

'No more than you have, my lord, for the son of a murderer
and usurper.'

In the dreadful silence that followed he could hear the hammering of his own heart as loud as a drum.

Then the king replied in a voice that was not so steady as it had
been. 'You are eager for death, it seems. Even to the wielding of
the axe yourself?' Then the king waved his hand around the
shocked and silent gathering. 'Leave us,' he said, 'save my
brothers and the lords Neville and Warwick.'

When the hall had emptied the king rose from his chair and
came slowly down the steps of the dais. He was close enough for
Hal to see the threads of silver that already streaked the smooth
dark cap of hair and the puckered scar on his cheek that he had
gained at the Shrewsbury fight. His full red mouth was almost
womanly but there was nothing of softness about it now.

'You say I am usurper, then?' he asked softly.

'Your father was.'

A shadow darkened the king's face. Did he not know it? Did he
not sleep and wake to it? The nagging doubt, the guilt.

There were no innocents, only the guilty. The only innocent
had been Richard himself. They must all bear the shame of it.
Easily said but in his heart Henry knew that all the shame of it
was his, his and his father's, but more his for he had loved
Richard. He had loved this man's father too, Harry Hotspur, his
idol and mentor who had taught him to handle a sword like no

other man in England, who had bullied and chivvied and praised him to perfection and then had that perfection turned against him at Shrewsbury. The king lowered his eyes. He had learnt since: Hotspur; Richard; now his beloved Scrope. Kings and princes had no friends. There was only loneliness and the dark void of death to come.

'You are your father's son and I am mine,' he said. 'I am also king. Crowned, anointed, hallowed, as much a king as Richard ever was. My only fault is that I am descended from the fourth son of King Edward instead of the second. Is that such a great fault? Would you plunge England into war against herself for such an accident of birth?' He smiled grimly. 'You said yourself that Edmund Mortimer would make a worse king and there is none else, no other choice. Am I such a bad one?'

Hal stared at him resentfully and wondered why Henry even cared what *he* thought. But he did care. The dark haunted gaze upon his face left no doubt as to that. He recalled Albany's words: 'He's plagued by conscience and unlaid ghosts.'

Then John of Bedford spoke. 'Why did you try to warn me at Berwick? It was conscience then. I know it.'

Hal avoided his gaze. 'Because I would not see a man slaughtered like a tame rabbit.' He threw the king a malevolent look. 'Even you.'

'Then why not tell all there and then?' Warwick said. 'These others meant nothing to you. You could have saved yourself if you had named them.'

'I swore an oath not to betray them,' Hal said stubbornly. 'I could not break it.'

'Do you hold an oath so dearly then?' Henry said quietly. 'Even above your own life?'

Hal did not answer and Henry went on. 'If you swore an oath to me, would you keep it? For all of your life?'

The question trembled on the air like a plucked chord. Hal looked past the king's head to the three leopards ramped in gold upon the wall. He knew what the king asked. The old allegiance: Lancaster. The loyalty of his father and grandfather that had destroyed them in the end.

He drew a long deep breath. 'Yes, I would keep it.'

'In God's name, my lord,' Gloucester blurted out, 'he's a Percy.' He was flushed with anger. He wore cloth of gold and plum velvet despite the heat, and sweat beaded his petulant upper lip. He had a vain and greedy face and Hal disliked him instantly. 'I'd not trust him further than I could spit. Treachery's in his blood as it was in Scrope's.'

Henry flinched as his brother's clumsy words probed the wound that was not yet fully healed. 'I am prepared to take his word for it,' he said sharply. 'If we all paid for the sins of our fathers I doubt if you would be wearing cloth of gold this day, Humphrey.' He looked at Neville and Warwick in turn. 'How say you, my lords?'

Neville nodded eagerly and Warwick sighed, an old man's deep and despairing sigh of remembrance. 'Aye, give him his chance,' he said. 'There's been enough lives lost already.'

'I think he's paid enough, sire,' Bedford said. 'Ten years is a long time for a man to be without kin or country.'

The king raised his eyes to Hal's. 'Then will you swear?' He held out his hands. 'We are cousins in blood. The thread's been broken but we can mend it. It can bind us as closely as it did our forefathers. Your grandfather and mine. You and I. All hatred's buried and past.'

Hal looked down at the pale outstretched hands, unadorned save for a jewelled seal upon his thumb: strong hands, capable hands with a grip that would not easily lose what they had seized.

'For Lancaster and England,' Henry murmured. 'And Northumberland.'

Hal heard the promise implicit in his voice and slowly he knelt and slipped his hands between the king's. They closed on his, strong as a vice, the hard calloused palms crushing his. He felt their unyielding pressure and knew himself more surely bound than if he still wore chains.

The next day he rode with the king into Southampton, past Henry Scrope's rotting fly-infested corpse, beneath Tom Grey's head on Bargate, shrivelled out of all recognition by the fierce August sun. He did not look up this time. He was the king's man now.

On the small rise of ground above the harbour they dismounted. The brilliance of sea and sun was almost blinding, the strident colours of the ships softened and warped by the haze. The quay itself was like a battleground. Men swarmed like ants among piles of stores and weaponry, shouting and swearing as they loaded the flat shallow-draught boats that ferried between the great warships. Henry walked among them as if he were one of them: checking that loads were securely tied; testing the sharpness of a sword with his thumb; soothing a terrified horse that balked at the ramp. The men called out to him familiarly. 'God bless you, Harry. Long live King Harry.' The king smiled and returned the greeting and the smile transformed him. He looked almost boyish, the wild young Harry of the Coldharbour days, the Harry that Jack Allbright had remembered.

The thought of Jack made Hal look harder at the faces that milled around him. He was bound to be here, as like as not already on his ship with his face buried in a jug of ale. Hal smiled faintly to himself. Jack had got his war after all.

The king returned to his vantage point on the hill, trailing his gaudy retinue like a peacock's tail. From the edge of the gathering Hal watched their faces; eager, attentive, assiduous, the moths around the flame that was the king. He could put names to some of their faces now: the king's brothers, Clarence, Gloucester and Bedford; the tall man with the pale ascetic face was Richard Courtney, Bishop of Norwich and Henry's close adviser; there was Edward, Duke of York, still pale and shaken from the execution of his brother Cambridge; the Earls of Oxford, Warwick and Suffolk; Sir Gilbert Umfraville, Thomas Erpingham and John Cornwall. There was a man standing close to the king who eyed him warily from time to time but never acknowledged him openly – Thomas, Lord Camoys, the husband of his mother, Elizabeth.

There were men of lesser importance, though not to the king: Leicester, Guienne and Ireland Kings of Arms; Hans Joye, the Dutch master-gunner; Thomas Morstede and William Bradwardyn, surgeons, and the king's physician, Nicholas Colnet; John Waterton, Master of the King's Horse and Allbright Mailmaker, royal armourer; Thomas Matthews and William Temple, master carpenters; Master Stephen Morpath, royal chaplain and Thomas Tunbrigge. Yeoman of the king's household; the king's minstrels, John Clif, Meysham Pyper, Thomas Norys Tromper, Snaith Fydler and Thomas Haliday; a hundred nameless clerks of napery, chancery, buttery and wardrobe: and this was only the hundredth part of it. Aboard the moored ships there were grooms and scurriers, carpenters, bowyers, fletchers, smiths, armourers and masons. A hundred and twenty miners, seventy-five gunners, two thousand knights and eight thousand archers. The enormity of it all was almost frightening.

Out on the Solent trumpets shrilled from ship to ship giving the signal to close up. The sails were being hoisted, blooming suddenly like bright gaudy flowers against the azure sky. The king's barge already nosed the quay waiting to take him and his retinue out to the *Trinité* where he would pass the night before sailing on the morning tide.

The king made his last farewells, embracing John of Bedford who was to remain behind as Lord Lieutenant. He even had a special word for the townsfolk who knelt with the priests on the quayside to pray for his safe journey. His rare and brilliant smile engulfed them like the sun. Then he paused for a final word with Neville and his glance encompassed Hal. For a moment he frowned distractedly, almost as if he had forgotten who he was.

Then he said with half challenging amusement, 'Will you wish me safe crossing, my lord?'

Hal looked steadily into the pale tireless face. 'God go with you, your Grace,' he said, and meant it.

The king nodded and turned away, his hand on Neville's sleeve. He stared out to where the ships manoeuvred sluggishly on the light summer tide. The sun was almost down and had lost its fierce heat. He closed his eyes to the pleasurable warmth and felt a sudden wave of tiredness. It was done. All the months and years of preparation had come down to this last moment of uncertainty. He counted the cost. Half of his crowns and his stepmother's jewels in pawn, the Great Harry broken up and given out piecemeal as pledges, the massive loans that would take him the rest of his life to repay: thirty-two thousand pounds from the Londoners, another fifty thousand from the Church. Beneath the fine wool doublet his skin began to sweat. Was it enough? Could he have done more? He opened his eyes on the solid reassurance of his fleet: fifteen hundred well-equipped ships and ten thousand hand-picked men below their decks. The doubt receded, leaving him calm again. With God's blessing he could not help but succeed.

Then Neville pointed skywards. A flock of swans had risen from the marsh behind the town and circled the fleet, skimming the turrets and banners of the *Trinité* and dipping their long graceful wings as if in salute.

'A good omen, sire,' Neville said.

Henry smiled. An omen. A sign from God that his prayers had been well received. Then his face assumed its habitual sternness again. He spoke of more earthly things: the safety of the Border, giving orders to increase the garrison at Berwick and Norham. Hal heard his own name spoken. The exchange with Albany's son was to go through as arranged. He stared at Henry's narrow back. So he was to be free at last, saving the restraint of Ralph Neville. But not free of past loyalty, not free of guilt. There was still one more thing to be done.

Boldly he touched the king's sleeve. Henry turned, preoccupied, irritation thinning the corners of his full mouth.

'Yes?' he asked almost coldly. 'Is there more?'

'One thing more, your Grace.' Hal knelt and looked up into the king's long pious face. 'My grandfather's head down from London Bridge.'

York

He walked the length of the Minster nave alone, his footsteps echoing eerily in the great vault of space and silence. On either side, the limestone pillars rose and blossomed into a tangle of oak- and vine-leaves, then looped themselves into slender fluted arches. Higher still, the great lancet windows soared to the ribs of the roof like arrowheads, each shaft imprisoning a rainbow of glass that showered a mosaic of soft-coloured light at his feet. He paused before the chancel arch where the sombre figures of kings and bishops stood sentinel over St William's shrine, then strode on past the choir and presbytery, past the high altar. Beneath the great East Window he saw the dark open pit of his father's grave.

He walked on, holding his precious burden close against his breast. Shrouded in regal velvet, it was all that was left of Northumberland. Where the rest of his bones lay, only God knew. It had seemed so frail at first that he had thought it might shatter at his touch, but the skull had been scoured and polished by wind and rain to a hard ivory whiteness. It was as indestructible as the memory of the man himself.

His mind had given it a semblance of life. It had not been so hard to fill those dark caverns with the fiery yellow of his eyes, to clothe the high cliff of his brow and the proud cast of the hollow cheek with bronzed and polished flesh. For a moment, beneath his trembling hands, the old man had lived again.

He stared down into the yawning darkness. The grave had been opened clumsily by the four monks who knelt praying at its edge. Flakes of mortar and limestone dulled the fine tissue of gold. Thin and worn with age it revealed the shape of the fragile bones beneath. Some kind and loving hands had composed them as best they could but still the broken remnants beneath the golden pall were those of only half a man. There was enough left to bring back the aching emptiness of loss: the proud head that had once stooped for his kiss; the long outflung arm that had once held him close; the broad cage of bone that had covered his heart before that dog Bolingbroke had torn it out. All the rest was dust and empty memory.

He leant down into the grave and the smell of damp earth and death engulfed him. In the cleft where his father's heart had been he laid the shrouded head. The bones shifted and settled as if he had stirred them to brief and sudden life and the long arm seemed to creep closer in a last welcoming embrace. They were together again, the lion and his wild unruly cub. None would ever part them now.

He stood, his face a white mask of agony. 'Cover them over,' he said. 'Let them rest.'

As he walked away he heard the slab grinding harshly into place and after it the silence. For the first time in ten years he wept.

*   *   *

Elizabeth stood quite still before her glass. Her face was starvation thin and the fine bones honed by grief to a razor sharpness showed white beneath the pale translucent skin. She was forty-four years old, yet the lines that etched her eyes and mouth were more of sorrow than of age. The hard bitter mouth was still perfect, her eyes as clear and colourless as glass and the hair that was loosed about her narrow shoulders was still bright as a candle's flame.

For the first time in twelve years she had put off her mourning black. Her gown was of soft grey silk trimmed with vair. It gave her a frail, ethereal look. She smiled at her own reflection. A long-dead Elizabeth came to life again.

Unhurriedly she moved to the open window. She walked with silent feline grace and her eyes as they looked out across the Weald were long and green, unblinking in the autumn sun. She remembered it had been September when they had first brought her here, when they'd taken Harry from her and given her an old man in his place. Ten years ago? More than that. The year was 1415 now. Harry had been dead twelve years this summer gone.

She stared blankly from the casement. Twelve years of waiting, each day running into the next with only a few nightmare hours of sleep between them. This had been all of her world since then, shut in by the narrow strip of the Channel to the south, the ridge of round, somnolent hills at her back; and all around the vast impenetrable forests of the Weald. She had been glad enough of the solitude then, even glad of her husband Thomas with his stolid kindness. Both had dragged her back from the edge of madness. Her eyes clouded with remembered grief. Harry, her beloved Harry, to end as a banquet for carrion. She'd been spared nothing. She'd felt every blow of the axe that had ripped his perfect body apart; she'd felt the crawl of the worm in his flesh, the sharp devouring beaks of the crows that had feasted on him. They'd brought him back to her eventually, a heap of broken and shattered bone, all that was left of the glory that had been Harry. And with it the death of all her dreams, all her wild high ambition. She smiled her small, enigmatic smile. No, not dead, such dreams never really died. They merely slept. She felt them stir inside her now like the kick of an unborn child.

She closed her eyes on the sunlight and the brightness remained. The visions rarely came to her now and when they did it was always in the guise of nightmare. There was always blood – her father's; her grandfather's; her brothers', Roger and Edmund; all dead before their fortieth year. It was the Mortimer curse, carried from generation to generation since the first Roger Mortimer had been hung like a common felon for the murder of a king. She herself was free from taint but she could pass the contagion on. She had passed it to Harry and his father; she could pass it to her son. The curse was laid now, the blood of a king for the blood of a king. It was Lancaster's burden now.

She picked up her stitchwork and began to sew placidly, an altar cloth for the monks at Steyning. The faint sound of laughter floated up from the courtyard below; the first of the men to be invalided back from the war, still faint with sickness yet recovered enough to mask the stink of death with the sweeter smell of glory. Harfleur had fallen, but at the price of two thousand dead from dysentery. Thomas had written to her of it: the heat, the flies, the tainted shellfish from the salt marshes that the army had gorged out of boredom. The disease had spread like wildfire, sparing none, high or low. Suffolk was dead from it; Bishop Courtney too. Clarence and her nephew Edmund, Earl of March, had been shipped home and it was doubted whether Arundel would survive. For a month Henry's guns had pounded the high castellated wall that ringed Harfleur. Toward the last even the air had become unbreathable – the choking gunsmoke and the noise, the worse stench of men purging and bleeding where they stood then lying down in sheer exhaustion to die in their own ordure. Death within and death without and none sure who'd had the worst of it. Both sides had died with agonising slowness, the French with their starved bellies swollen like gunstones, the English draining out their lives in blood and filth. Thomas' last letter had been full of despair. Harfleur was theirs but it would need a garrison of a thousand men to hold it. With a quarter of the army dead or dying, Henry's proposed march to Calais with less than five thousand men and winter approaching was tantamount to madness. Thomas had added that if any but Henry himself had asked it they would have had mutiny on their hands.

But Henry *had* asked it and they'd followed him as they always did, meek as lambs to the slaughter.

The needle slipped, pricking blood from her hand, and the pale pointed face turned ugly with hatred. Henry of Lancaster, the whelp of the dog that had murdered Harry. She had never met him. She had no need. The force of her hatred was strong enough to conjure him up. For a long time the image had been blurred and undefined. Her powers were dulled by introspection, by looking back and never forward. Until now there had been nothing to see. But the image now grew sharper. She knew a little of what went on behind that pale priestly face: the guilt, the uncertainty, the thoughts that lashed him like a penitent's whip. She knew how he fasted and spent hours in prayer to stifle the lusts of his flesh, how he courted the Church to ease his conscience and cover his ambition. He was all his father Bolingbroke had been and worse, for this Henry cloaked up his ambition with holiness. Perhaps she should be glad that he had a conscience. Her son would not be free if he had not. She smiled happily. Soon she could begin again. She was not alone any more.

For the first time in twelve years she looked upon her son. It was harder than she had thought to reconcile the boy with the man. There was nothing of Harry about him except perhaps the quick easy smile. All else was Northumberland. She resented him for that alone.

She offered him wine, aware that he had neither kissed nor touched her, nor even seemed to want to.

'You are well then, Hal?'

'Yes, I am well.' He took the wine and looked up reluctantly into her face and found he had nothing to say. She was a stranger to him now; a shadow of the lovely remote creature who'd always been part of his life yet had somehow always remained outside it. She was still lovely, he granted her that, but it was the cold inanimate beauty of perfect line and shape. His father had said once that she had no heart.

'And free.'

'Yes.' The exchange had gone through a month before. After Henry had sailed Neville had returned him briefly to Albany's charge and a week later had brought the Regent's son north. At Berwick, at dawn, Albany had got his son back. Hal and Albany had parted in amity, both aware that it was the last time they could ever do so. For all his freedom, he'd miss the scourge of the old man's tongue.

Then abruptly he said, 'You know I am wed to Alianore Neville?' Yes, of course she knew. It was one of the disturbing things about her, her habit of answering a question before it was ever voiced.

Elizabeth smiled. 'It means nothing. We have married Nevilles before. Your grandmother was one. Ralph Neville himself has his share of Percy blood. His mother was a Percy.' For a moment her face lost a little of its composure.

'And how is my lord of Westmorland?' she asked bitterly. 'Still growing fat on our lands?' She glanced covertly at her son. 'He'll not part with them without a struggle. Are you willing to fight, Hal? As your father and grandfather would have fought?'

'Yes, I am prepared for that,' he answered quietly. He would not be content with an empty title, any more than they would have been. There was still much to be won back. All that his grandfather had held and more. He was not without ambition himself.

He saw the small satisfied smile that curved her red mouth and thought it strange that she had said nothing of Cambridge's abortive rising. She must know of his death and her nephew Mortimer's shameful betrayal.

'Did you know that Cambridge approached me whilst I was held in Scotland? That he asked me to join with them in placing Edmund on the throne?'

She turned wide innocent eyes upon him. 'How could I know? I've not left these walls for nearly ten years.'

'And that I withdrew of my own accord rather than see that idiot cousin of mine as king?'

Her mouth tightened and froze the smile to her face. 'Idiot or not, he is still England's rightful king,' she murmured. 'Your father and grandfather died believing that.'

'They died for Richard, not Edmund. He was no more than a boy then.'

She turned wide incredulous eyes upon him. 'What are you saying? That you'd rather see Lancaster as king?'

He held the cold intimidating look and fought the urge to turn his eyes away. 'He *is* king,' he said stubbornly. 'And I swore an oath to uphold him as such before he sailed for France.'

There was a small empty silence, then Elizabeth smiled suddenly. She understood now. He was asking her forgiveness, her approval. He needed her reassurance that his oath could not bind him, that he had not betrayed her.

'Is that all?' she said softly. 'There's no shame in that. It was taken under threat of death. Such oaths are not binding.'

'Nevertheless I mean to keep it,' he said, and for a moment glimpsed the crazed and grieving woman of ten years ago.

'Keep it? Keep faith with the Usurper?' Her voice rose to a scream. 'Have you forgotten so easily, what his father did to yours?' With an effort she brought her voice back under control. She said piteously, 'Jesu. Don't desert me, Hal, else all's been for nothing.' She came and knelt beside him. 'Is it Edmund? Because he's weak and cowardly? I can understand that but it need not be Edmund. Cambridge has a son by Anne Mortimer. His right is as good. Even you, Hal. Your blood is as royal as Lancaster's.'

He stared down at her in pity and disgust. 'Dear God,' he said. 'You'd put a mad dog on the throne if it had Mortimer blood.'

She sat very still, crouched at his feet like that very dog. Then slowly she stumbled to her feet and backed away from him.

'Traitor,' she said softly. 'False ungrateful traitor, betrayer of your father's blood.' She turned her back on him and said so quietly that he barely heard it, 'May he forgive you. I shall not.'

When he had gone she stood for a long time staring into the darkness. Her eyes were quite dry but inside she wept: for Northumberland, for Harry, for all the dead and broken dreams that had come to nothing. Most of all she wept for herself. She was alone again.

Agincourt. The name was distorted and mispronounced by the revelling Londoners. It meant nothing to them and only a little more to the men who had actually fought there. Few were even aware that the small village overlooking the boggy field where they had decimated all of France's chivalry was so called. To King Henry, riding out from Eltham to the welcoming city it was synonymous with victory, with God's approval. It was the longed-for affirmation that he had been judged and found innocent, that his cause was right and just. It was the pall under which he buried all his doubts.

At Blackheath, the mayor and aldermen of the city waited to greet him, resplendent in scarlet coats with the arms of their companies blazoned in gold on their sleeves. The mayor, Nicholas Wolton ('Witless Nick' the citizens called him), looked almost childishly disappointed to see him so plainly attired. Bareheaded, the king wore only a mantle of imperial velvet over the inevitable black doublet and hose. He was whippet thin from fasting, his face gaunt and pale. He looked almost saintly in his pallor.

The mayor fell on his knees and fumbled his slack wet mouth against Henry's hand. 'Welcome,' he said fervently. 'Welcome, Conqueror and King.'

Though Henry said nothing the words pleased him, as did to a lesser degree the riotous and gaudy ceremony. On the gatehouse by the Stoops, a pair of mammoth jewelled figures held out the keys of the city in welcome. Every pillar and post was decked with the royal arms; his banners flew from every rooftop and turret: the antelope, the swan, the blood-red rose of Lancaster. On the far side of the bridge a triumphal arch spanned the street surmounted by a gargantuan statue of St George. He wore full armour and his helm glittered with pearls and precious stones. Were they real? Henry wondered, and thought of the cost.

Beneath the arcade a hundred boys with gilded faces and wings of swansdown shrilled an anthem.

> *Then went oure Kynge with alle his oste,*
> *Thorowe Fraunce for all the French boste,*
> *He spared not drede of leste, ne moste,*
> *Tyll he come to Agincourt coste.*
>
> > *Deo gratias:*
> *Deo gratias Anglia redde pro Victoria.*

Then for sother that Knyghte comely,
In Agincourt feld he faught manly,
Thorow grace of God most myghty,
He had both the felde, and the victory.

The words shivered down his spine. The glory and horror of it were still with him. It had so nearly been defeat. It had stared him full in the face on the banks of the Somme when he found that the force he had ordered to be sent from Calais to hold Blanche Tâque had been driven back and that now the crossing place was held strongly by the French. He had glanced behind him at his scarecrow army, weary and dispirited from the long hundred and fifty mile march from Harfleur. Some were still sick and feverish, some were without shoes and tramped barefoot through the squelching mud. Half the horses were lame and those that weren't were starved and nigh on dropping with fatigue. At his back, unseen, the French army under the Marshal d'Albret stalked him like a giant shadow. He had felt the doubt then, a dreadful corroding fear that had turned his bowels to water. There had been no thought of victory in his mind then.

The next day at dawn, in the pounding rain, they had taken the road to Voyennes. His thoughts had alternated between wild hope and abject despair – hope when a captured Frenchman had told them of a causeway across the marsh; despair when halfway across they had found the road broken up and submerged in slime and reeds. His iron determination had not weakened. He'd had his men fell trees and tear down abandoned houses and farms. For half a day they had waded waist deep in cold clinging mud, stopping the gaps with logs and thatch while the rain beat down heavy as hammer blows on their heads. But by noon he had a makeshift road. By sunset the last of his men were across. He had almost wept with relief, even though Calais was still a hundred miles away.

Henry blinked as rose petals showered on his head and the long tortuous procession crawled slowly up Fish Hill to the Corn-market by Leadenhall and down the narrow overhung streets that led to the Chepe. By the Tun in Cornhill they loosed a flight of gilded birds that fluttered unnervingly round him. In Leadenhall they were forced to dismount as there was no room for horsemen in the narrow street that had been thinned to half a yard's breadth by the crowds. They pressed close in adulation, touching his robe, kissing the ground he walked upon. They praised him for his victory and he answered them piously, 'Not mine, but God's.' Yet there was a vain little streak in him that could not yield all of the glory. It had been his in part. It was he who had held the despairing army together, he who had quelled their fears, comforted them, inspired them and finally led them to that glorious hour. It had all been done for love of him. He'd had proof of that.

After the crossing of the Somme there had been worse fears to come. The French, so quiescent while his army had struggled from Harfleur, had roused themselves. Bourbon and Orleans had brought their armies up to join d'Albret. While the English slept exhausted in the mud and rain, six miles away at Peronne the French made camp.

The next day Bourbon had sent his heralds to parley. With heavy courtesy they issued the challenge of war. Henry had answered them calmly, 'Be all things according to the will of God.' Yet in the next few days he wondered exactly what His will was. They marched on again at dawn, down into the valley and beneath the walls of Peronne. The French had moved on, hoping to outflank him, and the road north east to Bapaume was churned to a sea of mud by thousands of marching feet. But how many thousands? He had stared down the road in dismay. Too many. The French must outnumber him five to one.

They'd marched only sixteen miles that day and camped in howling wind and rain at Forceville, then on again to Lecheux and Frevant. Then at Blangy, for the first time he'd had sight of the enemy.

For a moment all hope had fled. Unmoving he'd sat on his horse and stared numbly at the tens of thousands who moved slowly and inexorably toward him. By nightfall they had completely blocked his road to Calais. He remembered it had been the eve of Saint Crispin and Crispinian.

When darkness fell he had walked alone through the camp. The rain had eased to a fine impenetrable drizzle that somehow seemed infinitely worse than the steady downpour of the day. He had viewed the wreck of his army with quiet despair. The men slept where they could, in ditches, beneath trees; some just lay in the open where they had fallen, from hunger and sheer exhaustion. Ragged and dirty, cold and tired, they were all he had to pit against the shining monster that was France. For some, like him, sleep was impossible. The priests moved silent as nighthawks through the darkness while men knelt in the mud, were confessed, shriven and absolved. Afterwards he spoke to them quietly and confidently of victory, of God's blessing on their cause, empty, useless words that he didn't even believe himself any more. And they didn't believe it either. But there was no reproach, no blame or accusation in their eyes when they looked at him. It made the failure all the harder to bear. He'd asked one man if he were afraid to die, a young archer with bright hair that had reminded him of Scrope. The archer had smiled and turned his face up to him, spattered with tears of rain. 'As well to die with you as with any,' he had said quietly.

Henry had almost wept. *As well to die with you as with any.* He'd brought them to this and still they loved him.

He prayed all through the night. Was he to be judged thus? The fear gnawed like rats in his belly. *Usurper.* The old guilt he'd smothered with dreams of glory came out of its dark hiding place to taunt him. Men would see it so: his punishment for Richard's death, for all the deaths. He had bowed his head and listened to the rain beating steadily against the walls of his tent. Tomorrow he would know. It was in God's hands.

He could smile now at his lack of faith, and with the London crowds roaring his name, it was hard to believe that he had ever conceived of failure.

They emerged into the Chepe where the walls were hung with mammoth tapestries of past glories: Crecy, Poitiers, the Black Prince's victory at Najera. He walked beneath awnings of silk and arches of green laurel and the scent of lavender and thyme rose up beneath his feet. The noise was deafening: the roar of the crowd; the frenzied bellow of horn and drum; the quavering falsetto of the angelic choir; and overriding all, the clamour of bells in every church from Billingsgate to Holburn. It was like the dreadful joyous sound of battle, like the noise that had filled his ears all that glorious day and had remained with him ever since.

At dawn he had risen stiffly from his knees and called to his squires. He'd stood immobile while they had dressed him. A soft padded shirt of finest Rhennes linen to cushion the weight of the scoured and polished silver breastplate engraved with his arms. On his feet were long steel shoes fitted with gilded spurs. His hands were encased in soft velvet gloves beneath the gauntlets of hardened leather. He lifted leaden arms while his *côte d'armes* was slipped over his head, the leopards of England and the lilies of France. Their colours had stabbed painfully at his tired eyes. Then he took the gilded helm from its cushion of silk. The crown that encircled it blazed like a beacon in the uncertain light; rubies and sapphires and one hundred and twenty-eight pearls set in fifteen pounds of solid Welsh gold. Almost all of his wealth now. He set it grimly on his head. It would take more than a crown to make a king of him today.

Yet when he emerged his face was pale and resolute and his dark eyes almost slumbrous in their calm. He knelt in the open amongst his men and heard the Mass. The raw wine of the sacrament burnt his mouth and he thought of John Badby, dying in an agony of flame and smoke. *The Bread is bread. The priest is only a man.* His lips moved in a convulsive prayer.

He was plagued by all manner of doubts. The priests' loud and plaintive exhortation did nothing to dispel them. 'Our enemies are gathered together and boast in their might. Scatter their strength and disperse them that they may know that there is none other that fighteth for us but only Thou, our God.'

A miracle, he thought. They're praying for a miracle. Nothing less would give him the victory out of this. He'd seen the enemy: the vast numbers; the superior strength of weaponry and cannon. There must be all of thirty thousand and well fed and shod at that. No wonder Bourbon's heralds had laughed at him.

Then he rose to his feet and mounted the sleek white destrier housed and tasselled in gold. From its height he surveyed the remains of his army. They looked even worse in the daylight, indescribably filthy, their jerkins and breeches torn and stiff with mud. Some had even lost these and stood bare-legged and shivering in the keen October wind. They raised their chapped, wind-burnt faces to him as he spoke the expected words of comfort and encouragement. Inside he was as cold and raw as they were. Who was there to comfort him?

For four hours the two armies faced each other across the mile of sodden cornfield. The French had made no move to attack. Were they trying to starve him out? To break his nerve hoping that he'd make a run for it? Henry smiled grimly. Better death than that. He looked again at the solid shining ranks. By now he knew their displacements better than his own. Behind the scarlet thread of the flaunting Oriflamme, a hundred banners licked the pallid sky. The Dukes of Bourbon, Orleans, Alençon and Bar. The veteran commanders Charles d'Albret and Boucicourt, the Counts of Eu, Vendôme and Lammartin, the cream of French chivalry. But not the king, or the Dauphin Louis. Was d'Albret not confident enough to risk them? He stared till his eyes filled with tears and the enemy lines blurred into a rainbow haze. There must be a flaw. He looked again. The front line heaved and stretched like some dread scaled monster as the heavily armoured chivalry jostled for precedence. Three thousand faceless steel-clad men, indistinguishable one from the other save for the jewelled colours of their banners. Behind them, the pikemen stood six deep, and wedged between, almost as an afterthought, were scattered companies of crossbowmen. Henry frowned. It was a weakness but not the Achilles heel he was looking for. The mounted men-at-arms brought up the rear, flanked by harrassed gunners who struggled to maintain their firing position against the surging front line. Henry's eyes narrowed. That was it. There were too many. Too many and too heavily armed for the wet and boggy terrain. As he looked on, the bulging front line broke under the pressure of eager knights forcing their way in from the rear. The trees that had sheltered them during the night now hemmed them in, the woods of Tramecourt on the left, the small but dense belt of scrubland below Agincourt on the right. There was no way for them to go but forward, down the narrowing field that culminated in his own front line. He drew a long deep breath and lowered his eyes lest the sudden hope should show too plainly. The French might outnumber him but their position was bad and he had mobility and freedom of movement. Above all he had the bowmen.

He turned his horse and rode back. Briefly he surveyed his own orderly ranks. The main body of foot soldiers and men-at-arms was broken up by taut spearheads of bowmen. The curving outer flanks were solidly bowmen: his hope, his strength, his David against France's Goliath. He called to his captains and commanders: Umfraville and John Cornwall with their grim quiet confidence; Dorset, Suffolk and young John Holland, Earl of Huntingdon now for his valour at Harfleur; old Erpingham, grey and grizzled as a badger but with the light springing step of a ten year-old; his brother Humphrey of Gloucester, his round face pink and freshly shaven; the one eyed Welshman, Daffyd ap Llewellyn ap Hywel; Thomas, Lord Camoys, still flushed with pride at Henry's choice of him to lead the left wing. His cousin, Edward Duke of York, was to lead the right. He himself would lead the centre.

'Avaunt banner,' he lifted his face and cried to the heavens. 'For Jesus, Mary and St George. Advance.'

The scream of the trumpets sent shock waves down the field and hurled a flight of scavenging crows skywards. Slowly, laboriously, they moved forward through the clinging mud till they came within bowshot. Then they dismounted and the horses were led back. The archers ran forward to plant their palisade of sharpened stakes.

Henry nodded to Erpingham who raised his hand, one eye on the steel wall that had begun to lumber steadily toward them. The bowmen took aim. They paused a moment on the advancing French then swept up to a point in the pale empty sky.

Erpingham's arm swept down like an executioner's axe.

'Loose.'

The scream of their going shivered down Henry's spine. Briefly he remembered Shrewsbury, the darkness of arrow clouds across the sun, the roar of torn and ruptured air, the shaft that had planted itself deep in Harry Hotspur's brow. He gripped his sword a little tighter and watched as the shafts plunged into the enemy flanks. The crossbowmen attempted a reply but their quarrels did not have the reach of the English shafts and fell far short. By the time they had fumbled with the complexities of winches and winders their line of fire was blocked by their own disordered ranks. There were a few ragged bursts of cannon fire and a gunstone skimmed Henry's cheek and ploughed down a dozen men behind him. He hardly noticed. His eyes were intent on the enemy front line, still stumbling toward him despite the onslaught of arrows. It seemed to shrink in toward its heart as the trees forced the ranks closer and a few horses stumbled and fell, out of sheer lack of space. They moved at a gallop now, the heavy horses finding purchase on the dryer untrampled ground of the cornfield.

Their battle cries filled his ears, the pounding weight of steel and horseflesh set his teeth rattling in his head and still they came, innocent, unaware until the very last. They rode straight onto the sharp angled teeth of the palisade. The first horses fell impaled to the heart and still they came on in great shining steel waves like a river in full spate. The exultant battle cries had turned to screams of panic as the oncoming riders fought desperately to turn their mounts from the tangle of dying men and horses that rose up like a wall before them. Few succeeded, nearly all fell, spilling like bright jewels at the feet of the English. Coffined in steel, they fell like the dead. The bowmen took them at their leisure.

The carnage grew as wounded horses bolted up the field straight into the path of the advancing foot soldiers under d'Albret. The columns broke, scattered and reformed again as the maddened horses charged them, but still they came on till they were shoulder to shoulder with hardly room to swing a pike between them, penned in the narrowing gap between the trees. It was what he had prayed for: chaos, disorder, the enemy hampered and rendered impotent by its very magnitude. The divisions of his archers fanned out, shooting at the exposed flanks of the enemy columns, forcing them even closer in upon themselves. Henry watched and saw them scythed down like ripened corn. There was hardly room for the dead to fall.

He turned and nodded to Camoys and York. He raised his sword. For the second time the trumpets sounded the advance.

He fought with a dreadful savage joy. There was a darkness in his mind that excluded all but the ecstasy of killing. The smell of blood filled his nostrils; it soaked the brave colours of his surcoat and dried and blackened on his flesh. It was a new baptism. He was washed and cleansed in blood.

The slaughter continued far into the day but long before its end he knew he had won. The French had lost heart and some were already slipping into the cover of the woods. D'Albret was dead, the Dukes of Orleans and Alençon and countless others prisoners. Even the stalwart Boucicourt had yielded. Henry had smiled his blood-red smile and watched the pale sun slide behind the tower at Agincourt. He'd had his miracle after all.

And now he gave thanks for it, with all his heart, with all his mind. He knelt in humility on the steps of St Pauls where eighteen bishops in full pontificals waited to receive him. The glittering figures of the twelve kings, martyrs and confessors of England watched him in approval and showered leaves of gold and silver on his bowed head. The choir soared to its deafening crescendo, the crowd roared his name: Harry of England, Conqueror and King. A small voice at the back of his mind added 'murderer'. Involuntarily he glanced behind him. The French prisoners he had flaunted through the streets stood impassive under the taunts and jeers of the crowd. The mild blue eyes of the captive Charles of Orleans accused him gently. *Murderer.*

He looked away, his hands suddenly damp with sweat. What else could he have done? When the French prisoners threatened to outnumber his own men? Victory had only been a hair's breadth away when Brabant's foolhardy attempt to rally his scattered countrymen had come. Foolish, reckless, utterly useless, yet it could have worked. The French were still in the field. They could still be rallied. The prisoners they held could easily turn against them. Coldly, without emotion, he had given the order for all the prisoners to be killed save those of the highest rank. Within minutes the field had stunk like a slaughterhouse. The enormity of what he had done had not touched him till now.

He smothered the small spark of uncertainty. More guilt? More innocent blood on his hands? Then the bishops came to raise him up and their joyful approving smiles were his absolution. It was God's will. Surely he'd had proof enough of that. He

raised his pale intense face and smiled. He was Henry the King –
no usurper now.

In York the great Minster bell tolled out the victory, the deep
sonorous notes caught and held in an endless echo by the hundred
and one churches that stood virtuous and aloof among sleazy
taverns and greasy pie shops. On the Ouse, the mayor's ceremo-
nial barge drifted regally down to King's Staith. Silver trumpets
blared from her prow and the throb of drums beat out the rise and
fall of the white oars. Garlands of laurel draped the hull, flung by
the joyous citizens that crowded Ousebridge and stood ten deep
along the narrow banks. They seemed undaunted by the lack of a
king.

In Coney Street and Ousegate where the merchants' high
gabled houses leant drunkenly together the crowds were worse:
soldiers come home from the war with their pockets full; merchants and whores eager to empty them. Cheapjacks screamed
themselves hoarse in every doorway selling spurious relics: mud
from the field at Agincourt; fragments from the gunstone that
had breached the wall at Harfleur. The cutpurses had a field day.
There was more French gold in York that day than in the whole of
Paris.

On Pavement belled dancers whirled and stamped in wooden
shoes. A choir of boys with mouths like rosy apples bawled Deo
Gratias from the steps of All Saints, their high sweet voices
drowned by the drums and timbrels of the Guild procession that
swept down Fossgate in pompous bannered splendour from the
Merchant Adventurers' hall. The Bridge across the Foss was
almost impassable; a surging tide of horses, carts and people
squeezed between the tenement houses on either side. From every
house a banner flew: the great scarlet cross of St George, the
crossed keys and crowned pike of the Fishmongers. Children
screeched with excitement and clung precariously to the backs of
overloaded carts. Horns blared, dogs barked and ran wildly
between the cartwheels to snuffle in the slime of scales and
fishskin in the Shambles. At the far end of the bridge, the thin
insistent chime of St Anne's struggled to make itself heard.
Beyond the river Walmgate stretched down the city wall and the

tiny church of St Peter Le Willows huddled in its shadow. On either side high timber-ribbed houses bellied out over the street so that the small leaded windows stood almost eye to eye. The peaks of their intricate turrets and gables showed like a row of teeth against the sky, a smiling facade that hid the mean little houses that crowded the stinking lanes at their back.

Hal eased his horse onto the soft muddy spine of the road between the ruts thrown up by the constant passage of carts toward the gates. The damp clinging smell of wet cloth and hot irons drifted up from the fullers' houses in Little Bretgate; a worse smell came from the stagnant ditch outside the walls. He glanced up at the gaudy painted crests that hung on poles outside every house: Neville's Inn, Mowbray's Inn, the twin churches of St Mary and Margaret, the blackened gap where the Cliffords' house had stood before the rebels had burned it down during the Hurling Time nearly forty years before. It was tall with weeds now and stray pigs grazed contentedly in the seeding grass. He rode on, past the gilded and painted shopfronts of mercers and apothecaries, beneath the squat tower of St Denys. On the corner by Bretgate, the blank shuttered windows of his grandfather's house looked down on him. The blue lion had been torn down long ago and yellow lichen festered between the stones. The corbels of the roof were crumbling, the carved lions at their head clawing through moss and bindweed. It was his again, what was left of it: the stripped and plundered hall, the rotting staircase, the upper rooms shrouded in dust, the bare walls furred with damp. It was the same everywhere he had been: Warkworth, Prudhoe, Langley, the manors of Leconfield and Tughall; all crumbling beneath the alien hand of neglect. All his again but he had been given only the empty shell. The plate and jewels were gone, the priceless library, the jewelled relics, the gifts of kings and princes over a hundred years, all were dispersed into the hands of strangers. Only Alnwick had seemed untouched. The great Crecy tapestry had gone but all else was as he remembered it. He smiled wryly. Not all else. There was no warmth to Alnwick now, no face that he knew except the old man still defiantly wearing his faded Percy colours who had been his grandfather's steward. He had not been old then. Hal remembered that he'd had a voice that could shiver the stones of the keep. Even he had lived in dread of him.

He kicked his mount disconsolately over the bridge in the wake of the noisy crowd. A few ragged urchins came and swung on his bridle, begging a penny for bread. He tossed a coin though he could ill spare it. He was not much better off than he had been when he had crossed the Border. The money granted by Parliament had been eaten up by repairs to Warkworth and Prudhoe and he'd already borrowed a thousand marks from Ralph Neville against his Michaelmas rents. It had been grudgingly lent. Neville meant to keep him in his pocket as long as he could.

Fossgate was almost deserted now. A few hens pecked hopefully in the runnels. A soldier fell out of an alehouse door and vomited noisily into the mud. In Colliergate where the great brass-headed conduit trickled free wine a group of soldiers swilled themselves into a red-faced sweat and passed the time by pelting with filth the poor wretch chained in the pillory. Others brawled happily in and out of alleyways and chased giggling tavern girls into doorways. There was one, taller and broader than the rest. His massive bare arms were thrust like hams from a jerkin of boiled leather and he roared obscenities at the unfortunate fishmonger who dangled limply from his grasp. Hal smiled. He would know that cracked raucous voice anywhere.

'Jack. Jack Allbright.'

Jack swung round and his eyes narrowed aggressively. He dropped the fishmonger and struck him a blow on the crown of his head that would have driven a smaller man into the ground.

'My lord,' he muttered awkwardly and flushed.

'So formal, Jack? When I all but carried you home that night?'

Jack rubbed his huge hands on his jerkin. 'I did not know,' he mumbled in an agony of embarrassment. 'If I said aught out of place that night, it was only the drink. I've got a great trap on me when I'm full of the drink.'

Hal grinned. 'That you have, Jack.'

Jack forced a nervous smile. 'I did not know who you were,' he said again.

'I was nobody then, Jack.' Hal dismounted and came to stand

85

beside him. 'What was said then was said between friends. Can we not keep it like that?'

Jack stared at him, looking suitably doubtful at the prospect of friendship between a common man-at-arms and a peer of the realm. But he was a man who'd take a gamble on most things. Perhaps old Wat was right. This one was different.

'Well then,' he said and grinned shyly, 'you're still all of a piece, then? I wagered two groats with one of Arundel's men that Harry would have your head.'

'I'm glad you lost,' Hal said drily.

'So am I.' Jack turned his back on the fishmonger who had come out of his daze and was preparing to lunge at him. He glanced at Hal's solitary horse in surprise. 'Are you alone? No escort?'

Hal gave a faint smile. Solitude was a habit hard to lose and he'd become even more withdrawn since he'd seen his mother, aware that his life and liberty were as precarious as her sanity and that she would plunge him back into the pit from which he'd just crawled for her own advantage. Even more disquieting had been the recognition of himself in her. The same evil streak ran in both of them, the same capacity for hatred, except that in him it was smothered by caution. Just lately he'd found that caution harder to maintain. He kept himself to himself when he could.

'I'm tired of escorts, Jack,' he said grimly. 'I've had one at my back for the last ten years. For the moment I'm enjoying the freedom.'

Jack nodded sagely, though it baffled him why a man should want to travel alone when he could have had a fancy escort to fetch and carry for him. He said nothing and fell in beside Hal as he turned toward the river.

The crowds were thinning in Spurriergate, moving with less purpose, pausing to gawp at the stalls and travelling sideshows. A girl in a faded sarcanet dress smiled coyly at Jack and he said without thinking, 'You married the Neville wench, then?'

Hal nodded. He'd not thought of Alianore nor seen her since that day at Berwick. As far as he knew she was still at Raby. He'd not asked after her and Neville had not seemed to expect him to. It was part of the tacit understanding that had grown between them. Alianore was only a link in the chain that bound him. He would break it as soon as he could.

Jack had subsided into awkward silence, knowing instinctively that he had trodden on dangerous ground. It was difficult to know what to say, how far he could go without overstepping the mark and being slapped back into his place.

Then Hal said, 'You had your war after all, Jack. It was a great victory. Only fifty men killed in all.'

'Only fifty that counted,' Jack answered grimly. 'There were two thousand poor sods left their innards in a ditch at Harfleur. Old Wat was one of them. Do you remember Wat?'

Hal nodded, saddened that another link with his grandfather was lost. Then he said, 'Was it worth it?'

'Aye, it was worth it.' Jack grinned. 'If only to see the look on those Frenchies' faces when he gave them the thrashing of their lives. We made little else out of it,' he added glumly. 'No prisoners, no ransoms. Well, not for the likes of us, anyway. The King ordered that all below the rank of earl were to be killed. I didn't like that much, I can tell you. Something not quite right about killing a man under the white pennon, and besides I had two fat little French knights that would have brought me a tidy bit. Offered me the earth and a ruby the size of a penny if I'd spare them. I took the ruby anyway after I'd slit their throats.' He sat heavily on an upturned lobster pot. 'Not that it did me any good. The bloody supply ships were late as usual and the prices went up as soon as we showed our faces in Calais. By God, I'd like to have one of those fat burghers on the end of my sword now. Two marks for a loaf of bread and us their own countrymen at that and half dead on our feet from three days' marching.' He sighed elaborately. 'I sold the ruby to a Jew for three marks and half a mouldy cheese that had maggots wriggling in it as big as eels.' He spat disgustedly. 'I'll know better next time. Next time I'll choke the heathen bastard and eat his heart instead.'

'Will there be a next time, Jack?'

'Oh, we'll be back,' Jack said, watching the fishermen hauling out their catches at the little jetties and quays by Ousebridge. 'Our Harry's had a taste of it now. We were hard put enough to ship him home at all. Panting for more he was before we'd even reached Calais. He'd got the French on the run and knows it. Half their leaders dead, the rest cooped up in the Tower. Who's there to stop him? Mad Charlie or that German whore of his?' He rubbed his huge hands together. 'No, Harry'll be back. Give him six months to get his wind and squeeze another loan from Parliament and he'll be back.'

'And you with him?'

Jack shrugged. 'What else? Better to die out there than of boredom at Berwick.'

Hal stared out across the river where the tattered garlands of the pageant bobbed on the sluggish water and children on the far bank pelted them with stones. 'What will you do till then?'

'Get drunk every night while I've money. Eat my heart out in that stinking garrison when I've not. I'm bound to Neville for another half year.'

Hal smiled wryly. 'So am I.' He skimmed a pebble across the water and watched it sink. 'You said once that if ever I needed a stout man by me . . .' He looked the big man hard in the eyes. 'Well, I do. A shilling a day and a sergeant's livery.' He grinned. 'You said you'd do anything for a shilling a day.'

'You don't have to bribe me,' Jack said and stared down at his feet. 'I'd come anyway.' He prodded the mud and shingle with the toe of his boot. 'Why me?' he asked suddenly. 'I'm nobody. You could find a hundred men like me for less than a shilling a day.'

'You can't buy friendship for that,' Hal answered quietly.

Jack looked away. 'What's there between you and me? I'm the son of a Southwark butcher and you're the son of Harry Hotspur.' His lip curled in a sneer. 'A fine pair we'd make.'

'It was the sons of butchers and bakers that kept me alive once, Jack,' Hal said pensively. 'I'd have starved many a time if it hadn't been for men like you, when they fed me and my grandfather and sometimes went without themselves. I need company sometimes. Someone to trust, someone to get drunk with now and again. There's none of my own kind that I'd trust, not yet anyway.'

'No, not yet. But you will. One day you will and then you'll have no time for clumsy old Jack.' He rose abruptly to his feet and came to stand beside him. 'I'll serve you and gladly. For nothing if need be. But it's a cruel thing to take a man from what he knows and then shove him back to it after you've given him a taste of something better.'

'No one knows that better than I, Jack. I've been as poor and hungry as you many a time. I wouldn't want to go back to it either.'

'Well then,' Jack nodded and grinned, his big face suffused with pleasure, 'you've got yourself a stout man. When do I start?'

Hal laughed and flung his arm round the thick bull neck. 'What better time than now?'

They rode out of York together, down Micklegate and past the cluttered roofs and spires of Holy Trinity. As he passed beneath the wide barbican gate that straddled the road Hal did not look up as he usually did. He could hear his mother's voice: 'Traitor. False, ungrateful traitor. Betrayer of your father's blood.' He turned his head and looked quickly at Jack riding beside him and the voice quietened and was still. He smiled to himself. There were no ghosts in the face of Jack Allbright.

Hal kept Christmas at Raby, a lean and hungry hawk among the gaudy Neville peacocks come home to roost, so many of them that he felt more isolated than ever, envying them their closeness, the easy laughter and affection which they took for granted. To him such feelings were only memories.

He had Jack with him. Neville had not queried it when he had asked for him. He had never heard of him. Men like Jack Allbright were ten a penny to Ralph Neville. Amazingly, he'd settled down at once, ousting the slovenly page who had previously cared for Hal and fussing among his meagre wardrobe as if it were the king's own; steaming velvets till they were as smooth and soft as a newly-cropped lawn; stamping the creases from Hal's shirts with a great box iron filled with charcoal; mending and darning with his thick clumsy fingers, till he was as at home with fine silk as he was with steel.

Hal had had new livery made, crimson and black, as aggressive and defiant as he was. Jack wore his colours like a whore in a new gown, swaggering round the yards with his sergeant's staff tucked under his arm and so anxious to be worthy of his advancement that he poked his nose into everything from the bakehouse to the coveted preserves of Neville's own steward. He'd even persuaded the chaplain to teach him French, though his lessons rarely lasted the hour before the chaplain would emerge in tears of frustration and Jack with a face that sent every page in his path scurrying for shelter. Hal and Jack made an incongruous pair, Hal with his arrogant stare and quiet aloofness, and Jack as potentially explosive as a primed tinder box. But Jack was loyal and did Hal's bidding unquestioningly. It was some sort of bulwark against the overwhelming hoards of Nevilles. Hal watched them closely, looking for any small thing that he might use against them, and for all their outward amity there were dissentions. John Neville was there with his Holland wife and his young son Ralph. John was the eldest son by Neville's first marriage, and the heir to the Westmorland earldom, a fact which never ceased to rankle with the Countess Joan. And she, lately delivered of yet another daughter, made her feelings quite plain. It was well known that her stepson was less than welcome at Raby.

Joan manipulated her own sons with the natural instinct of a breeding sow: Richard, the eldest, fair-haired and handsome and as aggressive as only a sixteen year-old could be; William, a year younger, a dark-haired boy with a drooping eyelid that gave him a look of slyness which was probably quite unwarranted; Robert, at thirteen the scholarly one and destined for the church; George, at nine the youngest and as yet of no account. There was also a flock of daughters, whose names Hal could never remember. And Alianore.

Tonight she'd put her hair up under a tall pointed hennin that set off the fine bones of her face to perfection. Her eyes were dark and languid in the candlelight and she was smiling, consoling her brother Edward, his cheek still red from his mother's hand because he'd stuffed himself unforgivably with syllabub and had then been sick on the floor. It hurt to admit even to himself that he desired her, but he did. In his mind he'd felt her soft flesh beneath his and had kissed her mouth to burning redness, but outwardly he still maintained his air of disinterest. He behaved toward her with perfect courtesy, pulling out her chair at supper, laying his cold mouth on her cheek when they met and parted. But at night he shut his chamber door behind him and did not open it till the morning. If she cared she did not show it. She matched his detachment word for word, look for look, and unknowingly drove him further away.

Hal's eyes moved fractionally from her face to the soft gleaming flesh at her throat. He'd had enough practice to gauge the moment when she would look up; then he would turn away before their eyes could meet and busy his hands with some trivial task. Tonight he filled Elizabeth Neville's already overful glass.

Elizabeth smiled at him prettily. They had much in common. Though she was John Neville's wife, she had once been a Holland and both her brother and uncle had lost their heads under Bolingbroke. Here at Raby she was as much an outsider as he was. He glanced toward the small intimate group from which they were so obviously excluded. They were speaking of John Oldcastle. The heretic was still at large in the west despite the vigilance of the Church's witch-hunters. Then Richard Neville looked across at Hal. He was more than a little drunk and his handsome face was flushed and sweating.

'Did you ever meet him?' he demanded loudly. 'When you were plotting your treasons with Cambridge?'

Hal did not rise to the bait. This was not the first of Richard Neville's clumsy attempts to provoke him.

'No. I did not,' he answered calmly.

'Just as well. You might not have got away with heresy so easily. I doubt if Arundel would have been as soft on you as the king. Still,' Richard glanced smugly around the now silent company and disregarded the warning in his father's eyes, 'it's comforting to know that the only penalty for plotting rebellion is restoration and favour.'

'Richard.' Ralph Neville raised his cold eyes to his son's flushed face. 'Watch your tongue.'

His son pursed his lips in mock surprise. 'Oh? Is it a secret? I thought that all knew that the Percys were traitors.'

Neville slammed his fist on the table. 'Be silent. Or I'll have you whipped.'

'Why should I?' Richard glared venomously at Hal. 'Just because he's wed to Alianore doesn't mean I have to like him. I

91

suffer him for her sake – we all do. Why should we pretend otherwise?'

'Because I command it,' Neville said coldly. 'Whatever your private feelings, you will keep them to yourself and pay your cousin the respect and deference due to his rank. He is Earl of Northumberland – you are nobody yet.'

'You don't have to remind me of that,' Richard shouted. 'Fifty years of Neville service and loyalty to Lancaster against twenty years of Percy treason!' He glared bitterly at his father. 'And how are you better than him now? What rank or privilege do you hold that he does not? Such loyalty hardly seems worth the effort.'

His father's voice was soft and almost inaudible with anger. 'For that I'll have you whipped till you cannot stand. And if I have one more word out of you then Northumberland can administer the punishment himself.'

'My lord,' the countess laid a restraining hand on his arm and threw a hostile look at Hal. 'How can you take *his* part against your own son?'

'I take no one's part,' Neville snapped. 'Richard needs a lesson in manners and obedience.' He looked coldly into his wife's plump avaricious face. 'Else he'll never attain those glittering heights you have planned for him, madam. He'll be nothing but crow's meat if he doesn't learn to keep his tongue between his teeth.' He turned to his son. 'You will apologise to our cousin, Richard, or I promise you that you'll know worse shame before the night is out.'

Richard held his father's furious look. 'There could be no worse shame,' he said defiantly.

'Very well.' Neville turned toward Hal. 'You have my leave, Northumberland.'

Hal raised his eyes from the idle contemplation of the ring that adorned his left hand. If any of Richard Neville's insults had gone home they had left no mark on the cold impassive face he turned toward them. He smiled his empty meaningless smile.

'You are gracious, my lord, but there is neither skill or pleasure in thrashing a boy. The apology can wait till he is a man.' His insolent gaze rested lightly on Richard's face. 'If he ever is.'

There was a little silence. Then with a scream of rage Richard flung himself at Hal, his hands reaching for his throat. The company rose in uproar, the ladies giving little yelps of outrage as spilt food and wine spattered their gowns, the men grinning with delight at the prospect of a rough-house.

It never happened. Before Richard's hands ever reached his throat Hal had caught his arms and pinned them effortlessly to his sides. Their faces were close; he could feel the boy's panting breath upon his cheek. For an instant their eyes met and Hal felt a shiver run down his spine. Here was a hatred that matched his own; not the passive antagonism of Neville or the veiled hostility of his wife. This was real, a tangible recognisable thing, the same ever-destructive thing that was in himself.

He glanced at Neville's set face. 'Let him be,' he said quietly. 'If the punishment was mine then so is the withholding of it.'

Richard squirmed in his grasp. 'I want no favours from you, Northumberland,' he yelled.

'You'll get none, I promise you.'

Suddenly Richard Neville was still. The iron grip on his arms was eased and he almost fell, so sudden was the release. Only Northumberland's eyes kept him on his feet, green, glittering and full of malice, narrowed in the parody of a smile.

'Not yet, Richard. Not yet,' Hal said softly. 'We've a wealth of time together yet.'

Richard took a step backwards. 'I'll not forget this,' he blustered.

Hal smiled. 'I've no mind that you should. I shall remind you of it from time to time.'

Alianore winced as her sister's furious brush-strokes smoothed her hair. She had drunk a little too much and her head felt as light and empty as a puff ball. She only heard the half of Katherine's loud castigation of their brother.

'Jesu. I could have whipped him myself. To shame us so and in front of Northumberland too. And then to bring his dinner up in the Bishop of Durham's lap . . .'

Alianore sighed. Katherine could clack a mill-wheel when she like – and tonight she did like.

'Mind you,' Katherine looked darkly at Alianore in their

shared reflection, 'I can't say that I blame him in a way. Richard knows what we all know – that there's naught between you and Northumberland at night save the thickness of your chamber wall. Jesu, Alianore. Wed twice before you're twenty and still as virgin as the rest of us.'

Alianore flushed. 'Mind your business, Katherine. And tell Richard to mind his. I can manage my husband very well myself.'

Katherine looked sulky. 'As you please.' She shook out the folds of Alianore's discarded gown and hung it on its pole.

'I just pray that Mowbray has more fire in him.'

'Oh, I'm sure he has,' Alianore said derisively. 'He's fathered bastards on half of England already. That must be recommendation enough, even for you, Katherine.'

'Well, at least he can,' her sister snapped. 'I'm beginning to wonder about Hal Percy.'

Alianore swung round from the glass and eyed her sister coldly. 'You seem to have caught Richard's disease, Katherine. You saw how it profited him to insult my husband. Will you risk a whipping also?' She turned her back on Katherine's furious face. 'You may go,' she said abruptly. 'I shall have no more need of you tonight.'

The door slammed on Katherine's stiff outraged back and the silence of the room grew oppressive and intense. Alianore stared at her reflection and fought back the tears. She felt the humiliation more than they knew. Katherine was right. Wed more than a year and still a virgin; Jesu, how they must snigger behind her back

She looked across at the great canopied bed. She'd waited all that first night for him, disbelieving and angry when he had not come, ashamed of herself for wanting him to. He'd made the rejection easy for her. He'd been polite, courteous, even mildly attentive sometimes, but no more than that. She'd never seen beneath the cold impassive exterior that even Richard with all his niggling had failed to penetrate. She'd made excuses. They had not laid eyes on each other since that dreadful parody of a marriage in Berwick and they might never have again if the king hadn't been so lenient over the Cambridge affair. He needed time, she told herself, that was all. But there was no more time left. Her father returned to Carlisle in the morning and Hal would go with him. God only knew when she might see him again.

She rose, shivering, and drew a furred cloak about her shoulders. The fire had burned down to pale crumbling ash. She was cold. She glanced again toward the great empty bed. She'd be colder still in there. She hesitated only for a moment, then went quickly out of the room. There would be cold nights enough once he had gone.

Outside his door her courage failed her. Dear God, what was she about, sneaking to his chamber to beg his bed like some common whore? Did she want him so much? She smiled grimly. Yes, she did. At least she wanted to know why he didn't want her.

He was still fully dressed, lounging in a chair by the spent fire. His eyes were cold and expressionless when he turned his head. They did not change when they saw her.

She stared at him for a long time, taking in the long languid body, the gilded hair, the fine hands that toyed absently with an empty goblet. She was the first to speak.

'My lord. I came to apologise for my brother Richard – and to thank you for not punishing him.' Did it sound as feeble to him as it did to her?

He stood and turned reluctantly to face her. 'There was no need. It was not done for him.'

Alianore swallowed hard and closed the door behind her. The rejection in his eyes hurt more than she had thought. He was not going to make it easy for her.

'I know that.' She advanced a little way toward him and saw his eyes drop to her breasts. She smiled in quiet triumph. So he did want her after all.

'His behaviour was shameful,' she began confidently. 'But he is young and proud . . .'

'And I am not?' His eyes were on her face again. 'Bad manners are nothing to do with being young and proud. Or is it just a perogative of the Nevilles?'

She flushed. 'I cannot argue with that.' His look put her on the defensive again. 'But sometimes you provoke him,' she added sharply.

Hal raised his brows. 'Indeed. In what way? What have I ever said that could provoke sweet Richard to such unseemly wrath?'

'You don't have to say anything. A look is as good as a hundred words. He is a boy and easily provoked. He resents you because he thinks you got Northumberland back without sacrifice.'

'And he doesn't think that ten years of my life is sacrifice?' She winced at the bitterness in his voice. 'Well, I resent the fact that your father holds land that should be mine. I resent the fact that he hacked off my grandfather's head and kept it on London Bridge for ten years. And most of all I resent the fact that I was forced to marry you to get back what was already mine.'

He could not have hurt her more if he had struck her. She understood now. Love, even desire, did not enter into it. She was being punished. She was to be the whipping boy for all the Neville sins. Unsteadily she said, 'I understand that. But we are wed, like it or not. Must we be enemies too? Must I always sleep alone?' She stretched out her hand and touched his. 'I am your wife, Hal.'

There was no response in him. His flesh was as cold as his eyes and the only pleasure in them was the pleasure of hurting her.

'Yes. You are my wife, but from necessity not from choice. At least let the choice of sharing your bed be mine. Or is that to be forced upon me also?'

Pride emptied her eyes of the pain and shock and after the first few agonising moments she could bring herself to look at him. It was longer before she could trust herself to speak.

'Did that please you, my lord?' She smiled at him almost pleasantly. 'Do you also kick dogs and pull the feathers from little birds?' She turned to go and said without looking at him, 'I shall not trouble you again, my lord. For all I care you may sleep in a ditch.'

He stared at the door long after she had gone. Had that pleased him? He closed his eyes in self disgust. Did he also kick dogs and pull the feathers from little birds?

He lay down wearily on the wide embroidered bed. His body ached with longing. Christ, how he had wanted to touch her, to hold her softness against him. He knew that she had wanted it too. It was why she had come. And he had turned her away because he had preferred to see pain rather than pleasure in her eyes. Now all the pain was his, all the pain and longing and emptiness. He closed his eyes wearily. Hatred was such a comfortless thing.

The next day he rode with Ralph Neville to Carlisle. He saw Alianore briefly before he left among the confusion of departure. Cool and distant as ever she raised her cheek for his kiss, and the action quelled the impulse he'd had to beg her forgiveness. They parted without a word between them. It was to be three years before he saw her again.

It was the end of summer and the moor was bleached to a dry brilliance that hurt the eyes. Yellow gorse blistered every hillside, in every crease and hollow white hawthorn glared and scorched russet flanks of heather rose from burnt stubbled fields. Only on the high ground was there wind enough to cool the blaze of noon.

On the roof of the great keep at Alnwick, Hal lifted his face to the fitful breeze. From here he could see almost all of Northumberland: the sprawling ridge of the Cheviots veined with black hags of peat and the shining headwaters of the Till. Beyond the river the moorland rolled toward him like a petrified sea, rising to the rounded head of Dod Law, falling gently down to the coast and the wide Roman road that led down to Durham. To the south the hills were harsher, struggling from black forest, their jagged tors like crouching giants against the sky. At their back, unseen in a haze of heat, the moor ran on, bleak and barren, down to Newcastle and the Tyne.

He followed the line of the West March where the hills dropped down like a flight of steps toward Westmorland: Black Hag and the Schill looped by the shining width of Kyle Water; Auchope; Windy Gyle and Bloodybush Edge; the dark sullen mound of Peel Fell laced by the last drove roads into Scotland. A rainbow haze marked Liddle Water as it plunged between steep wooded fells. It would emerge tamed and douce to join the Esk and flow quietly into the black mouth of Solway.

His mouth tightened: all Neville territory, from Carlisle to the Hanging Stone on Cheviot, then along the Tweed to Berwick. For all his new-found favour he had not succeeded in displacing Neville and his sons from the Wardenship. They still held the

Border and while they did he was impotent. A faint acquisitive smile eased his mouth from its grimness. He could wait. He had done more than well in the last few months. Cockermouth and Langley were his again and he'd had more joy from the look on Neville's face when he'd had to yield them than from all of the wealth they'd brought him. But that was then. He'd grown greedy since and had acquired a taste for richness: the feel of silk against his skin; the lambent fire of a perfect stone. The Crecy tapestry graced the wall of the great hall again and he'd begun to replace his grandfather's priceless books: an early copy of the Astrolabe; Chaucer's 'Legend of Good Women' bound in rose silk with a ruby and emerald clasp. There would have been more had not his conscience pricked him to send the copy of Boethius to Bishop Wardlaw. He still kept the worn and shabby volumes that had been his gift. Incongruous among the silk and velvet bindings, they reminded him of the times when they were all he had. It made his new treasures seem all the more precious.

He looked out again into the perfect day like a miser counting his hoard. All his — except for the canker of Neville lands festering in the heart of Redesdale. He thought again of his father-in-law. He'd seen little of him since the spring, and of Alianore nothing at all. Neville had remarked on it before he had departed for Carlisle.

'And how long do you intend to keep my daughter virgin?'

Hal's look had brought a flush to Neville's thin face. 'Does she complain of it then, my lord?'

'No. But I do,' Neville snapped. 'I'd hoped for a grandson by now.'

'To keep your shelves filled? How *do* you sell them, my lord? By the yard or the pound?'

'By God.' Neville turned as pale as the parchment held between his trembling fingers. 'If you were not kin I'd have your tongue out for that.' He thrust a long finger at Hal. 'And let me tell you this. If you've a notion of putting Alianore aside or asking for an annulment . . .'

Hal interrupted him coldly. 'I never go back on a bargain. And it was a bargain, was it not? Your daughter in exchange for Northumberland? Well, when I have Northumberland — all of it, including the Marches and the land which you hold in Redesdale – then I'll take your daughter.'

Neville advanced his face threateningly close. 'The Border is mine and I intend that it shall remain so. You've had Cockermouth and Langley, and God knows what more. Be content with that. It's more than you deserve.'

Hal had smiled. 'Then your daughter must bear her chastity as best she can,' he said softly. 'And you, Grocer Ralph, can replenish your shelves elsewhere.'

And he had meant it. What needed to be said between himself and Alianore was said through stewards and clerks. She'd asked his consent to move to their manor at Leconfield and with indifference he'd given it. Now the steward came once a month with the accounts and he paid them unquestioningly. There was never any word from her and he sent none by return. He was content to have it so. If he needed a woman there were plenty to be had on his own terms. Northumberland was both wife and mistress to him and filled all of his life: the restoration of Alnwick, of the house at York; the dragging up of the land itself from the dust of neglect. Ten years of Bolingbroke's penny-pinching rule had left its mark. John of Bedford had done his best but his father had been no more generous to him then he had been to Northumberland before him. Half of Wark's curtain had slid into the Tweed and Berwick had a breach in its walls the width of Durham nave. The land was barren again, the fields burnt and sterile. It had been too charitable a thought to believe that Albany would have allowed him a breathing space. He'd come in October when the cattle were sleek and pastured on the hills and the barns full of ripened corn. In two great sickening waves, Douglas in the west, Albany himself in the east, they'd burnt and ravaged their way as far down as Alnwick, then turned back upon Berwick to sit down before its crumbling walls. And he'd been as helpless as a babe waiting for Neville to come up to Carlisle. By the time he had mustered enough men for reprisal Alnwick was in flames and they were threatened with the loss of Berwick. It was Bedford who had saved them from that. He'd appeared almost miraculously with six thousand men at his back and Albany, never so sure of himself on the field, had retreated with such alacrity that the enterprise had been dubbed the Fool's Raid. He and Bedford had pursued the enemy as far as Melrose and here it was Hal who had the advantage. He knew every hill and forest on the Scottish side, every wood and valley, every peel tower and crossing place. He knew where they could hide, where they could lie in ambush. Better still, he knew Albany. The Regent would not stand and fight if he could run, and run he had, all the way back to Dalkeith. It had been some small revenge to see him scuttling back into Scotland with a pack of English borderers snapping at his heels. But the damage had been done. A year's harvest had been turned to black smouldering ash. The mills that had ground the abundance of corn were burnt and derelict, the barns that had housed it were charred, empty shells. He'd mended the mills and patched the barns and begged a grant from the king for the repair of Berwick. He had been refused, albeit with great courtesy. Henry had neither time nor money to spare. His eyes were fixed on France again.

He turned as Jack's heavy face appeared over the rim of the stair well.

'Bedford's here,' he announced. 'And that tart Mortimer with him.'

Hal allowed the disrespectful allusion to his cousin to pass. You got used to Jack after a while. And he supposed that any man who could call the king 'Harry lad' to his face and get away with it deserved some measure of indulgence.

Bedford waited for him in the great hall, his pale sombre face turned up in admiration to the Crécy tapestry. It stood twenty feet high. The gargantuan armoured figures of the first Edward and his son looked down with hard sapphire eyes. There were four hundred pearls worked into the gilded housings of their mounts and jasper and tourmaline studded their helms.

'It's magnificent,' Bedford said. 'Fit for a king.'

'Your father thought so,' Hal answered, thinking of the day Bolingbroke's men had come to take it down. It had taken thirty of them to carry it. His mother had been there. He remembered that she'd wept more for the loss of the tapestry than she'd ever done for the loss of him.

Bedford nodded absently and glanced round the hall. 'You have a taste for magnificence, Hal,' he observed.

Hal stiffened, sensing criticism. He looked into the pale open face and found none.

'It's bred from years of penury, John,' he said lightly. 'It makes me feel safe, like high walls and deep moats.' He turned his head fractionally so that his smile encompassed the man who stood uneasily by the fireplace.

'And how does our illustrious cousin of March and Ulster? I wonder that you ever wanted to be king, Edmund, when you hold half of England already.'

Mortimer's thin face flushed. 'I never wanted to be king,' he blurted out. 'It was Richard . . .'

'Don't speak ill of the dead, sweet Edmund. Cambridge has paid his debt.' Hal's face hardened. 'Which is more than you ever did. Still,' he smiled maliciously, 'all is not yet lost. Your Aunt Elizabeth still schemes and plots for your cause. You might be king yet.'

'Damn you,' Mortimer yelled. 'If you were not kin I'd make you pay for that.'

Hal laughed. The second time he'd had that said to him. 'Don't let that stand in your way, Edmund. I'd be more than glad to forget it.'

Mortimer stared at him like a rabbit hypnotised by a stoat. Then abruptly he turned and strode wordlessly from the hall.

Bedford stared after him. 'You were hard on him, Hal.'

'Only because he deserves it. He was as much involved in Cambridge's plot as Cambridge himself. Yet a good man like Tom Grey has to lose his head while sweet Edmund keeps his because . . .'

'Tom Grey was a traitor, Hal,' Bedford interrupted.

'Was he, John?' Hal handed him the brimming goblet of malmsey. 'And how do you define "traitor"? One who plots against his lawful king?' He smiled derisively. 'Well, even you would have been guilty of that once, John. It's not the treason that matters, it's being on the winning side that counts.'

'You're still bitter, Hal?'

Hal shrugged. 'No. Not bitter, John. Bored, frustrated, sick of being Ralph Neville's apprentice. While he holds the West and Middle Marches I'm powerless. And penniless. I can't mend the breach in Berwick's walls with promises. And that's all I've had.'

'Not from me.'

Hal sighed. 'No, not from you, John.' He turned and looked squarely at Bedford. 'Did you put it to the king? My restoration to the full wardenship?'

'I did. He said he'd think on it.'

'Not trusted well enough yet, eh John?'

Bedford frowned. 'That's unfair, Hal. Henry's got more on his mind than your wardenship.'

'Is there news then?'

Bedford's heavy face lit with sudden animation. 'Only the best. Falaise has fallen. Henry's moving south to Rouen. If he can take Rouen then all of lower Normandy will be his.'

Hal felt a flicker of excitement. Since the summer Henry had swept through France like plague. Touques had fallen within a week of his landing; Caen and Alençon after a long and bitter siege. His progress had been almost unopposed, while the French fought and squabbled amongst themselves for possession of Paris. His only setback had been the sudden defection of Burgundy who had allied himself to the banished Queen Isabeau both in council and in bed. It had not been enough to turn the tide against him. The French king still raved in squalor at Tours. The flagging Orlánists had found a new leader in Bernard, Count of Armagnac, and their possession of the Dauphin Charles had momentarily given them the edge, but Henry continued to play them off one against the other and almost leisurely to make his way into the heart of France. Whether by God's will or the Devil's, none doubted that by the end of the year Henry would be virtual master of France.

Hal turned his empty goblet restlessly between his fingers. Then abruptly he said, 'I want to go to France, John.'

Bedford raised his heavy brows. 'France? What about Albany? What about the Border? I thought you cared so much for it.'

'I do. But not as Ralph Neville's unpaid errand boy, and Warden of the East March or not that's all I am. Besides,' he smiled wryly, 'I need the money. Warkworth's falling about my ears and a good gust of wind could bring Prudhoe down. There's money in France, John. Ransoms, plunder . . .'

'There are other things as well,' Bedford said grimly. 'Cold, hunger, dysentery – even death.'

'I'll risk it. Christ, John, you know that you'd give half your revenues to go back yourself.'

Bedford smiled. That he would. It was the only thing he envied his brothers, Clarence and Gloucester: the war and the company of Henry.

'And Albany?' he said. 'Lord Warden or not, we could never have given him such a thrashing if it hadn't been for you. You know Albany and the Border, Hal. That counts for quite a lot.'

'Albany won't be back yet awhile. He's taken all we had and he'll not have the men to mount another attack.' Hal smiled archly. 'Did you know he's sending ten thousand men to the Dauphin?'

'Who told you that?'

'One of Albany's little birds. I caught him trying to fly the coop after we fired Melrose. He sang all the louder for Jack's knife at his throat.'

Bedford stared thoughtfully at his feet. 'Ten thousand, you say.'

'Oh, come on, John,' Hal said irritably. 'Henry's crying out for men. That's what Mortimer's over here for, to drum up recruits.'

Bedford did not look up but picked absently at a stray thread on his sleeve. 'How many men could you muster?'

'Enough. Fifty lances. A hundred men-at-arms – mounted.'

'And still leave a garrison at Alnwick?'

Hal nodded.

Bedford looked up and smiled. 'Then go. And I wish to God that I was coming with you.'

France

The gunsmoke hung in yellow stagnant clouds round the walls of Rouen, though the great guns had been silent for almost a week. It was the silence that was so unnerving, the silence of waiting, the silence of slow painful death.

For six months the garotte of English troops had held Rouen in its stranglehold as with elaborate care Henry choked the life from it. His cannon had pounded the walls to rubble, his army blockaded every gate and tower. As the weather broke the cord grew tighter and the rain of weeks had turned to snow, fine soft blinding snow that froze as soon as it touched the ground. It was another weapon in Henry's already merciless armoury. Those who had not died of hunger did so now from the cold.

Hal looked out across the frozen river at the ring of watchfires strung out like the jewels of some intricate collar. Beyond that nothing moved, no light showed. The towers of Philip Augustus' great fortress rose unseen. The great yawning ditch that girdled the city merged with the winter darkness. The ten thousand poor wretches huddled in the freezing mud of its depths made no sound – ten thousand useless hungry mouths that Rouen had thrown to the mercy of the English. Not so many now, for Henry had had no mercy and refused to let them pass the English lines. For two months now they'd lived in the no-man's-land of the ditch, surviving on the meagre slops that the monks of St Catherine's could spare. Even those had ceased now. There was nothing to spare anymore. They ate mice and beetles, their own ordure, even the dead that were heaved from the ditch each morning and ringed the town with their sickening stench: babies no more than a few hours old with the slime of afterbirth still on them; old men with limbs like kindling sticks; young girls scabbed and pussed with scurvy; a tangled undignified heap of skin and bone that made even the hardest blanch with shame. All except Henry. He was past all suffering, even his own. He was thin as a cadaver himself with fasting, the full voluptuous mouth narrowed by strain and lack of sleep. If he had a conscience over the refugees in the ditch he salved it by pointing out that it was the French, not he, who had put them there. It was enough for Henry, but not enough for Hal. His tent was close enough to hear their suffering. He'd seen it too. Babies born in filth and mud, hauled up to the ramparts for a hasty baptism then lowered to the pit again to die. Once the noise had been unbearable. They were quieter now. They needed all their strength just to stay alive.

He set his horse to the slippery planks of the timber bridge and the guard at its head danced with cold as he watched him approach. His greeting was cheerful. He was fat and well fed like all the English. The king had seen to that. A bribe to Portugal had ensured a friendly fleet off Harfleur and the free undisturbed passage of English supplies up the Seine. They had cheese and meat daily. In Rouen they ate rats and dogs and counted themselves lucky.

He dismounted and picked his way through the closely-set tents and the lattice of trenches that linked the camps. The snow was growing heavier, blown by a freezing wind into knife-edged drifts against the city walls. He heard the cry of a child from the ditch and turned his face away. Dear God. Even a dog shouldn't die like that.

Inside the tent there was warmth and the smell of freshly mulled wine. Jack looked up from the boots he was polishing with goosefat. 'Froze enough for one night then, have you?' he said. 'I've been keeping broth hot two hours since. It's not fit for pigswill now.'

Hal flung himself down on the low truckle bed and thrust out his foot for Jack to ease his boot off. 'It doesn't matter. I've no stomach for food tonight.'

Jack paused in mid pull. 'You sick?'

'Only sick of doing nothing.'

'Ah, well. That's sieges for you. Got to have patience for siegework you have. Like our Harry. He'll sit here till kingdom come before he'll back off.'

'I don't doubt it,' Hal said grimly. He locked his frozen hands round the cup of warm wine. 'For God's sake, how much longer, Jack?'

'Oh, not long now. The cold'll finish them off. A month. No more.'

'Unless Burgundy comes.'

Jack sat down with his knees touching the brazier of hot coals. 'Burgundy won't come. He's too worried that he'll lose his grip on Paris. It's too late now anyway. If he'd come a month ago he might have saved them. But not now.' He jerked his thumb behind him. 'They're half dead already, most of them. Eating all sorts of nameless filth and glad of it too. I've heard an onion costs six deniers. Christ. That's more than I earn in a month.'

Hal lay back among the furs of his bed and stared up at the roof sagging beneath its weight of snow. He was more than disappointed. The brief sorties when the French had still had the strength to fight had barely lasted a month and any hopes he'd had of persuading the king to restore the Border to him had died at the first glimpse of that pale fanatical face. Henry saw nothing but Rouen and the wider vision of France. So they waited like vultures for Rouen to fall. It seemed he'd spend all his life waiting.

He closed his eyes and listened to the relentless drip of melting snow onto the hard earth floor. There were other sounds: the helpless wail of a child; the drone of repeated unanswered prayers. He thought suddenly of Alianore and the north. A long time since he'd seen either. Did she even think of him? Why should she? He had never thought of her till now.

He pulled the furs over himself as Jack doused the lamp and moved the brazier closer between them. It was still early; the bell of St Ouen had not yet struck seven. An hour to curfew. Henry was such a stickler for curfews. From the adjoining tent came the sound of low furtive laughter, a warm companionable sound – his men playing at forbidden dice again. He glanced across at Jack and wondered if he'd done him such a great service by taking him from his own kind. He was viewed with suspicion by the common soldiers for keeping his master such close company and the knights had denounced him as an upstart, yet he seemed content and his loyalty and concern for Hal had never once wavered. Hal thought indulgently, they were two of a kind. They had no place save that which they made for themselves. Jack's was with him. He had no desire to change it.

It seemed he'd hardly fallen asleep before Jack's great hand clamped over his mouth. They both stared at the motionless shadow transfixed in the corner. Hal saw the gleam of terrified eyes, the cowering droop of a small untidy head. Jack's hand relaxed its merciless grip. 'It's no more than a lad,' he said softly.

The boy moved with the speed of a frightened rabbit and he'd wriggled halfway beneath the canvas before Jack grabbed him by the piece of twine that served as his belt. He hauled him back, struggling and kicking, then slapped him sharply across the head.

The boy was instantly still, dangling like a corpse on a gibbet from Jack's heavy hand.

Hal leapt from the bed and lit the lamp. Eyes hard and dry as pebbles stared back at him from a ravenous face. Only the soft trembling mouth betrayed his fear.

'And what are you after, you verminous little bastard?' Jack shook the boy so that his teeth rattled in his head.

Hal motioned Jack to let him go and held the lamp higher. The child was filthy. His clothes were sodden stinking rags, his feet were bare and bleeding from the cold.

'What do you want?' he asked softly in French.

The boy raised his head and looked at him. Hal saw by the flicker of his eyes that he was understood. Hal set the lamp down. He knew that look. It had been in his own eyes often enough.

He reached for the half-eaten loaf and held it out. 'Is it food? Is it food you've come for?'

The boy suddenly began to cry. He stared at the bread while great silent tears scored grey streaks in the filth of his face. Then he lunged and grabbed the bread, stuffing it uncontrollably into his mouth.

Hal snatched it back. 'No,' he said sharply. 'You'll kill yourself like that.' He looked at Jack. 'Get some wood on that fire and warm some wine.'

Jack pursed his mouth in disapproval. 'Still itching to lose your head, aren't you? Harbouring Frenchies and feeding them to boot. Harry'll like that, he will. Him sweatin' blood trying to starve them out and you filling them up twice as fast.'

'For pity's sake, Jack. He's just a child.'

'So were we all once.' Jack thrust the pot into the brazier's warmth. 'But he'll grow into a dirty great Frenchman one day and then slit your throat for your trouble.'

Hal eyed the thin cavernous cheeks. 'I'll risk it,' he said grimly. 'I'll not make war on children, King Henry or no King Henry.'

The boy had begun to shiver uncontrollably and Hal wrapped a fur from his bed around him. Jack glanced over his shoulder. 'Unless you want him howling the place down when his limbs thaw out, don't get him too warm. Besides, he'll never stand the cold again when he leaves.' He dumped the wine unceremoniously on the stool beside Hal and brushed a lively brown speck from his sleeve. 'Place'll be bloody crawling by the morning,' he muttered.

Hal crumbled the bread into the steaming wine. 'Slowly,' he said and held out the bowl. 'Eat it slowly or you'll bring it back before it's half down.'

The boy shovelled in a mouthful and choked on it. Hal took the bowl from him and began to spoon it carefully between his chattering teeth.

'How long since you've eaten?' he asked gently.

The boy spoke for the first time. 'A long time.' He shrugged his thin shoulders. 'I don't know. A long time.'

'Have you family? Mother? Father?'

'My mother. She is dying, though.' He said it quite calmly, without emotion. He was used to death by now.

'How old are you? How many years?'

'Ten, I think. I might be more. I was nine when my father died. That was two winters ago.'

'Then you are more. That makes you eleven.'

The boy nodded and Hal saw that his eyes were drooping with exhaustion. Swiftly he refilled the bowl and wrapped the rest of the loaf and the scraps of meat in a cloth. 'Take these,' he said. 'Give the bread and wine to your mother, but slowly as I showed you. Eat nothing more yourself till the morning.' He shook the boy gently. 'Do you understand?'

The boy nodded drowsily and rose unsteadily to his feet. 'Yes, I understand.'

Hal picked up the fur that had slipped from his shoulders. 'Take this also. It'll keep you from freezing.'

The boy fingered the rich sable longingly then dropped his hand. 'No,' he said. 'I'd not keep it long and the others would wonder where I got it.'

Hal nodded and spoke to Jack. 'See that it's clear.'

The boy looked up at him gravely then wordlessly he followed Jack out into the night. Hal watched him go, lurching unsteadily across the snow till the darkness and silence swallowed him up.

'Ungrateful little whelp,' Jack said. 'Not so much as a bloody thank-you.' He stamped the snow from his boots. 'Waste of time anyway. He'll not survive another week of this.'

'He might,' Hal said. 'If Rouen surrenders.'

'It won't be in time for those poor bastards out there.' Jack thrust his booted feet beneath the covers of his bed. 'Anyway, why do you care? What's he to you? One less Frenchman if he dies. That's the way to look at it. That's the way Harry looks at it.'

Hal said nothing but for an instant the boy looked out of the man's eyes. There was still enough of the boy left in him to see in himself the hungry desolate child he had sent back out into the cold to die.

It rained ceaselessly all the next day, a cold relentless downpour that kept them penned in their tents and turned the land into a sea of mud. Hal rode out but once, to the daily council that Henry's rigid discipline insisted upon. An air of strained boredom prevailed but they went through the ritual that Henry demanded for no better reason than that Henry demanded it.

Hal's eyes dwelt cautiously on the king's face. Henry did not care to be stared at these days, even in admiration. He had changed. France had changed him, hardened him and drained the humanity from him. His prominent eyes ringed with premature lines were as ruthless as a hangman's. He had developed a fanatical passion for detail, even to the precise distance that their tents must be set apart. Nothing was too small or insignificant to be brought to his notice. The loss of a weapon, the sickness and death of a penny-a-day pikeman, the king must know all and by knowing he maintained his iron control over sixteen thousand rough illiterate men who would have cut their own mother's throats for a penny. He glanced at the raison above the king's head: *Une sans plus*. Only one. How fitting. Only one dream, one ambition, the dream that had all but bankrupted his great-grandfather Edward. Would Henry succeed? Looking at that pitiless mouth, Hal knew that he would and wondered if he would still have kept his head if he'd faced Henry now.

The king was fretting over a bout of sickness in his brother Clarence's camp. Fever? What symptoms? How many dead? Was it spreading? Clarence yawned, unconcerned by the loss of fifteen archers till he caught the king's eye. Every life was precious, Henry told him. They needed every man they could get.

Hal wondered at the incongruity of it, remembering that less than a week ago Henry himself had hung two of his own men for straying from the confines of the camp. Their lives were not so precious, it seemed, if they thwarted Henry.

The plight of the refugees in the ditch was tentatively raised. Hal looked from the king's set face to the man who sat beside him, Humphrey of Gloucester, plump as a ripe damson in purple velvet and unquestioningly Henry's man in this. The refugees were the enemy. What did it matter whether they lived or died?

Archbishop Chichele worked his thin scholarly mouth, torn between conscience and his loyalty to the king. Clarence yawned again, and this time Henry did not reprimand him. This was a subject he did not care to debate. His face hardened. They were not his responsibility. *He* had not turned them from the city. Let the French feed them.

Henry looked bleakly at Sir Gilbert Umfraville as he rose to his feet. 'My liege, I was thinking of our own safety,' Sir Gilbert said. 'If they continue to die in such numbers there will be disease. The dead lie unburied. We are not so far off that it could not spread to our own men.'

Henry smiled thinly. 'You need have no fear, Sir Gilbert. The cold will kill any pestilence that threatens.'

Archbishop Chichele licked his lips. 'Your Grace, we should not see compassion as weakness. Next week is the Holy season of Christ's birth. Perhaps a small offering might be sent to these poor souls on this day. A gesture, in celebration of Our Lord's coming.'

'It's a fool's notion,' Gloucester stated baldly. 'You don't feed a wolf before it flies at your throat.'

'My lord, these are not wolves. There are women and children, helpless old men, the sick and the lame.'

'But French. Don't forget that.' Gloucester went back to the idle contemplation of the rings that banded his broad knuckles. 'The enemy is the enemy and that's all there is about it.'

'That is not necessarily so in this case.' A row of astonished eyes turned on Hal. He had surprised himself that he had had the courage to speak. 'Perhaps they are the enemy now,' he went on. 'But when the king has conquered they will be his subjects.' He dared to look at Henry and saw his brows raised in interest. 'If you want to tame a wild dog, you feed it. It'll follow you anywhere then.' He leant forward and addressed Henry directly. 'A taste of food might break them, your Grace. These people are dying, starving to death in filth and squalor without hope of reprieve. And by whose decree? Their own masters. Who is to be their hope, their salvation? Not Burgundy, chewing his nails in the safety of Paris, nor the Dauphin. But Henry, King of England and France, their rightful lord. The hand that fed them, that lifted them up from the pit of hell.' He thought he had overdone it when he saw the cynical twist of Henry's mouth and added more soberly, 'If you could tempt the people of Rouen to surrender it would save both time and money.'

'You mean a bribe?' said Henry with rare amusement.

'Of sorts, my liege,' Hal answered frankly.

Archbishop Chichele took up the idea eagerly. 'As Moses led the children of Israel from Egypt, so King Henry leads the French out of hell.' He smiled. 'A pleasing analogy, do you not think?'

'What good's feeding those wretches in the ditch? How will that influence the city?' Clarence said.

'Nothing travels faster than the smell of food to a starving man,' Hal said. 'It is the garrison that will not surrender. The people of Rouen outnumber the garrison fifty to one. If they could be brought to revolt.'

Henry's eyes narrowed speculatively. He didn't care if the refugees all died tomorrow but he did care about the prospect of shortening the siege. It meant a saving of time and money, money of which he had precious little.

'Very well,' he announced. 'A truce on Christmas Day, but only Christmas Day,' he added sharply, in case any thought him moved to weakness. He looked at Hal and smiled thinly. 'We will feed your dog, Northumberland. Let us see if it eats from our hand or bites it.'

Hal bowed and retreated to his previous obscurity while the king passed briskly on to the appalling loss of weaponry in my lord of Warwick's division. Hal almost laughed aloud with exhilaration. He had won a point and without even trying. And if it worked . . . He caught his lip between his teeth. He would think no further than that. Sufficient to the day thereof, as Bishop Wardlaw used to say. At least he had won those poor devils out there a day's grace. He lowered his eyes, suddenly aware of Gloucester's hostile look. That was an enmity, flourishing without any help from him. They had hardly spoken, but it was there, a hard core of dislike that grew stronger each time they met. He thought of the French boy and the risk he was taking. He'd come again last night, scratching at the tent flap like a drowned rat. Jack had dragged him in, cursing.

'You see? You'll not get rid of him now. Follow you like a bloody dog he will. And like as not you'll have a bevy of them out there soon, when the word gets around that there's an Englishman who's a soft touch.'

The boy had stared silently at Hal. His rags had dripped a pool of water and he'd shifted his bare feet nervously, treading mud. 'She's dead,' he said quietly. 'They smelt the food and went for her.'

'They killed her?'

The boy shrugged. 'She's dead. I don't know how. I ran away.'

'How do you know she is dead, then?'

'They threw her body from the ditch. I saw it.'

Hal glanced at Jack who folded his mouth tight into his beard and threw wood onto the fire without being asked. He looked back at the boy. 'Get these filthy rags off,' he said harshly. He watched as the boy peeled the sodden clothes from his body. He was so painfully thin, his belly swollen incongruously like a woman with child. His back was scarred from the weals of a whip and there was an ugly bruise in his groin.

'Who beat you?' Hal asked and wrapped his cloak round the pitiful nakedness.

The boy shrugged. 'I don't know. They kick you sometimes when you're sleeping. If you've a dry place in the ditch. They kick you till you move.'

'I meant your back. Who whipped you?'

The boy looked at him in surprise. 'My father,' he said almost proudly. 'No one else would dare.'

'Is he dead?'

'Yes.' The boy gobbled the stew that Jack thrust ungraciously under his nose and Hal did not stop him this time.

When he'd wiped the bowl clean with the last of the bread Hal said, 'How did he die?'

The boy regarded him innocently. 'The English killed him,' he said simply. 'We had a farm near Pont de l'Arche. The English came. They killed him and took my sister. My mother and I hid in a ditch.'

'Took your sister? Took her where?'

'Took her.' The boy looked uncomfortable. 'The soldiers took her. All of them. Till she died.'

Hal looked away and Jack cleared his throat noisily. 'So you have no one then?' Hal said.

'I think I have an uncle or something in Rouen. He's a tailor. My mother went to see him once, to see if he could stop them putting us out of the city.' He huddled deeper into the cloak and watched his own rags steaming by the brazier. 'Are you English?' he asked.

'Yes.' Hal smiled. 'I am English.'

'You don't speak like the English.'

'That's because I was taught French by a Frenchman,' Hal said. 'He came from Valognes. That's not far from here.'

The boy nodded. 'My grandfather had a mill there. It was burned, though, in the last war.' He spoke without malice. War and death were so much a part of life to him that he did not apportion blame. He accepted death as unquestioningly as he accepted hunger and the fact that his father should flay him raw. Then he said almost shyly, 'My name is Jean, after my father. What is yours?'

'Henry. Henry Percy, after my father.' Hal would not have sounded right in French.

'Percy?' The boy drew his thin brows together. 'There is a little village called Perci a few miles away.'

Hal nodded. 'That is where my ancestors came from. Before they came to England with the Conqueror. Have you heard of King William? He was Duke of Normandy before he was King of England.'

The boy nodded avidly. 'He is buried in the great abbey at Caen.' He smiled for the first time. 'So you are not all English then? If your forefathers came from Normandy?'

Hal returned the smile. 'No, I am not all English.'

Jean nodded and smiled drowsily.

Then Jack looked over. 'What now? He's half asleep as it is and them rags'll never be dry for an hour. You'll kill him if you send him out now.'

'He can sleep here. With me,' he added as he saw Jack's mouth open in protest.

'Fleas and all?'

Hal grinned. 'Fleas and all.' He picked the boy up and laid him on the low bed. 'You can sleep here till your clothes are dry but you must be gone before daylight. Do you understand?'

He shook the boy gently but he did not answer. Behind him Jack's voice muttered. 'Bloody fool. Bloody soft fool.'

The boy had been gone when he awoke, the cloak neatly folded on the end of the bed. It was still raining and he had thought anxiously of the boy being wet and cold. He pulled a wry face and tried to concentrate on the voice of the king's clerk adroitly accounting for a shortage in stores. Jack was right. He was a bloody soft fool.

He dined that night in the king's tent to the open displeasure of Gloucester, eating with restraint and drinking watered wine for the king strongly disapproved of gluttony. Henry himself picked disinterestedly at the succession of dishes that were set before him and most he sent away untouched: Hal wondered in God's name where he got his strength from. Yet the strain of the campaign was telling. Even the softness of candlelight could not hide the gauntness of his features that was so at odds with his high colour, as if some dreadful fire consumed him from within. He was thirty and looked twice that.

His mood had mellowed since the morning. He played for them on the ornate Welsh harp that went everywhere with him, and flushed like a schoolboy at their praise. He paused for a brief word with Hal before he left them.

'His Grace of Bedford wrote to me of your coming.' Henry's

shrewd dark eyes searched his face. 'His Grace speaks very highly of you.'

Hal inclined his head. 'You are gracious, Sire. I hope I prove worthy of his regard.'

Henry smiled at the empty courtesy. 'He says you want the Border back,' he said bluntly. 'Do you think you deserve it?'

Hal looked at him squarely. 'Yes,' he said. 'I do.'

'You think you could do better than Neville?'

'As good as,' Hal answered.

'As good as is not good enough. You must be the better for me to uproot Ralph Neville and his sons from the post they've held these twelve years past. It's considered theirs by right now.'

'They have no rights save those which you decree,' Hal said. 'None of us have.'

The remark pleased Henry and he smiled. 'Well, we'll see.' He patted Hal's arm absently and turned away. 'We'll see.'

Hal stared after him. Had he thrown his chance away? Had he been too forward, too sure of himself?

Then Humphrey of Gloucester's nasal voice sounded behind him. 'Quite the courtier, eh?' He smiled unpleasantly. 'You're wasting your time with Henry, though. He's immune to high words and flattery.'

'Just as well then, my lord,' Hal returned coldly, 'as I am skilled in neither.'

'No?' Gloucester seated himself on the edge of the table and swung his plump silk-clad legs. 'I would have thought there was some skill in drawing the king's attention to yourself twice in one day.'

'Do you object to it, my lord?'

'Yes.' Gloucester sprung down from the table and stood close to him. 'From a man like you I do.' His heavy face was flushed and sweating. 'I don't like you or that frozen wasteland you come from. Take my advice, Northumberland, and stay there. You're not welcome here.'

Hal raised his eyes and smiled, and the smile brought fresh sweat to Gloucester's lip. 'I am grateful for the warning,' he said softly. 'I shall not heed it, but forewarned is forearmed as they say.' He bowed with elaborate courtesy. 'I bid your Grace a good night.'

He moved on, aware of Gloucester's furious gaze on his back. Once outside he laughed recklessly into the cold night air. How Gloucester would have fumed if he had known about the boy.

He did not come that night, though Hal waited till long past midnight. The rain had ceased and the tent was filled with a hot steamy warmth that kept him awake long after he had given the boy up.

Jack propped himself up on his elbow, roused by his restlessness. 'For God's sake, Hal. It's only a dirty little urchin and French at that. You're acting as if he were kin.' He heaved himself round to face Hal. 'He's probably hightailed it off to Paris to inform Burgundy of our doings. You can't trust 'em. Young or old, they're as crafty as foxes.'

Hal said nothing. He didn't believe that. If the boy had been able to come he would have. There must be a reason. The worst and most obvious sprang unpleasantly into his mind. He was probably dead, if not at the hands of the English, then at those of his own kind. He flung himself irritably on his back. He didn't even know why he cared, perhaps only because the boy had roused old memories. There was no real comparison if Hal was honest. He had been hungry but he had never starved. He'd been alone and without family but never without identity. It was the boy's courage that he admired most, the brave spirit unbroken despite all.

Jack said, 'Well, he's got more sense than you have, anyway. Only a matter of time before he was caught sneaking in and out every night. And you with him. You wouldn't have talked your way out of that one. Had your head off your shoulders soon as look at you, Harry would.'

'I wonder who'd care?' Hal said with rare self pity.

'Well, I bloody well would,' Jack said. 'I'd lose my billet, for a start!'

Hal smothered a wave of laughter. 'Oh, Jack. You're so honest that it hurts.'

'Well.' Jack's voice grew hoarse with emotion. 'You know

better than that. Christ, I'd cut off my right arm for you but I'm blowed if I'll stand by and see you risk your neck over some fool boy. You want to get back to that little wife of yours and breed some of your own, if you ask me.'

'Well, I didn't ask you,' Hal snapped.

'Well, I'm telling you. It's not her fault that she's a Neville, any more than it's that lad's fault he's French.'

'Any more than it's your fault you're a loud-mouthed oaf who doesn't know when to keep it shut.'

'Oh, well. If that's what you want, some bloody toady full of yes, my lord, no, my lord, then you've picked a wrong'un in me. I told you that at the start. Boot lickin' don't come within my order of things, any more than silk breeches do.'

'Nor mine, Jack,' Hal said harshly. 'I married Alianore Neville because I had to. When I go back it'll be because I want to.'

Jack sighed and pillowed his hands behind his head.

'Aye, I suppose you know best, lad.' He turned to look at Hal in the dim light. 'I've no mind to poke my nose in where it's not wanted but I'm afraid for you sometimes. There's a reckless streak in you that turns me cold. I can understand a man taking a few risks for gain, out of spite even. But you seem to do it just for the hell of it, just to see how far your luck will take you.'

'It's an hereditary disease, Jack. Both my father and grand-father suffered from it.'

'Aye, and look how they ended up. I don't want that for you, lad. There's no man I think more highly of than you, not even King Harry himself. You're the only one who ever showed me any kindness or respect and I'd follow you into hell because of it. But don't expect me to sit on my arse and say nothing when I can see you're heading for trouble. Forget the boy, forget everything except what you came for, and that's to get the Border back. Just keep that in your mind. You'll maybe feel easier about the little maid when you're your own master again.'

Hal turned and smiled at him. 'Such a speech, Jack. I didn't know you had the words for it.'

'I've a darn sight too many of 'em sometimes. But I meant every one of those. Take it steady, my lord. Don't lose sight of what's really important. Forget the rest, including that snot-nosed little

French sod. I should have throttled him the first time I laid eyes on him. Saved us all a parcel of trouble if I had.'

Hal turned his face to the wall of the tent. He thought of Alianore the last time he had seen her, with her hair loose and wind blown from the open casement. He remembered that last night with shame. 'Did he kick dogs and pull the feathers from little birds?' And then he'd left her without even the courtesy of a farewell. He closed his eyes. How she must despise him.

He was almost asleep when the small hand touched his cheek.

'My lord?' He stared drowsily at the grubby face poised above his.

'Jean.' He sat up, unable to keep the pleasure from his voice.

'I could not come before. It has taken me hours to get through the camp.'

'Where from?'

'The hill above St Katherine's. In the woods. I found an old hut there. Not much, but it has a roof and it's dry.' He grinned. 'I caught a fish and ate it raw. It didn't taste very nice but it filled me up.'

Hal glanced across at Jack who was stirring restlessly. 'You must not come here again. If they catch you they'll hang you. It's too dangerous for you to cross the lines from the other side.'

He felt rather than saw the disappointment on the boy's face. 'Will I not see you again?' Jean asked quietly.

'Yes.' Hal winced and prayed that Jack would not wake. 'I'll come to you. Is there anything you need?'

'A blanket and a knife, that is all. I can manage very well for the rest.'

'I'll see to it. Now you must go. It'll take you an hour at least to get back.'

The boy nodded. 'When will you come?'

Hal smiled and ruffled the scarecrow hair. 'Tomorrow,' he said. 'I'll come tomorrow.'

He went the next day and every day for a week. The hut in the woods was a miserable affair, a tangle of branches and twine and straw, but it was dry and better than the ditch. The boy seemed happy enough. Hal brought him food and he caught the occasional fish himself, cooking it over a crackling fire that filled the hut with pungent warmth. It was strange the pleasure it gave Hal to see the thin cheeks filling out and blooming with faint colour. There was a faint easing of something in himself too, a debt repaid. He could not help but remember those who had fed and sheltered him, not just because he was Harry Hotspur's son, but because he was a small, frightened, hungry boy.

Jack knew full well where he went each day but his disapproval was silent. He'd said his piece and Jack was never one to harp. He even supplemented the smuggled ration with a piece of salt fish or an extra loaf now and again. It was not that he had anything against the boy, he said. He was just afraid for Hal.

On Christmas Eve it began to snow again. The boy was huddled beneath his blanket by the choking fire but he sprang up eagerly at Hal's approach and ran barefoot to meet him.

Hal hauled him up on the front of his horse. 'I did not think you'd come today,' the boy said breathlessly.

'I shan't be able to tomorrow,' Hal said and lifted him down. 'Or perhaps for a few days while the weather is bad.'

The boy looked solemn but nodded his understanding.

'I brought you an extra blanket.' He glanced down into the boy's expectant face. 'Do you know what day it is tomorrow?'

The boy's eyes grew wider. 'Christmas Day.'

Hal thrust the sack into his arms. 'Your Christmas feast,' he said gently.

The boy tore open the sack. There was half a fowl and a skin of wine, some soft fragrant cheese, a honey comb, a fat loaf of trencher bread and a thick slice of salt pork. But it was the shoes that the boy pounced on avidly. He held them up and laid his cheek against the soft leather. 'I've never had a pair of shoes before.'

'They're a little big, I'm afraid. It was the best I could do. There's a leather jerkin as well.'

'It doesn't matter,' said the boy, still entranced by the shoes. 'I can stuff them with rags.' Then he looked up shyly and fished inside his ragged jerkin. 'I've something for you. It's not much. I made it myself.' He held out the piece of carved wood and Hal took it silently.

'It's not very good. It's a lion,' the boy added. 'Like the one on your shield.'

Hal turned it in the light. It was crudely worked but he'd caught the essential savagery of the beast: the tangled mane; the snarling jaws; the power of the hindquarters.

'Do you like it?' the boy asked.

'Very much. Very much,' Hal said softly. 'I shall keep it always.'

'Perhaps your son might like it.'

Hal smiled into the boy's eyes. 'I have no sons. Not yet. But when I have I shall call him John and give him this.'

The boy seemed pleased. 'I would like that,' he said quietly. 'And when I have a son I shall call him Henry.'

'And give him the shoes? I doubt if he will be as pleased.'

They both laughed and Hal realised he had never heard him laugh before. He reached out and laid his hand on the boy's head. 'I must go now. I'll come again as soon as I can. 'You'll watch your step?' he added. 'Don't go near the camps unless you have to.'

The boy nodded and walked outside with him, still clutching the shoes. 'God keep you, my lord,' he said and smiled.

Hal mounted his horse and turned it to the path. 'And you, Jean. And you.'

The next day he watched the sickening spectacle of Henry's largesse. With great pomp and blaring of trumpets the food was given out. Thick slices of trencher bread ladled with stew. They fell on it like animals, fighting each other for a scrap of bread though there was plenty for all; stuffing it so violently down their throats that their shrunken empty bellies threw it straight back up again.

'Poor sods,' Jack said feelingly. 'Been better to have let them be.

Hal glanced up at the rim of the city wall. Desperate hungry faces had already begun to appear, calling down piteously for food. Some even wept and tore at their clothes. Henry's heralds trailed in the wake of the steaming cauldrons bawling out his terms. Surrender and receive the King of England's mercy. Resist and know all of his wrath.

Swathed in sable, Henry rode the perimeter of the ditch. He reined in his horse a few yards from Hal. His cold eye took in the mountain of dead beneath its pall of freshly fallen snow, rested briefly on the skeleton that crawled from the ditch to vomit its dinner then gobble it up again. Then he looked up to the screaming mob that crowded the walls. He smiled almost cheerfully. 'It promises well, Northumberland,' he said over his shoulder. 'It promises well.'

It took about three weeks for the French to sue for terms. In Henry's chilly quarters at the Charterhouse they sat and faced each other for the first time, the English splendid in furs and jewels, the French in funeral black. And after two days of wrangling, of proposals and counter proposals, of compromise and retreat, little had been resolved. Though the French had conceded almost all but their honour, Henry would concede nothing. He must have all. At the end of the two days the French retreated back behind the walls of Rouen in outrage. Henry looked at the doubtful faces of his council and his red mouth curved in its predatory smile. 'Have no fear, my lords. They'll be back,' he said quietly. 'Before the week's out they'll be back.'

It did not take even a week. The next day the envoys were back, driven out by the fury of their own starving citizens.

Henry was magnanimous in victory. He allowed them the eight days' grace that honour demanded to make a last appeal to Burgundy for relief. He was more than sure of himself. He knew with certainty that Burgundy would not come.

Hal had only managed to see the boy once in all that time, a last hurried visit while Henry was preoccupied with his entry into Rouen. The food had run out weeks before but he had managed to feed himself on roots and fish and once a rabbit that had carried even less flesh than he did. Hal did not stay long, only long enough to give him food and money and instructions to return to Rouen to seek out his uncle the tailor as soon as the English took possession of the town.

The boy stared doubtfully at the gold louis that Hal had pressed into his hand. 'Will I see you again, my lord?'

His voice had trembled on the verge of tears and Hal had looked away from the mute appeal in his eyes. 'Perhaps,' he answered cautiously. 'But even if you do not you must do as I have told you. Give half the money to your uncle if you can find him. It's more than enough to buy you an indenture.'

He smiled and ruffled the boy's hair. 'Wouldn't you like to be a tailor, Jean?' He tugged at the voluminous jerkin that hung like a tent to the boy's knees. 'You could make this fit then.'

Jean smiled and looked down at the long shoes stuffed and tied with rags. 'I think I would rather be a cobbler,' he said gravely.

He walked with Hal to the edge of the wood and for a moment they stood staring down at the English camp seething like ants round the walls of the near-dead city.

'Will King Henry be a good king?' the boy asked seriously.

'No worse than the one you've got,' Hal answered. He smiled down into the grave little face. 'At least he can eat his dinner without spilling it.'

It took a long time to say goodbye and when the moment eventually came the words stuck like a stone in his throat. The boy nodded and blinked rapidly, then suddenly threw his arms round Hal's neck. 'Goodbye, my lord,' he whispered fiercely. 'I shall not forget you, ever.'

Hal disentangled himself from the soft pungent embrace. 'Nor I you, Jean. Nor I you.'

Instinct warned him to leave well alone. He'd done all he could, more than he should. Yet the boy's soft warmth remained with him all through that day. By nightfall he'd talked himself into seeing that at least the boy was with his uncle in Rouen. He'd be on his own after that.

By the eighth day nothing had come from Burgundy save a brief message that no aid for the stricken town might be expected.

King Henry smiled faintly as he took the keys of the town from its captain, de Botelier, and passed them to Exeter. There was nothing in the inflexible lines of his face to betray his triumph and he gave his orders without emotion, announcing his intention to pass the rest of the day in prayer. Only then did a faint note of humour creep into his voice. Rouen had waited for him this seven months. It could wait a day longer.

At dawn the next morning the bells began to ring, a hollow empty sound. Henry rode in to the blare of trumpets, dressed in sombre black – a priest come to bury his dead. And there were enough of those, though the death carts had been at work all through the previous day and night. Corpses still littered the streets and dunghills and despite the food that came in Henry's wake they continued to die faster than the carts could carry them away. Fear of Henry had kept violence to a minimum. There had been retribution, for those who had added insult of Henry himself to resistance: Robert de Livet, the vicar general; Alain Blanchard, who had hanged an English prisoner. The rest of the garrison were granted amnesty – on terms that had them walking from the city stripped of all but their shirts. Looting was a different matter. The untended shops and booths were too much of a temptation for English soldiers kept inactive for nigh on six months. It was done discreetly. There were none to resist. Gold and silver had long ceased to matter to the people of Rouen.

Hal rode alone through the desolate streets and paused to watch the dead being cleared from a house. An old man and a child, a woman who might have been young or old, it was hard to tell. There was nothing left but skin and bone. The corpses were dragged from the doorways and flung with a crack of skeletal bones into the cart after a cursory examination to see if they still bore anything of value. The living were more pitiful. Pot-bellied children scrabbled dementedly in dunghills though there was bread in abundance to be had in the market square. Some were too weak to move and lay where they had fallen. They were piled in the cart with the rest. If they were not dead now, they soon would be.

In the market square a queue for bread stretched as far as the cathedral where Henry had given long and pious thanks before ensconcing himself in Philip Augustus' great fortress. The rows of empty shops looked bleakly on, picked as clean as the bones that littered the streets.

Hal paused before the peeling sign of a tailor's shop. There were seven in the town. This was the last.

In the ransacked upstairs room a man lay beneath the soiled sheet, his hands folded primly on a cross. The woman beside him had not died so well. Her limbs were twisted in the parody of a dance, her eyes were wide and staring. Her mouth was still full of the decaying bread that had choked her.

Hal stared for a long time at the grotesque face, his eyes fixed on the trickle of vomit that had crusted her chin. Then reluctantly he turned his eyes to the small figure huddled by the bed. The mark of the mailed fist that had killed him stood livid upon his cheek, patterned like the scales of a fish. A careless blow, probably for no better reason than that he had been there. The soldier had not even bothered to search him. The gold louis was still clutched firmly in his hand.

Hal cradled the boy in his arms. He had not been dead for long, no longer than a day. A tear glistened diamond-hard on the pale cheek and he brushed it gently away before he realised it was his own. Carefully he picked the body up and carried it outside, setting it astride the horse so that the bruised and broken head rested lightly against his shoulder. Then uncaring of the stares and whispers of his men he rode out through the gates of Rouen. By nightfall the little French boy rested in the soft fragrant earth of St Katherine's.

The whore and the lunatic held their beggars' court at Troyes, Isabeau sweating in purple velvet, King Charles ill at ease in a clean shirt and flinching from the page who wiped the persistent dribble of saliva from his chin. Between them sat the bait, the prize that had lured Henry the length of the Seine – the Princess Katherine, and a dowry of three hundred thousand crowns.

This was the second meeting of its kind. The first, almost a year before at Meulan, had failed, as Jean sans Peur had meant it to. For days they had haggled back and forth, Henry demanding a dowry of eight hundred thousand crowns, Burgundy refusing and offering two hundred thousand crowns, reminding Henry that the dowry of King Richard's queen Isabella had never been returned on his death. Henry harked back even further to thirty thousand crowns that still remained unpaid of the ransom of King John, captured by the English at Poitiers sixty years before. He also demanded the Regency of France whilst King Charles lived; all the conquests of his great-grandfather Edward the Third and the territories of the still unfulfilled Treaty of Bretigny; and on the death of King Charles, all of France to be held in his own right. He had pushed the already uneasy Burgundy too far and the talks had ground to an abrupt and hostile end. But Rouen had opened up all of the Seine to Henry. Within a month he'd taken Pontoise by storm. Gisorse, Meulan, St Germain and Chateau Gaillard had fallen like ripe plums into his lap. By summer he was close enough to the walls of Paris for Queen Isabeau to sue again for peace.

The meeting this time was one of caution and constraint. Though outwardly Henry had the upper hand, his reserves were almost as low as those of the French. And for her part Isabeau could not afford to let Henry walk away again. At heart they both knew there was nothing for it but peace, and the young girl who sat mute and still between them was its instrument. If Henry was pleased by what he saw he did not show it, though he stared for a long time at the tall thin girl who might have been beautiful save for the long Valois nose and the slightly vacuous look that reminded him uncomfortably of her father. But like her father she was only a puppet here. It was Isabeau who dominated, Isabeau and the new Duke of Burgundy, so much more Henry's man since the brutal murder of his father by the Armagnacs. That had been near disaster for Henry. The late duke's spleen at the loss of Rouen and at Henry's outrageous demands at Meulan had driven him uncomfortably close to an alliance with the Dauphin Charles. They had met at Montereau, ostensibly to join forces against the English invader. Instead they had split France as surely as the Dauphin's henchman, de Chatel, had split Burgundy's skull. Now his young son Philip burned for vengeance with a passion that bordered on insanity. He was a quiet dark young man, astute enough to know that Henry of England was the only man who could give him what he sought.

Hal's eyes dwelt thoughtfully on King Henry's face. Startling in his plainness against the jewelled brilliance of Isabeau, Henry played the courtier. His red mouth curved obediently in answer to Isabeau's nervous heartiness, then turned down again in pity at the mumblings of King Charles. It tightened in outward sympathy at Burgundy's grief, though none was more jubilant than Henry that the crafty old fox, his father, was dead. Occasionally he would glance at Katherine sitting taut as a coiled spring beside her mother. Only then did the smile reach his eyes. But if he found his future bride pleasing he did not allow it to distract him from the terms of the treaty.

All was as he demanded. Two days later in the draughty unfinished cathedral of Saint Pierre he was formally named as the heir to Charles the Sixth of France. For a moment his cold eyes rested on the feeble old man who nodded and mumbled his vague assent. Then he turned and smiled into the dark frightened eyes of his betrothed.

They were married a week later in the church of St Jean and for a day and a night the horror of war was forgotten. But if any had hoped for respite they were to be disappointed. The next day Henry was on the move again. By nightfall they were camped in pouring rain outside the walls of Sens.

Sens fell within the month and they moved up river to Montereau where Duke Philip exacted bloody revenge for the death of Jean sans Peur. Then south again, on to Melun where the hard core of Armagnac resistance sat smug and unassailable behind high walls.

Hal surveyed the island fortress gloomily, his heart sinking at the prospect of another long and weary siege. Yet there was no other way: the town straddled the river, linked to walled suburbs on either bank by fortified bridges. Everywhere the English were met by water and stone yet Henry was unperturbed. He would be master of the town by Christmas he assured them. And knowing Henry as they did, they believed him.

The king was sick. It showed in the dark pain-filled eyes and the high burning colour that could fade in minutes to a pale unhealthy grey. Hal, seeing him at close quarters for the first time in weeks, felt the shock of the wasted limbs and hollowed cheeks. He thought desperately, dear God, he's eaten up with it.

Henry's long capable hands moved restlessly among his papers and clenched in sudden agony as a spasm of pain ran through him. His glance warded Hal off. 'It's nothing,' he said and his anguished mouth assayed a smile. 'A slight fever. Nothing more.'

Hal accepted the lie without comment. He knew dysentery when he saw it. He woke to the stench of it every morning and he'd seen the pitiful wrecks of men that were buried in the limepits at night. He felt a tremor almost of fear. One had always thought of Henry as invincible.

The king looked away from the knowing glance and re-arranged his papers and charts for the third time. The quick precise movement helped to take his mind from the burning core of pain in his belly. It would pass. It always did. The pain was bearable; the knowledge that he was vulnerable was not. He felt a sudden wave of despair. It was Harfleur all over again: the heat, the flies, the rotten tainted food, the stench of blood and ordure that overlay even the acrid stink of the guns. He listened to the dull distant pounding of his cannon. A useless empty noise. As well to set a rat to gnaw his way through the walls, for as fast as he breached them, the French filled them up. For every mine he sunk the French blocked it with one of their own till the land was a maze of burrows and trenches that led nowhere. They were well provisioned too, more so than they had been at Rouen. They also had more men, a great deal more than he had bargained for. He glanced up at Hal. 'You know there are Scots in the town? Douglas' men? Five thousand or more, by my reckoning.'

Hal nodded. It was common knowledge. The Douglas was not one to let his presence go unheeded.

Henry sucked at his full underlip for a while. Then he said, 'What kind of man is James of Scotland?'

Hal looked mildly surprised. 'I would have thought you knew that better than I, Sire. I have not seen him since he was a boy.'

The king smiled bleakly. 'Men do not change in spirit. The boy becomes a man but at the heart of him the boy remains constant.' His eyes sparked suddenly with their old malignant fire. 'Can he be won? Bribed? Bought? Threatened?'

'Not as I remember him,' Hal answered.

'Every man has his price. Even I.' The king smiled grimly. 'Find out what James of Scotland's price is for me. Bring him here.'

'Here?'

'Yes. Here. Let us see what scruples Douglas has about making war on his own king.'

'I can tell you that, Sire,' said Hal flatly. 'None at all. I know the Douglas better than I know King James. He'd not care if James never saw the light of day again. He's Albany's man.'

'But the others?' Henry queried. 'The common men. Might they not feel it?'

'They might.' Hal smiled. 'Free or not, a king is still a king.'

Henry smiled wryly. 'I am glad you think so.' He paused, nodding thoughtfully to himself. 'Yes. Go and fetch him here. Let us see what James of Scotland is made of.'

Outside in the blazing heat of the July day Hal paused and looked across at the needle spires of Melun glittering beneath the rabid eye of the sun. Beside the dark-quilled Porcupine of the Armagnacs, the Bleeding Heart of Douglas flew. He smiled, remembering the barbarous old man. He thought of Jamie. Was it fourteen years since they had met? All of that. The wheel had come full circle. He was free. It was Jamie who was the prisoner now.

He passed swiftly by the crowded tent where the groans of dying men turned his stomach. He averted his head from the dreadful stench, the smell of hideous painful death, the smell that King Henry carried with him.

The man standing by the window did not turn his head even after Hal had closed the door loudly behind him.

'Your Grace.' He had no need of sight of his face. He would have known the set of those shoulders and that shock of russet hair anywhere.

James Stewart, King of Scots and England's prisoner for the last fourteen years swung slowly round. The light brows drew sharply together over the shrewd blue eyes. 'Hal. Hal Percy? It is. By God, it is.'

Hal raised his brows at the warmth of his welcome. 'I've never known you so pleased to see me before, James,' he commented dryly.

'I'm pleased to see anyone these days,' James said fervently and flung himself into the least comfortable of the two chairs the room possessed. He motioned Hal to the other but for a moment Hal remained standing. He lifted a sheet of parchment from the table and narrowed his eyes to read the untidy scribbled verse.

> *The bird, the beste, the fisch eke in the see*
> *They lyre in fredome everich in his kynd . .*
> *And I a man, and lakith libertee.*

'I did not know you were a poet, James.'

James flushed. 'I'm not,' he said. 'It just passes the time.'

Hal came and sat beside him without comment. He knew only too well the feeling behind the poem's poignant words.

Then James said, 'I'd heard you were free. Exchanged for Albany's brat. No doubt my dear uncle made a profit on the deal?'

'Would you doubt it? When did he ever do ought for nothing?'

James nodded. 'Still as mean as ever, then?'

'Meaner.'

'Mean enough to let me rot in here for ever?'

Hal met the shrewd blue eyes squarely. 'He's an old man, Jamie. He'll not last forever. There'll be changes then.'

James pulled a face. 'You think his son will be any the more generous? I'm not a fool, Hal. I know well enough that while I'm stuck in here they've got the field to themselves. Why would they want me back? And have to pay for the privilege into the bargain?'

'Neither Albany nor his son are Scotland, James. And Murdac will never hold the regency as his father has. When Albany's dead they'll fetch you home, James.'

'And who are they?'

'Those who'd prefer even you to Murdac. He's not well liked. He's weak and stupid. A pig and a drunkard. He'd have Scotland penniless within a year.'

James stared down at his short square hands then brought them up to cover his face. 'God. I wish I could believe that,' he said wearily. 'Fourteen years is a long time. You don't know what it is like.'

'Do I not, James?' Hal said softly.

James lifted his head. 'Of course. I'd forgotten.' Then he said sharply, 'That's not why you're saying all this? Out of pity?'

'I'd not be that cruel, Jamie. False hope is no hope at all. I know that well enough. But truly, my lord, you've not been forgotten. There are many who'd bring you home tomorrow if it were not for Albany. Bishop Thomas never ceases to work in your interest.'

James's face softened. 'How is he?' he asked.

'Old and frail and refusing to die till he's set the crown on your head at Scone. You remember that ramshackle old hut where we had our schooling?'

'Do I not.'

'You'd not believe the thing that's risen in its place. All turrets and pinnacles of shining grey stone with windows like flown arrows and a roof that you could lose Scone Palace in.'

James smiled. 'Aye. It was his dream wasn't it? The first university in Scotland.'

'And you remember how impossible that dream seemed when he was hard put to raise the price of a loaf?'

'And my dream is no more impossible. Is that what you're saying?'

'If he can raise the price of a university he can raise it to buy you home. But that's all he can do. The rest is up to you, James.' He paused and weighed his promise to Bishop Thomas against the slight disloyalty to Henry. The old man won and he said, 'Those aren't my words, James. I was asked to tell, to beg, you to bend a little. Scotland needs a king, a real king, not one wasting out his days in an English prison. Whatever Henry wants, give it to him, saving your honour.'

'Ah. Now there's the flaw, Hal. Saving my honour. And what honour is there for a king who swears away his kingdom?'

'Henry's not asked you for that.'

'As good as,' James answered sullenly. 'Overlordship. What does that mean? Overlordship, and what more? Give him an inch and he'll take a yard. Then when he's won France it'll be Scotland's turn.'

'Are you afraid of him, then? Are you afraid you couldn't win if it came to it?'

'No. I'm not,' James said, his fair face flushing with anger. 'But I'll not furnish him with a paper claim to my kingdom. It's all mine or nothing.'

'Then let it be nothing,' Hal said, remembering that Albany had said almost the same words to him once. 'While you're Henry's prisoner you're king of nought but these four walls. As you say, when he's done with France, Scotland will be waiting for him, with none to keep him out because the Regent is an incompetent drunkard and her king is cossetting his honour four hundred miles away.'

'A man is nothing without honour,' James said pompously.

'Damn your bloody stupid honour, James. What about the poor wretches who are supposed to be your subjects, left to fend for themselves against the likes of Douglas and Fife? There's none to make laws, let alone see they're kept. For God's sake, James, why do you think you've been kept under lock and key for all this time? Because Albany and Douglas have been too busy feathering their own nests to spare a thought for you. And you're more use to Henry where he can keep an eye on you. God knows he's needed the money often enough. Even now your ransom could make all the difference between a battle won and lost. While he can find a pretext to keep you here he will, because without you Scotland is vulnerable, his for the taking. Will you let him take it, James, without even a fight?' His voice had grown soft and hypnotic and the angry colour had left the Scots king's young face. 'Is this all being a king means to you, James? An empty meaningless title, for that's all it is? A king without a king-dom is as useless as a cannon without shot. Kingship is craft and guile and winning. You must want to win, James, or you cannot begin to fight. Will your honour be comfort enough when you are dispossessed and Henry is king of Scotland, as soon he will be king of France? Will honour suffice then James?'

James looked up. 'Did King Henry send you?' he asked dully. 'To talk me round?'

'No. He did not. Not for this, anyway. If I speak for anyone, it's Bishop Thomas. He did not think you could be aware of Scot-land's need, to have left her to fend for herself for so long.' Then, seeing the misery on the other man's face his voice softened. It was easy enough now to judge, but he'd had his own doubts once, his own agony of indecision. He would let it lie for now. He added gently, 'Think on it, James. Just think on it. That's all I ask.'

James nodded. 'What did he send you for, then? Henry, I mean.'

'To take you to France.' He smiled at the look on James's face. 'You're to have a holiday, James. A taste of freedom.' (Like the poor wretches in the ditch of Rouen had tasted food.) Hal made no mention of Douglas or the Scots at Melun. He was learning from Henry. One step at a time was enough.

James turned his back on him and stared silently from the window. It was a habit that Hal knew well. The reaching out towards the forbidden air, the imperceptible stretching of the whole body towards the elusive distance, like a young hawk poised for flight. It was the nearest a captive ever got to freedom.

King Henry was smiling, the wide predatory smile of a wolf about to devour his prey. He beckoned his brother Clarence forward with wine and motioned to James to sit beside him. To Hal he gave a brief questioning glance before he spoke. Hal nodded imperceptibly. Jamie was ready for the pot.

Henry's smile broadened and he said softly, 'Welcome, cousin. We are glad that you could come.'

James raised a flushed uncertain face to Henry's. 'Did I have a choice, Sire?'

'Oh yes,' Henry said innocently. 'All men have a choice. To comply or defy. To advance or retreat. You chose to advance, James.' He patted the Scottish king's broad shoulder. 'A wise choice. A warrior's choice. One I have always chosen myself where possible.'

Clarence, standing beside Hal, raised an eyebrow and whispered, 'Christ. He's overdoing it a bit, isn't he?'

Hal glanced at James's face and saw the struggle between inbred distrust of the English and the desperate hope that things at last might be different. Hope as always won. James would believe what he wanted to believe.

Henry touched the goblet of wine to his full lips but he did not drink. 'We thought to broaden your learning, James. I doubt if there is more you can learn in the tiltyard.' He smiled blandly.

'We thought to give you a taste of the real thing. We could not send you back to Scotland untried, could we?' The promise hung soft and quivering in the air. For one dreadful moment Hal thought that James was going to pursue it and ask Henry bluntly, '*When?*' But James had his own share of guile. He smiled, though the smile lacked confidence. He had waited this long. What was a week or two more? He had not even heard the price yet.

Henry did not keep him waiting long. The next day he escorted James round his prime and orderly encampment. Across the river, Burgundy's disorderly camp sprawled in squalid and comfortable contrast. There was wine to be had there and women too if you had food or money. That some of his men had at some time or other sneaked across for both, Henry did not know. He would have hung those involved if he had.

Hal saw James grow pale at the stench that seemed to grow worse each day though there had been fewer deaths since the chill autumn weather had lessened the spread of the disease. They still used a full bushel of lime each day to dispose of the dead, but it had not increased. The king regarded this as a hopeful sign that the sickness was on the wane. But not for him. Hal glanced at the king's set face as he led the way through the labyrinth of open trenches. By almost continuous fasting he'd kept the worst at bay but it was still there, the pain burning like hot coals in his bowels. The physic that he poured down his throat daily did little but make him vomit. It was a miracle that he was still on his feet. Yet to the men who cheered and saluted him as he passed he showed no sign of weakness. He smiled and raised his hand to them, a soldier's greeting, and permitted a degree of familiarity that he would never have brooked from the greatest of his lords. The bonds still held, despite his growing harshness, despite hunger and cold and sickness. They would still have followed him into hell.

The king paused and waited for James to come alongside. He flung out his long arm toward the scarred but still intact walls of Meulan. 'Behold the object of our desire.' He spoke softly as if he spoke of a woman. Then suddenly his voice and eyes hardened. 'And full of your countrymen also,' he snapped. 'Defying us, insulting us.'

James blinked at the abrupt change in Henry's manner. Then as suddenly Henry was smiling again. 'What manner of subjects are these that fight against their own sovereign lord?'

'I doubt if they are aware of my presence, Sire,' James said defensively, and too late saw the trap Henry had so cleverly laid.

'Then tell them, James,' Henry said quietly. 'Tell them that the king of Scots is come and that further resistance will be treason.'

James's face had flushed an angry red. 'Is that why you brought me here?' he shouted. 'To trick my countrymen into betraying their loyalty?'

'Betrayal? Loyalty?' Henry's mouth drew into a thin red line. 'Do we credit such feelings to men who are no better than paid mercenaries, who sell their loyalty to any that's able to fill their bellies with wine twice daily?'

'Their loyalty is to Scotland,' James flung back. 'They'll fight with any who fight the English.'

Henry smiled thinly. 'Is that so, James? Is that so? I've not seen them so eager to fight the English without the skirts of the Dauphin to hide behind. Perhaps they feel that the disgrace of further defeat will be lessened if it is shared.'

'If you are so sure of victory, why do you need me?'

'I do not need you, my lord,' Henry said coldly. 'You could be useful, as my horse or my sword is useful, but never necessary. Melun will fall, this month, next month, but it will surely fall sooner or later, as did Sens and Caen and Rouen. If it is sooner, it will save time and money and lives, perhaps even the lives of your precious Scotsmen.' His voice dropped an octave to a reasoning note. 'All I ask is that you declare yourself and give your men the opportunity to fight with you or against you, or even to remain neutral if they choose.'

'They would not take it as binding, even if I did as you asked. They know I am a prisoner, speaking under duress.'

'Duress?' Henry interrupted him sharply. 'With what have I threatened you except your freedom?' He smiled maliciously. 'Is that what you are afraid of, my lord? Have you grown too comfortable in captivity, like your grandfather the Bruce?'

James' head jerked up at the magic word. *Freedom*. The promise was there, implicit in the cold eyes and beneath it the threat. Yet James was too young and raw to know the difference between the two. He merely felt confused and completely and utterly out of his depth. There were tears of rage and frustration in his eyes as he turned and walked away from them.

Henry pursed his lips and stared after the broad retreating back. 'As you said, Northumberland, a virgin from the cloister.' He turned and looked directly at Hal. 'But his eye burns with a reformer's zeal. There's fire in him somewhere.' He smiled thinly. 'We must douse it before we set him free.'

Hal walked with the king as far as the group of courtiers and clerks who waited anxiously behind the gun lines. The wind was coming up, cold and from the north. He thought of Alnwick and the cold clean sea off Bamburgh. He would not be sorry to get home.

He glanced up at the silent walls of Melun. How much longer? In a month it would be Christmas. Could the French hold out that long? They'd been without fresh food for nearly three weeks now. He smiled grimly at the irony of it: the French dying from lack of food; the English from too much.

He paused by the tent that housed the wounded and dying. Behind it the lime pit bubbled and churned and gave off its filthy stench. He hurried on. He was not afraid of death but he was afraid of that; of dying in his own blood and filth with only the lime pit to cleanse him.

In his tent an elderly man fretted and fidgeted under Jack's malevolent glare. He rose at Hal's appearance and gave Jack a freezing backward glance. 'My lord.' He twitched back his cloak so that the Neville bull on his livery could be seen. 'I bring a message from Sir John Neville. He begs that you spare him a few moments within the hour.'

Hal stripped off his embroidered gloves and tossed them on the bed. 'Where is he?'

The steward's face twitched. 'In his tent, my lord. I fear he is dying.'

Hal paused, the cup of warmed wine that Jack had thrust at him half way to his lips. 'Of what?' he asked.

135

The steward licked his lips. 'Of the bowel rot, my lord. He's been sick these last two weeks.'

Hal followed him wordlessly from the tent. Neville was dying. Should he have been pleased? One less, one less of the hated breed that had soured all of his life. Yet he felt no pleasure, only a strange regret that of all of them it had to be John.

He stooped his head beneath the flap of the tent and paused. There was no light, only the dusty filtered daylight through the heavy canvas. But even that was enough to illumine the dreadful wreck of a man who lay quite still on the low bed. John Neville turned his head slowly; the dark fevered eyes burned like hot coals in his skull. His thin emaciated limbs hardly caused a ripple in the thick fur covering. He winced with pain as he heaved himself up onto the bolster. 'You've come, then.' He smiled faintly. 'I did not think that you would.'

Hal swallowed on the nausea that rose in his throat at the stench coming from the curtained privy.

Neville saw his look. 'Forgive me for subjecting you to this. But I had to see you.'

'Why?'

'Well, we're kin, aren't we? Or have you forgotten that you're wed to my half-sister Alianore?'

'No, I have not forgotten,' Hal answered quietly.

'She thinks you have. She says she has not seen hide nor hair of you since you left Raby.'

'You've seen her?' It came out more eagerly than he had meant.

'Before I left England. She was at Leconfield trying to stop it falling round her ears.'

'She does not have to remain there,' Hal said stiffly. 'There are plenty of other manors she could live in.'

'But not with you, eh?'

'I did not say that,' Hal snapped. 'Is this all you asked me here for, a lecture on my mistreatment of my wife?'

'No. As long as you remember that she is your wife and that it's not her fault she's a Neville, any more than it's yours you're a Percy. Oh, there's room for hatred on both sides. You know. I was bred on it too.'

Hal said heavily. 'What *did* you ask me here for?'

John Neville smiled wanly. 'Yes, I'm sorry. I'm wandering. I just wanted you to see how futile it was. So many things look rather pointless when you're dying, but especially this. I should hate you but I don't. Being a Percy just doesn't seem a good enough reason. A man must be judged by what he is, not his blood, and I've enough of yours and you've enough of mine for me to be confused.' He opened his eyes. 'But Beaufort blood. That's another thing. And that's why I asked you here.' He struggled up onto his elbow. 'When I die, Westmorland goes to my son Ralph – but not if that old harridan Joan has anything to do with it. She wants the earldom for her own son, Richard.'

'I'm sure your father will not see your son cheated,' said Hal.

'Father is an old man. If he dies before Ralph comes of age, then he'll never see Westmorland. There'll only be his mother left to fight for him, and Elizabeth's no match for that greedy pack.' His thin fingers reached out and clasped Hal's wrist. 'If you want to start a feud with the Nevilles, then this is your chance. The Countess Joan and her lovesome sons are more worthwhile prey than my Ralph.' His eyes grew desperate. 'Protect my son. If it comes to it, take his part against Richard. I saw you and Richard that Christmas at Raby. His hatred for you is no less than it is for me, albeit we are brothers. I had thought to see to it myself: that Ralph would be a man before it came to it, that I would be Westmorland before him.' He smiled weakly. 'It's not much to ask. Spare the runt of the litter and slaughter the sow and all her fat piglets.'

'And Alianore,' Hal said gravely. 'She's a Neville as well.'

'No. Not anymore. Alianore's a Percy now if you'll let her be.' Neville was quiet for a while. Then he said, 'Will you do it? Out of hatred for the Nevilles, if nothing else? So that I might die easy.'

Hal stared down at his hands and Richard Neville's arrogant face swam before him, so close, as close as it had been that night at Raby when his hands had reached for Hal's throat. 'Yes. I'll do it,' he said quietly.

John Neville died two days later among the filth and squalor of his own body. King Henry received the news grimly and for a moment something like fear showed in the dark melancholy eyes.

It was too close. Henry was far removed from the hundreds who were buried in the lime pit at night but John Neville was kin, close kin. It was a reminder that death was no respecter of rank or privilege.

Henry busied himself among his papers for a moment, then said, 'Well, it's an ill wind, Northumberland, as they say.' He raised his gimlet eyes to Hal. 'John Neville is dead, or more to the point, the Warden of the West March is dead. Well, it's what you wanted, is it not? What you came for? You know I could not have dispossessed Neville without loss of conscience. Now I shall not have to. The Lord is bountiful to some, is he not? He giveth and He taketh away.'

Hal cleared his throat uncomfortably but the king did not even seem to be aware of him. Henry stared broodingly at the faltering candle. It was so quiet. The quiet of death? He closed his eyes. He would not think of it. The thought would destroy him more surely than the obscene disease within him. He must think of Katherine waiting for him at Corbeil. He half smiled, remembering her virgin caresses. He had forgotten there was such delight, such warmth. Then he thought of his own body, his skin veined and blotched with privation, the starved and shrivelled flesh shrouding his skeletal bones. Even Katherine had cried out in pity at the thinness of him. And he had wept. He had not thought that love could be so painful. His full mouth twisted wryly. Pain. He should be immune to that by now. It was kept well to heel like a vicious beast that once unleashed would tear him limb from limb. None knew, save his physician, of the secret hours of agony when he could hardly rise from the privy for weakness, or of the sickening potions he swallowed in sheer desperation – tincture of emerald to stop the flux, mandragora for easement. But there was no easement. The pain never left him. It was always there, grinding his bowels to a bloody pulp, reducing him to less than a man, let alone a king.

He glanced up at Hal, waiting with blank courtesy, and was suddenly resentful of his strength, his vibrant health. There was no justice, he thought. Why not him instead of me? The Lord giveth and the Lord taketh away. But why always from him? All that he had ever loved: his mother; Richard; poor Scrope; his beloved Hotspur. What crueller punishment than to give a man all then snatch it away the minute his hand closed around it? *Punishment*. The word echoed in his aching head. For Richard, for Hotspur, for all the poor starving souls at Rouen? *No*. He almost cried the word aloud. He was absolved. Had not Agincourt and all the catalogue of victories since proved that? He was so close, so tantalisingly close. Only a feeble crackbrained old man stood between him and the reality. He began to laugh softly to himself. He could see the irony: for Mad Charlie to outlive him, for it all to come to nothing. It would be the supreme punishment, for all to be taken from him and he be left poorer than ever before. *Usurper*. The word cut through him sharper than the pain that suddenly flamed in his belly. *Usurper. Murderer. Violater*. He screamed, a high womanly sound that brought Hal swiftly to his side.

'It's nothing. All's well.' The king was breathing deeply like a woman in childbirth and the pupils of his eyes had shrunk to dark needles of pain. He pushed away the hand that rested in concern upon his sleeve, then as quickly gripped it again. 'It's not true, is it Northumberland? That the sins of the fathers are visited upon the sons? I've proved that wrong. You've all that your father ever had and more. All paid. The debts are all paid.'

'Gently, my lord.' Hal pulled the furred cloak a little closer around Henry's trembling shoulders.

'I cared for your father very much, you know,' the king said. 'Such a waste. All that fire and brilliance gone for nothing. And it needn't have been.' He looked up, his eyes brilliant with fever. 'It needn't have been, you know. Even to the last my father would have made peace. He wanted peace. In his own way he loved your father too. But not Hotspur, not Hotspur.' He laughed shrilly. 'Christ. If ever a man deserved that name he did. He wouldn't listen. He couldn't wait, not for Glyn Dwr or Northumberland. He could have won if he had waited.' He smiled faintly as the pain subsided. 'But then I would never have been king.' He stared down at his clenched hands. The spasm had passed and he uncurled his long fingers slowly, watching his white knuckles fill with blood. 'You'd rather have had it so, would you not, Hal? You're close kin to Mortimer.'

'I'm close kin to you, sire.' Hal answered softly. 'I am content.'

'Are you Hal?' Henry looked up eagerly in his face. 'Are you really content? You called me usurper once.'

'But only once. I did not know you then.'

'And you do now? What do you call me now?'

'The king – as you are, my lord.'

'The king. No usurper?'

'No usurper.'

Henry smiled as the tension eased from his body. Even the pain was dulled. *Henry the king.* He repeated it over and over to himself. It was a better salve than all the physic he could swallow.

Hal said softly, 'Shall I send for your physician, sire?'

'No. I have no need of leeches tonight. You have been physician enough.' Henry rose stiffly and leant with his hands on the table. He looked up into Hal's knowing eyes. 'I'll not let it beat me,' he said quietly. 'I'll conquer it as I conquered the French.'

'I don't doubt it, my lord,' Hal said. If any man could it was Henry.

Melun fell a week later, a grisly repetition of Rouen though the sense of victory was dulled by the enormity of their own dead. Then Henry moved on to Paris, a fifty-mile march through a starved and desolate land where nothing lived and nothing grew. There was death everywhere, in the burnt and barren fields, in the empty villages, and most virulent of all, in the harsh lines in the King of England's face.

Leconfield

He was coming home. After three long years he was coming home. Alianore laid aside the brief formal letter. He had not even cared to write it himself, only the long sprawling signature. The one word. *Northumberland.* All there was of him.

She looked up into her father's stern face. 'When?'

Ralph Neville flexed his long fingers to the fire's dying warmth. 'A month, perhaps less. The king plans to sail within the week, weather permitting. I doubt if Northumberland will tarry in London. He's heartily sick of the war from what I hear.' His long face grew bleaker. Were not they all? Such waste, such loss of money and life. He'd not yet recovered from the news of his son John's death. Such an undignified, almost dishonourable death. He would much rather his skull had been split by a Frenchman.

'And I doubt if he'll stay here long either.' His tender thoughts were broken by his daughter's voice. 'Why should he alter his habits now?'

'He'll be changed,' Neville said absently. 'Three years is a long time. Every man has his needs, even Northumberland.'

'So he'll resort to me in desperation,' Alianore snapped. 'Well, I have my needs too. I need to be left alone.'

Neville stared at her uneasily. He had little knowledge of women, even less of his own daughters. His wife Joan was the only woman he had ever understood. She was hard and ruthless and totally unscrupulous – almost a mirror image of himself as he had been once. He thought of the way Joan's hot little eyes had lit up when she had heard of John's death. Bitch. But then he'd never deceived himself that she'd ever felt anything but pure hatred for his children by Margaret Stafford. John in particular had suffered, for John would have had Westmorland and Joan had wanted that for her precious Richard. It had not worried him unduly then. John had been a man and well able to fend for himself. But a boy of twelve? He knew how easily the rights of a boy of twelve could be set aside. He straightened the long back that had begun to curve only of late. He was good for another ten years yet. Ralph would be a man by then.

He turned to look again at his daughter. She was almost as tall as he was and looked as thin in that plain fustian gown. Her lustrous hair was bundled carelessly in a tarnished caul. He noticed too that her shoes were frayed and spotted with wax. There was no lack of money, though. A glance round the long spacious hall told him that. Arras silk graced every wall and the carved oak trestles gleamed with plate. To give Northumberland his due, he'd not stinted her – except with his presence. His mouth pursed in disapproval. Alianore had grown even wilder this last year. Not that he blamed her, living at Leconfield like a cloistered nun with none to keep her in check save a dozen old knights and dames who were too fond of a soft billet to disturb the pattern of things. Neither did he blame her for leaving Raby.

She had peace and quiet at Leconfield, if nothing else. It was half the reason he came as often as he did himself.

'Alianore,' he said awkwardly. 'Are you so unhappy?'

She gave him a hard cynical look that was all her mother. 'Do you care?'

'I wouldn't have asked if I didn't.'

'Then if you cared you should not have wed me to Northumberland.'

'Why not?' he said defensively. 'You didn't speak against it. You didn't even care yourself then. Who was to know he would treat you so badly?'

'You knew,' Alianore shouted. 'You knew how bitter he was, how much he hated us. You made me the whipping boy for all of you so that you could keep your hold on the Border.'

Her father turned away from her. It was true, though even he had not known how deep Northumberland's bitterness had gone. He said stiffly, 'I did not think he would be so cowardly as to take his revenge on a woman.'

Alianore laughed mirthlessly. 'You see? You still deceive yourself. I am only the smallest part of it. He means to have us all down, you know. Down to the very last one of us.'

Neville said nothing. He could believe that. Hatred and vengeance were emotions not unknown to him either, but they'd always taken second place to ambition. It was Northumberland's singleness of purpose that was so unnerving. He got that from the old man, Neville thought grimly. He'd sacrificed all he had to gratify his honour.

Then Alianore said, 'Whatever did you do to him that made him hate us so much?'

Her father eyed her bleakly. It was all so long ago. He'd forgotten so much. So much was best forgotten. 'It's a long story,' he said wearily. 'A long story with a dozen facets depending how the light falls. There's no right or wrong to it now and that's the great pity of it. We were both right, we were both wrong. But as Northumberland sees it,' he looked away and stared hard into the flames of the fire, 'as Northumberland sees it, we took all that he loved and broke it for no better reason than to see it smashed and dishonoured at our feet.'

'And is it true?'

'Some. As I said, there's no right or wrong to it now. It's a long time ago.'

'A long time to you, Father. But not to me. I have suffered for it daily these past four years.'

'I know.' He came and laid his arm around her. 'And you've borne up bravely.' He lifted her face towards him, suddenly eager to see her smile. 'Perhaps it will be different now. He was too close to his captivity last time. He's had three years to purge himself of it. It'll come right this time, you'll see.'

She smiled and took the sop obediently, raising her face for his kiss. Whatever the right or wrong of it she loved him. He was her father. There was no help for that.

When he had gone she rose and slowly crossed the long vaulted room. The four white hounds who'd slumbered by the hearth raised their great heads and watched her, then fell back yawning as she stood motionless by the open window. There was nothing to see. The great house closed her in on all sides, fencing the sweep of sallow grass and the sapling trees that struggled up in the sunless court. Ivy still clung tenaciously to the south side, choking the shuttered windows and the graceful merlons of the roof, the last to be stripped to reveal the soft York stone and gleaming lattices. She turned back abruptly to the room. Once there had been little else here but mould and dust. Now new mortar patched the weeping cracks. The sunken floor was planked with oak and the choked and crumbling hearths gave out a welcoming heat. All her doing, her achievement – till now. She sat down abruptly. He was coming home.

She sighed aloud and the largest of the dogs padded toward her and thrust his fearsome head beneath her hand. She stroked his ears absently. *He was coming home.* She should have felt nothing. She'd been without him so long that the memory of that last night and the long silence ever since had ceased to hurt. She had grown used to the solitude, even revelled in it now. She'd thought she had need of none, least of all him.

She began to pace angrily, the dog following till she told it curtly to lie down. A month, perhaps less, and then what? Her freedom curtailed and a horde of soldiers and hangers-on to fetch and carry for. And at night, the humiliation of sleeping alone and every scullion in the manor knowing of it. No, not that. Not ever that. She'd take herself off to Raby before she'd suffer that again. Then the thought came that perhaps he would not even stay. And if he left she might be forced to accompany him. *Leave Leconfield?* Spend her days trailing from dreary manor to dreary manor at her lord's pleasure? She kicked out viciously at a small carved stool and scattered the dogs. They retreated, growling softly, and stared at her with hurt amber eyes. For once she did not see them. She felt sick with rage and despair. If she thought she'd suffered by his absence, how much more could she be hurt when he was here?

She ran, blinded by tears of frustration. She didn't want him back. She didn't ever want to set eyes on him again.

In her chamber a plump woman swathed in shawls unravelled a bolt of emerald cloth. 'It's stained,' she announced without turning her head. 'And a flaw in it the size of an egg.'

Alianore dragged the caul from her head and shook her hair loose. 'Send it back. There'll be no money to pay for it anyway,' she said grimly. 'Not with my lord coming back.'

The woman turned round blue eyes on her. 'Coming back? When?'

Alianore pulled an old cloak round her and headed for the door. 'Too soon, Bess,' she muttered in anguish. 'Much too soon.'

She rode as if the Devil were after her and in her mind he was. She pushed the horse to its limit, the dogs pounding noisily in her wake. Mud spattered her clothes, thorns tore at her face and tangled in her flying hair but she did not loose the reins till she reached the open swathe of Southwood. She leant panting against the horse's steaming neck. The anger had drained out of her and had been replaced by something harder, less transient. She looked down toward the manor ringed with trees and the silver loop of the moat. It looked small and insignificant now in the wide sweep of the deer park that ran as far as Stork Dyke and the river. Beyond lay Arram and the few damp fields they had rescued from the marsh that spread insidiously inland from the banks of the Hull. Hagg Dyke drained the fields to the north, a black crooked scar scored through the soft green fields. Ugly but necessary: before the dyke there had been only water. Alianore dragged her hair back from her face and smiled ruefully. How strange to feel love for such an unlovely place; unlovely perhaps compared with Raby but it had a beauty of its own in the summer when all was soft and luminous green and a silver mist hid the marsh and spread across the valley in a rainbow haze. It was beautiful then beyond Raby, beyond Alnwick even, simply because it was hers.

'And I'll not give it up.' She spoke aloud and the dogs ceased their scuffling in the undergrowth and stared at her inquisitively.

No, she'd not give it up, not without a fight anyway. Richard would help her and be more than glad to side with her against Hal. If anything her brother resented her husband's treatment of her more than she did. She smiled affectionately and glanced towards the great white hounds that had been his gift – to be with you when I cannot, he had said, and that was nearly always now. He still came, but less often this past year. The Border took all of his time and when it didn't he danced attendance on his new Montague wife. She thought none the less of him for it. He came when he could. It was enough.

She sat a while longer till her horse had caught its wind, then started back along the narrow road. The mill stood idle in its field, inert and creaking in the windless day. A few ragged children pelted the sails with mud, pausing to stare at her as she passed. She was used to that. At least they had something to stare at today. She paused for the last time where the road forked and ran down to Beverley. In a month, perhaps less, her father had said. She smiled grimly. Let him come then. She was ready for him now.

The month lacked only a day – the longest month of her life. All through it she had struggled to maintain her anger, fuelling it with visions of losing Leconfield, of those last painful hours they had spent together. Yet as the days past her resolve weakened. She found excuses. Her father was right. He had been raw from captivity, resentful at the price he'd had to pay for freedom. Three years was a long time, long enough to blunt even the worst hatred. And even if it wasn't, to meet hatred with hatred was so futile. It had gone on long enough. It was time for peace.

Then on the last day the doubts came crowding in. Perhaps she made too much of it all. Perhaps he had forgotten that she even existed. He might come only to pay his respects and then leave her again, to grow old and sour alone at Leconfield. It was the more subtle rejection but she believed him quite capable of it. She shivered with cold premonition and screamed at Bess for creasing her gown. She was still angry, but with herself. It was she who was the fool to love him still.

She paced out another square of the hall. The tight gown of crimson velvet hung on her, heavy as chains, and the narrow shoes pinched at her feet. Pearls collared her throat and drooped from her ears. She wore her hair loose, disdaining the high fashionable hennin. She had height enough without being steepled like Beverley Minster.

From their corner the dogs watched her warily, uncertain of her mood. Then Connor growled softly in his throat. He had already caught the distant thud of horsemen. She too heard it now and breathed deeply to ease the constriction of her gown. Sharply she called to her steward and saw with relief that his livery was clean – Percy livery, though he was in fact her father's man. She'd made sure that there was nothing here today to remind him of Raby.

She saw him long before he saw her. From the window she watched him dismount. There were less than a dozen men with him, including that great bear of a man that he'd had by him at Raby, John Grey and John Clifford. The rest she did not know. Softly she called the dogs to her as if for protection. She would have gone out to greet him had her feet not been so firmly rooted to the floor. She felt near to tears. Oh Jesu, she prayed. Let him love me. This time let him love me. Yet when he came into the room she turned on him the cold formal smile she kept for strangers. The dogs sensed her distress and Connor leapt forward snarling at Hal's approach.

His eyes dropped from her face to the massive dog and swiftly he stripped off his glove and held out his hand. The dog was quickly submissive and Hal raised his cold eyes to her face again.

'Would that I could tame you so easily, madam,' he said dryly. He came towards her. She'd forgotten how tall he was. He seemed changed.

'Such a welcome,' he said. 'Did you feel yourself in need of such formidable protection?'

'They are not used to strangers,' Alianore said stiffly. 'No more am I.'

He almost visibly withdrew from her. 'If my presence here disturbs you I can easily go elsewhere,' he began.

'No.' Alianore moved away from him into the centre of the room. 'No. You are more than welcome.'

'As welcome as plague by the look on your face.'

She was saved from a reply by the noisy entrance of John Grey. She could have wept. There seemed no middle road between outright coldness and flinging her arms wantonly around his neck. She would have done better to have chosen the latter. If he had been alone she knew that he would have been long gone by now.

They supped almost immediately: venison from the deer park; mutton and lamb in crisp hot pastry. She sat through the first three courses in utter silence. She forced food between her stiff lips, stretching them obediently in a hospitable smile when she had to, keeping them pressed tightly together in desperate self-control when she didn't. The wine thawed her a little and banished the temptation to scream aloud. She discovered that the big man's name was Jack. Sir Jack? Master Jack? It didn't seem to matter to the others and when she'd grown accustomed to his outrageous familiarity it didn't seem to matter to her either. He was amusing and kindly and he doubly endeared himself to her by his efforts to draw her into the conversation from which Hal so pointedly excluded her. Wisely she resisted. This was not the time to shine in wit and perception.

A page came and refilled her glass for the fifth time. She sipped a little and set it down again. The malmsey burned her throat and gave her a kind of courage. She turned her head to watch him. His skin had lost the pallor of three years ago and he was leaner, harder than she remembered. All else was the same: the arrogant gilded head: the chameleon eyes; the mouth. She longed to reach out and touch him. That was all it needed. Some small gesture from her. She knew him well enough now to know that it must come from her. She smiled at the thought. She did not know him at all. She had never kissed him, never touched him except with cold public formality. Yet she knew instinctively that he needed love. What was it her father had said? 'We took all that he loved and broke it for no better reason than to see it smashed and dishonoured at our feet.' And what had there ever been to replace it? An unasked-for Neville wife, a constant reminder of the cause of his loss. Her mouth softened with tenderness, remembering his eyes before her impulsive tongue had turned them cold again. Whether he knew it or not he had need of her. They had need of each other. She would not sleep alone tonight.

Deliberately she overturned her glass. The wine splashed his hand and stained the sleeve of his doublet and quickly she snatched a cloth from the page at her elbow.

'Forgive me. How clumsy.' She drew his hand into her lap and held it fast even when he made to withdraw it. She looked up into his eyes. 'Forgive me,' she whispered softly.

He smiled uncertainly. 'For what?'

'For not telling you how glad I am that you are home.'

He said nothing, only stared at her. His eyes held the candle-light, burning green and gold like marshfire. And then slowly he smiled and raised her hand to his mouth. It was enough. She had no need to hear more.

She watched the candles inch slowly down, waiting for the moment when she could decently retire. The steward brought more wine and she bit her lip in irritation, thinking, Jesu, would they never be done? She smiled encouragingly at Jack as he yawned, and discreetly moved the malmsey from John Grey's reach. A half hour more, then she rose and smiled graciously, begging them all to excuse her. She turned towards Hal. The shadows masked his eyes and he was unsmiling. 'Goodnight, my lord,' she said softly.

She sat quite still before the little dressing glass. She was naked beneath the crimson robe and her flesh was chilled with waiting. It had been an hour, perhaps more. Despairingly she threw down the ivory comb. He was not coming. He hated her still.

Angrily she brushed the sudden tears from her eyes. She'd see him in hell before she'd weep again, though she could have filled all of Hagg Dyke at the thought of how she'd demeaned herself. She stared down at the emerald with its greedy green fire then slowly turned her head as she heard the door open quietly and close. He stood with his back against it, watching her.

'Alianore.' He spoke her name softly.

He awoke from the dream and reached out for her in panic. She was there, soft and fragrant as lilies against him, her skin still warm and damp from loving. He pushed the heavy fall of hair from her face. She slept like a child, her lips slightly parted. Her honeyed breath stirred a tendril of hair that lay across his hand. He kissed her softly but she did not stir.

He turned on his back and stared blindly into the shadows of the room. The moonlight slid in latticed squares across the bed. The crimson robe she had so hastily discarded lay on the floor like a pool of blood. He closed his eyes. His father's blood, his grandfather's blood, their blood on Nevilles' hands, Nevilles' hands on Alianore's, Alianore's on him, touching, caressing, drenching him in blood. His eyes flew wide in fear. The dream. He remembered the dream now. His mother's voice whispering soft, 'Traitor. Betrayer of your father's blood.' He had seen her face, the pale lovely face that had enslaved his father all his life. The long hair floated wide, malevolent as fire. The small red mouth was smiling. She bent toward him as if to drop a kiss on his brow. Then suddenly her lips had parted and her mouth had spurted blood.

He turned his face into the bolster. A dream, a hideous dream, nothing more; yet it was a long time before he was still. He reached out for Alianore's warmth. This was real, her long lissom body beside him, her small perfect breasts against his ice-cold flesh. She still slept but her arms slid softly around him and his need for warmth and love smothered all guilt. He kissed her softly awake. 'Alianore,' he whispered. 'I love you, Alianore.'

The Bishop of Winchester leant back in his chair and smiled benignly at his host. 'A most handsome feast, Northumberland,' he pronounced cordially. 'And the best Bordeaux I ever tasted.'

Hal obligingly refilled Henry Beaufort's empty hanap and moved the dish of sweetmeats a little nearer his jewelled hand. At the end of the hall his vast retinue fidgeted and yawned and drank themselves into a drowsy stupor. It was past midnight but the bishop talked on, oblivious to their grumbles and his stiffly polite host. Like the devil, Henry Beaufort had no need of sleep.

The steward came and bent to Hal's ear and he nodded his assent for another cask of wine to be broached. He wondered vaguely if the Bordeaux would last the night. Four tuns had been consumed in as many days, besides the hundred sheep and young deer slaughtered on the farms. Not that he had grudged any of it. For the first time in years the sound of laughter had filled Leconfield; laughter, music, the brilliance of jewels, the soft sheen of furs still worn against the chill of early spring. Two kings, a queen and half a score of dukes had graced his table: Charles, the captive Duke of Orleans with his sad, poetic face; James of Scotland, momentarily charmed from his sullen resentment by Bishop Beaufort's niece, Joan. It was well known that the king hoped to enforce James's captivity with chains of a gentler kind. All the Beauforts had been there: the bishop and his brothers, Thomas, Duke of Exeter, John, Duke of Somerset and their youngest brother Edmund, who had earned the king's displeasure by falling drunk beneath the table before the fifth course had been served. The king himself had eaten frugally, though Queen Katherine had gorged enough for two, smiling nervously at the jests and little courtesies which flowed around her, only half of which she understood. Her eyes had held a vague sadness which had aroused Hal's pity. Moreover, the queen disliked Duke Humphrey. He could have loved her for that alone.

Gloucester had been there, flushed and out of temper at the king's refusal to allow his marriage to the Hainault heiress. That the lady was already wed and to a coveted English ally at that had not deterred Humphrey. Only his brother's extreme displeasure and the width of the Channel between himself and the Countess

Jacqueline had momentarily cooled his ardour. He had sulked throughout the day and had vented his spleen on Bishop Henry, loudly insinuating that the bishop's riches came more from filching royal revenues than from careful investment and that in any case, such wealth did not become a man of the cloth, let alone that he should employ it usury.

The bishop seemed unperturbed by Gloucester's open dislike. He'd eaten bigger men than Gloucester for breakfast and spat them out again. Hal, glancing at his heavy face, now thought that he would be a dangerous man to cross. He wondered uneasily why he was still here. It took more than a good Bordeaux to keep him till this hour.

Bishop Henry murmured his thanks as he filled his cup for the third time, then fixed Hal with his worldly gaze.

'His Grace, the king, looked well.'

'I thought so.' Hal refused more wine and laid his goblet pointedly aside. A man did not drink so deeply when he drank alone.

'Better than he did when he first came home?'

'Greatly so.'

There was a pause while the bishop lodged his teeth in a sugared violet. Then Hal said, 'Will his Grace return to York now?'

'After Beverley.' The bishop sipped his wine appreciatively. 'He goes to pray for victory at the shrine of St John tomorrow.' He winked at Hal. 'Pray for money more like, eh?'

Hal smiled faintly and felt the tension ease from his bones a little. Perhaps now they were coming to it, the purpose of this last wasted hour.

'And will his prayers be answered?' he enquired mildly.

'To the tune of fourteen thousand pounds from my own coffers. I know not what else he has managed to scrounge on his progress north.'

'Fourteen thousand pounds,' Hal murmured. 'A goodly sum. It must gratify his Grace no end to have such direct communication with the Lord,' he added dryly.

The bishop smiled. 'It keeps him content.'

'And dependent?'

The long reptilian eyes blinked in mild surprise at the sudden thrust. 'A happy thought, but not so in Henry's case,' Bishop Henry said regretfully. 'He would have the money in any case. I deem it wiser to give freely and be thought a generous man.'

'Such generosity is no doubt profitable though, my lord.'

The bishop shrugged. 'Nothing is without profit, my son: of the pocket; of the soul; of the conscience. If a man gives all his wealth to the poor he profits by knowing his place in the kingdom of heaven is secure.' The long mouth assayed a smile. 'I merely happen to prefer my reward to be a little more earthly.'

Hal laughed aloud. He could not help but admire Beaufort though he knew little of him as a man: the legitimised bastard of John of Gaunt, now churchman, scholar and money-lender in chief to his nephew the king. He was a large man, well fed to the point of obesity but surprisingly agile despite his size. He had a clever face, a brow furrowed by constant scheming, a mouth that looked as if it tried not to smile at the folly of others. His robes proclaimed unpriestly wealth. A collar of rubies stemmed the fall of his chins and his cope was faced with ermine and pearls. He wore no crucifix or other token of his calling, only the gold collar of Lancaster around his heavy shoulders. The bishop made no secret of where his allegiance lay. He said slowly, 'There was a moment when the king came home, when I first saw him.' The pale eyes snapped Hal from his straying thoughts. 'It crossed my mind that he was not long for this world and that if he died before *la belle* Katherine gave us an heir we should be in sad case with only Clarence, Bedford or Gloucester to choose from. Unless,' the smile upon his face became as fixed as steel, 'Unless we choose to examine the reverse side of the coin.'

'Meaning?'

'Meaning Edmund of March and after him, young Richard of York.'

Hal stared at him in amazement. Beaufort? Coming as near to treason as made no difference?

'Is that a suggestion or merely an observation?' he asked.

'It's a fact,' Beaufort stated bluntly. 'King Richard's designated heir was Roger Mortimer and the heirs of his blood.'

Hal drained the remnants of the wine into his cup. 'Richard is dead,' he said slowly. 'Dead and buried and best forgotten.'

'Some wish that he weren't.' Beaufort smiled thinly. 'One never sees the good in a man till he is past all evil!'

Hal stared hard into the lizard-like eyes. What was Beaufort after? More than he was prepared to say outright, yet on the face of it he was suggesting a change of sides. He'd have believed it of any but Henry Beaufort. He'd been faithful to Lancaster all his life. The king trusted him implicitly though it occurred to Hal now, not enough to allow him the Cardinal's hat that Rome had conferred upon him. Did Beaufort resent it so much?

Then he saw, in the quick sideways shift of the bishop's eyes, that it was not Beaufort's loyalty that was in doubt but his own. He said coldly, 'And you think I am one of those who wish that Richard was still king?'

'I did not say that,' the bishop countered mildly. 'But I knew your father and your grandfather. Both died attainted rebels and traitors in Richard's cause.' He shrugged his heavy shoulders. 'Such habits are sometimes hard to lose.'

'And if you remember, my lord, it was Northumberland who raised Lancaster to the throne in the first place.'

'And regretted it till the day he died.' Beaufort's mouth turned in a sad little smile. 'As did my brother Lancaster himself many a time.'

'It's a long time ago,' Hal said wearily. 'It's best forgotten now.'

'Not forgotten, I fear. Merely laid aside.' Beaufort glanced meaningly at Hal. 'You know that well enough. As long as there is a choice, a doubt, it can never be forgotten.' He leant back in his chair and regarded Hal over the high bridge of his nose. 'I think that we may speak freely, Northumberland. I am greatly concerned for the king. He is sick, grievously sick. I fear this war will destroy him and at worst he'll leave England to be fought over by his brothers; at best he'll leave us a babe in arms. The one is no better than the other. Both will be disastrous for the realm. It is Henry who has made England what she is: stable; respected; feared even. But what of his succession? Clarence cares for nothing but brawling. Bedford lacks imagination and my lord of

Gloucester has far too much of it and dreams he is greater than he is. At such a time old loyalties are remembered, old grievances dragged up. It was not so long ago that you nearly lost your own head over a like happening.' The bishop paused delicately, then said, 'Your mother, Lady Camoys as she now is. Have you seen her of late?'

Hal felt his mouth grow dry with fear. 'No. Not of late. Not since I was released.'

The bishop nodded sagely. 'As well. As well. Your mother bears a grudge too well and too long.' He paused again, averting his eyes to pluck a stray hair from his sleeve. 'I should perhaps tell you that your kinsman John Mortimer has been arrested for treason.'

The words froze Hal like ice water. Faintly he asked, 'What treason?'

Bishop Henry smiled wearily. 'What else but scheming to place our noble Edmund on the throne? The old story: Scots and Welsh mercenaries and the king's untimely demise. I doubt if it got further than furtive gatherings and treacherous talk but,' he smiled thinly, 'it must be stopped before it develops.'

'And Edmund?'

'Innocent as always, or so he pleads, though he turned out at Shrewsbury to greet the king with such a force of men at his back that Henry thought it politic to pack him off to his Irish estates for a time. Who knows but beneath that milk-and-water exterior there does not beat an ambitious heart?'

'And my mother? The Lady Elizabeth? Was she involved?'

The bishop fixed him with his shrewd dark eyes. 'She's a Mortimer too and can't forget it,' he said. 'There's nothing proven but it's known that their paths have crossed lately.' He shrugged. 'It's not the first time she's meddled, but then I'm sure you know that. His Grace is inclined to leniency. She's Harry Hotspur's widow and that counts for something with him. Nevertheless, Henry feels that it would be unwise to leave her to her own devices. The Devil makes work for idle hands, don't you agree?' He smiled blandly. 'The king would feel easier if she were more closely supervised. Here, in the north, where you could keep an eye on her.'

Hal turned away from the bishop's probing stare. Elizabeth, Elizabeth. What fresh madness had seized her now? 'Was it because of her that you questioned my loyalty?'

Bishop Henry stretched his long mouth. 'No. It was not because of that. A shared blood does not always mean a shared loyalty.'

'What was it then?'

'The north. You hold the north. There could be no rebellion without the north.'

'Is that all?' The bishop's very stillness told him that there was more.

'No. Not all. Certain information was laid before me that led to Mortimer's discovery and arrest. Names were mentioned. Yours was one.'

Hal held the bright unwavering gaze. 'May I ask by whom?'

'You may.' The bishop smiled with happy malice. 'It was your brother-in-law, Richard Neville.'

'I don't believe it,' Alianore said faintly. The shattered vial of jasmine that he had struck from her hand lay between them and its perfume rose and engulfed her in a sickening cloud. She stared blindly at the cold bitter face turned toward her. It was the face of a stranger, the man she had married at Berwick five years ago.

'Believe what you like, madam. Unholy devil that Beaufort is he'd not lie so blatantly and about his own kin at that.' Hal looked away from her stricken face. He felt so cold, so empty, like that time at Portchester. He had been close to death then and for a like reason. It was not so long ago that he could not remember the fear. It was the fear that made him angry. Bitterly he said, 'Make peace, you said. Let it lie. It's over. Forgotten.' He swung round violently to face her. 'And I almost believed you, believed that it didn't matter that you were a Neville.'

'It doesn't,' Alianore said desperately. 'It doesn't any more.'

'Then prove it. Stop defending that precious brother of yours. Believe it, Alianore. Believe that he falsely accused me to Beaufort. Believe that he'd see me swinging from a gibbet and think it a good day's work.'

'And you him.' The sneer of his voice stung her to anger. 'Are you so saintly that you never bore Richard a malicious thought?'

'The thought is one thing, the deed another. I'd not stoop so low as to falsely accuse a man.'

'And neither would Richard.' Vainly she clung to the hope that it was not true. If it was, then these last few months together might never have been. She would be plunged back into that dreadful world of hatred and violence that she'd thought almost banished. 'You've only that old mischief-maker's word for it. Beaufort would say anything to serve his own ends.'

'And you would say anything to protect Richard.'

'That's not true. But neither will I condemn him till I've heard it from his own mouth.'

'Well, that you'll never hear. Richard Neville will never enter this house again nor will you go to him. As far as you are concerned, Alianore, your brother is dead.'

'Don't order me as if I was some kitchen wench. Richard is my brother. I grew up with him and loved him before I ever loved you. You'll not force me to choose between you.'

'Choose?' The quiet violence of him unnerved her more than all his rage. 'I said nothing of choice, Alianore. You'll remove yourself and your household to Alnwick and stay there till I say otherwise. I shall leave word that Richard Neville is not to be admitted. Nor shall you leave without my consent.'

She screamed at him in pure rage, 'I will not go. You'll not shut me up at Alnwick with only the wind for company. I've had three years of it here. I'll not suffer it again.'

He smiled, such a cold smile that fear overcame the choking rage and she fell silent. 'Oh, if it's company you lack you need not fret.' His smile widened to soft mocking laughter. 'I'll give you such company that will freeze your blood, Alianore. A woman who can out match you a thousand times in loyalty to her kin, a woman whose hatred for Neville blood is greater even than mine.' He smiled slowly. 'You should do well together, you and my mother Elizabeth.'

From the sickly pit of her stomach she dragged up her voice. 'I'll not go.' The useless protest came faintly then gathered strength under the scornful gaze. 'You'll not rule me, Hal. I'll do as I please, as I have always done.'

'Then you'll do it alone, Alianore,' he said quietly. 'It'll be a long time before you see me again.'

She leant her back against the door after it had closed behind him. The dogs whined for admittance and scored the oak with their claws. Richard's gift. To care for her when he could not. She closed her eyes and squeezed the hot bitter tears from beneath her lids. How could he have hurt her so when they had always loved each other so well? But then she had never told him that she loved her husband more. He'd have hated her for that as Hal had for her loyalty to him. That was all there was now, hatred and suspicion, vengeful and bitter words. It was too strong to stop it now. Involuntarily her hand slid down to her waist and she smiled faintly through the burning tears. She had not even told him yet that she was with child.

For the third time that morning the needle stabbed at her hand. Alianore sucked absently at the pinprick of blood and laid her stitch work irritably aside. Jesu Mary, she was bored. Bored and hot and out of temper. The child seemed to weigh more heavily on her today. She glanced across at the woman who sat on the far side of the room, so small and slight in her nunly black. Her hands worked swiftly at the tapestry square but all else about her was utter stillness. Even when Alianore rose laboriously to her feet she did not raise her eyes. Alianore did not exist as far as Elizabeth was concerned.

She crossed wearily to the open casement. The stillness of the woman behind her was reflected in the breathless day. Nothing moved, there was no sound, as if the burning heat had slowed all the world and only she moved on. She stared blindly out, though there was nothing to see. Beyond the high walls the Aln ran sluggishly and the fields were a glare of yellow corn. It would be a good harvest if the rievers did not come and she'd heard that the Scots were too busy squabbling among themselves to spare a thought for England. She thought pityingly of James of Scotland, under close restraint now since the news had come that the Douglas and his men had slain the king's brother Clarence at Bauge. She smiled faintly. His freedom had been almost as brief as her happiness.

She'd not seen Hal since the night of their quarrel. In the morning he'd been gone. With Beaufort? With the king to avenge Clarence in France? He'd left no word except to order their removal to Alnwick. Out of sheer defiance she'd gone to Raby, though she'd found no refuge there. Her mother's welcome had been less than warm but it had seemed warmth enough to be home again. All her sisters had gone except Cecily the youngest. They were near strangers now and she'd felt little affection for this coldly beautiful child who was a replica of their mother in her youth. She had the same arrogance, the same perfect fairness. She seemed to dominate though she was barely nine years old, especially the fair-haired boy who trailed constantly in her wake. This was Richard of York, her father's ward and the son of the traitor Cambridge, heir to the dukedom of York and the earl-doms of March, Ulster and Cambridge. He was also Cecily's betrothed. Alianore had raised a cynical brow. No wonder he was cossetted so well.

Her brothers were home, save Robert who was making his way in the church. Edward, wayward as ever, strutting like a peacock in garish red silk, was there. George was quieter, sulking over his betrothal to the poor stunted child that was Lord Latimer's heiress. William she hardly recognised, he had grown so fat. And Richard – her dearly beloved Richard.

At the sight of him all her doubts fled. He kissed her soundly and twirled her round. 'Jesu. You're as thin as a broomstick, Nel. Does that swine Northumberland not feed you?'

She had laughed out of sheer relief. It was not true. He would not jest about a man he had just betrayed. She curled herself happily in the window seat. Richard spliced a peach with the knife at his belt and gave her half.

'How is father?' she asked softly and wiped a trickle of juice from her chin.

'Old and irritable and unbearable as ever.' Richard pulled a face. 'I'd hoped for the wardenship long before now but it looks like the old skinflint will hang on till he drops.'

Alianore smiled faintly. She had forgotten that such blatant ambition was encouraged at Raby. With her back to the warmth of the sun she listened while he talked, about their father and brothers but mostly about himself. He spoke vaguely about his young wife Anne. He was more enthusiastic about the fact that her father Salisbury was ailing and not likely to last the year. It would make up in part for being cheated of Westmorland, he added with a little avaricious smile.

Alianore raised her eyes innocently. 'Cheated? But surely there was never any question but that the earldom went to Ralph?'

'The earldom, yes. I don't grudge the boy the title. But not the lands. Not Raby, Sheriff Hutton, and Middleham. Those are family lands. Our lands. I hardly think that Ralph represents the family. Besides, he's only a boy. It would be madness to leave control of Raby to a boy.'

'Nevertheless, as the eldest son of the eldest son, Raby is his,' Alianore pointed out quietly.

'The eldest son of the first marriage.' Richard answered sulkily. 'John is dead. I am the eldest son now. It's only right that Raby comes to me.'

'What does father say?'

'What do you think he says? That Raby must go to John's son. He says I'm well enough provided for and I dare say I am. But it's not just land, Nel, it's Raby.' He touched the soft golden stone of the embrasure reverently. 'I'll tell you this, Nel. I'll not give it up without a fight. We'll see when father dies. We'll see who gets Raby then.'

Alianore said nothing but she watched his handsome brooding face and saw how he had changed, not obviously but in small ways: the bright laughing eyes overlaid with greed; the handsome mouth had acquired a spiteful twist.

He was speaking of their father again. 'It's the waiting, Nel.' He sprang to his feet as if the very thought made him restless. 'Father's too old and sour and he's not the heart for the Border now. But he'll not yield it up. He says I've not the wisdom for it yet.' His face suddenly turned spiteful as a woman's. 'I should have had the West March when John died and I would have had if it hadn't been for that usurping bastard Northumberland. It's not as if he even attends to his duties. Half the time he's whoring it around France with Henry.' He shifted his feet uncomfortably, seeing her look. 'Sorry, Nel,' he muttered. 'But even for your sake I can never think anything but the worst of him.'

Alianore kept her eyes fast on his face. She had meant to work round to it, put it more subtly, but now she asked him outright. 'Did you accuse Hal of treason to our uncle of Beaufort?'

He returned her look without flinching and she thought for one joyous moment he would deny it. Then he said, 'Well, what if I did? I don't suffer traitors, Nel, even if they are wed to you.'

Alianore sat limp and still as if all the breath had gone from her. Then quietly she said, 'Hal is no traitor, and well you know it, Richard.'

'His kind are always traitors if it suits them. Like father, like son. And I know for a fact that meddling Mortimer witch had a hand in it. Like mother, like son.'

'And you thought those grounds enough to accuse a man for his life? Would you have been so sure, so quick to point the finger if it had been other than Hal?'

He turned away from the scorn in her eyes. 'I did what I thought was best,' he said pompously.

'Best for you, Richard. Best for the Nevilles.'

'And why not? You're a Neville too, in case you had forgotten.'

Alianore turned away from the once-loved face. 'Yes Richard,' she said softly. 'To my shame. To my eternal shame.'

She'd come back to Alnwick sick at heart and longing for Hal. She'd found Elizabeth instead, a pale wraith-like creature that seemed to need neither sleep nor sustenance. By day she sat silent and unmoving. At night she walked the dim passageways like a ghost. And that was all she had for comfort. The great tomb that was Alnwick, the wind, and Elizabeth. There had been nothing from Hal and she'd given up hope of word from him now. All she knew was that he was with Henry in France and that the war was going less than well. Disease was rife. There had been many deaths. Fear of rejection forbade that she should write and there was no certainty that he would receive it. Her only hope lay in the approach of winter. Perhaps Henry would cease campaigning then. And what did he know of her? Perhaps not even that she was soon to bear his child. She glanced to where the narrow bridge spanned the Aln and the road swung up to Berwick. She closed her eyes. Let him come home soon. For pity's sake, let him come home soon.

Then Elizabeth's low malicious voice echoed softly across the room. She came in a whisper of mourning silk to stand at Alianore's back. 'He will not come. He'll not come until he has to,' she said. 'He can bear a grudge almost as well as I.'

If she was unnerved at Elizabeth's reading of her thoughts she did not show it. She had grown used to Elizabeth now. The hours of silent brooding that she broke only to exercise her malicious tongue had ceased to trouble her. She was still a little afraid of her as they all were, for there were no secrets from Elizabeth. The most private intimate thoughts could be laid bare at a glance from those long malevolent eyes. Those that could avoid her did so. Alianore was one of the few who could not. It made life only a little more bleak. She said coldly, 'If he bears a grudge it's only because you taught him so well.'

Elizabeth smiled her thin pointed smile. 'Not well enough, it seems, or you'd not be mistress of Alnwick and heavy with his child.' She moved closer and the vervain at her throat was strong and bitter in the heat. 'You'll not win him, Alianore.' The soft malicious voice laid ice on Alianore's heart. 'You might be Countess of Northumberland and the mother of his sons but you'll never possess him. He might even care for you a little in return, but those that he loved long before you will never let him forget. He'll always resent you and despise you for what you are.'

'I am his wife,' Alianore answered steadily. 'I am Alianore Percy, Countess of Northumberland. No more, no less.'

'As you were Lady Despencer before that? As I am Lady Camoys?' Elizabeth's cold fingers closed round her wrist. 'Don't deceive yourself with empty titles, child. You are Alianore Neville and I am Elizabeth Mortimer. I was born such and will die such. It's blood that counts. Blood and heritage and not even the greatest love can overcome that legacy. Can you rise above your blood, Alianore? Could you cast off your own kin so easily? Could you see them suffer pain and degradation for Hal's sake? Your father, your brothers . . .'

Alianore wrenched herself free from the clinging grasp. 'For pity's sake, Elizabeth. Let it die. It's all past now.'

'Past?' Elizabeth's long eyes widened. 'Past, you say? All that pain and grief past? Then why do I still suffer it daily? Why do I still wake and see Harry's torn and mangled body before me, see his empty eyes looking down from Micklegate? Grief is never past. It lies quiet and dormant inside you till another grief takes its place and makes it less. It's always there; it never really dies.'

Alianore lowered her eyes. The anguish in Elizabeth's face was real enough for her to feel pity. 'Only because you keep it alive,' she said. 'Because you feed it with hatred and thoughts of revenge.'

'Because that keeps *me* alive.'

'But what of love? Could you not have lived for love? You had your son.'

Elizabeth smiled bleakly. 'My son was taken from me when he was nine years old. I did not know if I would ever see him again and when I did he'd become a man and lost all need of me. Love is fickle and transient. It can fade and die as quickly as it is born. Hatred is indestructible, eternal.' She looked hard into Alianore's eyes. 'It's all I've had these past seventeen years.'

'And do you hate me?'

'No.' Elizabeth turned her evil eyes to the sunlit world outside. Alianore was not important enough for such intensity of feeling. She was a bright lovely flower that would fade and die in its own time. It was the root that must be destroyed and the root was Lancaster. She gave a swift sideways glance at the woman beside her. No. There was no hatred there, perhaps if anything there was a grudging admiration. The child had pride and spirit, all that she would have cherished in a daughter. The thought went no further. It was too late for her to reach out now. Her world had narrowed long ago to a single thought. Ambition had become obsession and there was no room for affection in the crowded shadows of her mind. Sometimes there was brightness, a shining light that drove the shadows back. She saw him quite clearly. Tall as a forest oak with hair like molten gold, the redeemer of her waning sanity, the pure flame that would burn out the canker that was Lancaster. It would not be Edmund, not silly timid Edmund who wanted all but would risk nothing. Twice she had put herself in jeopardy for him and twice he had failed her. There would be no third time. Edmund's dim fire was spent. He was childless and like to remain so. She could not look for salvation there. Who then? Who then would carry the torch of her ambition? There was only one, only one would have the right of blood and birth: Richard of York, whose father had lost his head for Edmund's cause. And when Edmund died all of the vast Mortimer lands would come to him, more land and power than Lancaster had when he first thought to make himself king. Her brilliant eyes clouded. *Lancaster*. They would have to be rid of Lancaster first. Then she smiled, a slow rapturous smile that stripped half her years from her. It would not be long. She had seen him die, seen the dreadful agony that lessened hers.

'Soon. It will be soon. Less than a year and the usurper will be dead. And such a death, wallowing in his own blood and filth, his dream unfulfilled.' Her eyes had darkened with ecstasy and she spoke aloud, oblivious to Alianore's pale stricken face. 'You'll think of Hotspur then, my lord. Think of his torn and bleeding body and his pain. But his pain will be nothing to yours. In the end you'll pray for such a death as his.'

'Elizabeth.' Alianore leant against the wall fighting against the nausea in her throat.

Elizabeth turned slowly to look at her, her mouth parted in a triumphant smile. 'You have no stomach for death then, sweet Alianore? Yet death is the only reality, the only certainty. All else are dreams and shadows.' She turned her face to the light again. 'Lancaster will die in pain and humiliation as I have willed it. He will leave nothing of himself save a half-wit child who will bring all his great achievement to nought. I have seen it, Alianore. I am never wrong.' She turned the serene smiling face of a child towards her. 'You think I am crazed, don't you? A poor crazed old hag whose mind has been turned by grief. But look upon me well, Alianore. You see yourself, forty years hence. Old and alone with all you loved beneath cold barren earth.' Then she reached out and brushed a tear from Alianore's cold cheek. 'Hush, child,' she said softly. 'The time's not for weeping yet.'

It was not yet three o'clock but the gathering clouds had snatched at the last of the day and it was dark by the time they reached Newcastle. The spittle of rain drove in Hal's face and stung the raw wound on his cheek. He paused as they came within sight of the gates and waited for the straggling column of men to come up. They moved slowly, with a dreadful weariness that was more of the spirit than of the body. Henry of Lancaster was dead and every man still trembled with the shock of it.

Tom Mowbray edged his horse alongside. His face was grim and unsmiling. He'd lost his luxuriant beard and most of his hair, his thin cheeks were seamed and scared with frostbite. There was not a man come out of France that did not bear the mark of that dreadful winter siege at Meaux. There were more who had not come back, thousands who had died from cold and starvation and the filthy virulent disease that had dogged them since Harfleur. And Henry of Lancaster was one of them. All that splendour of endurance had failed in the end. At the last he had been carried like a babe to die like a dog at Vincennes. The king was dead, yet Hal grieved more for the loss of one common soldier. Jack had died at Meaux, the slow lingering death he had always feared. John Clifford too; more grief for his sister Bess.

Hal spurred his horse forward, heavy with the sense of loss. It was finished now, the dream tarnished. Though Bedford had been left to carry on the war the spirit had gone from all of them. Now the substance would slowly rot and die.

In the great hall of the keep Ralph Neville awaited him. He had aged since Hal had seen him last. The thinning hair was almost white and his mouth was perpetually creased with pain. He smiled a welcome. Only the dark intelligent eyes reminded Hal that they were adversaries.

'It's ill news, Northumberland.' Neville led him to the banked fire and offered him wine. 'I had almost thought Henry indestructible.'

Hal took the cup of warmed wine and drank deeply. Jesu, he was cold. Cold and hungry and desperate for sleep. He eyed Neville bleakly. 'He thought himself indestructible,' he said. 'I never saw a man fight death so long and so well.'

Neville nodded. 'A great man. A great man. All England will

mourn him.' He placed his elegant doeskin boots on the rim of the hearth. 'I hear he suffered greatly.'

'We all suffered,' said Hal sharply, then thought perhaps none so much as Henry, for his suffering had been of the mind as well as the body. He stared grimly into the roaring flames that somehow still left him cold, remembering how Henry had driven himself day after day till his thin stricken body had barely been able to stand. He'd never complained, but all had known of the pain. Some days he'd had to be dragged half fainting from his horse. They'd seen the saddle wet with his blood, smelt the indescribable stench of his agony. Yet still he'd gone on. And because of it he'd kept thousands of starved frost-bitten men on their feet. They'd endured the frozen hell of Meaux because of him. Because of him they'd been glad to die. Meaux had fallen after seven months but there had been no rejoicing. They were in no better case than the poor wretches they had starved into submission. Besides, they had dead enough of their own to mourn. As soon as the weather allowed they had moved south to Paris. Queen Katherine had joined Henry there, and they had rejoiced belatedly in the birth of the son born six months before at Windsor. But Paris was hostile and Henry's sickness worsened in the summer heat. They'd removed to Senlis, then Corbeil. It was there that Henry had at last given up and they'd taken him by river back to Vincennes where he had died the next day. It had not been an easy death. Whatever guilt had haunted Henry in his life had stayed with him till his last hour. At the end he'd cried out in protest, 'No. No. Thou liest. My portion is with the Lord Jesus Christ.'

Hal shivered and drew his furred robe a little closer.

Neville was still watching him with shrewd narrowed eyes. 'What now, then?' he said.

Hal shrugged. What now, with France slipping visibly from their grasp despite Bedford's vigilance, and England with a year-old babe to rule her? Humphrey of Gloucester was already straining at the leash. They'd been hard put to keep him from seizing power.

As if he read his thoughts, Neville said, 'I hear that Gloucester is to be Lord Protector during the young king's minority.' He sipped sparingly at his wine, and added almost as an after-thought, 'He must not be allowed full power.'

Hal looked up at him. 'I had thought you Gloucester's man.'

'I am nobody's man now. I was Henry of Lancaster's man and now he is dead I am his son's. Inasmuch as a man can feel loyalty to a king who still fills his breeches,' he added with a rare touch of humour. 'It's Gloucester who will rule, and unchecked there's no telling the harm he can do. He's greedy and feckless and would bring us all to ruin to have his own way. He must be kept to heel.'

Hal raised his brows. 'Do I hear Bishop Beaufort's voice in this?' he enquired mildly.

'Albeit the bishop is my kinsman – and yours,' he added with a little smile, 'he's a fine statesman and at the moment our greatest asset. He is the only counter to Gloucester.' He leant forward to refill Hal's cup. 'King Henry willed the Protectorate to Gloucester and the Regency of France to Bedford unless Burgundy should want the title for himself, which I doubt. But even Henry saw the wisdom of laying restraint on Gloucester. He's to take no major decision concerning the realm without Bedford's agreement. Bishop Beaufort seeks to widen that concept: a strong Regency council to curb Gloucester's wild schemes. Let him have the Protectorate but not the Regency. There is a world of difference.'

Hal nodded dully. At this moment he did not care if an ape ruled England.

'If and when such a council is formed, Beaufort has named you to stand.' Neville paused, remembering his son-in-law's unpre-dictability. 'Would you be willing?'

Hal roused himself with an effort. What was Neville offering him? Nothing that had not been sifted to the last grain between himself and wily Beaufort. Cautiously he answered, 'I have no objection to serving England in such a way.'

Neville pursed his mouth at the careful evasion. 'That's well, then. I shall inform the bishop of your patriotic feelings. One thing more,' he added as Hal rose to his feet, 'nearer home. You have no doubt heard that the bishop is pressing for the release of the King of Scots?'

'Which of course is nothing to do with the fact that his niece will be Queen of Scots if James is released.'

Neville frowned. 'Irrespective of that, we cannot keep him prisoner forever.'

'Why not? It would be madness to let him go.'

Neville's shrewd eyes widened. 'Madness? For whom?'

'For England. For the Border. He's changed, you know. He's not the boy you shut up in the Tower and left to scribble melancholy verse. He's a man now, a hard bitter man, twenty seven years old, who's been a prisoner for fifteen of them, and he holds England responsible for every miserable day. King Henry dragged him round France on and off for the last five years to see how he could use him. Well, I fear James is tired of being used. Wed to the bishop's niece or not, he'll have his revenge on England. He'll ally himself with France, for one thing. Bedford needs every man he can get over there. He'll not be well pleased if he loses men to guard our rear into Scotland.' The rush of words left him exhausted. 'James has changed,' he ended quietly. 'More than any thought possible.'

'As you have, I think.' Neville regarded him steadily and saw how thin he was. His face had a gauntness, a hard worldly quality that had not been there before. His eyes were dull and empty and the thin scar showed raw and livid on his pale and unshaven cheek. 'Will you go to Alnwick?' Neville asked quietly.

Hal stiffened. 'Perhaps. I have business here that will keep me a few days and then . . .'

Neville interrupted him harshly. 'You think it manly to desert your wife for over a year?'

Hal flushed. 'She sent no word that she had need of me.'

'As you sent none to her.'

'And what would I have said?' shouted Hal. 'That we were half dead from cold and hunger?'

'Better that than no word at all.' Neville curbed his rising temper. 'Did you never think of her at all?'

Hal sank down wearily and buried his face in his hands. Yes, he had thought of her, thought of her every dreadful day as if it was his last, and if anything the horror of war had intensified his need of her. Yet it had been a long time before he could think of her without anger and when he could his pride had stopped him sending word to her. His had been the hurt and betrayal. The first move must come from her. None had, and by then the misery of being without her was overwhelmed by the war. He had counted himself lucky to be alive. Love and desire had had no place at Meaux.

He said wearily, 'Leave it be, my lord. We'll talk of it later. You do not know the circumstances.'

'Oh I know the circumstances. Richard falsely accused you to Beaufort, and Alianore unthinkingly took his part. Well, you should have brought your grievance to me. I would have believed you and seen him punished.' He smiled grimly. 'I have no illusions about Richard. He's his mother's son and will stoop to anything if it brings him reward. Carry on your feud with Richard if you must, but leave Alianore be. Christ, she's just a child. She's known little of love and much of grief and shame, all the affection she's ever had came from her brothers. It's a hard bond to break. No man who cares for her would even have asked it.' He leant forward and touched Hal's arm. 'Must we go on? Is it not time past for peace, at least between us? Hatred is only cousin to fear and what do you see now to fear? I am an old man and long past all earthly desire.'

'My grandfather was an old man, but you did not spare him.'

'I told you before, only because I feared him, and he feared nothing. I was not so brave. I tell you this though, he would not have harboured a grudge so long and he would never have revenged himself on a woman.'

It was true, Hal thought. The old man would never have been so petty. John of Gaunt had been his life-long enemy yet he'd embraced him at the last and risked all he had to fulfil his promise to a dying man. 'I fear I do not have his generosity of spirit,' he said tightly. 'And neither do you, my lord. I would have thought it's a little late in the day for an olive branch between us.'

'Perhaps. But not too late for you and Alianore. Go to her, Hal. She's waiting. She's been waiting this past long year.'

Hal swallowed hard. 'Yes. I'll go. In a day or so.'

'Not sooner?' Neville smiled his malicious smile. 'I would have thought you more eager to see the child.' Hal swung round on him, his face pale with shock. 'Did I not tell you? Your wife gave birth to a son six months ago.'

Both she and the child were still sleeping and the great lofty room hung between shadow and light. Hal leant back unsteadily against the door. He was filthy and unshaven and his legs still trembled from his furious ride. Outside the door her attendants still muttered in outrage at his intrusion. He had cursed them softly to silence. He must be the one to wake her.

It was barely dawn but there was light enough to see. He came silently to the bedside and looked down on her sleeping face. She looked so young and defenceless with her hair all tumbled about her. He smiled tenderly. Dear God, what a fool he had been. He loved her. He would have loved her had she been kin to the devil himself. Then he knelt beside the little gilded cradle that had been his, and his father's before that. The babe was out of swaddling bands and a plump arm had thrust back the mountain of furs that covered it. Tentatively, he touched the tuft of gilded hair so like his own. His son, his dear beloved son. He saw the futility and waste of it all now. He could no more condemn Alianore for her Neville blood than he could this child. She was his wife; this was his child. They would be as one and let all else outside go its own way.

He went and stood by the window. Across the river the abbey bell tolled for matins and a pale silver sun struggled through the morning mist. He heard the watch called from the Falconer's Tower and the answering drag of reluctant feet like faint discordant music. The castle was stirring; the rattle of chains, the groan of bolts, the strident scarlet of his livery against the muted golden stone. A thin pile of smoke began to curl from the bakehouse chimney, and he suddenly remembered that he had not eaten for nearly two days. He smiled and felt a sense of warmth and belonging. He was home. For the first time in all his life he was home.

He turned back into the room and saw her watching him. 'Alianore,' he whispered. 'Oh Alianore, forgive me.'

The sweet warmth of her enfolded him. He was in her arms and weeping, the hard bitter tears of twenty loveless years.

'Oh my love, my dearest love.' She kissed his trembling mouth. 'Forgive me. Forgive me.'

They clung together and she felt his desperate need of her. She held him close, whispering softly to him as to a child till he was quiet. Then she touched his scarred cheek with her mouth. 'You are hurt, my love?'

'Not any more,' he whispered. 'Not unless you send me away again.' He stroked her hair back from her face. 'About Richard. I had no right to make you choose. If it would make you happy . . .'

She stopped him with her mouth and then turned her shining face towards him. 'You are my happiness,' she said. 'I need no other. I am with you, Hal. Against all the world if need be.'

The soft drone of plainsong lifted Ralph Neville from his fitful sleep. He was dying, a slow dignified death without pain or excitement. A death almost dull, as all his life had been. Each time he slept he did not expect to wake again, yet wake he did, each time a little farther removed from the crowded room in which his mammoth family had gathered to watch him die. He grew as impatient as they. He was sixty-one. He had lived long enough.

Through half-closed eyes he watched them, praying, fidgeting, staring from the windows in undisguised boredom. His wife prayed solicitously, her fat knees cushioned on velvet. A wry smile twisted his thin mouth. Scheming, more like. Plotting to cheat young Ralph out of Westmorland. Well, he'd seen to that. Joan wouldn't have her way this time. At least he'd lived long enough to see Ralph a man.

He sighed and his thin ribs creaked with effort. He supposed he shouldn't complain. He'd thought it all the world to have Joan once. The daughter of John of Gaunt, bastard or no, had been a feather in his cap. He'd been ambitious then, climbing the ladder hand over fist and not caring who he trampled on the way. Then Joan's ambition had dwarfed his own and made it seem almost trivial. Her schemes were always so much greater, so much more than he had dreamed of. And to give her her due, she'd given him the sons to back it with: ten children still living to add to the eight that he already had. Eighteen in all, each set like the link in a chain so that every great family in England was bound to them. He'd found rich heiresses for all his sons: Katherine had gone to John Mowbray; Anne to Buckingham; and little Cecily had married

Richard of York a month ago. There was the prize: Richard, Duke of York, and Earl of March and Cambridge, since the death of Edmund Mortimer, the wealthiest man in England saving the king. He smiled faintly. Surely there was achievement in that? Not that he'd had any joy from it. They all despised him except perhaps his Nel. His eyes wandered vaguely over their blurred faces. All his life's work gathered here in this one room. His strong manly sons, his comely girls. It was an effort to remember all of their names. And such a credit to him, he thought with bitterness, as selfish and uncaring as he had been. He could die content. He'd seen all his dreams fulfilled – except love and affection and friendship. For all his great family he was a lonely man.

The muted sounds of the room were dimmed a little, the soft images blurred. He remembered a long time ago – what did he remember? The memory had slipped by too swiftly and he was left with only a fleeting remembered warmth.

It was cold again now, cold and dim with nothing but shadows. And yet he knew the shadows better than all the faces here. Perhaps because he was closer to them now. Were they waiting, across the dark void that drew imperceptibly closer? He knew one that was. The tall unmistakable shadow had been there for days. Was that the archbishop with him? Poor murdered Scrope that he had betrayed to his death with soft words and cunning? The shame of it had come upon him gradually, seen first in other men's faces and then in his own heart. Somewhere outside his fading consciousness a priest intoned the Mass. Faintly he heard his wife's shrill voice. 'And we shall lay up a store of treasure in heaven.'

A tear slid beneath his heavy lids. What treasure had he laid up for himself after a lifetime of avarice and greed? What hell fire would punish him for Scrope's death, for all the dead and maimed and destitute? He shivered uncontrollably. Dear Christ, he was afraid. Then a ministering hand drew the furs closer about his chin. There was care and concern in the touch and he opened his eyes. He smiled. It was Nel, come at last.

He slept for a while and woke to the brightness of candlelight. Another day past. Would he see the next? There were voices outside the sphere of flickering light, a blur of discordant sound like the unruly chatter of birdsong at dawn. As he stirred they fell silent, all save one and he had no need to open his eyes to see Richard, pacing and impatient. He'd grown even more unbearable since he'd wed the Montague girl. Is the waiting so hard, my son? he thought bitterly. And then: no. Not my son. Not Richard nor Edward nor any of them. They were somehow separate and apart from him as if he'd done no more than plant the seed of their being and then passed on: the Neville bull serving the Beaufort cow. He'd heard it said in jest often enough. This was the first time it had ever amused him.

Nel's hand was still there, warm and comforting. And Northumberland. He could sense that Hal was there in the shadows beyond the bed. He smiled grimly to himself. Once he would have balked at the thought of Northumberland at his deathbed. It did not seem so important now and at least he'd given his little Nel a mite of happiness for all their poor start. His eyes were not too weak or tired to see the quiet radiance of her. She'd grown quite beautiful, with a warmth and strength about her that none of the others had. She'd filled out a bit too, and not before time. Three sons was it now, or four? Harry, Thomas, George and, of course, the baby Ralph, named for him. There were no resentments now. And Hal? If he still harboured a grudge he never showed it. They'd worked together peaceably enough since Hal had come back from France. Yet still he was not sure. Sometimes he thought it was still there, deep beneath the veneer of contentment that Alianore had laid upon him. And festering the worse for lack of air.

Premonition seized him. It would need only a spark and his death could provide it. The wardenship would go to Richard; greedy, unforgiving Richard who never forgot a slight. Poor Nel. She'd suffered enough for Richard as it was.

He groaned and his fingers plucked fretfully at the sheet. There was no true peace. No peace with France, no peace at home. Three years now since King Harry had gone and John of Bedford was still struggling vainly to press England's claim. Charles of France had gone raving to his grave in Harry's wake. And every year the Dauphin grew stronger, bolstered by Scottish aid. Only last year the Douglas and his son had been killed fighting for the French at Vernuil. Hal had been right there. Freedom had gone to James of Scotland's head like raw wine and he'd proved even more ruthless than any had thought. Within a month of his crowning, old Albany's son Murdac and two of his sons had gone to the block; aged Lennox too. He'd not turned his eyes to England yet but he would. The alliance with France was but the first step. If Beaufort had had any hopes of influencing James through his marriage he had been disappointed. If indeed the aging bishop had time for peace-making, his quarrel with Gloucester reaching new heights. Twice Bedford had been re-called from France to intercede when Gloucester had roused the Londoners to near riot against Beaufort. Both times his efforts had come to nought and at his departure both antagonists had returned to the fight with fresh venom. Up till now Gloucester had maintained the upper hand. Though a strong Regency council had kept him from the worst of his follies, he still meddled and all France had been affronted by his marriage to the Hainault heiress, doubly so when he had put her aside within a year in favour of a strumpet called Eleanor Cobham. Bedford had been left to pick up the pieces, and had married Burgundy's daughter in an effort to patch the alliance. It was all so futile. Nothing was ventured in France now with true hope of success. Henry's dream was ended. It had died with the man, as all dreams did. All the glory was gone, all the strong men gone. England was ruled by babes and old men, old men like him, past their best with all their fire dimmed. He closed his eyes. It was not his care now.

The shadows filled all of his mind now and his vision was a blur of palest grey, like the sky that day at Bramham Moor. He heard a woman weeping softly and felt the warmth of tears upon his hand. No tears, Nel, he thought sadly. No tears for one who never shed any. His only regret was in leaving her, the only sweetness of his life.

Then his breath caught and strangled in his throat as the shadows grew strong and definitive. He felt a coolness on his face, a darkness in his mind. He saw the great bowed head, the mane of hair streaked with blood. So much blood that it had been hard to believe that the old man was still alive. Yet he was, terribly and agonisingly alive. He'd lifted his head and looked at him; those yellow pitiless eyes that had struck terror into him all his life had met his. He had understood and for the first time in his life felt compassion. It had been swift and clean and when that proud old head had fallen at last it was as if part of himself had died too. Strange how the fear of him had lived on till now. He was filled with a ridiculous, belated, sense of triumph. He was not afraid any more.

'Northumberland.' His feeble shout brought them crowding round. 'Northumberland.'

Hal bent close to the bed but Neville said no more. He had seen the gilded head come close. The burning eyes were his guide. Then the long scarred mouth twisted in its familiar provoking smile. He smiled in return. The old wolf was come. It was time.

1435–1437

*Right as the fresshe redde rose newe
Against the summer sun coloured is
Right so, for shame, al waxen gan the hewe.*

– Chaucer

The long hall at Dalkeith was still familiar, even after twenty years. The threadbare hangings had been replaced by fine tapestries, the rough-hewn benches with chairs of polished oak. But the dark-banded ceiling was still oppressive. It still smelt of fish oil and sour wine.

Hal sat uneasily among the English Marcher lords. It was against his better judgement that they were here at all; thirty miles into Scotland with only three hundred men between them. Dalkeith held its share of bitter memories, and worse, he saw it as a concession to James. He glanced to where the Scottish king sat among his sparse nobility, resplendent in saffron velvet and seed pearls. The great yellow topaz on his thumb winked like a jaundiced eye. He's grown fat, Hal thought maliciously. Fat and coarse and vengeful as a scorned woman. Could a man change so much in ten years? The question struck a raw note within him. Why not? He had.

He thought back to the day he'd brought James home. They'd reached Berwick by noon and stood together for a moment on the ramparts. They could see for miles: the verdant green of Ettrick Forest, the grey unchanging hills where they had hunted as boys. Hal had said quietly, 'It's just like old times, James.'

It was a while before James had answered him and when he did his eyes were cold and bitter. 'No, Hal, it's not like old times. We were friends then.'

He had spoken truly. There had been nothing but enmity between them since. But then James was someone who made enemies with ease. Hal's eyes moved thoughtfully to the handful of men who flanked the king. The Earls of Atholl, Douglas, Crawford and Moray, a few of the survivors of James's savage purge. Their faces were closed and withdrawn, their eyes were cautious but sometimes in a rare unguarded moment they would rest fleetingly on James's heavy face. Then it would show, the fear and resentment, the outright loathing. Hal smiled. So James was not well-loved, even by his own kind. He thought fleetingly of old Albany. James had had the full measure of his revenge there. All his sons dead or gone to the block. He was glad the old man had not lived to see it.

Then the thin querulous voice of the Bishop of Carlisle opened the proceedings. Hal winced at the servile phrases, the humble tone that left the Scots in no doubt of the English need for peace. Placate him, Beaufort had said, concede all that you need to but not too much. *Not too much.* Hal closed his eyes in anguish as the bishop rambled on, yielding all but his soul. He suddenly felt unutterably tired, tired of compromise and concession, of smiling to conceal his bitterest thoughts. He felt soiled and dishonoured and humiliated. And not only because of this farce of a parley. He'd sold himself for a woman's body: his mother's words, said unthinkingly but never forgotten. Nothing Elizabeth said was ever forgotten. And there was truth enough in it. All his grand schemes of vengeance had come to nothing. For Alianore he had swallowed all of his pride. She'd wanted peace and he'd given it to her, throwing himself into such an orgy of reconciliation that his mother kept to her chamber for weeks in disgust. He'd even wed his sister Bess to Alianore's nephew Ralph. In return he'd had the love he craved, a son every other year and three beautiful daughters. It should have been enough, but it wasn't. There was still an empty corner of him that even she could not reach; old loves, old loyalties that would never quite die. It was Elizabeth who kept them alive, with her perpetual mourning, and accusing eyes. Perhaps if he was totally honest, it was Elizabeth rather than

Alianore who had made him so tame. He was afraid of his own unfulfilled need for vengeance, of what it might begin. It was ten years of Elizabeth that had changed him so. He'd have sent her packing if he could have, if he hadn't been afraid of the mischief she could cause – another compromise like the one he prepared himself for now.

James's full mouth curved smugly as the bishop resumed his seat. He had the upper hand here and knew it. He was as well informed as they and knew perhaps better than they how the war dragged on in France. Thirteen years on from King Harry's death, and no real headway had been made. Towns were won and lost again a day, frontiers pushed forward then snatched back again and all with great loss of life and money. It had made an old man of Bedford. And James himself had not helped: he pursued the French alliance with a vengeance. Only last year he'd wed his daughter Margaret to the son of the Dauphin, Charles; King Charles now, since his unbelievable coronation at Rheims. Hal still thought of it with faint disbelief. Weak, timid, milksop Charles, King of France and through a woman at that. *La Pucelle de Dieu*, the Maid of Orleans. There were a myriad names for Jeanne d'Arc and none could deny that there was an air of the miraculous about her relief of Orleans. Salisbury and a thousand good men had died that day. Then Auxerre, Chalons and Rheims where she had taken that travesty of a prince and made him king. God's handmaiden? The Devil's daughter? At least her flesh had been mortal enough to be wounded and captured outside Paris. It was said she had burnt as well as any other.

Her death had brought the English no advantage. The belated crowning of their own little king at Notre Dame had been a shambles. Lack of money, lack of faith. Only Bedford still believed in the dream. At home the people screamed for peace. Cardinal Beaufort saw it clearly enough and manoeuvred for truce and treaty in every quarter. He'd had short shrift from James when he'd tried to prevent the French marriage and was like to get it again, Hal thought grimly, as James made ready to speak. For a moment their eyes met and quite clearly Hal saw his intent. There would be no renewal of the truce, no payment of the ransom instalment that was long overdue despite the twenty-eight Scots hostages that languished in the Tower at English expense. This was just a game to James, to buy time, to consolidate and perhaps to exact a small measure of revenge for those lost eighteen years. Hal could understand that. Once he had not felt so differently himself.

James said slowly, 'When we speak of truce, we speak of peace and amity. And there can be no true amity while one holds that which belongs to another.' His pale glassy eyes fixed particularly on Hal. 'I speak more especially of Berwick and Roxburgh, possessions of the Scottish crown held unlawfully by yourselves.'

Hal almost laughed aloud. So obvious an opening gambit and from such a skilled master as James. The game was null and void, the moves all led to an inevitable stalemate. Hal rose grimly to his feet. Dear God. How had they come to such a pass, to let the likes of James best them without even a fight? He could not let James leave the board entirely unscathed.

'You say "unlawfully", sire. By whose law? God's law? Or that which you have invented yourself to suit your own taste?'

James's complacent smile faded with his colour and from his own ranks Hal heard the Bishop of Carlisle's strangled groan.

'I say unlawful, Northumberland, because in the time of my forefathers Berwick was a Scots possession, till it was seized by Edward Longshanks for England.'

'Nearly a hundred and fifty years ago,' Hal countered smoothly. 'I would have thought that gave us good enough title. The Stewarts have not been kings of Scotland for even half of that.'

James heaved his bulk out of the chair, then sat heavily back again. 'I'm not here to be called to task, Northumberland,' he yelled. 'Berwick and Roxburgh. Those are my terms. Take it or leave it.'

'Don't inflame him,' Bishop Thomas whispered piteously in his ear. 'Remember why we are here.'

'As if I could forget,' Hal thought savagely. It was too late now. A ridiculous childish rebelliousness filled him. He was not going to humble himself for no return. Self-abasement had never come easily.

'Well, sire, if those are your terms then I can do no other but put them to Council in Westminster. But in the mean time,' his voice hardened as James openly smirked, 'in the mean time, perhaps we could clarify exactly what we shall get in return for such major concessions. When *we*, the English, speak of truce, we take it to mean just that. No burning or looting, no sheep stealing or cattle raiding, no crossing into England without lawful cause. I must take it from the burning and harrying of my lands these last six months that it means other to your Grace.'

James looked uncomfortable and glanced at his uncle Atholl for support. Atholl frowned but said nothing. It was clear they had not expected to be opposed. Then James said haughtily, 'I cannot be held to account for every pig and cow that strays across the Border.'

'Then your kingship is less than it should be and it seems to me that Berwick and Roxburgh are too high a price to pay for a pledge that cannot be kept.' Oh, what joy to see James's face red and mottled as a rotten plum. Now this really was like old times. The Scots king leapt furiously to his feet but it was Atholl who spoke.

'You go too far, Northumberland,' he said deeply. 'Remember to whom you speak.'

'I do not forget, my lord,' Hal said. 'His Grace reminds us of it too often for that.'

James answered him then, his voice thick and heavy with rage. 'Damn you, Northumberland. Damn you and your truce. I'll not treat with you again, not for Berwick or Roxburgh or half of England. You hear that?' he cried shrilly to the men who stood in silence at Hal's back. 'Go and tell your fat cardinal that if he wants peace he must send other than Northumberland to get it.'

Among the muttered uproar on both sides, Hal bowed insultingly low and smiled happily into James's engorged face. 'You need send no messenger, your Grace. I shall tell him myself with pleasure.'

When they reached Norham the repercussions began in earnest.

'Well, you made a fine hash of that, Northumberland,' the Bishop of Carlisle said wretchedly. He wrung his thin hands together in despair. The failure was bound to be laid at his door. Failures always were.

'Don't fret, Thomas,' Hal said kindly. 'I'll take full blame for it.'

'And so you should. A common dog could have barked as loud.'

Hal turned his head to meet the speaker's hostile gaze. Richard Neville, Earl of Salisbury since his father-in-law's fall at Orleans, came toward him. He was smiling faintly and only his hard round eyes betrayed the virulent dislike that was still between them. It never went further than that. Richard Neville rarely uttered a thought or a word that could prejudice his rise. He was more the politician now, grown hard in the company of men like Richard of York, and Gloucester. Hal took the insult calmly. Perhaps this was his greatest compromise, that he'd left Richard alone and even let him have the advantage once or twice. Instinctively, he'd always known that Salisbury's rise would be his own fall but he'd done nothing, said nothing – till now. The mood of rebelliousness that had seized him at Dalkeith touched him again now.

'And you could have done better, my lord? As you did in France, perhaps, to the shame of us all.'

The blood came readily into Salisbury's face at the mention of his last ignominious campaign. Belligerently, he said, 'I could have done no worse.'

'You may well have the chance to prove it, if King James is as good as his word,' Hal said amiably. 'I have no doubt that you could be servile enough to please even James.'

'I doubt if there's anything to be salvaged now since you deliberately wrecked our hopes of truce.' Salisbury answered him savagely.

'Truce? What truce? The same truce that we've had these five years past with Norham and Berwick garrisoned to the hilt because we're not sure which way the Scots will jump?' Hal eyed Salisbury as if he were a half-wit. 'Bedford is crying out for those men in France but we dare not lose them because that is exactly what James is waiting for. An undefended Border. He'd not be asking for Berwick then; he'd be taking it.'

'And what of the burnings and night raids?' his nephew Tom

Clifford said. 'Common rievers? I've not known rievers come with shod hooves and broadswords before.' He spat disgustedly. 'They're James's men, right enough. I know damn fine they are. Sent to keep us on the defensive.'

Bishop Thomas chewed fretfully at his lip. 'I must say I don't trust a man who courts France so openly and so well,' he observed.

Richard Neville's lip curled. 'My God, listen to you all. You've exempted Northumberland from blame already.' He strode in among them, his face red and angry. 'Let us not forget our mission – to effect a peace with the Scots and settle terms for the prolonging of the truce. It was not our policy to insult James to his face and incense him further against us. Our instructions from the cardinal were to concede where we could.'

'Concede what? Berwick? Roxburgh? And perhaps Windsor too, if James has a fancy for it. I understand Windsor can be most pleasant in the spring. Perhaps we should have told him that.' The rich sarcasm of Hal's voice brought the tell-tale flush to Salisbury's fair skin. It was strange how such a little thing filled him with such exhilaration. For all his veneer of sophistication, Neville could still be drawn – at least by Hal. He smiled at his sudden inner warmth. It was as if he had been sleeping for ten years and had woken to a glorious day. 'You have much to learn yet, Richard,' he said pityingly. 'And your first lesson is not to pay lip service to a man like James of Scotland.' He addressed them all gravely. 'There will be no extension of the truce. If we'd all gone on our knees for it the result would have been the same. James's policy should be clear enough now: subtle aggression to distract our attention from France. Impossible demands – can you see Beaufort yielding Berwick? James is hand in glove with the French and we'll get no truce till we've given one or the other of them a beating.'

'You advocate war, then?' Salisbury demanded.

'No. I advocate reality. It is useless to attempt to change that which cannot be changed.' His eyes sought and held his brother-in-law's. 'A pretence is never lasting, is it, Richard? Sooner or later what has to be said must be said, what has to be done must be done.' The statement brought a sudden intense relief. There would be no more pretence, no more compromise. The men around him felt it too and moved imperceptibly closer. Tom Clifford handed him a cup of wine. Hal raised it smilingly to Salisbury. 'To reality, Richard,' he said softly. 'To the end of pretence.'

Alnwick

Alianore dappled her feet in the swirling stream. The water was cool and clear, foaming like syllabub round the black oily rocks, and beneath the rippling surface little fronds of weed swayed and danced to the water's rushing song. Alianore sighed and closed her eyes as the wind lifted her sleek hair. Such solitude was rare, away from her clamorous sons and complaining daughters. She stretched herself contentedly in the long damp grass. They would have missed her by now. Dame Isobel would be searching for her, her thin mouth pulled down in grievance – the wine was sour, the cheese rancid, Thomas had put worms in her bed and Catherine had torn her best summer gown. She watched a spider crawl unchecked across her skirts and frowned to see the seams straining at her waist. She was with child again, the twelfth in as many years. Only two had not survived; a son named John and a girl who had barely lived an hour. She smiled wryly. No one could say that the Nevilles were not breeders. Yet this time there was no joy in it, this time she was afraid. She'd almost died bearing her last child and would have if it hadn't been for Elizabeth. She opened her eyes. *Elizabeth.* Elizabeth had potions and cure-alls that could all but raise the dead. Would she have aught for killing? The thought brought a flush of guilty colour to her face and she sat up abruptly. Her tender breasts throbbed painfully against the tightness of the gown. She thought angrily, why not? Had she no rights? Was an unknown life so much more precious than hers? She was tired of childbearing, tired of the pain and ugliness. She smoothed down the skirts of her rumpled gown. She rarely wore one for longer than three months before it had to be let out again. Broodingly she looked to where the river narrowed and slid darkly beneath the bridge. If only Hal were here. She plucked a flower from the clump that cowered beneath her skirts and tore it nervously to shreds. Perhaps tomorrow, no later than the next day, for she'd already had word that the conclave at Dalkeith had dispersed. The news that Hal and King James had quarrelled was only rumour as yet, though rumour had an unpleasant way of becoming fact. What joy for her brother Richard if it were true. It was just the opening he had been looking for. She had no illusions about Richard now. She'd watched him grow crueller and greedier over the years. She'd almost wept with disbelief when he had openly stripped young Ralph of the Westmorland lands except for the pittance of Brancepath and a few manors in Lincolnshire. Ever since, she'd felt as if she walked on hot coals. Ralph's bitterness infected them all and his marriage to Bess had laid a strong claim on Hal's loyalty if it came to it. If it came to what? Her heart pounded suddenly in fear. If it came to taking sides, if it came to pressing Ralph's claim. They would all be caught up in it and all her careful peacemaking of the last ten years would have been for nothing. Then she gave a faint wry smile. Sometimes her capacity for self-deception amazed even herself. Did she really believe that this stifling of tongues and tempers between Hal and Richard was a peace? Nothing was ever said. Nothing needed to be said. She could feel the hatred between them as strongly as intense heat or cold – carefully hidden for her sake, at least on Hal's part. About Richard she was not so sure. It was more policy with Richard. He had not been sure enough of himself until this last year. Now he had the backing of men like York and Gloucester. Gloucester all but controlled the court, checked only by his aging uncle Beaufort and the occasional grudging presence of Bedford. The king was a nonentity, a sickly timid boy who cared more for prayer than power. He'd need all his prayers to avert the disaster that was so openly brewing. She did not think that York and Gloucester would be content with second best for long. Richard was one of their number, openly covetous, openly flouting the law because there were none to enforce it. Richard would not have dared to touch Ralph's inheritance if the old king had been alive. Apprehension chilled her. The peace was ending, if peace it had ever been. Ralph would see to that for he had married Bess, almost twice his age, merely to ally himself to Hal. Eventually he would seek Hal's support against Richard, and rightly Hal would give it. Gladly, she wondered? Yes. Gladly, with all his heart and soul. She was a fool to think she could change him so easily.

Then she screamed as a pair of hands slid over her eyes. 'Thomas,' she cried. 'Oh, you fool, Thomas.'

Her second eldest son came out from behind her. 'How did you know it was me?'

'No one else would play such foolish tricks,' she said crossly. 'See. You've made me wet my gown.'

Thomas sat down crosslegged beside her. 'Why are you angry?' he said. 'You've never been angry before.'

Alianore smiled into his anxious face. He was such a handsome child with his pale delicately-boned face and dark curling hair. He had the most remarkable eyes, of such a bright penetrating blue that at first one instinctively avoided his glance. 'I'm not angry, Tom,' she said. 'You startled me, that's all. I was thinking things I shouldn't have been.'

'Wicked thoughts?' asked Thomas with interest. 'I'm always thinking wicked thoughts,' he added happily. 'Uncle Beaufort says it is better to think the thought than do the deed.'

'It's better to do neither,' Alianore said firmly and slipped her feet into the loose velvet shoes.

They walked hand in hand down the river path. Thomas's grip was firm, unchildlike. It was he who led and she who followed. There was warmth and protection in his touch. Suddenly she remembered the child within her and her dreadful sacrilegious thought. It could be another Thomas, another George or Ralph. All her children were so different, like the facets of a brilliant gem. Each shone in his or her own way. Harry's quiet solidarity was balm to Ralph's wildness. George was a little frail, but this last year or so had seen the emergence of a dry, acid wit and a clever mind. Richard had been named for her brother and that was a travesty; poor Richard with his short crippled leg and gentle heartbreaking smile. William was the youngest, clumsy and shy as an unbroken colt. Her daughters she did not care for so much. Catherine was vain, though Alianore had to admit with good cause. Anne was plainer but had a kinder heart. Joan was the baby that had all but killed her. And then there was Eleanor, Harry's betrothed, a sly, sullen child who hated the north and liked them no better. She was not a pretty child but she had a certain ageless quality about her that reminded one of Elizabeth. Perhaps that was why they had been drawn to each other, both outcasts untouched by love or kindness for Eleanor Poyning's total family was a perpetually absent brother. She was a great heiress and the match was considered a good one. Only she had her doubts. She did not think Eleanor was possessed of the temperament that could be happy or content with Harry. Alianore sighed. She had done her best to draw the girl out but so far Elizabeth had been the only one to penetrate her sullen remoteness – except perhaps for Thomas. She glanced down at the dark curling head that already reached to her shoulder. Though she would never have admitted it she loved him the best, wild, unpredictable Thomas with his mazarine eyes that could draw the very soul from you. She ruffled his black curls and said reproachfully, 'And why aren't you at your books with the others?'

Thomas smiled disarmingly. 'I have had a surfeit of learning for one day.' He skimmed a pebble at some feeding ducks and laughed delightedly as they rose shrieking into the air. 'Besides,' he added, 'George studies enough for all of us.'

They had come within sight of Alnwick and Thomas paused for a moment, staring at the clustered golden towers. He said quietly, 'When father dies is it Harry who will be Earl of Northumberland in his place?'

Alianore looked at him in sudden concern. 'Yes,' she said. 'Harry will have Northumberland. You will have the lordship of Egremont.'

He did not answer her and she looked at him in sudden concern. Already she could see the man behind the child's face. His eyes were narrowed against the sun. His mouth was – she searched for a kinder word but there was none – his mouth was cruel, like her brother Richard's. 'Thomas,' she said sharply. 'Northumberland is Harry's. You must have no thought of it.'

'I know,' he said, and smiled. 'And I'd not grudge it him if I thought he cared for it. But he's never here. He spends all his time at court with the king.'

'That is the king's wish, not Harry's. They have been friends since they were young children and naturally the king wants to keep Harry by him. The poor soul has few enough.'

Thomas's expression said that he was not surprised. He could not envisage friendship with such as Henry. The king was drab and dowdy and smelt of tallow. But then that would suit Harry. Harry was drab and dull himself. He smiled up into his mother's face. It troubled him when she looked like that, uneasy, almost afraid, as if she saw something that he did not. She was the only one he really cared about. His brothers irritated him, his sisters bored him and his father he saw too little of to inspire anything but a mild affection and respect. But his mother he really loved, almost passionately.

He caught at her hand and kissed it. 'You are sad, sweet Nel.' He laughed his light infectious laugh. 'Are you worried that I shall grow into a mannerless clod because I do not slave over pen and parchment all day? Shall I give you proof of my wit and scholarship? What shall it be? Chaucer? Gower? Rustically erudite Langland? Or perhaps a little dreary Virgil? I know all of the Aeneid by heart.'

Alianore regarded him sadly. She needed no proof of her son's cleverness. He absorbed knowledge like a thirsty sponge and used words to baffle and confuse the enemy. This was the first time he had ever regarded her as such. She looked hard into the brilliant callous eyes. 'Thomas,' she said, 'there are other worlds besides Northumberland.'

He looked away toward the hills. 'Perhaps,' he said dreamily. 'But I have need of no other.'

When she reached her apartments uproar awaited her. Catherine was screaming like an eelwife. Ralph yelled back at her and Anne shouted loudest of all to quieten them. From his corner George looked on in grim disapproval and the baby Joan wailed from her cot.

Dame Isobel flew toward her, her downy upper lip trembling on the verge of tears. 'Oh, my lady,' she wailed. 'The Lady

Catherine is in one of her rages. I can do naught with any of them.'

Catherine screamed, 'She stole my comb. She's a thief. A thief.'

Ralph pushed his sister roughly aside. 'You've no proof of that. You just can't find the damn thing.'

Alianore's mouth tightened and she looked frowningly toward the cause of the trouble. She sat with her eyes downcast, remote and aloof as if she saw and heard nothing of the tumult around her. 'Eleanor,' she said quietly, 'what have you to say?'

'She's taken my comb,' Catherine interrupted. 'The one set with pearls that uncle Beaufort gave me.'

Eleanor raised limpid blue eyes. 'I did not,' she said calmly. 'What need have I of her tawdry finery?'

With a scream Catherine flew at her and slapped her hard in the face. 'Liar. Who else could it have been? You've always coveted it. You took it just for spite.'

Then the door opened sharply and even Catherine fell silent. Elizabeth stood there, tall, ageless, unsmiling. 'For God's sake, Alianore. Can you not quieten these brats?'

She came slowly into the silence she had made and her cold eyes moved from face to face. Catherine flushed and glanced nervously at her mother. Ralph stared at his feet and for no apparent reason William screamed and ran snivelling to Alianore's skirts.

Elizabeth paused beside Eleanor and her long fingers gently touched the red weal upon her cheek. 'Who struck you, child?' she asked.

'Catherine struck her,' Alianore said before anyone else could.

'And you condone this?'

'No. I do not condone it. But Catherine was provoked.'

'How so?' Elizabeth laid a protective hand on Eleanor's shoulder. 'What did Eleanor say to provoke Catherine to such viciousness?'

'Nothing was said,' Alianore answered in mild exasperation. Jesu. Why did Elizabeth always make her feel like a child herself? 'It seems that Catherine believes Eleanor to have taken her comb.'

'And of course you have proof of this?' Elizabeth demanded

coldly. 'I take it the comb has been found in her possession or that she was seen to take it?'

There was silence, an angry awkward silence that brought a smug little smile to Eleanor's full mouth.

'Well, then,' Elizabeth said, 'it seems that Catherine acted rashly which out of charity we shall attribute more to lack of wit than malice.' She smiled her thin, pointed smile. 'I have no doubt that Eleanor will accept such apology as Catherine cares to make.'

Catherine flushed an angry red and looked wildly at her mother for support. Alianore merely shook her head. Elizabeth had all their measure well enough. She knew the punishment that would hurt the most. Catherine would rather have had a beating than apologise.

'We await your pleasure, Catherine,' Elizabeth said icily. She looked at Alianore. 'Do you encourage such open defiance then, Alianore?'

'Make your apology and be done with it, Kate,' Alianore snapped. 'You are at fault here and it's best you own it.'

Catherine lifted her head defiantly. 'I will not apologise,' she said loudly. 'And I still say she took my comb.'

Elizabeth's face grew white. She spoke to Alianore but her malevolent eyes never left Catherine's face. 'I am sure you will agree, Alianore, that a few days in her chamber on bread and water is a lesser punishment than she deserves.'

Alianore went and slipped her arm round her daughter's trembling shoulders. 'Come, Kate,' she pleaded. 'It's only a few words. They won't kill you.'

'No,' Catherine whispered. 'I won't. I won't.'

'Very well then,' Alianore withdrew her arm. 'It must be as Elizabeth says. I can't help you if you won't help yourself.'

Elizabeth smiled in quiet triumph and drew Eleanor to her feet. 'And I suggest you remove the glass from her chamber also. She'll only spend the time preening otherwise.'

Alianore stared resentfully at Elizabeth's retreating back. Dear God, she thought. Would the woman never die?

Elizabeth spread her skirts in the shadow of the wall and stared thoughtfully at the child who plucked daisies at her feet. No beauty, though the narrow face had a certain sensual fascination. Her hair was long and pale and colourless as were her eyes. Only her mouth had definition, firm and bold and passionate as a courtesan's. Elizabeth looked away, watching the ambling figure of the guard pacing the walk above the garden. How strange to feel warmth and compassion after all this time, stranger still that a child like Eleanor should be the one to rouse it. Perhaps it was merely a sense of identity that drew her. She could still remember her own loneliness and isolation when she had first come to Alnwick as Harry's bride. She had been nine years old then. Jesu, had she ever been so young? All had seemed so easy then, all within her grasp. There was nothing now. Nothing to fight or care for. Had it all been taken from her or had she merely let it go? Too long ago to remember, too long ago to care. How many years? Ten at least. More than thirty since Harry had died, and all still unavenged. At least the dog Lancaster was dead. How she'd revelled in that, her last remembered joy. She'd watched him die, hour by hour, minute by minute, clinging to the vision of his agony till she was all but dead herself. There had been nothing since. She was empty, a void, a decaying hulk filled with fading memories. How old was she now? Sixty-five and not even ailing. How it must irk Hal to see her so resolutely clinging on. But now there was Eleanor, young and untried and full of vibrant life and though she would never have her own perception or her gift, she was ripe for mischief.

Quietly, Elizabeth said, 'And what did you do with Catherine's comb, Eleanor?'

The child raised her innocent eyes. 'I dropped it down the well.'

Elizabeth smiled. A childish trick but then Eleanor was a child, in years at least. Only a little past twelve. Young enough to learn, old enough to use the knowledge perhaps to both their advantage. 'And you think yourself the victor in this?' she said.

'Should I not, then? Catherine is confined to her chamber and without her precious comb.'

'Only through my intervention,' Elizabeth reminded her. 'Would things have gone so well for you if I had not been there? I say this only to show you the better way, the cleverer way.'

She rose and walked the narrow path, her skirts rousing strange scents from the clustering herbs. 'Tell me, Eleanor. What is it you want from life?'

The child answered her with perfect honesty. 'I want Thomas,' she said simply.

Elizabeth smiled. Yes, she could understand that. Wild, handsome Thomas, so like her own beloved Hotspur. He was the only one of Hal's children for whom she had even the remotest liking. Thomas always called her *ma reine*. Under Thomas's eyes, every woman was. Poor Eleanor, she thought, saddled to dull, joyless Harry. 'Is that all?' she said mockingly. 'Does your soul see no further than a mere man? Will that content you, Eleanor? To be some man's chattel all your life, bearing a child year after year as Alianore does?'

Eleanor frowned. 'What other way is there?'

Elizabeth's eyes gleamed with green fire. 'My way, Eleanor. The way of power and domination. With my way you can have all; any man, any jewel. A crown even.' Her eyes clouded suddenly. 'But you must never falter, you must never divert. I faltered, Eleanor, and lost. The way is sure, it is only we who are fallible.' She held out her hand. 'Come. I'll show you.'

She led her slowly down the scented path. 'You see this garden, Eleanor? I raised it all myself from barren soil. There is naught here save that which I have planted, nothing that does not earn its keep or give me reward. So must life be. Harbour nothing which you cannot use.' She knelt and cradled the head of a drooping flower in her palm. 'And this is the face you must show to the world — innocent and smiling, without stain or blemish.' She plucked it swiftly and held it out. 'You think it pretty, Eleanor?' She flung it down and crushed it beneath her heel. 'The juice from one leaf could kill ten men. All the world is here, Eleanor. Pleasure and pain; agony and ecstasy; madness and death. Learn their secrets and revere them and they will serve you well. See here.' She gathered a handful at random. 'Agrimony, sacred to Jupiter. Basil, governed by Mars. Sorrel and Valerian, herbs of Venus. Centaury, sacred to the sun. Wormwood for Artemis, sister to Apollo — a bitter herb, but used sparingly can bend a man's will. Rue, under Leo, the herb of Grace. Dittany mixed with verbena and pennyroyal will bring the Archangel himself to your bed. Jessamine will keep him there. Hellebore for purging – in strength it will make a man rave and see all the devils in hell. And henbane.' She touched the trampled flower with her foot. 'For paralysis, madness and death.'

Elizabeth moved closer to the child. 'You see? There are other ways, subtler ways, infallible ways. A way that can leave you inviolate and untouchable, yet can give you your heart's desire.' She lifted Eleanor's hand and held it between her own. 'I could teach you that way, Eleanor, if you would let me.'

For a moment Eleanor was spell-bound, then the hypnotic voice loosed her. She had not grasped the half of what Elizabeth had said, yet she knew that Elizabeth offered her something she craved, though she could never have put a name to it. She felt her hand grow cold in Elizabeth's, then warm again with belonging. 'Yes,' she said eagerly. 'Teach me, Elizabeth. Teach me to be as you are.'

Elizabeth merely smiled.

'I think I shall go to Leconfield,' Alianore said. Anywhere, she thought. Anywhere away from Alnwick and this dreadful insidious feeling of impending doom she'd had ever since Hal had returned from Scotland.

He answered her without looking up from the gilded manuscript he was reading. 'Yes. Why not? I can ride with you as far as York.'

She looked at him with quick anxiety. 'Will you be away long at Westminster?'

He looked up then and smiled wryly. 'As long as it takes to pacify the Council that your brother will have so joyously stirred up against me.'

She said nothing and he came and slipped his arm around her waist. 'It had to come, Nel,' he said softly. 'It had to come in the end. I tried. Dear God, how I tried, till I was sick with shame at the hypocrisy of it all.' He tilted her small face toward him. 'Don't deceive yourself, Nel, that it was all forgotten and mended. I might have kept it down for your sake but Richard has no such compunction. He's a powerful man now and would be more powerful still. I have to protect what is mine, what is ours.'

Alianore nodded bleakly. 'I know, Hal. I know the right of it but it still doesn't stop me being afraid. If Richard is strong enough to disinherit Ralph, what more could he do to us?'

'Only that which we allow him. We've let him rise too high as it is. He should have been stopped years ago when your father died.'

'And you blame me for that, I suppose?'

He smiled and shook his fair head. 'There's no blame to any, Nel. I wanted peace as much as you did then – or I thought I did.'

He bent to kiss her, then drew back sharply. Elizabeth stood framed in the doorway. 'So you are returned,' she said mockingly. 'Did you not think to come and greet me, Hal?'

Alianore felt him stiffen and grow tense as he always did in his mother's presence. She wondered sometimes if he had held his hand where her family was concerned more to spite Elizabeth than to please her. She knew he would go to any lengths to see his mother thwarted.

Elizabeth advanced into the room. 'What news from Scotland then, my son?'

Hal stared at her coldly. 'You would not have asked unless you already knew the answer.'

'I know that you have quarrelled with James and that he has refused to treat with you. I was quite overjoyed to hear that you still had some fire left in you.' She sat and spread her funereal skirts on the long hard bench. 'Is the fire already quenched? Do you go cap in hand to Westminster to placate fat Beaufort? Do we fumble Lecher Gloucester's hand and beg pardon for speaking out of turn? Or by some miracle could you be half the man that your father was and tell them all to go to hell?'

Hal turned slowly to face her. His eyes were dark with rage and hatred yet his voice was quiet, almost amiable. 'Was it with such insults that you provoked him? Was it with such taunts that you sent him to Shrewsbury to be butchered like a pig? What good was he to you dead? What good was he to your wonderful ambition with his head spiked on Micklegate Bar?' He went toward her and pulled her roughly from the bench. 'Is that what you want for me? Will you not be content till you have used us all up in your mindless revenge?'

He let her go but she remained standing. 'I have often thought you stubborn and perverse but never a fool. Do you think all the world peopled with saints and angels then? Do you think there is no man who wishes you and yours harm?' She moved imperceptibly closer to him. 'Richard Neville wishes you harm. Do you think hatred is my sole prerogative? Do you think that each time you have turned the other cheek and let him gain the advantage he thought you a better man? You've let him run on until now he has the power to harm you. You should have listened to me years ago, Hal. If you'd listened he would never have grown to be a man.'

He left her then, without a word or look. Only when the door had closed behind him did Elizabeth turn to Alianore. Her look was blatantly triumphant.

Alianore returned her look with cold fury. 'Were you listening at the door, Elizabeth, to know so well the way his thoughts were running.'

Elizabeth shrugged. 'I saw the spark. I fanned it into flame, that is all. Besides, you should know by now that I do not have to listen at doors. I know things without being told – like the fact that you are with child again.'

Alianore flushed. 'What of it? It will hardly be the first time.'

'But it should be the last.' Elizabeth drew nearer. 'I care nothing whether you live or die, Alianore, but my son does. He'll be no use to man or beast half crazed with grief. The last child nearly killed you, Alianore. This one certainly will.'

Alianore suppressed the desire to weep. She hated Elizabeth as never before. Always there, unseen, unchanged, undying. Was there never to be any peace? Her whole life seemed to be overlaid with fear.

'It need not be, Alianore.' Elizabeth's voice dripped honey-soft in her ears. 'I have told you before. There are ways.'

Alianore kept her eyes tightly shut. In her mind her unborn child screamed in protest. The very thought was sacrilege. What did Holy Church say? Or was it such a grievous sin that Holy Church did not countenance its existence? The fear rose sour as vomit in her throat and her hand crept to the barely discernible swell beneath her gown. Herein lay her murderer. Her eyes flew wide and met Elizabeth's. She remembered Joan, the unbearable pain and afterwards the bleeding that would not stop.

Elizabeth said, 'It is nothing. A few herbs taken in wine for three days. On the fourth the child will come away.' She reached out and touched Alianore's hand. 'Why do you pull away from me in disgust? I offer you life. The other way is surely death.'

Alianore stood abruptly. 'I'm not sure that I wouldn't prefer it, Elizabeth. At least I might find a little peace.'

Elizabeth smiled cynically. 'You think death an escape, then? Are you sure there is such peace to be had? What if there is only darkness and emptiness? What if there is nothing?' She moved away and poured herself a little measure of the hippocras. 'Shall I prepare the potion for you, Alianore, or will you settle for eternal peace?'

She had emptied the goblet before Alianore answered. 'Yes. Prepare it.' She babbled on, burying the fear in an avalanche of words. 'I shall go to Leconfield, I think. And take the children, of course. We can ride with Hal when he leaves for Westminster.' Her voice tailed off into silence.

'And I of course shall stay here.' Elizabeth lowered her eyes so that Alianore should not see their sudden light. 'Will you not leave me Eleanor for comfort?' she asked plaintively.

Alianore nodded absently. 'Yes,' she said. 'Eleanor may stay.' Then she went quickly from the room and Elizabeth's unsettling presence. She would be glad to be rid of both of them.

John, Duke of Bedford, stared broodingly from the high turret window. The view was familiar yet strange, unchanged yet changed. He saw it all with the eyes of a newcomer. It was five years since he had been home.

The city was just a shimmer of spires in the distance shut in behind the ancient walls. From Ludgate the muddy line of the Strand ran down to Charing. On either side, the bishops' houses smiled in the sun like white gleaming teeth. They had much to smile upon. The wealth of the Church stretched lushly toward

Westminster, the orchards heavy with fruit, the fields golden with corn. Bedford sighed. He had forgotten how beautiful England was. He had forgotten how much he loved it.

He closed his eyes. Christ's Passion, but he was tired, so desperately tired. All for nothing, all his life and dreams for nothing. How Harry would have wept to see all his hard-won conquests slipping away. Would Harry have judged him? Could Harry have done more? Not more perhaps, but with greater effect. He acknowledged without rancour that his brother Harry had been the better man. Harry had been the inspiration, the creator, the builder of dreams. His had merely been the task of holding the crumbling, unstable edifice together as best he could. And he had failed, miserably and utterly. After twenty years of interminable war and suffering what was there to show for it? What were they masters of but a burnt and sterile land, a ravenous and hostile peasantry? Little enough after all those years of effort. And then to be called to task like an errant clerk, to have his judgement questioned, to be accused of failure and neglect. His full mouth thinned with anger. What more did they expect, when Parliament grudged every subsidy if they paid it at all? Promises did not feed grumbling garrisons. Now Parliament pressed for peace with a wealth of words, yet for Harry's sake he could not countenance a peace without honour and the French king would settle for nothing less. Oh, he could lay the blame at countless doors; shuffling Burgundy, perfidious England, that she-devil from Domremy – his heart hammered painfully against the wall of his chest and he steeled himself against the thoughts that inevitably followed. His nostrils flared against the remembered sickly-sweet smell of her burning flesh, his eyes misted with choking smoke. He recalled her eyes; wide and innocent, a child's eyes, a martyr's eyes. They still watched him, waking and sleeping, sometimes hard with accusation, sometimes soft with forgiveness. He had never doubted her guilt till that last day. He had called her devil and sorceress with all the rest. He had seen her put to the question without a qualm, seen her tortured and ill used. Virgin to whore in less than a day, one of her guards had boasted. Even then his conscience had been clear. Not till that last hour had he doubted. Her head had been shaven and her slim young limbs still bore the marks of her suffering. She had passed close to him and he had heard her clear young voice. No hellish mumbling though – a prayer, a simple prayer, and then as the flames had crackled wickedly around her, 'Jesus. Jesus. Jesus. Blessed be God.'

He stood up abruptly, biting hard at his lip to sever the thought. No. He could not have been wrong. Had not her own churchmen condemned her? Only out of spite, the inexorable voice of his conscience said. 'No.' He spoke the word aloud and stumbled like an old man to the chair. That would render his whole life meaningless: that he had been wrong; that Harry had been wrong before him; that they were both murderers of innocent souls. How many innocent souls? Yet only this one irked him.

He went back to the window and flung it wide. The warm sultry air brought sweat to his brow and he leant forward to catch what breeze there was. Beneath him a page in his brother Gloucester's livery struggled with an over-full flagon of wine. He frowned, diverted. He had troubles enough without imagining them and Humphrey was the foremost. The frown deepened to a scowl. Though Humphrey was his strongest supporter in the pursuit of the war he had become a dubious ally. Always meddling, always stirring up trouble whenever he showed his belligerent face. He knew that the scurrilous charges against him had come from Gloucester. It had been his reckless marriage to Jacqueline of Hainault that had caused the breach with Burgundy in the first place. And then to put her aside after a year and marry his mistress Eleanor Cobham! Not that he could afford to judge, he reminded himself bitterly. He was no better, marrying Jacquetta before his beloved Anne had been dead three months. He often felt faintly surprised that Jacquetta of Luxembourg was his wife. He still wondered why. Out of panic to replace the crumbling alliance with Burgundy? If it was, he'd badly miscalculated there. Duke Philip's spleen at Humphrey's former marriage had paled into insignificance beside the rage he had shown to Bedford. He shrugged. He knew what they thought. She was young and beautiful but he had never been swayed by such transitory considerations. No. It was none of those reasons. He smiled bemusedly. If he was honest, he had married her . . . He shrugged again. Almost because she had commanded it.

The tiredness swept over him again, a physical thing that made his heavy eyelids droop. Tired. Tired of endless war and now this empty talk of peace, of placating Burgundy and courting France; haggling, promising, reneging, then back to where they had started from while Burgundy flitted from him to King Charles like a cautious moth, anxious to throw off his tie with England, yet afraid to sever it completely lest he and Charles make a peace that excluded him. He had a breathing space now. Burgundy and Charles were momentarily at odds. If he could persuade Parliament to a substantial grant, if he could . . . He jerked upright as a tap came at the door. His heavy face broke into a smile. 'Northumberland.' He rose and went toward Hal, his hands outstretched.

Hal clasped them warmly. 'My lord.' He tried to keep the shock from his voice. Jesu, how Bedford had aged. An old man yet there could not have been that many years between them. 'I hope I do not disturb you, my lord?' he said.

'No indeed.' Bedford eagerly poured wine for them both. 'I'm glad of it, Hal. I was alone with my thoughts and that's not good for any man.' He raised his hanap and smiled. 'How goes it then, Hal? You are well, I hope?'

Hal grinned ruefully. 'Not as well as I could be, John. It seems that we are both out of favour with my lord of Gloucester. He seeks to take command of the Border from me and give it to Salisbury. He thinks I am here to beg pardon for my misdeeds and is savouring the thought of telling me to go to hell.'

'And have you? Come to beg pardon?'

'No.'

'Then why have you come?'

'To yield gracefully. What else can I do? King James refuses to treat with me. Someone must.'

'Yet you never struck me as the yielding kind.'

'No. I'm not. I said gracefully, not gladly. I'd rather resign the Border than have it taken from me. I'm not so tame yet that I'd afford Salisbury that pleasure.'

'Why did you put the Wardenship at risk in the first place?'

Bedford said curiously. 'It has always been so much your special care.'

'Oh, I don't know,' said Hal irritably. 'Because at the time I needed to thwart James more than I did Salisbury. You must have guessed that James is bent on outright war and that the French are backing him to the hilt. Cardinal Beaufort sent instructions for peace at any price.' He shrugged. 'I'm afraid the price was too high for me. James's demands were impossible.'

Bedford smiled sympathetically. 'It seems we tread the same path, Hal. I am not a great advocate of peace at any price myself.' He rose and paced to the window again. 'So you'll yield gracefully, then, Hal. I admire you for that. It's more than I could do.'

'Backing away from an unsheathed sword comes quite naturally to me now, John,' Hal said dryly. 'I suppose it never occurred to me that one day it would be levelled at my throat and I'd have to fight back. I don't know that I haven't left it too long. Salisbury is a powerful man with powerful friends, or is that merely my excuse for backing down? I was so full of rage and spleen at Dalkeith and here I am now, cheerfully yielding up years of hard work and effort to a man I have detested all of my life.'

'Then why do it?'

Hal was silent for a while. Yes. Why do it? He had friends enough here to turn the tables on Salisbury. Beaufort would have backed him at a pinch and he could count on Bedford's support. Then why? Because here at Westminster the fear that lurked in the back of his mind grew more real, more solid. He supposed he'd never really recovered from that time at Portchester when the headman's axe had only been a hair's breadth away. Since then he'd not meddled in the affairs of kings and if anything the fear had grown, not diminished. He saw too that other men felt it now. Even his young son Harry was disturbed by it. They'd walked together that morning in the palace grounds, the first time they'd met more than fleetingly for a year. Harry was taller, graver, with a slow, uncertain manner of speech that was slightly irritating. They had walked in silence for a while when Harry had said, 'When you ride home, father, I'd like to come with you,'

Hal had looked at him in surprise. 'Tired of the court already?'

Harry had smiled. 'No. I think it's more that the court is tired of me. At least Gloucester is. It's for the king's sake that I feel I ought to leave.'

'Does Gloucester persecute you, then?'

'No. Not me. But he bullies Henry unmercifully. He dislikes and resents our friendship and the king suffers for it. I feel it might be easier for him if I were not here to antagonise Gloucester. That might seem disloyal,' he went on, 'but a champion is the last thing Henry needs. He would not fight if every man in England stood behind him. He's very much a pacifist at heart.'

Hal groaned inwardly. A pacifist? The son of the victor of Agincourt a pacifist? He could well believe it. He had seen the king that morning, tall for his thirteen years and thin as a broomstick. And that long defenceless face, those martyr's eyes. It was the eyes that disquieted him the most. They were the eyes of his grandfather, Charles the Mad. He said, 'Is his Grace . . .' He paused, searching for a word that would not offend.

Harry flushed defensively. 'He's not a half-wit, if that's what you mean, but he soon will be if Gloucester continues to torment him.' He caught at his father's arm. 'Henry's kind and gentle. His heart is good, truly good. He would give his last coin to a beggar if he thought his need was greater and he loves God better than any I know.'

Hal stared thoughtfully at his son. 'I believe that, Harry,' he said gently. 'And I believe you truly care for him and would not desert him unless you thought it for his own good. But you must face reality, as the king himself must in the end. All these virtues would be praiseworthy in a priest but not in a king. And he is king, Harry. For better or worse, he's King of England. If you want to keep him so, then stay by him. Watch for him. Guard him, for he knows not how to himself.'

Harry was silent for a moment. Then he said, 'Is it Richard of York you're afraid of?'

Hal had looked at him sharply. 'Why do you say that?'

'Oh, nothing really. Nothing of importance. Except that I've seen him looking at Henry sometimes and sometimes he will stand very close to the king, and look around him as if to say, "See what you could have instead of this weak, puny creature." He flaunts himself, but no more. I think inwardly he's a very cautious man.'

'Let us pray for it, Harry,' Hal had said quietly. 'Let us heartily pray for it.' It had been enough. The tension was there in every man close to the little king. Only Bedford seemed oblivious.

At last Hal said, 'I think perhaps because I am too afraid of the alternative. I was weaned on vengeance and I saw how it warped and corrupted. Remember who my father and grandfather were, who my mother still is. Doesn't the name of Mortimer still strike a chill in you, John?'

'But your quarrel is with Salisbury, no other.'

'My father's quarrel was with Henry of Lancaster and no other but it went further than that. That's what I am afraid of, John. I'm afraid of starting it all over again.'

'Christ, Hal,' Bedford laughed a hollow laugh. 'That's all forgotten. It was forgotten years ago.'

'Do you really believe that, John? Richard of York has not forgotten. He remembers very well who his father was and more to the point, who was his great-grandfather. If it were only blood that counted, in all honesty he's a better right to the crown than any man.'

'That's treason, Hal, and well you know it,' Bedford warned him.

'Not between us, it isn't. Surely you and I can speak openly?'

'Yes, yes, of course,' Bedford ran a hand distractedly over his close-cropped head. 'I think you're wrong, Hal,' he persisted. 'Lancaster has held the crown for over thirty-six years. It's too late to change now.'

'Possession is not absolute security, John,' Hal reminded him. 'It didn't stop Richard from being deposed. It won't stop Henry.'

Bedford stared thoughtfully into his wine. 'You consider Richard of York treasonous, then?'

'In thought, yes. Do you see how he styles himself now? Richard Plantagenet. I wonder how many men remember that the last Richard Plantagenet was king of England? I think it's a point that tells. Cardinal Beaufort has suspected it for some time,' he went on. 'He spoke to me of it once when King Henry was alive. Only it was Mortimer then, and my own loyalty was in question.' He smiled thinly. 'If I remember rightly it was Richard Neville who stirred up that particular hornets' nest. As you say, John, my quarrel is only with him, but it's like a pebble thrown into a pond. The ripples spread wide.'

'You and I do truly tread the same path,' Bedford said gravely. 'Outright peace or outright war. The road in between leads nowhere except to hell.' He buried his face in his sweating hands. Hal was right. It was not forgotten. It had never ceased to plague his brother Harry until his dying hour. He dropped his hands and raised his goblet to his lips. He caught his misted reflection in the dark, sweet wine. An old man, all old men. How many years had he left? And after him Humphrey, cruel, greedy Humphrey with his colossal vanity and only Beaufort to keep him in check — another old man whose tenacious grip on life must surely wane soon. And between them Henry, poor, timid, weak Henry with his taint of madness. He raised his eyes and stared at Hal, remembering the holocaust of their fathers' time.

'Wait a while, Hal,' he said quietly. 'For my sake and little Harry's do nothing rash yet. Let's see which way the wind is blowing. Let Salisbury have the Border, for if James is set on war then he'll have bitten off more than he can chew. Let him choke on it, Hal.' The duke sipped appreciatively at his wine, his thoughts already drifting back to France. 'From Gascony,' he said, raising his glass, and smiled grimly. 'At least that's still ours.'

King Henry the Sixth of England and Second of France blinked nervously as Lancaster Herald bawled out his long and mostly mythical list of titles. He picked agitatedly at the stain of tallow wax that soiled his gown. His hand had been shaking when he had placed his votive candle that morning. It always did; in fact he trembled from head to foot at the very thought of his uncle of Gloucester. He glanced sideways at the resplendent figure who lolled familiarly against his throne. God be praised, Henry thought, that he had forsaken silk hose for a seemly robe. Yesterday the sight of his uncle's bulging thighs had turned him sick with shame. Henry judged vanity of dress to be the worst of sins.

Lancaster Herald shattered the air again with his shrill cry. Like a raven, Henry thought, the ugly, raucous birds that swarmed over Tower Hill. He smiled vaguely at the tall man who knelt and kissed his hand. He withdrew it quickly. He did not care to be touched except by his mother. He sighed wistfully. He had not seen her for a long time, though he prayed for her daily, for her and for Master Tydier and the two happy boys who he knew in some vague way were connected to him. He liked Master Tydier. He was kind to him and had given Henry a hunting bow that he had made himself the last time they had met. It was small and sturdy and suited Henry's light frame to perfection. It was his one delight, to hunt the fleet deer and ride like the wind through forest and glade. Then his pale face grew troubled at the thought. Did he delight in it too much? Was it sinful to kill such a beautiful creature, God's creature? He had asked the question of his confessor and had received the curt reply that man must eat. He frowned, remembering. That had not been his meaning. He had meant, was it wrong to enjoy killing?

He blinked at the slight but firm pressure of the cardinal's hand upon his arm. The tall man was speaking and Henry frantically tried to recall his name from the herald's garbled screech. Northumberland. That was it. He smiled happily, pleased with himself. Of course: Northumberland, his dear Harry's sire.

'– and if it please your Grace as I can no longer serve you in this matter, I would rather yield up the office to those who think they can.'

There was a long and empty silence. Henry stared at Northumberland in panic. What matter? What office? He glanced at his uncle of Gloucester and saw his cruel mouth grow tight with displeasure. The king swallowed hard. Was it he who had displeased him? Had he noticed his attention wandering or perhaps it was the stain on his gown? Then he sighed with relief. It was not him that Gloucester glared at with such dislike but Northumberland. Anxiety returned swiftly. It was still he who would bear the brunt of it, no matter what the cause. And doubly so, for he would spend the day in a sweat of fear till the dreaded summons came. Then his uncle would pace round him like a beast stalking its prey. First he would sneer and draw out all of his faults: timid; cowardly; simple minded; a travesty of all that his father had been. He knew the list by heart. Then Gloucester would shout, his glassy eyes bulging, his heavy face purple and veined. There was a great vein in his neck which throbbed and twisted like an imprisoned serpent. Henry had nightmares that one day it would burst and twist itself bloodily around him. Eventually his uncle would strike him and there was almost pleasure in the sharp stinging blow for it meant that his misery was at an end. He was free to go then, free to run blubbering to the chapel and beg forgiveness for only God knew what sins, for he certainly did not. He only knew that he must have sinned or he would not be punished so.

Then Beaufort's soft voice slid into his ear like balm. He looked round gratefully. He loved his uncle Beaufort. He was kind to him and talked to him of God. He did not sneer or shout at him as Gloucester did.

'Your Grace. My lords,' the mellow voice eased the fear out of all but the heart of him. The warm dark eyes encompassed him, included him. He felt less a nonentity when the cardinal was there. 'If it were not for our desperate need for peace in the north, I would be loathe to let my lord of Northumberland give up the office in which he has served us so long and so well. But as it is,' the cardinal spread his jewelled hands, 'temporarily, at least, the needs of England must come before those of any one man.'

'It's a pity you didn't have those sentiments before, when you emptied the Treasury to feather your own nest,' Gloucester interrupted loudly.

The cardinal smiled blandly. 'If the Treasury is empty then I fear it is because you have rewarded followers who apparently would follow you for no other reason than for what they could get.'

Gloucester's eyes bulged in a prelude to rage. John of Bedford stepped quietly forward. 'We digress, my lords. The matter in hand is the Wardenship of the Border.' He turned to Hal and smiled. 'If we cannot dissuade you, my lord, who then do you name to negotiate this peace in your stead?'

Hal turned his amused gaze on Richard Neville's astounded face. 'Who else but my lord of Salisbury?' he murmured. 'I feel

sure his ingratiating manner will more than soothe King James.'
He cast one satisfied look at Salisbury's mortified face then he
bowed low and took his leave of the little king while the court
sniggered at Salisbury's expense. When he rose every eye was
fixed admiringly upon him for he had come dressed for the
occasion in deep sapphire velvet and there were sapphires at his
throat and sleeves. When he turned and walked from the chamber, any who remembered old Northumberland could have been
forgiven for thinking that he lived again.

The snow came early that year, pale and silent as death, frail
gossamer flakes blown by a cold and killing wind into house-high
drifts that had them immured and helpless within a week.
Alnwick sat out the siege, impregnable, its turrets sheathed in
ice, a dark secret island in an endless frozen sea. Then in
December the thaw came with a vengeance, swelling every hill,
stream and river to a black dangerous flood that overran all of the
land and stripped it clean and bare as a plague of crows. The
stores of precious winter grain were scattered; sheep and cattle
drowned. Men waded waist high in frozen mud salvaging what
they could from their wrecked homes. Then the wind dropped,
the rain ceased. They waited out the silence cowed like dogs as the
days shortened to a lead-grey hour and the sky turned yellow and
sulphurous with snow. On the first day of the new year the
blizzard began, the worst that any had ever known. It merged
land and sky into a white impenetrable wall. It closed them in,
narrowing their world to dark smoke-filled rooms where day and
night were as one. Outside it swept over the land, a great
suffocating wave that smothered all life, smothered all hope of
life. For a week the blizzard raged. Then it ceased as suddenly as it
had begun. It left a faceless anonymous land where all was silence
– a soft white pall covering the dead.

It had been the savage culmination of a bleak and bitter year. In
May the truce with the Scots had ended. As Hal had predicted,
the raids had begun, small, tentative at first; merely foraging
parties, till the word had gone out that he was mewed of his own
accord at Alnwick and that the man with whom they would have
to deal was Salisbury. Then they came in earnest, hordes of

savage rievers who would burn a village to the ground for the prize of a single hen. Salisbury had been well out of his depth by then. Experienced soldier that he was, he was at a loss with men who blatantly disregarded his orders and went their own way; for since he had ceded the Border Hal had gone about subtly undermining Salisbury's authority. He had given no direct order, there had been no need. The north had no fond memories of Neville rule. They had wanted none of him and had showed it, giving grudging obedience when forced to it but no more. Salisbury himself had made it worse. His arrogance had offended all, billetting his men without thought or care and always on those who could least afford it. Discontent had been rife and Hal had fostered it carefully, blocking Salisbury at every turn. He had supplied the necessary quota of men for the Border's defence but had pleaded sickness himself. He had balked at actually being seen to be Salisbury's underling. The raids had become more ferocious, both Scots and English taking the law into their own hands. Then in late summer, a retaliatory raid into Scotland had brought matters to a head. That the English had received a thrashing at Piperden had not mattered. The affront had been excuse enough to bring King James down from Scone to lay open siege at Roxburgh. So the day Hal had schemed for so long had come. Salisbury's livery had been like a blare of trumpets in the crowded hall and none of the carefully worded message had disguised Salisbury's desperate need. It had occurred to him to refuse, to plead his mythical illness and let Salisbury bear the full brunt of the disgrace of the loss of Roxburgh, for Salisbury must think it imminent to have sent for him at all. Instead he had drawn it out, prevaricating, so when pressed to it, there was no help for it but for Salisbury's man to say the longed-for words, 'My lord of Salisbury begs your presence at Roxburgh.'

He had ridden out within the hour, the Lion flying proudly at his head, his sons at his back. Word had gone out to every manor and if they'd held back for Salisbury they offered their life's blood for him. Every knight, every burgher, every man who could wield stick or stave turned out. By the time they reached Roxburgh they were three thousand strong. If he had needed more, it waited for him there – James had fled at the very sight of him. Not a blow was struck. Roxburgh was theirs again by dusk.

It was a triumph that even the dreadful winter that had followed could not dim. It had warmed him through all the bleak and empty days. He had fed on it, reliving each sweet, vengeful moment. He had received commendation from Westminster and a grant of a hundred pounds a year. It had been enough, till now. Now it was February with no sign of a thaw. And still Salisbury hung on.

Hal rose from his cramped and chilled position by the sullen fire. He paced a while and went to stand by the tall window that looked westward toward the hills. The moor showed a blank, austere face. Could any man fight this? He smiled wryly. How ironic if for all his scheming it was the elements that brought Salisbury down. His spies had brought him rumours of riots at Berwick, the garrison refusing duty for lack of food. He bit his lip in frustration. All hearsay. They were trapped like rats themselves. No news came in, none went out. A journey of a mile was impossible let alone further. Still, if this last year had taught him anything, it had taught him patience. It had etched deep lines round his mouth and eyes and he had acquired the habit of turning the heavy seal upon his thumb when he was distressed. He did so now as he peered into the gathering dusk. The days were so short, a few grey hours then darkness. He hated the darkness; he hated the snow. So cold and beautiful and deadly – like Elizabeth.

He looked to where his mother sat. The white lead upon her cheeks was cracked with cold and her red mouth was like a wound. She was no longer beautiful, unless there was still a vestige of it in the sharp arrogant bones. He felt a sudden rush of pity; poor Elizabeth, poor, sad, empty Elizabeth. She caught his eye and smiled, the sly, secret smile that irritated him so, as if in some way he worked her will unknowingly. Beside her, Eleanor sat demurely, her long hands folded at her waist to emphasise the pregnant swell of her gown. Thank God, he thought, that she and Harry were wed at last though the marriage had done little to diminish Elizabeth's influence. They were always together, set apart from the rest of them like some rare, alien breed. He noticed too that Eleanor had acquired that unnerving air of repose that was peculiarly Elizabeth's. He frowned. She needed to be with Harry more. Perhaps in the spring she should join him at court. The frown softened a little as he thought of Harry, still keeping his vigil over the king. His allies were thin on the ground now, for two years before, John of Bedford had died at Rouen and Hal thought sadly of the last time they had met. Hard to believe that six months later he would be dead and with so little to show for his gallant and noble life. Of course, Gloucester was supreme now with the restraining hand of his brother gone. Richard of York had the Regency of France in Bedford's stead. A step higher. A move nearer.

He turned abruptly back into the room. His thoughts came full circle again. York was Salisbury's mentor and Salisbury still held what he desired most, what was his by right. He hunched himself irritably over the fire again. A page came with fresh logs and retreated hastily at his look. The new wood spat and smouldered and he kicked it viciously into a grudging flame. They were all giving him a wide berth today since he had ordered Thomas to his chamber for brawling. If the favourite had fallen so easily from grace, what worse could they expect? He sighed, regretting bitterly that he had struck Thomas so hard. Cold and confinement had strained his temper to the limit and Thomas had more than overstepped the mark by his blunt and stubborn refusal of an apology to his battered and bloody opponent. Hal smiled with grudging admiration. Thomas had more spirit and fire than all of them put together. He was fiercely proud of him, of all his sons, but especially Thomas. He reminded him so vividly of his own father. He closed his eyes in sudden weariness. Strange how he had thought of him more these past few months than he had ever done. That was all there was to do now: think, plot, plan – scheme how to bring that dog Salisbury down. He was becoming obsessed, he thought dully. As obsessed and vengeful as Elizabeth. He opened his eyes and looked again to where his mother sat: old and withered and frail yet seemingly indestructible. Elizabeth lived on while other, better mortals died. He sighed. It had been such a time of loss these past two years. Bedford gone and three months after Roxburgh, James of Scotland had been murdered like a rat in a cellar by his own nobles. Not that he mourned James but like Bedford it was another familiar part of his life gone. His sister Bess was dead too, her frail, sad little life snuffed out giving birth to Westmorland's longed-for son. Another irony, that the daughter of Harry Hotspur should die giving life to a Neville. He thought again of his father and the bitter, vengeful creature he had left as his memorial. Was that the only bond between himself and Elizabeth? A dead man, still loved and mourned so passionately by both? Why then had he always stood between them? Why then did he still hold them apart after all these years? As a boy his mother had terrified him with her awful hatred but he was not a boy now. Was his hatred so much less than hers because he had kept it hidden and tempered with caution? Perhaps the one might have balanced the other if he had not shut himself away. He might have softened her if he had loved her more. He looked away. How ridiculous to think of Elizabeth and love. Passion, desire, sensuality, all these she would have been capable of, but not love, not that frail, tender emotion. Then he rebuked himself for the presumption. What did he really know of Elizabeth, of those dead, empty years? They had shaped himself out of all recognition. What more had they done to her? It was only her power that he had feared, that dark, secret inner knowledge that had set her apart. Yet now he would gladly have had a share in it if it could bring Salisbury and his pack down. He strained his mind toward her. Did she know? Did she really know?

He stiffened, staring hard into the fire, aware that Elizabeth had risen and was coming unbidden to stand beside him. For once her presence did not unnerve him. He had called. She had merely answered him.

'Will Salisbury fall?' he asked quietly.

She sat down beside him. With her back to the light she did not look so old. The firelight softened her fleshless cheek and lent her faded hair something of its old glory. 'Yes,' she said. 'In the spring when the thaw comes.'

He believed her and nodded.

'And what then, my son?' she questioned mildly. 'Shall you sleep again?'

He looked at her then. Their eyes, so alike, met and held like the merging of winter seas. He had been afraid of her once, of her power and the sheer force of her will. He had withstood it when no other could, yet he was no more free of her now than he had ever been. He was her son, for good or evil he was of her blood. For the first time in his life he acknowledged her. He was no longer afraid.

'Elizabeth.' His voice was so quiet that he hardly heard it himself. 'Elizabeth. Could you settle for less than all?'

She looked away from him to keep the longing from her eyes. She knew what he asked. That she should abandon her dream, that she should come down from the pinnacle that saw only kings and crowns. And in that moment of her own deep need she would have. She would have given all for the merest touch of his hand. But now it was not her dream to give up. It lived apart from her now and dwelt in the hearts and minds of other men. They would bring it to reality, not she. The only dream that she had now was that she should see its beginning. She raised her long feline eyes to her son's face. And that beginning would be his end. She had already seen the manner of his death and wept in her mind's eye over his broken and shattered bones. But not yet, not yet. There was time still. He had need of her, perhaps only for this one brief moment out of all of their lives. She smiled her lovely, evil smile and said, 'If that is all you have to offer me then it will suffice.'

Tentatively, he reached out and took her cold hand between his own. 'Then I shall not sleep,' he said hoarsely. 'Not until his name no longer lies heavy between us, not till we can speak of him together in love and honour.'

Elizabeth shivered at the unaccustomed warmth of his touch. 'Then I am content,' she said, and for that one small moment, she was.

In her chamber above the hall Alianore stood with her back to the room watching the night shadows grow tall. The faint sound of music came wandering on the wind and tapped discordantly on the glass as if demanding admittance. She thought longingly of the warmth, the laughter, the company of Hal and their sons. She might have gone down if it had not been for Elizabeth and her arch knowing stare. And Eleanor – worst of all Eleanor, flaunting her belly like a trophy.

She moved away and drew her robe a little closer. She was cold, unbearably cold for all her furs and the fire that burned day and night in the hearth. Nothing would penetrate the chill of misery that had settled round her heart. She had gone to Leconfield that summer as she had planned. It was the last time she had been happy, the last time she had been free of guilt, free of Elizabeth who was a constant reminder of what she had done. Even now, a year later, she still mourned the child she had destroyed. It had been a boy, small and perfect – and dead. It had been a year of destruction, burning and killing, flood and famine. They had been roasted, frozen and half drowned in turn. Now they froze again – and starved. That morning she had counted the sacks of grain. Only twelve left. Barely enough to feed themselves let alone the poor, homeless wretches who came each day to beg bread. They would wait from dawn till dusk for a mere crust. It was that dreadful quiet patience that disturbed her. Even the children, silent as corpses, only their great hungry eyes alive. Seven more had died yesterday, frozen like effigies. There would be more tomorrow and nothing she could do. They would be on short commons themselves in a week or two and still there was no sign of a thaw.

She shivered and moved to the fire. She heard the wind like a caged beast in the chimney wall. She hated the wind. Even here, behind their high protective walls, it snarled and worried like an angry dog, tearing at the hangings, dousing the fires and filling the rooms with choking, useless smoke. She rose and prowled restlessly, wondering if Hal would come. He came less and less now and she could not blame him. She could offer him nothing but the empty sterile shell she had become. They were both obsessed; he with Salisbury, she with her guilt. Damn Salisbury, she thought savagely. She bit her lip in shame. *Salisbury*. No more her beloved Richard, no more her dear and tender brother. He was Salisbury now, even to her. Salisbury, the enemy who had changed and warped all their lives. Her pacing grew more restive and she thought of Thomas, sullen and resentful in confinement. Should she go and offer him comfort? The word rang mockingly in her head. Jesu, if any needed comfort it was she, and who was there to give it now. The boys were grown and past need of her. Catherine had gone to Edmund Grey, Anne to Thomas Hungerford. There was only Joan and she was nothing but remembered pain. There was no help in God, for by her own grievous sin she had placed herself beyond that comfort. She felt the tears well up inside her but they never came. It would have been comfort enough just to have wept, to cleanse herself in tears. All her tears were ice, frozen deep inside that small, pathetic corpse buried at Leconfield.

She lay down wearily among the furs of the bed. The music had stopped. There were voices, a shout of laughter, crisp stumbling footsteps across the snow. She closed her eyes. Tomorrow, she thought drowsily. Tomorrow she would venture down, despite Elizabeth, despite Eleanor. She'd wear green satin and bind her hair with pearls. There would be dancing; music to drive out the demons, a fire to warm the cold from her. Perhaps there would be fresh meat — a suckling pig, a peacock roast and glazed with honey. She smiled dreamily at the thought and saw Hal resplendent in dark velvet. Diamonds blazed hotly at his throat and he was smiling, the slow tender smile that always turned her weak with love. He held out a hand that glittered with rings. She felt a ridiculous desire to laugh. Such wealth and only salt fish for supper! Then they were all laughing. Elizabeth, demure and nunly, showed sharp white teeth. Eleanor simpered, painted and rouged like a harlot. Hal, still smiling, led her to the high table where a feast was spread. Haunches of venison glazed with frumenty, a roast swan done up in its feathers with a gilded beak. There was a blare of trumpets and a great silver dish was borne in and laid before her. With a flourish Hal lifted the lid. The laughter grew. There, roast to perfection, was the body of her dead child. An apple was stuffed obscenely in its mouth.

She screamed and the sound tore through the great vaulted rooms so that the stone itself trembled. She felt strong arms around her, heard her name called dementedly and still she screamed till in despair Hal struck her. It was still dark but she knew it was Hal who held her.

'Oh, Nel. My dear, sweet, Nel. What is it? For pity's sake, what is it?'

Her lips moved wordlessly against his face. He held her away from him, stroking her hair. 'It was a dream, Nel. Only a dream. You're safe. There's nothing to be afraid of.'

She clung to his warmth, to the strong, steady sound of his voice. When she could speak, all she said was, 'Hold me,' over and over again. Only within his arms was she truly safe.

He held her in the darkness. How thin she was, how pitifully thin. Had he been so preoccupied that he could not have seen this quiet inner wasting? Was it Salisbury? Did she still care? Was it his persecution of her brother that had brought her so low? He dismissed the frightening thought before it took shape. He was too far gone to turn back now. He kissed her gently. 'Poor Nel. It's all right. It'll come all right. This can't last forever. All of us are half demented with it but it'll pass. It'll be spring soon.' He laughed softly. 'Do you remember spring, Nel? Soft and green and warm?'

She smiled despite herself. 'Yes. I remember.'

'Think on that then, my love. In the spring we'll go to Court. We'll see what manner of courtier they've made out of Harry, shall we? And what manner of king he's made out of Henry.'

She looked up at him then, straining her eyes to his face. There was a new confidence in his voice, an eagerness that she had not heard for years. Something had happened tonight. Had he received news of Salisbury? She relinquished him while he lit the candle. The flame guttered then steadied between his cupped hands. Alianore stared at him. He seemed younger, more assured than ever she'd seen him. Then he turned to her and smiled. She looked full into the long green eyes of Elizabeth.

The hart turned at bay, its nostrils streaming white, vaporous cloud. It plunged once in a wild, angry circle, the broken shaft in its hindquarters streaking the snow with blood. Then it stood mute and quivering, its proud head raised, the long velvety throat stretched and bared as if for the knife.

Hal dismounted and waited whilst the huntsmen whipped back the clamourous dogs. They were no better than dogs themselves, wild-eyed and slavering at the raw smell of blood. Swiftly he drew the knife against the submissive throat. The blood spurted in hot, rich jets against his hands and brought howls of delight from the men. They danced like children round the dismembered corpse and Hal smiled grimly. That it had come to this; that the thought of fresh meat could turn them silly as boys. It had been weeks since they had tasted anything but broth and coarse bread, weeks since they'd stretched their legs farther than the hall's length, since they'd breathed anything but stifling smoke and their own sweat. This was more than just food. This was freedom and release from the long, dark prison of winter.

They rode home by the winding forest track, the steady drip of melting snow like music in their ears. Tom Clifford rode silently beside Hal, the only one among them who would have presumed so much. Neither man spoke. It was one of his nephew's virtues that he never did so without good cause. Then Thomas careered past them at a reckless pace. Hal checked the reproof that rose to his lips. He felt almost light-headed himself. The very air was intoxicating, cold and clear, burning his throat like strong young wine. Overhead tiny buds pricked from spindly branches and spears of green thrust stubbornly from their prison of frozen earth. There was one taller than the rest, and a half-formed flower dropped bravely from its stem. Hal smiled. A survivor – as he was. He remembered that Albany had said that of him once. He had been flattered then. But just to survive. Was that enough? It was only one better than mere existence. Never to run a risk, to gamble on winning or losing. He had never lost but then he had never really won either. Elizabeth always said, better to be an eagle for a day than a sparrow for all of your life.

He blinked as they emerged from the darkness of the forest. The snow still lay thickly on the fields, irridescent as pearls in the last rays of the sun. Below him the river ran at full spate, fed by the thaw. He looked up toward Alnwick and saw how the sun had burnished the stone to a fiery glow. The shadows crept up from the river like thieves, devouring the light and warmth, climbing the long ridge hand over hand to settle darkly in the hollows of the curtain wall. Above the wide sweep of the ramparts the intricate towers strained toward the fading light; the squat drum towers of the Barbican, the great octagonal keep, the rounded bastions of the watchtowers, all burning like candle flames in a corona of amber light as the sun plunged earthward at their back. No nest for sparrows, Hal thought. Only an eagle would have dared to make his eyrie there. Then he stiffened with premonition. Across the dark, empty space his mother's voice called softly.

He kicked his horse to a gallop, thundering across the flooded bridge, cursing as the clinging mud held him back. Elizabeth's voice still murmured above the rushing stream. He laughed with sheer elation. They had won, together they had won.

She waited to greet him, her pale face burning white with triumph. Her long fingers clenched the letter to her breast. The king's seal hung like a gobbet of blood against her wrist. He had no need to hear it but she said, 'Salisbury has resigned. The king bids you take command of the Border with all speed.'

1445–1450

'Si douce est la Marguerite'

– Jean Froissart

The noise of the revelling continued long into the summer night. It was well past curfew but the Londoners still celebrated, rolling in a glorious, drunken tide from street to street. Drums banged, trumpets shrilled, the king and queen's device flapped in mad ecstasy from every roof, their names were cried with raucous joy: 'Henry and Margaret. Henry and Margaret. Long live King Henry and Queen Margaret.'

Down by the water's edge bonfires flared and stained the sky like blood. The flames leapt higher, blown by a sudden and treacherous wind and threw off a vortex of sparks that spun and whirled like golden chaff. The crowds danced dementedly, shoulder to shoulder, arm in arm: beggars in rags; burghers in soft velvet; fishmongers in reeking homespun; and all the while the golden rain blew about them, hot needles of fire streaming westward on a veering wind. None saw the huddle of little boats moored in the shadow of the tall Hanse warehouses that stored all England's wealth of wool, or noticed the stray sparks feeding hungrily on the dry, oily decks. The flames roared suddenly from stem to stern, mastheads blazed like beacons. Then all the wooden jetty was ablaze and the warehouse was engulfed in a solid sheet of flame.

The crowds stood in stunned and sober silence as the stench of burning wool and fleece filled the air. A priest ran from their midst and crossed himself at this fearful omen and a voice cried out to God to preserve them from the 'Frenchwoman'. Rats slithered out from their damp lairs to bask in the fiery glow. The priest muttered fervently. The crowd wept. The river coiled like the Oriflamme down to Westminster.

In the great vaulted hall the dancers spun and swayed with courtly restraint. The minstrels played softly, the high clear treble of horn and rebec subdued by the bass of dancing feet. There was wine in abundance, the light, dry vintage of Anjou to honour the king's bride. They had been feasted well and royally, every delicacy of which their starved Lenten palates could conceive, yet still the laughter was discreet, the glitter of jewels subdued. Candles had been lit to ward off the night for none wanted to relinquish this glorious day. Only the king himself seemed weary of it.

He sat at the head of the throng, his narrow head drooping beneath the weight of the crown. His robes were of crimson velvet trimmed with ermine. He wore them like shackles, his thin shoulders slumped beneath some invisible burden. Elizabeth from her close vantage point below the dais regarded him with scornful pity. So this was the heir of Agincourt, the son of the man who had humbled all France? Could fate have dealt a crueller blow to the might of Lancaster? She smiled happily. As well to set a log on the throne.

At the young girl beside him, basking in his foolish smile, she looked more closely. Margaret of Anjou was small and fair but with a sharpness both of feature and wit that made her look older than her fifteen years. The Pauper Queen, Elizabeth had heard some say, for all knew that she had brought England nothing in the way of dowry, arriving with little more than the gown she stood up in and an equally destitute retinue. That had soured the match once and for all as far as Parliament was concerned. Proud, penniless, and French at that! But she had been the king's choice, and the Council had been desperate enough for an heir not to cross him. That quiet desperation still showed in the faces of the men who stood round the throne. New faces, though strangers only to her, for William de la Pole, Earl of Suffolk was already well entrenched with the queen. It was he who had negotiated so hard and so long for this marriage. It was also Suffolk, though few knew of it yet, who had bartered away England's prized possession of Maine to do it. Close by him, a tall man poured wine for the queen. Edmund Beaufort, Earl of Somerset, young, dark, handsome, a contender for the recently abandoned Regency of France and Richard of York's greatest rival. He wore burgundy velvet worked all over with the queen's device. His eyes dwelling long and lustfully on her face proclaimed where both his interest and ambition lay.

Elizabeth's eyes went again to the young queen. She had dismissed her as a nonentity and yet . . . She turned, her thoughts diverted as a shadow fell across her. Henry, Cardinal Beaufort and Bishop of Winchester, inclined his huge body in a mocking bow.

'Madam,' he said breathlessly, 'we are well met. It has been a long time.'

Elizabeth waited courteously whilst he seated himself. She remembered that the last time they had met she had been on her knees before his half-brother Bolingbroke. 'Indeed, your Grace, a long time,' she said coolly. 'I had thought you long dead by now.'

'And so I should be. So should we both be.' The long reptilian eyes were lost in the semblance of a smile. 'I sometimes wonder if there is some reason why we linger on. Or is it just the spleen of the gods to parade all this youth and beauty before us and taunt us with the knowledge that we shall never have such ourselves again?'

The shrewd and worldly gaze appraised her and there was enough vanity still left in her to be glad that for the first time in forty years she had put off her mourning. She wore deep and somnolent green, the sleeves and bodice latched with gold. A thin gold fillet held her veil in place. It fell soft and flattering as candlelight around her sharp, arrogant face. She said, 'Is youth and beauty so much to be desired, then, my lord? I would not rate it above wit and perception.'

'No. Perhaps not.' Beaufort smiled cynically. 'Indeed, I have never felt the loss of it. I was born old and ugly. But you, Isabella. You had great beauty once. I remember that as a raw young clerk

I cherished a most unholy passion for you. Do you not miss that, Isabella? Do you never mourn its passing?'

He had used her old courtly name and for a moment beneath his passionate stare she was young and beautiful again with all the world and Harry Hotspur at her feet. Then she smiled bleakly. 'I fear I have had greater things to mourn since then. What matters age or youth or beauty if one is alone?'

'And yet,' he leant forward so that she could see the purple threading of veins beneath his florid skin, 'and yet I have never thought of you as being anything else. You were always a rare creature. Aloof, separate, so much more than us mere mortals.'

Elizabeth smiled at the subtle thrust. 'Sarcasm becomes you even less than your cardinal's hat,' she retorted. 'And you're too unholy a wretch yourself to sit in judgement on me.'

Beaufort laughed soft and deep in his throat. 'Well said and well deserved.' He reached out and raised her hand to his full lips. 'You still have wit and perception, Isabella, a beauty of a more enduring kind.'

'You flatter me, my lord. And unnecessarily. I am long past the need for such a sop.'

He relinquished her hand regretfully. 'Then you are even less human than I thought.' He cocked his head inquisitively. 'What are your needs then, Isabella? Love, kindness, admiration? None of these, it seems. What has kept you alive then? What has kept you sane all these long and lonely years?'

He spoke mockingly to provoke her and Elizabeth laughed. 'Oh, my dear Cardinal. For a man so skilled in guile and deceit you are remarkably transparent. What is it you want me to say? That I still plot and scheme and call up the Devil against Lancaster?' She looked past the cardinal's bloated face to the drooping figure of the king. 'What need is there for scheming now?' she said softly. 'He will be his own downfall.'

Beaufort's eyes hardened and he maintained his attitude of friendly familiarity only with an effort. 'And do not deny that you won't be glad of it.'

Elizabeth merely smiled. 'I doubt I shall be here to be glad or otherwise. I am an old woman, Cardinal. Contrary to rumour, I am not immortal.'

She had struck at some hidden despair in him for he turned quite pale and sickly. 'Wish to God that you were,' he murmured irreverently. 'I'd sell my soul this moment for a share in it.' Then he gave a short, hard laugh. 'You see? Senility touches me already – to make such a blasphemous statement. And publicly.'

Elizabeth said gravely, 'Are you so afraid of death then, my lord?'

'Not death so much as its prelude.' Beaufort raised a jaundiced eye to her face. 'I resent the decay, the mouldering of my wits. I resent the thought of having to leave the field with only half the battle won.'

'I thought your battle *was* won. I do not see my lord of Gloucester here.'

Beaufort gave a grim smile. No. Gloucester was not here nor like to be for a while if he had any sense. Too many bore him a grudge for him ever to want to show his face at Court again. The king for one, whose long sufferance of Gloucester had shown him to be the stuff that martyrs were made of. Beaufort thought acidly that no doubt he would still be suffering in pious silence if Gloucester had not turned his spleen on Queen Katherine. Poor Katherine, even he'd shed a tear or two at her death. She'd had so little happiness that if she'd found it at last, albeit illicitly with a common Welsh squire, well, he for one had not grudged it. All had known of it. All had turned a blind eye – all except Gloucester. Out of nothing more than spite he'd hounded her to a bleak and lonely death at Bermondsey, sealed off from the world and her lusty Welsh paramour who still languished for his sins in Newgate gaol. They said her mind had gone at the last, shattered like a flawed crystal, and knowing the harsh sadistic rule at Bermondsey, he could well believe it. Almost eight years ago now but Henry had not forgotten. It must have made Gloucester's eventual fall all the sweeter. But Beaufort was too prudent a man to gloat openly and he said mildly, 'Gloucester is merely in disgrace through the downfall of that strumpet wife of his. I do not doubt that like the phoenix he will rise again.'

'But not without his plumage badly singed, I think,' Elizabeth observed. 'A man can survive all manner of disgrace but to be publicly branded the consort of a witch.' Her voice grew soft and malicious. 'And I'm sure it was publicly, my lord. As public as you could make it. I hear that his duchess was paraded half naked through the streets before you had her immured for life.'

'*I?*' Beaufort protested in mock innocence. 'Not I but justice. Eleanor Cobham was tried by her peers and found guilty of employing the black arts against our sovereign lord the king. She had leech books in her possession meant for killing, not curing and an image was found beneath her mattress stuck with steel pins. What more proof was needed that she intended the king's demise and to place that oaf Gloucester on the throne?' He smiled his broken, unpleasant smile. 'She was fortunate, my lady. It is the custom here in England for witches to be burnt.'

Elizabeth turned to look at him. 'You think I should remember that, my lord?'

He replied gravely. 'It would be as well, perhaps, madam.'

Elizabeth sighed wearily. 'Is that a warning, my lord? I see by your face that there is a moral to this anecdote of poor Eleanor's fall. Well then, we have fenced with words long enough. Put up your sword, Cardinal. I shall tell you what you came to hear.' She leant toward him and for a moment the world narrowed to the cold fire in her eyes. 'Firstly, do not threaten me, my lord, for I have been dead too long to fear death, a prisoner too long to fear captivity. What's to come will come and there's naught that you or I can do to hasten or divert it. Lancaster will fall in God's good time and neither you nor I will be here to mourn or rejoice. And secondly,' she leant closer still, 'I use nothing so crude as effigies and steel pins.'

He recoiled from her visibly, shaking his scarlet robes free as if from some contagion. 'You dare to lay your blasphemous tongue to God's name?' he hissed. 'Out of charity, I'll say your mind is touched, turned by grief and loneliness. But I know. I know you for the enemy as I did the first time I laid eyes on you all those years ago.'

'And I you, my lord,' she answered him calmly. 'I have never tried to hide it. Why have you?'

He drew himself up and smiled his bland smile to cover his fear and rage. 'Remember, madam,' he said heavily, 'It is our custom to burn witches.'

He left her smiling, a quiet inscrutable smile that showed nothing of the pleasurable surge of power that pounded through her tired veins. So it was not over. She was still a force to be reckoned with, still to be feared, even by one as fearless as Beaufort himself. She leant back in the small gilded chair that had been placed for her comfort. She watched the dancers drifting past and saw how they watched her, speculating on her age, her past, why she was even here at all. It still seemed incredible to her that she was. Freedom after so many years: its sweetness was undreamt of, like the first heady taste of a fine rare wine. She had thought herself past vanity, past the tortuous delights of intrigue and scandal, past the stimulation of argument and debate. She had forgotten so much, she who thought she remembered all.

There was another infinitely sweeter freedom. Her mind had been loosed at last from its chains. The dream had passed into solid reality. She had touched it, kissed it, heard its young, arrogant voice like a clarion call. At first she had felt almost abandoned. All her life had moved slowly and painfully toward that moment. She had suffered such loss and grief for it and now in the moment of its fulfilment she saw only emptiness beyond. And far worse had been the realisation that her own part had been so small, so unimportant – so needless. All would have run its course with or without her. Had she sacrificed her beloved Harry for nothing? Had she driven her own son to the limits of his affection and endurance without cause? Later she had seen that there had been no help for it. She had *known* and the knowledge had driven her on. Like a leaf in a vortex, whether she willed it or not, she had been drawn inexorably down. And all else with her, she thought bitterly. Whatever she had touched she had corrupted. Her eyes sought Hal in the throng. Was it too late to turn him from Lancaster's doomed cause? But then, she reminded herself, when had she ever swayed him from anything that his heart was set upon? She could lead him, advise him, but in the matter of loyalty he was essentially his own master. Once, a few years ago, she thought she'd had him tamed. After Salisbury's disgrace and resignation they'd made a tacit peace. He had consulted her daily, seeking her advice, using her mind, her knowledge. And she had shared it gladly. What joy to be needed, revered, to be united at last even if only against a common enemy. He had not failed her in that. He'd fought long and hard against Salisbury and even though this last year Salisbury had regained control of the West March, it had taken him eight years to do it. Then she rose with the body of the Court and sank into a deep, mocking obeisance as the king and queen made ready to retire. A voice, equally mocking, spoke softly in her ear. 'I fear our royal rose is wilting.'

She turned and looked into the pale eyes of her great-nephew Richard of York. 'Yes,' she answered, turning back toward the king. 'I think he will always tire easily. He has not the stomach for a long fight.'

'But she has, I fancy. Our fair flower of Anjou.'

Elizabeth frowned. Yes. Margaret! She might perhaps be a force to be reckoned with in time. If she had the fight and spirit she might compensate for the lack of it in Henry. Well enough to be a rallying point for dispirited and disillusioned Lancastrians? Elizabeth doubted it and said confidently, 'Do not trouble yourself, nephew. All will be York's in time.'

York looked away and made an elaborate pretence of calling for wine. He was too cautious to declare himself openly, even to her. And sadly, it would be through that very caution that success would always elude him. Elizabeth had had great hopes of him once. She had thought him the chosen one, the vehicle that would carry her Mortimer blood to the glory of kingship. Who else was more fitted? Who else had the absolute and undeniable right of heritage? Yet one look into that fair cunning face had dispelled her illusions. There had been something reminiscent in those pale eyes of her old enemy John of Gaunt. A loser? Yes, Richard of York was a loser; always a close runner but never quite able to grasp the prize. Like her, he was merely an instrument, a tool in the building of a dynasty. She had known this for almost a year now, since the day she had first laid eyes on him in the hall at Fotheringay. The discovery had shattered her. Who then? she had thought. Where else was there to turn? Then the frosty gleam of heavy silk had caught her eyes. Across the room York's duchess advanced, gowned and jewelled like a queen. She had bestowed a condescending smile upon her sister Alianore. At

Elizabeth, standing close beside her husband, she had looked with suspicion. Elizabeth had asked him there and then. 'Have you sons, my lord?' He had, a brood of healthy, boisterous sons bred from that tainted Neville womb. The bitter irony of it had struck her like a blow. This would be no particular victory for her, no triumph of York over Lancaster, Mortimer over Neville. All their blood was united in this child's veins. His name was Edward, a fair handsome boy so tall and broad that he had looked twice his years. He wore cloth of gold and the sun had gilded his hair to pure flame. Trembling, she had thought of the prophesy: 'And there shall come a giant, snow white in colour, and he shall beget a people that is radiant.' Edward had advanced toward her, smiling with faint curiosity. His eyes were blue and full of charm and when they rested on her eager face she was no longer a withered crone. For one brief moment she was young and beautiful and infinitely desirable again; for all his life, Edward Plantagenet would look at women like that. She had known then with such certainty that all the blood had drained from her and left her pale and staring. No vision, this. No figment of her tired imagination. This dream had mortal shape. She had knelt and taken his small hand to her mouth. Against the soft fragrant flesh she had whispered passionately, 'Oh, my lord. My gracious lord.'

Of those watching most had thought her crazed. Only the boy's mother had seemed undisturbed. Cecily Neville had come herself to raise Elizabeth up. Face to face, eye to eye, the two had exchanged a look of perfect understanding.

Now she took the cup of wine from York's ringed hand and gave a covert glance around the hall and saw how they were watched discreetly. She murmured, 'And what follows now, nephew? What shall you do, now that you have relinquished the Regency of France? Where higher can you climb?'

Still he would not be drawn, though his eyes said more than he himself was prepared to. 'I do not count the Regency a loss,' he said carefully. 'It was and is a thankless task and one that I was not prepared to finance indefinitely from my own revenues. If the king wishes to maintain his possessions in France, then he must provide the money to do so or find some other fool prepared to empty his pockets for glory.' His mouth turned down sulkily. Vanity forbade that he own to abandoning Normandy to anarchy because he could not stem the rising tide of French power, yet for the term of his Regency disaster had followed disaster, culminating in the humiliating loss of Pontoise and all its garrison. And still Beaufort whined for peace, sanctioning the release of Charles of Orleans after twenty-five years as a sop to Burgundy. It had gained them nothing but a paltry two-year truce. Nor had this farce of a marriage gained any greater reward. He swallowed hard on his rage and disgust. Parliament blamed him, he knew that. And then to have the gall to ask him to be patient with regard to the twenty thousand pounds they owed him. And who could have done better? he thought savagely. Who could have done better with an empty treasury and all this mealy-mouthed talk of peace? Edmund Beaufort for one thought he could. York glanced sullenly to where Somerset sat and become suddenly aware that the earl was observing him closely. His fair skin flushed with irritation and he said hotly, 'Somerset is watching us like a hawk and I've no mind to give his scurrilous tongue greater licence than it already has.' His mouth twitched into an embarrassed smile. 'I fear, Elizabeth, that your reputation is well known, even now.'

'You make me sound like a whore,' Elizabeth remarked drily.

York flushed a deeper red. 'I referred to your past allegiances, my lady.'

Elizabeth looked at him with mild disdain. 'Not past, my lord. Not ever past – though I think that if my loyalty rested only in you it might waver.'

She let him go, watching him scurry like a frightened rabbit to the safety of his Neville ranks. And Jesu, but there were enough of them, she thought bitterly. Like a private army they filled half the hall. Salisbury and his four brothers, his numerous sons and well-married daughters. There was gall: for Salisbury to have married his eldest son to the Beauchamp girl and then within the year to have all the vast earldom of Warwick swept into his grasp by her father's untimely death. She sipped irritably at the tepid wine. The room was growing hot, the music louder and more frenzied since the king's departure. Her frail body was tiring yet her mind ran ceaselessly on, memorising faces, striving to put names to them before they came to make themselves known. Some came out of courtesy: her granddaughter Catherine and her husband Edmund Grey; and this thin, sallow youth must be Lord Greystoke's son, a travesty indeed of the tall black-browed giant she had known. Some came out of sheer curiosity. Some, like old Talbot of Shrewsbury, out of remembrance. At Jacquetta, the widow of John of Bedford, she looked long and hard, as if into a mirror. She had married again with most unseemly haste, an unknown knight called Woodville. Now as the fathomless eyes met hers she felt a power that equalled her own, surpassed it even, for as hers was waning, this other grew and waxed strong.

The brief encounter took the last of her strength and she searched the hall wearily for Hal. Instead she found Eleanor dancing sensuously with a tall, dark man. She pursed her mouth in disapproval. Eleanor had proved a grave disappointment; all that early promise diverted into the sensual gratification of her flesh, all her art employed in nothing more malevolent than coaxing Thomas into her bed. As Elizabeth had pointed out scathingly, if a man had to be coaxed, he was not worthy of the honour. Not that this latest admirer would need coaxing. He all but devoured Eleanor with his eyes. His face was disturbingly familiar though he was too young to be known to her. The effort of recollection became too much and she closed her eyes, only to open them again as a light kiss fell upon her cheek.

Thomas' vivid gaze roused her immediately. 'Come, *ma reine*,' he said teasingly. 'I have watched you holding court all night and though you must be weary of flattery, I shall tell you that ancient withered crone though you are, you have outshone every woman here tonight.'

Elizabeth raised a thin brow. 'That is flattery, Thomas?'

He grinned and then said with real concern, 'You look tired, *ma reine*.'

She smiled the rare, loving smile she kept only for him and for Hal. 'Yes, Thomas,' she said. 'I am.' Until now she had not realised how desperately tired she was.

Through the wide-flung windows of the tall London house the night sounds came, disturbing the silence of the small, panelled chamber where Eleanor sat alone. The night was hot and plagued by tiny flies that hung in a buzzing haze beneath the roof. A dog barked, a bell chimed. There were footsteps, the slow, ponderous tread of the Watch. Somewhere a woman laughed drunkenly. Eleanor stretched herself like a cat on the rumpled silks of her bed. Music, the exquisite, heady music of life, and Jesu, could she not have danced to its tune if she'd had half the chance. It was here she belonged, among the noise and laughter, among the vivid, squalid luxury of the narrow streets and tall gabled houses. She thought longingly of the Court, of the elegant women in their fine silks and velvets, of the men – especially of the men. Not dull, witless louts like Harry but smooth, polished, jewel-bright men who flattered and courted her. Men like Richard Neville, Earl of Warwick. She smiled languorously, remembering his dark intense eyes upon her face. Jesu, how he had wanted her. And he could have had her too if there had been time or opportunity. Never in all her life had a man made her feel so wanton, so provocative. The very touch of him had been fire.

She rose from the bed, her flesh burning at the thought. She was naked beneath the thin nightrobe and she paused before the long silver glass. Her eyes moved critically from the firm, high breasts to the slender waist that could still be spanned by a man's two hands despite the birth of three daughters. Her head was tilted back and her unbound hair streamed like quicksilver to her waist. Beneath thin, querulous brows her eyes gleamed under heavy milk-white lids. Her lips were parted eagerly as if in expectation of a kiss. She laughed softly. Yes. Warwick had wanted her – the only question was, how much?

She sighed. Elizabeth was right. She had the soul of a harlot. She would never dream of yielding without advantage to herself, especially to a man like Warwick who could provide so much. Her red mouth curved in a calculating little smile. What price then the rich prize of her body? What did she long for most? Not jewels or trinkets, she had those in plenty. Position she also had. But influence, a place at Court, the ear of Henry's malleable young queen. It was what she desired most in all the world –

except perhaps for Thomas. Her face hardened as she thought of him. They had danced together once that night, a stiff tortuous rondeau that had kept their bodies tantalisingly apart. Only their hands had touched. It had been pain and pleasure both. The ecstasy of his nearness, the torment of his eyes, for he knew that she wanted him. He knew he roused her like a bitch on heat. Swiftly she conjured up Warwick's lustful face as a salve, then thought weakly, Thomas sometimes looked at her like that; when he was bored, when he was drunk, when he emerged from one of those long brooding silences that were usually the prelude to a violent quarrel with one or other of them. Nine times out of ten it was Harry and once she had foolishly thought that the friction between the two brothers was because of her, because Thomas desired and coveted her and only honour held him back. He had soon dispelled that pretty dream. She had learnt since that Thomas took whatever he wanted with little thought for the consequences. It was the only real despair she had ever known: that he had never wanted her.

Unsteadily she poured herself wine from the gilded pitcher by the bed. She disliked the taste but enjoyed the pleasurable warmth that spread through her limbs. Then she turned, startled, as the door opened softly. 'Harry?' She frowned. 'I did not hear you knock.'

Her husband smiled thinly. 'That is because I did not. Should I have? After all, you are my wife, or have you forgotten?'

She saw his eyes dwelling on her breasts, not hard and lustful as Warwick's had been, but half apologetic, grateful almost, like a hopeful mistreated dog. She drew her robe closer. 'What is it you want, Harry?' she asked wearily. 'I am tired.'

'I have no doubt of that,' he said grimly. 'Though you might not be quite so weary if you had not flaunted yourself all night like a whore.'

'And what would you know of such women, Harry?' Eleanor retorted scornfully. 'You've barely the stamina to keep your own wife content let alone a woman whose living depends on it.' She smiled spitefully as she saw the anguish in his eyes. 'It seems to me that you keep too close company with the king, Harry. You've become as monkish and dull as he is.' She sighed. 'Poor Margaret.

I don't envy her this night. I've no doubt that his Grace will be on his knees, but not astride the queen.' She laughed raucously as she saw her husband's mortified look. He hated her to be coarse. 'You're blushing like a virgin, Harry. Do I shame you so?' She moved toward him, loosening the robe so that it fell open to show her nakedness. 'Do you want me, Harry?' she whispered, knowing full well that even if he did she had already rendered him impotent with her sneers. 'No, of course not.' She laughed as she turned away. 'I forgot. You have to be drunk for that.'

'Eleanor.' He cried out in such a terrible voice that for a moment she thought she had gone too far. Then slowly the blood showed again beneath his ashen skin. His angry mouth was firm, controlled. It was that iron control that she resented so much. She could bait him till kingdom come but never once had she provoked him beyond that silent grimness he showed to her now. If just once he had thrashed her as she deserved, she might have cared for him more.

'Eleanor.' His voice held no tremor now, nothing to show that he had come as near to breaking point as he ever would. Flat, calm, dull, like a priest intoning the Mass, he spoke as if nothing more weighty than the time of day had passed between them. 'I came to tell you to make ready to leave tomorrow. We are returning to the north.'

Now it was her turn to reach breaking point and she'd not been brought to it slowly as Harry had. She was flung hard up against it so that her whole body trembled from the force of the blow. 'Leave?' Her voice was an outraged scream. 'Why? I thought we were to stay for the Parliament.'

'Well, we are not. Our plans are changed. My lord Northumberland decrees it.'

She glared at him in cold fury. 'My lord Northumberland decrees it.' Dear God, how pompous and self important he sounded, like one of his father's mealy-mouthed clerks. And why had he said it at all? As if she cared by whose word she was to be plunged into boredom and misery. Then her eyes narrowed. 'You,' she hissed. 'It's you who have instigated this. You want to pack me off back to the north, back to that God-forsaken wilderness.'

He returned her venomous look unflinchingly though she spat and screeched like a cat. Stiffly he said above her howling, 'Now that father has resigned the East March into my care, I cannot stay in London indefinitely. I have my duties to attend to.'

'Then *you* go,' she screamed at him. 'I'll not pine for you, Harry. I can promise you that.'

He turned his back on her and moved toward the door. 'Be ready, Eleanor,' he said before he closed it on her contorted face. 'We shall leave at noon.'

Furiously she paced the narrow room. She wouldn't go. Not now she'd tasted this. She chewed at her lip till it bled. What of Warwick? What of the court and all her carefully laid plans? She snatched up the goblet of wine, then retched in disgust at the cluster of flies feeding on the rim. She sank back, defeated, on to the bed. The defiance and rage ebbed slowly from her. Of course she would go. What other choice was there but to follow Harry? She'd been a fool to push him so far. Perhaps if she'd been kinder she might have coaxed him into letting her stay. The rage gnawed at her again. Jesu, what a prospect, living out all her life dependent on his whim, coaxing and cajoling him from what did not please. She thought with loathing of his pale ineffectual hands upon her flesh, groping, probing, rousing her to nothing but a screaming pitch of revulsion while he grunted and strained with pent-up breath to maintain the surge of blood to that limp and lifeless scrap of flesh laying inert upon her thigh. She had roused him well enough once, too well, for he was always quickly spent while she still jerked and thrashed towards a culmination that always seemed to elude her. She had grown colder and he more of a failure in his desperate anxiety to please. It had degenerated into a pleasureless ritual for both of them. Harry only attempted it now when he was desperate or drunk or both.

She sat up, plucking distractedly at the braiding of her robe. Jesu Mary, she thought. She could not live like that, yet what else? Who else? Who was there to turn to? Elizabeth. The very name was balm to her savage thoughts.

Elizabeth was still asleep when the discreet but urgent rapping came. She rarely slept longer than a few hours, the rest of the time

229

she drifted in shadow, projecting her mind back and forth at will. But this night sleep had lain upon her like a heavy suffocating pall. When she finally struggled awake her mind was stagnant and void. She stared blankly at Eleanor shivering by the door. 'What is it?' she asked in a strange, distant voice.

Eleanor sat heavily on the edge of the bed. 'It's Harry,' she said sullenly. 'Did you know that we were returning home tomorrow?'

Elizabeth lay back on her pillows. No, she had not known, but suddenly there were a great many things she did not know. 'And I presume that you do not want to go,' she said faintly.

'Of course I do not want to go.' Eleanor was suddenly assailed with a vision of endless purposeless days at Alnwick, or Berwick or Warkworth, or whichever cold stone vault Harry chose to immure her in. She saw Alianore's sad reproachful face as she mothered her neglected daughters. Thomas would be there to torment her. Thomas, Ralph, Richard, George, William, all that hearty masculine company and never one flattering look for her. 'Do you blame me? You suffered it long enough,' she said, 'You know what it is like.' She wrung her hands wretchedly. 'I had such high hopes of this time at Court.'

'Was my lord of Warwick one of those hopes?' Elizabeth questioned sharply.

'And if he was? What matters the means if the end is achieved? You have told me that yourself often enough.'

'Yes. I told you that. And at the time I did not think I had to qualify it. It seems that I must. I had not thought you so witless, Eleanor.' She laid her pale hands together as if in prayer. 'What end do you think Warwick can bring you to? None but the worst, for though he is possessed of great lands he is still young and relatively without power. I can assure you that his father Salisbury has him well in harness still. Moreover, his family are the bitterest enemies of your own.'

'What is that to me? I feel no loyalty to Northumberland nor ever will.'

'It is not of loyalty that I speak,' Elizabeth said wearily. 'It is disloyalty, such as you flung in your husband's face when you flaunted yourself so openly with Warwick. Such blatant disregard for family feeling calls for retribution, Eleanor, such as you have called down upon yourself today. Why else are you to be sent packing? Discretion, Eleanor, my child,' she said more gently. 'Discretion and patience and self-discipline. You cannot control others till you have learnt to control yourself.' She spoke without hope for she knew that Eleanor, despite her strenuous efforts, would never possess any of these.

Eleanor pouted. 'Is that your advice then? Wait, wait, wait, till I am old and ugly and have lost what advantage I have?' She caught possessively at Elizabeth's hands. 'It is now that I have the power. Now, while I am young and fair.'

Elizabeth smiled sadly. Indeed, she was fair, with her pale ruthless face flushed with passion. 'Beauty fades, Eleanor, more swiftly in a woman than in a man. You only have to look at me to know that. What will you have to offer then; the empty begging bowl of your body, the hope that some kind soul will set it rattling again out of charity? All women possess the power that you speak of. There is more, Eleanor. I have shown you what more, yet you push it aside and follow your instincts like a base animal. Indulge your body if you must, but sparingly. Use it as the falconer uses the lure. The hawk always comes back, does it not? Again and again it will return, and for what? A few paltry scraps when it could have had all. Don't settle for scraps, Eleanor, when so easily, with patience, you might have all.'

Elizabeth fell back, suddenly exhausted. A haze had gathered before her eyes, a fog of swirling amber light like the embers of a dying fire. And at the heart of it she saw herself, burning and writhing in torment.

Eleanor chafed her ice cold hands. 'Elizabeth,' she cried. 'Elizabeth. Are you ill?'

It was a long time before she spoke. Then Elizabeth said with faint surprise, 'No. I am not ill. I think at last I am dying.'

It took her a long time to die. For a week she lay in the high sunlit room, each day withdrawing a little further from the conscious world. Some days her mind was clear and still, then faces came and peered down at her. Eleanor, pale and grieving, though not so much that it kept her from the Court. Her grandsons were there, awkward and ill at ease in this close proximity to death. Alianore came and prayed ceaselessly, for Elizabeth had scorned a priest and sent the whey-faced chaplain muttering darkly from the room about God and the Devil. She would die as she had lived, in the shadowy world between the two. At other times, her thoughts like scattered petals on an ebb tide whirled and eddied in confusion. Then her mind drifted slowly back and she shed the dragging weight of years. She was a child again, running wild along the banks of the Usk, with the Welsh mountains like black-browed giants at her back. She was proud and haughty Isabella with the blood of kings and princes coursing hotly in her veins; she was Bess, the loved and lovesome wife of Harry Hotspur. At night she lay cold and sleepless watching the distortion of light and shade that took on the semblance of human form. In the swart, dark hangings her father lurked, sulky and discontented as she remembered him, worn out by the impossible dream that was all he had bequeathed to her. Henry Bolingbroke was there in the oily vapourous smoke of the cresset lamp, and shallow, vain Richard looked down on her from the clouded silver glass. Her brothers Roger and Edmund, both dead so long that she could hardly recognise the faces that swam bloodily in the pool of spilt wine by her bed. And overshadowing them all, burning hot and malevolent in every candle flame, that gaunt and splendid face with its bright unquenchable stare, the old man himself – Northumberland. Yet nowhere could she find Harry. All night she roamed the dark labyrinth of her mind searching for him. There was nowhere she could recall that was particularly sacred to him, perhaps because there was no place vast enough to hold him. If he was anywhere, it would be in the north, in the hills and valleys that were as wild and untamed as he had been. Perhaps he was to be kept from her till the last. Would he come when it was time?

On the last night Hal came and sat with her. The evening was hot and breathless, incredibly and terrifyingly still. The moon scudded across a black thunderous sky and illumined a city crouched and watchful before the coming storm. The bell of St Martin's chimed the hour. Elizabeth sighed. Only seven o'clock? The day had seemed so long.

Hal looked down on all that was left of her. She seemed so small, so old, her wasted body no more than a ripple beneath the silk sheet, her skin so transparent that the narrow shrunken veins stood out like cords. He thought of all the times he had wished her dead, yet now it was come he grieved as if for a well-loved child. She was all that was left of that distant world where his father and grandfather had walked and laughed and warmed him with their very presence, the last link in the chain that still bound him in love and honour to their memory. He would comfort her as he had never been able to comfort them.

'Hal.' Her voice was no more than a whisper of air against his cheek as she turned to look at him. He seemed so young, or was that only because she was so very old? His hair still grew thick and curling onto his neck, the silver merging imperceptibly with the gold. His mouth was taut and narrowed. With grief? With restraint? With distaste that he must sit out the night in this closed fetid room with the smell of death reeking in his nostrils? She did not know, for his eyes were pools of lambent green shadow in the whiteness of his face. That was all there was of her in him, the long green eyes. So little of her, nothing of Harry; all was the old man, as if he had imprinted his likeness upon her unborn child lest she should forget how much he had loathed and despised her. She had not forgotten. How could she, when his image stared down at her even now? How sweet must his vengeance be, to watch her die, to see all her beauty turned to dust and swept away whilst he lived on, incarnate in her own son.

She looked at him now with gentle eyes and wondered what manner of man he would have been if she had not reached out and touched him with her corruptness. What manner of woman would she have been? Not one who would have sacrificed her only son for ambition's sake. She thought of York and his sons growing fat on Hal's corpse; of Harry and Thomas and Ralph overwhelmed by the holocaust that she in her madness had inspired. 'Hal,' she said again. 'York. You must beware of York . . .'

He laid her gently back against the swan's down pillow. 'I know,' he said quietly. 'I know all there is to know of York and his schemes.' He stroked the quenched fire of her hair. 'Do you know more, Elizabeth?'

Elizabeth looked away. She would not tell him. What advantage was it to a man to know the measured span of his years? She could alter nothing now. 'No,' she lied. 'And even if I did I should not tell you. It would be a dreadful burden, to know with certainty whether the battle was won or lost before ever it was fought.'

'It would not matter. I cannot change my path, though I know it is in your mind to ask it. I swore to live and die with Harry the king and if it is to die, then I shall do so without complaint or regret. I would not suffer the grief that grandfather did for a broken oath.'

Elizabeth's mouth tightened at the mention of the old man's name. 'Yet he died fighting for Richard, for the true king,' she said. 'If you set so much store by what the old man said and did, does it not follow that you uphold the cause for which he died? He died for Richard. York and his sons are his rightful heirs and our close kin.' Even now she must cling to the belief that she had been right, that she had not sacrificed all in vain.

Hal turned his face away and she thought for a moment that she had angered him, yet when he spoke again his voice was kind. 'He did not die for Richard, Elizabeth. He died to absolve himself, to vindicate the dishonour of a broken oath and the murder of a king.' He looked at her with solemn eyes. 'Weak and witless Henry may be but nevertheless he is king, and perhaps in his simplicity and innocence he is beyond all our vengeance. Lancaster of York, I care not which, Henry is king, my lawful annointed king. I cannot see past that. Not even for you, Elizabeth.'

'Not even for you.' As if he cared, as if she mattered, as if she were truly loved. She reached out and gently touched his face and the small, tentative gesture broke down the last of the barriers. He lifted her cold shrunken hand and laid it tenderly against his cheek. A deep sigh ebbed out of her. Where now in this dark quiet room were all the hatreds and vengeances that had held them apart for so many years? Where was the loneliness, the grief, the terrible sense of loss? All swept away by the touching of their hands in love.

She lay very still, the warmth of feeling held cupped in her hand like a fledgling bird. It had come upon her so suddenly and softly that she hardly dare draw breath lest it fly from her grasp and she be as lost and alone as before. They had come full circle, from the time when she had been strong and he the helpless, dependent child. Now she was the child, as helpless, as needful, craving love and warmth as once she had power. She assayed a scornful little smile. What place had power here with death waiting so impatiently at the door? Still, she was afraid to speak and disturb the soft contentment that lay upon her. And what was there to say now? They had long grown past the need for words and explanations and if grief and suspicion had held them back from perfect understanding, love had dispelled them. All the complexities and sorrows of her life were resolved by the simple act of dying. So she lay quiet, content in the wonderful eloquence of their silence till softly Hal said, 'The priest, Elizabeth. Let me send for the priest. However you have lived, I would have you die with God.'

She smiled, undisturbed by this reminder that her new-found joy was to be so brief. To die with God? Was there a God? She had never really thought so till now. There were good and evil and the power of choice. She believed that. And strangely, looking back, she had never deliberately chosen evil. It was more as if it had chosen her. She had never fought it but had welcomed and nurtured it, letting it breed and multiply in her heart. She had served none but herself, neither Devil nor God, neither man nor beast. She'd had no faith save in her own destiny, no allegiance save to the wind and earth and the deep corrupting power within her. Why then should she change now? Only because he asked it. She could deny him nothing now.

'Very well,' she said and closed her eyes so that he should not see their mocking look. 'If it pleases you. Let the priest come.'

Almost with amusement she prepared herself for the final hypocrisy. The priest stood over her, lean and black as a hungry crow. She heard his muttered exhortations with scorn. Recant, repent, renounce. Did he really believe that a few trite phrases could atone for a life such as hers? Then his cold dry hands thrust a crucifix into hers, and her brow was smeared with chrism. She was absolved of whatever unnamed and unnameable sins he had judged her guilty of. She was free of all sin, free to die.

Then the growl of thunder drowned out the thin piping of his voice. Elizabeth turned her head as the first of the rain struck the lattice. Lightning flashed and showed her eyes void as glass. Her hand tightened fractionally on the cross. 'Hold me, Hal,' she whispered. 'Hold me till I am dead.'

All night the storm screamed and roared about them and still Elizabeth lived. She was gone from any conscious thought, her spirit long departed into the darkness to meet whatever awaited her there. Yet still she breathed, still her heart pulsed faintly.

In her chamber Eleanor stood shivering and watched the battle waged for Elizabeth's soul. All was darkness and silence within the besieged and trembling walls. Outside the wind shrieked dementedly and flung the rain like arrowheads against the rattling panes. Lightning veined a fathomless sky and lit the streets with its baleful glare. The city looked cowed and defeated, colourless, stripped of all life and vigour. There was a frightening stillness about the closed and shuttered buildings, a deathly silence that was apart from the raging storm. She thought in terror that it was like the end of the world.

She moved away from the window and hid in the shadows of the room, pouring out the last of the wine with a sweating, trembling hand. Jesu Mary, she was so afraid. What was this nameless terrible thing that Elizabeth had bequeathed her? What was it that roared and bellowed outside the door? Was it God or the Devil that had been cheated of its prey?

Her scalp lifted as a fresh onslaught of wind and rain shook the house and she raised the wine cup so sharply that it bruised her lip and the sweet redness trickled from her mouth like blood. 'Elizabeth,' she cried piteously. 'Elizabeth.'

The wind took up her sobbing cry and flung it back into the darkness. She thought of Elizabeth as she had seen her last: a few frail bones shrouded in yellow flesh, a few wisps of white hair, all held so lovingly in her son's last tender embrace. She had not stayed. The dim shuttered room with its drone of prayers and clacking beads had sickened her. Hypocrites. Hypocrites all, she had thought savagely. Only she had truly loved her. She shivered now. The sight of Elizabeth dying had been too strong a reminder of what she herself could become. Dear God, what gain was there in all the world that could justify such an end? She could feel Elizabeth's torment, see in her mind's eye the horned and winged creature that fought so furiously for possession. Eleanor reeled to her knees like a drunkard. For her it was not too late. She had not gone so far forward that she could not retreat. Mindlessly she began to pray, long-forgotten phrases falling heavy as millstones from her lips, a babble of senseless ritual remembered from the Mass. She invoked all the saints, promising penance and alms in abundance – her jewels to the monks of St Leonard's at Alnwick, her revenues to the poor. Then she screamed loud and long above the wind, 'In God's name, let her go. Let my poor Elizabeth go.'

She sank into a stupor against the skirts of the bed. After a while she became aware of the silence, of the moon filling the chamber with its clear, cleansing light. She began to weep quietly. It was over. Elizabeth was dead.

York

For the second time that year Eleanor made low and reverent obeisance before the king. Her gown was seemly, almost demure, her abundant hair concealed beneath a simple coif. A silver reliquary hung conspicuously to her narrow waist. She did not offend, and Henry, robed in his customary dusty black, smiled at her vaguely though he hardly saw her, nor any of the long glittering procession that came to lay their mouths on his white flaccid hand. His mind still dwelt on the glory of St John of Beverley from whose shrine he was lately come. The queen remembered her though, and to Eleanor's delight murmured smiling acknowledgement. She had changed since that time at Westminster two years before; she was harder, warier, the wide blue eyes fixed searchingly on every face that came before her as if to see where their loyalty lay.

Suffolk danced close attendance at her side like a persistent shadow. He had waxed even greater since Humphrey of Gloucester's death earlier that year. Murdered, or so York and his henchmen would have it, and Eleanor, dropping her eyes before his pale ruthless gaze, could well believe it. Gloucester had signed his own death warrant by his violent opposition to this man.

Eleanor returned to her place at the foot of the dais, thrusting herself blatantly between two unknown knights. Nine months incarcerated at Berwick had done nothing to quell her longing for the Court. There was little she did not know of its distant doings, for she had no compunction about eavesdropping on the whispered conversations of chamber and hall – discreetly though, for Harry did not consider it fitting that a woman should have a grasp of politics. She looked again thoughtfully at Suffolk. When his shameful dealings over Maine had become common knowledge, the shock had reverberated throughout the realm. To give up Maine, fought for so hard and so long? And for what? A queen who had so far brought them nothing but unrest. It had brought Gloucester out from his lair to uphold York in his violent criticism of the young queen and her ministers, especially Suffolk and Gloucester's old enemy, Beaufort. It was Margaret herself, now openly reviled as the 'Frenchwoman' who had borne the brunt of it. No blame could be attached to King Henry, who by his very simplicity had endeared himself to a commons perpetually kept to heel by men like Suffolk. It soon became quite clear to any who had the young queen's interests at heart that Gloucester must be silenced.

It had been done swiftly and discreetly: arrest, confinement and sudden death, all within the space of a week. Apoplexy, the court physician had given out to a sceptical and uneasy populace and the flaunting of his bloated but unmarked corpse had not dispelled suspicion. Nothing was said, none openly accused, but York and his henchmen had trod the more warily since.

Whatever the manner of Gloucester's death it had left the cardinal in clear possession of the field, though only briefly. A few months later Beaufort too had succumbed, less violently than his rival but just as surely. It had narrowed the field to two clear factions: York had taken the stance of reformer, and contented himself for the moment with issues of misgovernment, though always his criticisms were subtly directed against Margaret or

Suffolk or both. The queen had kept closer council and it had been conjecture as to how she could retaliate, as the king would countenance nothing that smacked of discord. In the event, she had persuaded Henry to endow York with the prestigious but isolated Governorship of Ireland. It was virtual banishment, but loaded with such honour that York could do nothing but meekly accede. Only the certain knowledge that York was well out of harm's way had tempted Margaret from the fastness of Westminster on this progress in the north.

Then Eleanor's attention was claimed by the king. He had risen, duty done, anxious to resume his debate with Archbishop Kemp on a knotty point of canon law. The queen remained, gathering a few chosen favourites around her. Eleanor looked on enviously, promising herself that one day she would be one of their number. She ventured a covert glance to where Salisbury and his son stood, pointedly excluded. She had not seen young Richard Neville since the revel at Westminster, despite the week's grace that Elizabeth's death had given her. She could not think that he had cooled, yet the look he gave her was controlled and cautious. Eleanor felt the colour staining her cheeks, deepening as she became aware of Thomas's amused stare.

'Faith, Eleanor,' he came close to whisper maliciously in her ear, 'how you can discomfort a man. Didn't you know that it is most unseemly to ogle, especially at a man like Warwick?' His brilliant eyes dwelt mockingly on her white angry face. 'I swear it is your only fault, Eleanor, my love. You are too eager. You devour the dish before it is even set on the table. You should never deny a man the delight of anticipation. There is little sport in so easy a kill.'

She broke away from him, moving through the crowded hall with as much dignity as she could muster. For once she was not aware of Richard Neville's eyes upon her.

Outside in the pleasaunce the soft breeze cooled her rage. She walked through the maze of tall box hedges to the little arbour in their midst. Here pale roses drooped on thorny stems and twined possessively round the old stone seat. Tiny flowers of souvenance thrust from the crowded paving, the exact colour of Thomas's eyes Vindictively she ground her heel on a bright upturned blossom. 'An easy kill.' Was that how he thought of her? Was that how Warwick thought of her? It was an echo of all that Elizabeth had said: 'Indulge your body if you must, but sparingly.' Sparingly! She smiled inwardly with sickly amusement; a year since she had had a man in her bed and the last a drunkard at that. It had been the night on which Elizabeth had died. Dear God, what a coupling, she thought disgustedly. Harry drunk and as violent as the storm that had all but left her witless. And she, half crazed with grief and fear, lying passive and detached beneath his sweating weight. Their son had been conceived that night and she had been almost glad to return to the north and hide the swift and gross distortion of her body that had kept her sickly from morning to night as none of the others had done. It had been a long and strenuous birth and the child when it had eventually appeared had been puny and dark, so alien to her own and Harry's fairness. She had viewed it almost with revulsion and abandoned it swiftly to Alianore's care as she had her daughters. She shivered, remembering the swart ugly little creature. There was no doubt that the Devil had been abroad that night.

She turned sharply, suddenly aware that she was being watched. Richard Neville swept his long lean body into a courtly bow. Eleanor smiled. The look in his eyes never failed to restore her pride. She said in a low seductive voice, 'What kept you so long, my lord?'

There was the merest flicker of annoyance in his eyes when he answered. 'Were you so sure I would come then?'

'No. No more sure than you were of finding me here.'

The first exchange was like the slither of keen blades and Warwick smiled, stimulated as much by her voice as her body.

They walked in silence, each intensely aware of the other. Warwick stared at the silken flesh of her long throat. She was at her peak now, like a perfect rose, though her beauty was more a radiance of skin and eyes than any cast of features. Her body was perfection and his eyes dwelt longingly on her heavy breasts and slender thighs. He would have liked to have seen her hair loosed. His mind conceived lustfully of her clothed in nothing else. Then he looked away and considered the dancing flight of a lone swallow above his head. He more than desired her, but he knew there was much at stake here other than the brief satisfaction of that desire. She was a Percy for one thing and his father would frown strongly upon any liaison there unless she could be of use to them. Well, he considered again the perfect curve of her throat, perhaps she could be. He said in a low voice, 'Have you thought what comment it would cause if we were discovered thus, walking like lovers amid roses in the sun?'

Eleanor looked at him boldly. 'Have you, my lord? I would not have thought that you did aught without pondering the consequences first.'

'I do not. And the consequences would be shame for you, censure for me and the widening of the already unbridgeable gulf between our families. Have you forgotten who you are? Who I am?' He sighed elaborately. 'It is a pity above all things, Eleanor, that you are a Percy.'

'Only by marriage,' she corrected him. 'I could just as easily have been a Neville or a Clifford, so why should my allegiance lie there particularly?'

He smiled with quiet satisfaction. So she could be disloyal – and indiscreet, his instinct warned him. He also thought that she could be clinging; these women of pure temperament usually were. All in all she was a risk and one that he was not sure he was prepared to take. He would need some other gain besides the mere gratification of his lust. He sounded her cautiously. 'You are changed since I last saw you,' he said lightly. His eyes encompassed the plain gown and the nunly coif. 'Is this for the benefit of our chaste and saintly king?' he enquired with amusement. The amusement deepened to laughter as he saw her uncertainty. 'I like that. It shows a certain cunning.' He reached out and touched her cheek lightly as she flushed angrily. 'Now you feel insulted. You should not. I am a man who looks for strange virtues in a woman.' He waited till he thought he had soothed her, then went on in his dry voice. 'And you, Eleanor? What is it you seek in a man?'

'Merely the man,' she answered boldly. 'A man is all I suffer the lack of.'

He laughed. 'I fear your husband bores you then.'

'Interminably.'

'Yet there must be more. I would not have thought you the kind of woman to be content with mere domesticity.'

'I am not.'

'What more then, Eleanor?'

She paused and plucked a young leaf, tearing it nervously to shreds with her sharp nails. Yes. What more? More than Harry and his drunken lechery. More than perpetual childbirth and the stink of urine and sour milk. All that Elizabeth had promised her, except that she had not had the courage to follow that path. She shrugged and said lightly. 'Influence, excitement. The thought that each day might not be the same, that it might be changed because I was there or because I was not.'

'And you think that our little French queen can give you this? I saw that you were eager for her favour.'

She flushed. He made it sound as if she had demeaned herself in some way.

He went on, his dry incisive voice slicing at all her dreams. 'Influence? Yes. She could give you influence of a kind. Excitement, certainly. I have no doubt that there is a certain thrill in being hounded and reviled. Will your love for the Frenchwoman carry you into exile with her?'

It was said deliberately to provoke and quietly Eleanor said, 'That is a rash statement for such a cautious man, my lord.'

'Is it not? Now there is a rare opportunity for favour, Eleanor. You could denounce me to the Frenchwoman; better still, to her paramour Somerset.' He came close and tilted her face toward him. 'But you will not because you're not sure yet, are you, Eleanor? You're not sure if you are on the winning side and that counts for a lot with you, doesn't it? To win and be seen to have won.' He loosed her, almost thrusting her away. 'I shall always win, Eleanor,' he said gravely. 'But then you know that, do you not? Why else are you so drawn, so fascinated? Because you can see beyond me to the glory. You can see the riches and the power, the land and the jewels . . .' He broke off abruptly. He had already said more than he had meant to but looking at her avid face it had been enough.

They had come to the last concealment before the maze opened out onto the spacious lawn. He took her hand and laid his sensuous mouth against it. 'So you see how we are divided, Eleanor. I could make you all my heart's desire if you did not cleave so well to Lancaster.' Warwick smiled deep into her eyes. 'Think on it, Eleanor,' he said softly. 'I beg you, think on it.'

She supped that night at Lord Hungerford's house in the presence of the queen; a small intimate gathering, all totally loyal, all totally Lancastrian. Great urns of crimson roses flanked the dais, white marguerites starred every gown. A minstrel played a sad courtly song of France and a jester in green and yellow silks parodied York as a braying ass. To end the long and dreary evening Hungerford's plump and simpering daughters disported themselves aptly as St Margaret and the Foolish Virgins.

Eleanor from her place beside Tom Clifford watched the queen. Tonight she shone with a quiet brilliance, removed from the dimming presence of the king (his royal Grace, it seemed, was fasting). Often her bright glance fell on Eleanor and she had drawn her once or twice into the light desultory conversation that flowed as easily as the wine. But tonight the queen's smile had lost its lustre for Eleanor. She viewed all through a veil of discontent. She could think of nothing but Warwick. She stole another glance at Margaret. Was her cause really doomed? Elizabeth had always thought so. Heart and mind she had believed in York. It had been all of her creed and religion. Elizabeth had seen the glory, the same glory that Warwick saw, that Warwick thought she saw. The sad truth of it was that she saw only herself. She had never looked for more.

Lord Hungerford's great booming laugh rang out, ceasing abruptly as his steward came and bent to his ear. There was a late arrival and one whose very name should have precluded him from this assembly. But Ralph Neville, Earl of Westmorland, was a rarity among his breed; the disaffected nephew of Salisbury, he was strong in Margaret's cause. Eleanor viewed him with interest, seeing perhaps a faint reflection of herself as she might be if she abandoned Lancaster. Here was one who had gone against the tie of family and allied himself with the enemy. There any resemblance ended. Westmorland had better reason to turn his back on his family than she would ever have. More than fifteen years since old Ralph Neville's death and still he wrangled and pestered the courts for the restoration of his inheritance. All in vain, for was not every justice and commissioner of rank in the land linked by blood or marriage to Salisbury? She listened intently as he complained that his last petition, like the others, had foundered in a sea of ambiguous legality. He pressed for action. Could the king not demand that Salisbury relinquish that to which he was so obviously not entitled? Was the king not the highest law?

Eleanor saw Margaret demur. Suffolk prevaricated, chewing irritably at his fat lower lip. Somerset made loud noises of sympathy then declared weakly that he did not think the time quite right. Only Northumberland shared Westmorland's discontent. When *was* the time, then? he demanded loudly. They had waited long enough, through all the long wearisome excuses that the Council had previously offered as cause for inaction: the king's minority, the quarrels of Gloucester, the war in France. Well, all these were past and the king would never be any more of a man than he was now. With respect, Northumberland said, was it not more to the point that they feared any affront to Salisbury whilst York still stood at his back?

Eleanor saw the weakness in their hesitant and uneasy faces. She thought suddenly, there is no king. They were ruled by an illusion, a simple-minded fool who saw the world as he would have it, not as it actually was. She knew that it took weeks of careful persuasion to bring Henry to any firm decision and then he could reverse it in an instant if the appeal of another touched his heart more. No blame could ever be attached to saintly Henry but it could to these men, it could to Margaret. So they hesitated and disdained action till the time when it would have given them advantage was long past. And set against all this weakness and complacency were York and Salisbury — and Warwick.

Then Thomas spoke in his clear firm voice. 'With respect, your Grace. I doubt that my lord of Westmorland will ever win his case through the courts where all are Salisbury or York's paid men. And if the law is corrupt then I say we take it into our own hands. Let Westmorland take what belongs to him by force, as it is kept from him by force. Harassment, sabotage, outright violence if necessary. These are the only terms on which Salisbury could be brought to treat. He might be less reluctant to yield the lands if they gave him less profit.'

'My Lord Egremont.' Lord Say's round eyes bulged from his small head. 'What you suggest is . . .'

'Justice,' Westmorland interrupted harshly.

'I was about to say unlawful,' Say reproved him.

'And Salisbury's blatant disregard of my father's will is not?' Westmorland demanded hotly.

'The terms of your father's will were ambiguous to say the least. None but the courts can determine the exact dispersement of the lands.'

'Then why do they not? Now we come to it. Because they are Salisbury's creatures. We are back where we started. The Chancellor and Chief Justice are his brothers-in-law, the sheriffs of three counties are his sons.'

'I do not dispute there are certain weaknesses,' Suffolk said. 'But the rough justice that Egremont proposes is no better. Surely you do not expect us to condone it?'

Westmorland raised an ironic eyebrow, for Suffolk's dealings with law and property were not always above reproach. He said angrily, 'If you can keep such long silence on my past requests for help then you can keep silent whilst I help myself.'

'My lords,' the queen's softly accented voice brought them all to sudden and uncomfortable awareness of her almost forgotten presence. Eleanor watched admiringly as she soothed and promised, weaving the torn and ruptured threads of argument into a smooth and even pattern of accord. She became aware of Margaret as a woman rather than a queen. She couldn't help but recognise the concern for self that was born out of fear and uncertainty. Margaret cared whether Ralph Neville regained his lands only in as much as it would swell the power of her cause. She did not particularly care for England or Henry except as a solid and unshakeable foundation on which to base her power. Eleanor wondered idly how many others who attended her so loyally now knew that she built on quicksand. She thought that perhaps Northumberland did.

Cynically she glanced at the ring of faces clustered round the jewel that was the queen. What indeed was there to keep her here? Northumberland, who regarded her as some pale and ineffectual imitation of Elizabeth? Her husband Harry sitting stonily beside him? And Thomas, who didn't care whether she lived or died or who she bedded with, as long as it was not him? She felt suddenly isolated, shut out from the warmth of family that did not include her. She allowed her goblet to be replenished despite Harry's scowl. She stared down into the dark glowing depths. There was warmth enough there, warmth and reassurance and fulfilment. She heard Warwick's soft eloquent voice, 'I could make you all my heart's desire if you did not cleave so well to Lancaster.'

'Elizabeth.' The child's name, sharply called, woke Alianore from the dream. She blinked and turned her face from the shaft of sunlight that fell blindingly across her chair. 'Elizabeth.' The plaintive cry came again and she shook her head drowsily. Was she still dreaming? Elizabeth, surely, was dead. But the child who flung itself laughingly upon her was real enough. She twined plump silk-clad arms about her neck and Alianore smiled. This was another Elizabeth, lovely, lovesome, wicked Bess whose laughter turned abruptly to tears as the irate nurse bore down upon them.

Bess shrieked and clung possessively to Alianore's skirts. 'Grandmère, she hit me. Dame Margaret hit me.'

'And with good cause, my lady,' the nurse said grimly. 'She was insolent. Even more so than usual. She called me . . .' The foremost of her chins trembled with outrage. 'I could not even lay my tongue to such a foulness.'

Alianore tilted the child's tear-streaked face toward her. The blow had been a hard one. The mark of the heavy ringed hand was still livid on her cheek. She raised cold eyes to Dame Margaret's indignant face. 'It would seem that you have even less self-control than the child you profess to have charge of. I suggest that in future you confine your punishments to those of a less physical nature or else consult the Lady Eleanor if you feel that more stringent measures are necessary.'

'And where might I be expected to find the Lady Eleanor on

this or any other day? The child will be a mother herself before her own takes any heed of her.'

'You are insolent, Dame Margaret,' Alianore snapped. 'And not, I would remind you, indispensable. Your duties are the sole care and welfare of the lady Elizabeth and if you would not be dismissed from them, I would attend to them more diligently than you have today.' Alianore turned away in dismissal and from the corner of her eye saw Bess' triumphant, smirking face. She sighed. That had been a mistake, to let Bess see that she had gained the upper hand. And of course, poor Dame Margaret was right. Eleanor could not have cared if the child were beaten daily.

She walked across to the window seat where earlier Eleanor had sat reading aloud. The book lay discarded, its thin vellum pages curling in the sun. Alianore smoothed it shut and carefully tied the silken cords. Eleanor, she thought grimly, had respect and reverence for none, not even Chaucer. She stared broodingly from the window. The gardens looked desolate, all the fruit and flowers had been harvested for drying. The trees were almost bare, stripped before their time by a vicious easterly wind that already held the threat of winter. Only the sun had colour and warmth.

She turned back into the room. The diversion of Elizabeth past, the day had resumed its quiet pattern. Joan Clifford played sweetly on her lute. The two Musgrave girls combed and preened their little French dog and Lady Ogle had again succumbed to the heat and snored gently in her corner. Alianore turned her eyes from the slack drooping jaw. Perhaps she would be like that in ten years, she thought fearfully; old and fat, her wits addled by boredom, with nothing left to do but sleep in the sun. She smiled absently as little Anne Dacre held out a crudely-worked sampler for her approval. A suitably dreary subject for an equally dreary child – the raising of Lazarus from the dead. She frowned, recalling her vivid waking dream: Elizabeth alive and malevolent as ever, a young vibrant Elizabeth with hair like fire and eyes like a sparkling summer sea. The rest of the dream was lost to her, driven out by Dame Margaret's raucous cry. All that was left was a vague sense of unease.

She looked down into the girl's plump face, murmuring vague

and undeserved praise as she gave the stitching back into her large clumsy hands. She tapped her foot in silent frustration. Dear God, she had never thought that she would miss Elizabeth, yet since her death it seemed that life had slowed to a crawling pace. She had been the focal point of their lives for so long, absorbing their discontents, keeping them alive with her scorn, their wits sharp and keen as against an adversary. Now each day was as well ordered and predictable as the one gone before. She woke and slept to the same bland faces, the same petty quarrels and intrigues. Such a dull passive life, for her at least. Hal, by contrast, was cursed with a frenzied activity of mind and body, living each day almost as if it were his last. He was often away and when he was not he was secretly closeted with Westmorland and lately Henry Holland, Duke of Exeter. Her sons were less comfort. Harry was Lord Poynings now, since the death of Eleanor's brother, and as Lord Warden of the East and Middle Marches, since the resignation of his father, had immured himself at Berwick. Ralph had replaced him as their man at Court and George and William were both at Durham in holy orders. Thomas and Richard she hardly saw at all, so close did they cling to their father. There was only Eleanor, and she was worse than no company at all. She filled all of the house with her discontent. Some days she did not leave her bed till noon and when she did her face was as blank and languid as if she still slept. She picked fault everywhere and yesterday she had reduced poor Anne Dacre to hysterical tears. Yet strangely it was Eleanor herself that Alianore pitied. To live in such an empty void, to see nothing but her own lifeless image. Only the presence of Thomas seemed to rouse her at all. Eleanor and Thomas. A flood of uneasiness assailed her. What was there between them? Perhaps only that which Eleanor imagined, for she thought that Thomas had more sense and on the surface he did not seem to care for her overmuch. It was Eleanor herself who was the danger. She needed a greater excitement than any here could provide. She thought sadly of Harry who loved her so well and was only despised for it. He had grown ever more silent and withdrawn of late, retreating so far within himself that even she could not reach him. The worst thing he could have done was to leave Eleanor to her own devices. Did he think she would turn to him when she had burnt out all her lusts elsewhere? Would any man still want a wife whom all the world had used? Then she reproached herself silently. That was unfair, for she doubted if Eleanor had actually been unfaithful to Harry. It was just that she gave the strong impression that she would be.

She stood abruptly and pushed the lattice wide. It was then that she saw Eleanor.

She sat coiled like a serpent beneath the rowan tree, her rapt unwavering gaze fixed on a distant solitary cloud. Only when Alianore stood beside her did she look up though she had long been aware of her careful approach. She smiled and once again Alianore was forcibly reminded of Elizabeth. She thought, Elizabeth is dead. It is only Eleanor who keeps her alive. Poor Eleanor. Did she find the living such worthless company? Alianore said brightly, 'I see we are of a like mind. It is a pity to waste such a day. The air in the solar is indeed stifling.'

Eleanor drew a basket of cut roses toward her and began to strip the petals for drying with ruthless predatory fingers. 'Not so stifling as those witless creatures who pretend to serve you,' she said sulkily. 'It was they who drove me out. You only suffer them out of charity; that Ogle woman, forever complaining of her ailments.' She mimicked the thin griping voice. ' "Oh, my lady. Could I beg a salve for this little swelling? The last you gave me brought such relief." ' Her lip curled in its familiar sneer. 'There's naught ails her that a good bath would not cure. I'll swear the stink of her flesh turns me sick.'

Alianore swallowed hard on the surge of annoyance. She said, 'I will speak to her. She is old and fat. I expect she finds bathing difficult.'

Eleanor crushed a flower-head ruthlessly. 'For God's sake, Alianore, must you always excuse?'

'Must you always sneer and find fault?' Alianore took a handful of roses into her lap. Jesu, why did they always rile each other so? She said, attempting lightness again, 'I think my lord has plans to return to Alnwick at the end of the month. No doubt you will be pleased to see Harry again.'

Eleanor said nothing and merely looked sulky. The prospect of

Harry and Alnwick turned her sick. She thought longingly of Westminster; of the light and airy apartments, the painted and gilded hall where Margaret would be scheming and plotting and arming herself against York who still languished in his Irish bogs. Salisbury would be there, though, working tirelessly in his stead, sneering, deprecating, demeaning, holding the king up to subtle ridicule, denouncing Margaret as the author of all their ills. And without her, all without her. She thought with equal longing of Warwick. It was three months since she had seen him last, three months since she had betrayed . . . No, betrayal was too strong a word for the little she had told him of Westmorland's intent against his father. It would have gained him nothing but the advantage of being forewarned and if she had known it, she had told him nothing that he did not already know. His pleasure at the disclosure of that brief and violent conversation in Lord Hungerford's house had been more at the knowledge that he could bend her to his will, that she could be used. The next day she had received her reward; a silver box inlaid with pearls and inside a single perfect white rose, the emblem of her new loyalty. There had been no message, only a scrap of parchment twined round the stem and written in his large ornate hand the one word: Warwick. She looked down at the crushed flower in her hand. Was that all she was ever to have of him?

Then Alianore said, 'Carefully, Eleanor. If you bruise the petals they will not retain their scent.'

At the implied criticism Eleanor thrust the basket away from her. 'Perhaps you had best see to them yourself then,' she said sullenly. 'I was bored with it anyway.'

'As you are bored with all humanity by the sound of it,' Alianore said tightly. 'I fear I am at a loss to know how to entertain or amuse you. You have a husband, children, wealth and position, yet you still crave after . . .' She shrugged. 'I know not what. Do you know, Eleanor?'

'You must forgive me, Alianore, if I do not share your passion for perpetual childbirth. Unfortunately, I do not possess your inherited aptitude for breeding.'

Alianore let the subtle insult pass. 'You speak as if bearing children was something shameful.'

'It is. Shameful, degrading, ugly. I am more than just a breeding sow.'

'What more?' Alianore demanded angrily. 'How are you so different, so special? What gifts has God given you that set you so far above poor creatures like myself?'

Eleanor's face took on that rapt innocent expression that concealed her ugliest thoughts. 'Not God,' she said, 'but Elizabeth. Elizabeth made me special. You know that, don't you, Alianore?'

Alianore stared at her in pity and disgust. At last she said quietly, 'I know that Elizabeth herself had a rare gift. Whether it was from God or the Devil I am less well informed. But Elizabeth had a purpose. She had dignity and restraint and a nobility of blood that you could never match, Eleanor. What is your purpose? To lure my son Thomas into your bed and shame yourself and your husband even further?' Her own lip curled in a sneer. 'Is this how you are special, Eleanor? Because you have no shame or dignity? Lust and greed and covetousness are no rare gifts. I have them too and the only thing that sets us apart is that I know how to control them, while you do not.' She smiled as if at an erring child. 'You are not different, Eleanor. Elizabeth only made you think you were.'

Eleanor said nothing. She sat with her shoulders bowed, staring at the rose that slowly blackened in her clenched and bloodless hand. Then she looked up at the sound of running feet. Thomas ran wildly toward them. His face was white and his eyes burned with a ferocious blue flame. He swept Alianore violently into his arms. 'The Scots are over the Border,' he said breathlessly. 'They've burnt Alnwick.' He kissed her soundly on the mouth. 'There's to be war,' he cried and laughed like a delighted child. 'Glorious, bloody war.'

The moon rode high in a clear ebony sky and from the summit of the rock Harry could see all of Annandale spread out before him. Below, the Sark river was a dark oily gleam with tortuous crags of unscalable rock rising sheer from the water. The farther bank was wider and easily passable but the hills were soft and ambiguous here with pockets of darkness that could each have housed a hundred men in ambush. He turned away and narrowed his eyes against the smoke that blew with the veering wind. In the distance Dunbar still blazed like a beacon, ringed with pinpoints of tired light that marked the gutted towns and villages of their homeward march – a glorious riposte for the destruction of Alnwick. But now it seemed that they themselves were trapped. Impenetrable hills blocked their path and their rear was cut off by pursuing Scots. He frowned in consternation. It had been a mistake to swing so far west out of Dunbar, another to have let his father go his own way, though the tension between Northumberland and Salisbury had risen to such a pitch that none had demurred at his suggestion that the command be divided between them. As Lord Warden, Harry had remained with the main force while his father had driven west into Lauderdale. He would have given much to have reversed that decision now. Northumberland could have led them out blindfold.

He dismounted wearily in the outer confines of the sprawling camp. Salisbury's contingent held the higher ground, his own the river bank, though there was more than just a stretch of trampled grass between them. His father's discreet withdrawal had solved nothing. The daily squabbles over strategy and procedure continued still.

He smiled shyly at the eager boy who took his horse and raised his hand to the men who called out to him as he passed. He always felt faintly surprised at their admiration for him as a soldier. If they had but known it, he loathed the war, though none would have guessed it from the ruthless and efficient way in which he pursued it. The uncertainty, the lack of self-esteem, he kept well concealed and even that had diminished these last few months. Only at night when he lay alone did the misery of it return. It was then that he thought of Eleanor.

Salisbury waited for him, pacing the limits of his tent in silent frustration. 'Well?' he demanded curtly as Harry thrust his head through the flap. 'I trust you bring better news than these fools here.' He glanced balefully at the two scurriers who had preceded Harry.

'I doubt you'll think so, my lord.' Harry stripped off his gloves and flung them down. 'There's no way out by the river road.'

'How so?' Salisbury halted in his pacing. 'My own man says there's more than room to pass on the east side.'

'So there is – but not at night,' Harry answered him. 'It's too open to ambush.'

'Ambush? What is this of ambush?' Salisbury's colour rose with his temper. 'It's behind us the enemy are, not in front. Behind, do you hear? Almost snapping at our heels.'

'The main host under Douglas is behind us,' Harry said. 'But there may be others. Our own force is divided, why not theirs?'

'Conjecture. Pure conjecture. It's facts we must face, unpalatable as they might be. And as I see it the fact is that with the enemy so close we must move from our present position or be snared like rabbits. There is no way to go but forward. We must take the river road.' Salisbury's eyes scanned the ring of faces, his meaningful glance telling them what was expected. The men nodded and murmured agreement. There were none there who would have dared question their lord's judgement.

Then loudly Harry said, 'I disagree. My father has been sighted less than twenty miles away. If we wait for him to come up then we'll have more than enough men to equal Douglas.'

Salisbury stared at him, the breath coming loudly through his pinched nostrils. 'Do I hear aright?' he said incredulously. 'You suggest that we give battle here? With the hills at our back and the river flanking our left?' He gave a scornful bark of laughter. 'Do you hear, my lords? We are to be schooled in strategy by this young cub here who has never fought anything more frightening than his own shadow. And such daring tactics – to wait for his father to come up.' Then he thrust his sneering face close to Harry's. 'Are you Lord Warden or no? Must you still be wet-nursed by Northumberland?'

Harry grew visibly pale as Salisbury's men sniggered loudly. The blue eyes mocked him steadily, Eleanor's eyes, with that same mixture of compassion and disgust as if they saw some low pathetic inhuman thing instead of him. Rage and bitterness scoured his mouth and he grew hot with the desire to strike the sneer from Salisbury's face. Then it all fell away like the warmth of a winter cloak. The old crippling uncertainty rushed in and for one brief moment left him cold and naked and less than half a man.

It was long enough. Salisbury turned away from him, smug in the knowledge of total victory. 'We are agreed, then? We must move quickly whilst darkness and the moon combine to our advantage. It will be a long night. We can be through and away on the homeward road well before dawn.'

Harry struggled to free his frozen mind. He looked wildly at the handful of men he could once have relied upon to back him but they no longer looked to him. Salisbury held all their eyes, strutting confidently in their midst, bright and malevolent and glittering with the assurance of a battle already won. Quietly Harry withdrew into the darkness.

They had gone barely a mile before it began to rain and they were plunged into darkness. The moon was obscured by dark threatening cloud, the wind had swung east and drove the stinging rain hard into their eyes, the wide river bank that had comfortably allowed four men to ride abreast had unpredictably narrowed down to the bare width of two. Still they blundered on toward the break in the hills. Their only guide was the dull treacherous roar of the river that hemmed them in.

Harry rode at Salisbury's flank, plunged into a misery as dark and fathomless as the night. Even the knowledge that his uncle's earlier confidence was waning fast was no consolation. He had lost the thing he valued most, the respect and admiration of his men, and though the news of his humiliation had not yet spread through the ranks, it soon would. Salisbury would make certain of that. Tears of mortification stung his eyes. He remembered all too vividly how he had stood and quailed like a raw boy beneath Salisbury's eyes. Again he thought savagely of Eleanor. Where was she now? Whoring herself with this man's son or any other who could meet her body's insatiable need? The thought raised a film of sweat on his icy skin and he thrust it violently back into a dark corner of his mind. He had long ago schooled himself not to think of her and if his mind ever strayed beyond the Border and his duty it was to the son that she had so grudgingly conceived and borne him. He even took a strange perverse pleasure in her loathing for the child. It somehow made the boy all the more his special care. In the darkness a smile softened his mouth. The boy would not lack for love. There was enough in him to make up for any lack in Eleanor.

Then Salisbury's raised and trembling hand halted him. The head of the column had emerged into the flat open grassland beyond the hills and the moon slid briefly from her hiding to show them a glimpse of the road home. Still Salisbury hesitated and Harry listened with him and heard nothing but the wind. Yet was it the wind, or more the long sighing release of a thousand pent breaths? Both men turned and looked back to where the rest of their army struggled from the darkness. They were still staring, rigid with shock when the first of the arrows fell.

Hal squinted into the rain, peering along the river road till it was swallowed by the hills. Then he glanced uneasily about him. Salisbury had not been gone long; the ashes of his watchfires still pitted the ground and the soft earth bore the sharp clear imprint of a wheel. Again he looked toward the granite cleft. But not that way, surely? The road was well enough for a single horseman but not for an army laden with wagons and packs. Would Salisbury have been such a fool?

He turned his horse and rode to where Clifford sat sucking rain from his dripping beard. 'They've taken the river road,' he said grimly.

'More bloody fools them,' Clifford answered dourly and spat.

'And the Douglas after them?' Thomas asked from the shadow of his sodden hood.

'No.' Hal shook his head. 'James Douglas would have more sense.' He pointed westward. 'There's another road up ahead; steep and rough in places but a shorter and less hazardous route. Douglas will have gone that way and no doubt he'll be waiting to welcome Salisbury when he reaches open ground.'

Thomas groaned. 'And Harry with him.'

Hal's mouth tightened. He might have gained some perverse pleasure from Salisbury's obvious blunder if Harry had not been part of it. He frowned in exasperation. What in God's name was Harry about to have taken such a risk?

The uneasiness pursued him as they took the steep uphill path, stronger upon him than it usually was, for anxiety and disquiet were an integral part of him now. He felt sometimes as if he were smitten with some dread disease, knowing that each road he took led nowhere, that the future was a dark cavern of emptiness from which he would never emerge. He lived with it well enough now. He was past all fear of it, past all hope that Elizabeth, for once, might have been wrong. A while ago he had almost convinced himself of it, in those first strange days after her death. He had felt a wild and joyous sense of freedom. He was like a child emerging from a dark and frightening room; all had been bright and wondrous colour. Then slowly, as the days passed, the shadows had returned. He felt her presence often now, watchful and loving and benign. He did not resent it. She came only out of love, because he was her child and she would stay with him till the end. Almost he derived a sense of peace from it now. All his pleasure and pain was outside himself. He thought only of Alianore and his sons, for although he knew that he would not survive, they might. And in the meantime, even if the ultimate victory was not to be his, he would give Salisbury a fine run. There was a certain advantage in knowing that one's days were so neatly and precisely numbered. It had bred an air of reckless defiance in him that was some compensation for all the careful and stilted years that had gone before. He said and did as he pleased and feared neither the law nor the men who made it. For this small space of time at least, he was inviolate. He intended to make the most of it, yet for all his fearlessness, fear could still touch him; through Alianore, through his sons. He thought again of Harry. If any harm had come to Harry through this piece of folly . . .

Then they were standing on the low brow of the hill looking down on the unbelievable slaughter of their army. Not more than half had managed to gain the open ground beyond the ravine and make a stand. The rest had perished miserably where they stood, cut down by the enemy concealed in the rocks, or thrust into the river as they ran for their lives. Jesus, he thought. It was like looking down into the bowels of hell.

The rain had ceased and the moon shone like a single baleful eye. The pale crystalline light lent a terrible unreality to the men who moved beneath him like an army of the dead. Shadow upon shadow, light upon light, their armour glowed with a ghostly sheen. Their banners flew bland and colourless, yet he knew all their devices: Ross, Livingstone, Kerr and Home, the bleeding heart of Douglas. Their own were fewer: Salisbury, Latimer, Grey and with heart-stopping relief, the silver crescent of his son. He smiled. Harry was alive.

He drew his sword and filled his lungs with the cold night air. 'Espérance. Espérance Percy.' His cry rang out all over the valley, rebounding from the hills as the thousand men at his back took it up. It reached the ears of the tired men who fought below him and they fought harder, knowing that he was at hand.

The hillside drummed and quivered with the force of their headlong ride and Hal did not check their pace even when the enemy were less than a bow's length away. The impact alone felled two hundred men and swept them into the heart of the fight. Thomas and Richard fought close by him, matching him blow for blow, sharing his charmed and protected life. They cut down thirty men between them in minutes. It was little effort to run through a man already dulled by an hour of carnage.

He saw Harry fighting grimly and silently and shouted aloud his relief that he was whole and sound. Then suddenly Harry's face was torn from his vision. He felt the dragging numbing weight of the flail wrapped round his arm, the dull agonising thud of the ball lodged in his shoulder. Then he was down, clawing at silk and leather and the sweating flanks of his horse. He anchored himself to the stirrup, thrusting his forearm through the loop. The horse dragged him wildly along through a mire of mud and trampled bloody flesh. Then a hand checked and steadied the beast and Harry danced his own horse round to protect him while he rose. He heard Harry's voice urging him up. 'Mount up, my lord, for pity's sake. I cannot hold them off for long.'

Hal forced himself to his knees and felt with his broken trembling hand for the reins. Harry helped him the rest of the way and only waited to see him safely in the saddle before he was gone again. Thomas led him solicitously from the field. Above the drumming of blood in his ears he heard Salisbury's trumpeters shrilling the retreat. He closed his eyes in weary resignation. If only he could. Dear God, if only he could.

The next day he stood in the open and viewed the horrific toll of the dead. Two thousand at the last count and still more to come. Since dawn he had waited and his tired eyes had seen each battered and mangled corpse as it came in. It was noon now and he was beyond shock, beyond all horror or regret, beyond all feeling save that of his own bitter grief. The tears ran unchecked down his face. His son Harry was not among the living.

Eleanor was aware of Thomas long before he entered the room. Her flesh grew warm and moist, her heart beat with sharp painful strokes. Familiarity, absence, the cruel disdainful way he used her; nothing had ever lessened her desperate longing for him. She heard him close the door quietly. His footsteps moved with a slow, soft, dragging tread. Only when he was close enough to touch her did she look round. Her eyes dilated in shock. He was filthy and unshaven and his left arm hung limp and useless by his side. He smiled his twisted, resentful smile. 'Forgive my dishevelment,' he said mockingly. 'I have ridden hard all night. I knew that you would be too eager for news of Harry to reproach me for soiled linen.'

He was sneering at her as always but for once she didn't care. Her heart beat faster, pumping the blood hotly into her face. 'What news?' she asked faintly.

He quirked his dark sleek brows at her. 'You have to ask, Eleanor? Surely you must have dreamt of it often enough. I had thought to find you revelling already.'

She rose abruptly and the jewelled book upon her lap clattered to the floor. She stared down at it, not daring to look at him lest he see the hope in her eyes. Her voice when she spoke was a thin pale thread. 'Is he dead?'

Thomas came and stood close to her. There was wine on his breath and a great purple bruise stained his cheek beneath the pallor of dust. She would have put out a hand to touch it but the relentless eyes checked her. 'Harry,' she said again. 'Is he dead?' This time she could not keep the shameful eagerness from her voice and for a moment his eyes seemed to affirm and enlarge the hope. Harry was dead. She was free. They were both free.

Then Thomas smiled with sad mockery. 'I fear not, sweet sister.' He laughed as he saw the colour leave her face. 'You see, Eleanor, how I am always bound to disappoint you?'

He moved away from her and dropped awkwardly into the high-backed chair by the hearth while she stood mute and trembling with anger and despair. He spoke tauntingly to her rigid back. 'Poor Eleanor. I fear there is no escape yet. Harry is alive and well, albeit in captivity. He'll soon be back among us. At a price.'

There was something in his voice that made her turn and look at him. He was slumped wearily on the chair, his eyes half closed as if he would sleep, yet there was a tension in the long lines of his body, a resentment in the blue eyes that for once was not for her. Softly she said, 'And you think the price is too high perhaps, Thomas?'

Instantly his guard was up again. 'Harry is my true and well beloved brother. What price could be too high?' It was said with his usual irony but she held his look, refusing to relinquish this rare true glimpse of him. Then his head dropped back and he closed his eyes, too weary to fight even her.

'Let us say I think the money could be better spent,' he said. 'It was his own damned stupid fault.'

She heard the whole sorry tale of it then: Salisbury's gross and unforgiveable error and Harry's enforced complicity. Her lip curled. How like him to be swayed so easily from his judgement. Both Salisbury, and Northumberland in Harry's stead, had been called to account for the debacle. There had been more than three thousand lost and half as many again maimed and crippled. She looked at his own crudely bandaged arm. 'Does it pain you?'

'Not overmuch. Not as much as will putting my revenues in pawn to free Harry. Douglas is demanding an extortionate sum. It'll keep us in penury for years.' He smiled weakly. 'That will irk you, will it not, Eleanor? To yield up all your furs and jewels to buy Harry back: was a worse bargain ever struck?'

She smiled back at him, almost afraid to speak and shatter this new and fragile peace between them. She said carefully, 'I have no doubt I shall survive the lack of them.'

259

'Yes. No doubt we will all survive, enriched in mind and spirit by the sacrifice. After all, what are lands and riches compared to dear Harry's life?' The sneer was smothered by an exclamation of pain as he shifted his weight in the comfortless chair.

Eleanor remained silent and unmoving though she longed to put a pillow at his back and change the filthy binding of his wound. She doubted that it had even been properly cleansed.

Thomas looked quickly away from her caring glance and studied the rich velvet-clad elegance of the room. His eyes lingered on the high carved bed spread with skins of vair and fox and curtained with tussore silk. At length he said in a voice hoarse with pain, 'Eleanor. In all this regal and feminine splendour is there anything so coarse and profligate as a cup of wine?'

She went to fetch it wordlessly, her hands trembling with the depth of her feeling. For the first time in years there was something more than bitterness and conflict between them. And even if it was only his weakness and pain that had brought him to this softness, it was enough that he was here, within reach of her love and tenderness.

When she returned with the wine he was already asleep. She stood and watched him for a while and smoothed the damp curls from his brow. Then quietly she sank down at his feet and laid her head against him. If all her life were to be had again, she would wish for nothing better than this.

When he woke his face was flushed and sweating with fever. For a moment he stared at her blankly. His dry lips moved soundlessly before they shaped themselves into a scream of pain as he tried to stand. His bright fevered gaze clung to her face as if she were all that held him upright. Then the fire was quenched and he fell heavily against her. His weight almost felled her to the ground and she cried out for a page to attend her. Together they half dragged, half carried him to the bed. Eleanor laid her fingers on his burning flesh and felt for the slow dragging pulse.

'Fetch the Countess Alianore,' she commanded. 'Tell her that the lord Thomas is grievously sick.'

Alianore came swiftly with the black-polled leech fluttering in her wake. She watched anxiously as he settled by the bed like a vulture, then she turned her sharp accusing gaze on Eleanor. 'Why did you not send for me sooner?'

'He slept. I thought it better that he did so.' Eleanor saw the older woman's gaze rest suspiciously on the ornate bed that held her son. 'He came to tell me the news of Harry and fell asleep in the chair. I summoned a page to help me carry him to the bed.'

Alianore nodded dully, her face pale and taut with worry. She had hardly recovered from the news of Harry's capture. It was almost too much, to be struck at again so soon. And through Thomas at that, who held so much of her heart.

The physician rose and sucked in his cheeks gloomily. He had cut away the stained bandaging to reveal swollen and discoloured flesh. 'The wound is badly tainted, I fear,' he said almost happily. 'We must cauterise immediately or the arm will be lost – if we can save it at all.'

'No.' Eleanor went and stood beside him. The wound indeed was tainted, the torn edges of flesh seeping a sickly yellow pus. She felt again for his threadlike pulse. 'He would not survive the shock of burning,' she told the affronted leech. Then to Alianore she said, 'Let me try. There are other cures beside the brand and the knife.'

Alianore raised dull passive eyes. She wished suddenly that Hal were here. He would have known the best course to take, for suddenly the decision was beyond her. She looked from the hot offended countenance of the leech toward Eleanor. Her eyes were soft and wide and calming, overwhelming in their persuasion. Alianore nodded. She knew that Eleanor would not let Thomas die.

She beckoned the grumbling leech away and together they retreated to the shadows though Eleanor had long ceased to be aware of any save the stricken man upon the bed. She called for more light and candles were brought and set funereally round the bed. She cleansed her hands with a scalded cloth and fetched the little sandlewood box that had been Elizabeth's. She viewed the wound dispassionately. It was long and deep and stinking of contagion, the flesh almost riven to the bone. His fever was mounting. Sweat poured from him in great rivulets and soaked the furs at his back. She glanced once more at his face to be certain that unconsciousness still held him. Then she drew the little silver knife from its sheath and held it in the candle flame till it glowed redly. She thought tenderly, let this be all the pain I ever cause him.

For three days and nights she nursed him while the flesh steamed and pared from his bones. Alternately he roared like a drunkard and whimpered and cried like a frightened child. Then she brewed the dried root of valerian for his easement; she forced water and bitter herbs down his parched and closed throat; and when his fever reached its zenith she held him swathed in furs and velvets till it had burnt itself out. On the fourth day the fever ebbed from him and he slept peacefully. She was with him when he woke, cleansing and rebinding his wound as she had done each day. It was healing swiftly, the purpled angry flesh diminishing to a deep but well-knit scar. She glanced up and blushed faintly to find his eyes upon her.

He said, 'I had not thought you so gentle, Eleanor.' His voice was soft and slurred with weakness and the mere sound of it filled her with a joyous warmth.

He lay back among the silken pillows and gazed wonderingly about him. 'Dear God. Is this your bed?' He began to laugh weakly. 'I've often thought of being in it but not like this.'

There was a little silence as the realisation of what he had said dawned upon him. Imperceptibly he drew himself away from her and attempted lightness again. 'And how long have I languished here at your mercy? Three days? Is that all? It seems a lifetime. My mouth tasted like the pitting end of a tavern floor.' The dry eloquent voice spilled out of him, the words falling heavy as stones between them as he tried to rebuild the wall. 'And what of the prodigal Harry? Does he still fret, quite deservedly, in Douglas's cells?'

She did not listen. Her thoughts had not progressed beyond that first unguarded admission. He wanted her. He loved her. His voice went on, cruel and dispassionate, reducing everything to the trivial empty mockery that was his only defence.

'Thomas,' she said desperately. 'Thomas. Look at me.'

He lay still and silent for a long time, then slowly he turned his head. 'There,' he said softly. 'Are you content now, Pandora, now that I have raised the lid? Will the knowledge of what you can see in my eyes suffice when it is Harry lying in this bed instead of me? Will either of us be happier for knowing?' He saw the tears in her eyes and smiled. 'I see that you have a woman's admirable facility for weeping,' he said. 'I had rather hoped that you would not. Tears are such a cowardly weapon. A woman sins, she weeps and *ergo*, is forgiven. Not so with us men of honour. We must fight the good fight with a steady hand and a dry eye. I always feel that is rather unfair.' He turned away from her and stared pensively at the ceiling. 'Do you think that love unrequited is worse than love denied? That to know is all? There are some things that it is better not to know, not to feel, where ignorance is truly bliss. We are neither of us made of strong enough stuff to resist. Today perhaps we are content to smile, to look, to dream. Tomorrow that will have palled and we will touch and once we have touched we must consummate that touching. Then we are lost beyond recall till we are found and discovered, as surely we must be. What then, Pandora? What will our consolation be then?'

He smiled. 'You are such a child, my love. Greedy, demanding, snatching all the sweets from the dish and stuffing yourself unforgivably till you are sick. All is such a game to you.' He lifted a hand as if to touch her then let it fall. 'Shall we play the game of living, then, Eleanor? Shall we pretend, disguise ourselves? You will be Aphrodite, sprung from the foam of the sea. And which of your many lovers shall I be? Hermes, perhaps, patron of rogues and vagabonds – or Mars, mentor of thieves, and robbers, night walkers, quarrel pickers, mockers and scoffers? And Harry? He must be Hephaistos, her blind and cuckolded spouse . . .'

Then Eleanor reached for his hand lying inert upon the covers. Their fingers twined and locked convulsively. Thomas smiled and sighed deeply. 'Today at least, my love, I do not have the strength to fight you.' He looked deep into her tear-filled eyes. 'Will I ever have again, do you think?'

For all of that day and the next she moved in a bright euphoric haze that even Alianore's hard suspicious stare could not dispel. There was a softness and a radiance in her that lit the dark wintry rooms and turned every head toward her. The covert sniggers and thin-lipped disapproval barely touched her consciousness. Nothing could penetrate her shining contentment. She loved and was loved and her happiness overflowed and spilled out of her. She smiled, she laughed and dealt so gently with little Anne Dacre that the foolish child burst into tears. Only Alianore's face sobered her and she kept her eyes lowered as she moved about the chamber they had shared since Thomas's illness. It seemed, however, that she was already betrayed.

Alianore said coolly as they dressed for supper, 'I was happy to see Thomas so well recovered today. He tells me that he is well enough to leave his bed and return to his own apartments.' She smiled thinly. 'No doubt you will wish to do the same. It will be of great comfort to me to know that you are so near at hand.' She paused and lifted her cold knowing eyes to Eleanor's face. 'In case he should wake in the night and have need of you.' She smiled as the blush suffused Eleanor's cheeks. 'But there. How selfish of me. As if you had not done enough. You must be in need of rest yourself after so long a vigil. His brother Richard shall sleep with him and see to his needs. You need not fear that you will be disturbed, Eleanor.'

The two women stared each other out and Alianore's glance was so assured and proprietory that it was Eleanor who looked away first. Then she turned and almost ran from the room, colliding with her little Flemish tiring maid at the door. She thrust her back into the passage way. 'Is Thomas alone, Rene?' she whispered urgently, afraid that Richard had already taken up his guard duty.

Rene nodded above the stack of linen in her arms and Eleanor smiled with relief. 'Keep the countess as long as you can,' she said. 'I would not be disturbed.'

She slipped silently along the dark gallery. Tears of frustration stung in her eyes. Thomas was right; knowing was not enough. She had to see him. She had to be with him and Alianore plainly was going to make sure that she was not.

Thomas was risen and dressed when she entered, standing with his back to the room. He was thin from the fever yet somehow the leanness suited him. It matched his wit and sharp derisive tongue.

She went eagerly toward him, unwarned by the dreadful stillness of him that anything had changed. 'Thomas,' she said passionately. Then he turned toward her and she flinched at the look in his eyes. She reached out a hand toward him. 'Thomas?'

He flung her off with such violence that she fell to her knees. 'Don't touch me. Don't ever touch me.' She saw then what lay beneath his hand; the white rose, faded and yellow in its little silver box and, still twined around the stem, the tell-tale scrap of parchment with its one condemning word: Warwick.

'You slut,' he said softly. 'You filthy treacherous little slut.'

The blood and breath drained slowly from her. Her eyes were dark with terror as she watched him walk slowly away. The door slammed thunderously behind him and the echo dwindled down to an awful empty silence that contained only her. She had not moved from where he had thrust her. Her eyes, still glazed, stared blindly after him. She shivered as her heart grew cold within her and slowly broke.

To Eleanor's amazement life went on; drearily, emptily, but still inexorably on. She woke and ate and slept and woke again, all within a dreamless void. Sometimes reality touched her, when Thomas's cold remorseless eyes met hers, when she remembered how close she had come to the dream and how cruelly it had been snatched away. And all for Warwick whom she had never thought of once in half a year and he probably never at all of her. The cruellest thing was that she had never been able to vindicate herself. Never once had she been alone with Thomas again, a circumstance with which Alianore happily connived. And if there ever had been words with which she could have redeemed herself the time for them was long past. She rarely even saw him now and what little news she had of him was second and third hand. She would not have demeaned herself further by asking after him. The only relief in her sad colourless world was the continued absence of Harry. Northumberland still bargained and haggled for his release but it seemed that the Scots had their eye on a greater prize. They now demanded the release of the hostages that had been given years ago as surety for the murdered King James's release. This was totally beyond Northumberland's power, so Harry stayed where he was, his life as meaningless and stilted as hers, had he but known it.

In the spring they returned to Alnwick and her despair increased. The town still bore the scars of the burning: the scorched and smoke-blackened walls of the dwellings; the charred remains of the guild's timbered hall. There was a black empty space in the heart of the town where the wooden houses of the weavers had been. And around all this, flung like a long protective arm, the first few courses of the wall that Northumberland had begged licence of the king to build. Eleanor watched it rise, stone by golden stone. Each day the carts rumbled back and forth with irritating monotony, spilling out their cargo of stones on to the cleared and levelled site where they were split and dressed and filled the air with a fine yellow dust that infiltrated even the high and lofty rooms of the keep. By April the skeletal framework of the East Gate stood like a gallows against the sky and all she could see of the moor was a faint dismembered curve. Her misery grew. She felt as if she were being walled in alive.

Distraction came and briefly roused her. There was news from Court, and of the worst for the queen and her party. Her choice of Somerset for the command of France had cost them dear. Vire, Bayeux, Avranches, Caen; the list of their losses was terrifying, and by June Somerset's bungling had cost them the whole of Normandy and Guienne and now Bordeaux was threatened. Someone had to pay for it and if Somerset himself was untouchable, he had minions enough who were not. Bishop Moleyn's head had been the first to roll, murdered by the mob as he knelt at Mass. Then Suffolk himself had been impeached, on such a long and grievous list of charges that he had feared for his very life. The queen's intervention had temporarily saved him and the ultimate sentence had been commuted to exile. He got no further than Portsmouth strand, where he had been captured and taken aboard the king's vessel, the *Nicolas of the Tower*. There he had been summarily tried and beheaded by a jeering mob.

Margaret had raged impotently. There was no doubt that York was the instigator of the crime for within a month the men of Kent were in open rebellion, their leader, significantly, calling himself John Mortimer. That his claim to be a cousin of York was so obvious a fabrication did not matter. It stirred up the long-dead fire. Roger Mortimer had been the designated heir of Richard the Second; Richard of York was his only direct descendant. The fire spread, fanned by the partisans of York and in June the rebels had appeared in strength at Blackheath screaming for blood. They had had it in the complete and utter rout of the royal army sent against them. The king and queen had fled to Kenilworth and left London to be taken almost peaceably. The citizens, disillusioned by the king's cowardly flight, had allowed them free rein, even to the savage and brutal murder of Lord Say. Only when the wholesale plundering of the city began did they rouse themselves to its defence. The rebels were quickly dispersed, slain by the irate Londoners or bought off by a timorous Lancastrian council. John Mortimer, or Jack Cade, or whatever he was called, had been taken mortally wounded to the Tower. Yet the point had been made. The government was weak, the king weaker, and though this first sparking of rebellion had been doused the smoke continued to drift. York's name was on every man's lips and his instant recall demanded. Only the king's obvious virtue kept his name unsullied. Margaret's was spat upon and openly reviled and all her power suddenly lost beneath a wave of hatred and contempt. It was on the crest of this wave that Richard of York came home.

Even this portentous news barely stirred her. Margaret, Somerset, Warwick and York? Pale shadows of another world. Had she really ever longed so much to be part of it? It seemed so futile and distant now; a long time since her heart and mind had strayed beyond the man who sat so agonisingly close to her now, for Northumberland had judged the news to be of sufficient import to call them all together for the hearing of it. She and Thomas might well have been a thousand miles apart for all the recognition he gave her, though she thought that his mouth had tightened fractionally at the mention of Warwick. She watched him openly as he joined his father and brother to discuss the implications of York's return from Ireland. Her hungry eyes saw so little of him that this was indeed a feast. He was so often away, on his father's business at Berwick or York or else to his own lordship at Egremont. Then he would be gone for days on end, always returning after dark, always dusty and dishevelled and obviously drunk. Not so obviously that it caused comment, but she whose every day was regulated by the hope of a glimpse of him noticed. She noticed too that he saw a great deal of Westmorland.

Then almost as an extension of her own thoughts she heard Northumberland say, 'Does Westmorland know?'

'Even before we did, I should think,' Thomas replied.

'Then we must . . .' Northumberland broke off as Thomas touched his arm in warning. She saw the earl's eyes come to rest coldly and accusingly upon her. She felt herself grow hot with shame. They thought her a spy. Dear God, they thought her Warwick's spy. And had she not almost been so once? her conscience reminded her. She had laid her paltry little treacheries at Warwick's feet as if he were a god.

From the corner of her eye she saw them draw away from her, shutting her out of their confidences and their lives. So they all knew about Warwick, she thought despairingly. She was the intruder, the Judas in their midst. The knowledge that Thomas had made them all party to his discovery of her trivial and half-hearted liaison was the cruellest blow of all.

She rose with stiff dignity and left them to their whispering. Outside the door she paused and heard the high wild sound of Thomas's laughter. She covered her face with trembling hands. She had never felt so forsaken and alone.

She often went to Elizabeth's old apartments, still empty, for none had cared to inhabit them after her death. The memories there were always welcoming; the silence and quiet order of the rooms soothed her. Hardly anything had changed. Even stripped of all ornament the high turret room was almost as it had been in Elizabeth's time. The bare stone floor lacked its silk rugs and the hangings had been removed from the wide bed. All else was the same. The carved Venetian desk with its secret opening still stood by the window, the massive high backed chair was set close to the hearth as Elizabeth had liked it. The chests and presses were still full of her gowns; all black, all alike, different only in feel and texture. She touched them pensively. Soft mossy wools, rich velvets, the unmistakable crispness of tussore silk; and all with the sharp scent of vervain clinging to their folds. Eleanor buried her face in the poignant softness. 'Oh, Elizabeth,' she breathed. 'Elizabeth. Help me.'

She blinked back the tears ferociously. Like Thomas, Elizabeth had despised tears – tears, weakness, failure, and she was guilty of all three.

She moved idly round the room, remembering that she had once been happy here. She could still picture Elizabeth sitting aloof and remote at the little desk, the room redolent with the scent of herbs and flowers. And herself, cramped and uncomfortable at her feet, struggling through the French poem it had taken her more than a week to learn. It was not that she had lacked the wit. It was concentration that she had lacked, the dedication to her task that would have kept Elizabeth penned inside all day no matter how the sun shone or what manner of delights were offered elsewhere. She knew she had disappointed Elizabeth in that, as in other things she had disappointed everyone else, including herself. How she had envied Elizabeth; her learning, her skill, that cool, mysterious detachment that had commanded instant respect and fear. She had never been afraid of her. Elizabeth had embodied all love and kindness for her once, her refuge against a cold and unfriendly world. She had longed so much to be like her, aping her every look and gesture, even to the low musical inflection of her voice. It was only now that she saw what a poor imitation she had been. Alianore had been right in that. She was only the merest shadow of the brilliance that had been Elizabeth. Was that Elizabeth's fault, for attempting to impregnate her with her failing image or her own for abandoning hers for one that pleased her better? She saw now how vastly different they had been. Elizabeth had never needed love. She needed nothing else.

She sat at the small carved desk. Her fingers traced a pattern in the dust, then felt hesitantly for the hidden spring beneath it. She drew out the ancient leather book but did not open it. She knew its contents by heart; cures, potions, ointments, salves, harmless herbal remedies for all manner of ills. And at the back, written in a cramped black hand, the recipe for death and damnation. She thrust it back and slammed the panel shut. Once she had thought that knowledge her protection and salvation; once she would not have hesitated to use it – when Elizabeth had been alive. The delusion was resolved with frightening clarity now. Elizabeth had been her only protection. Could she still protect her from the grave?

Miserably she continued to stare through the high arched window. It was almost dusk and the sun that had warmed the room all day was bloodily impaled on the ramparts. She watched it slip down behind the blackened keep and light the turrets like lanterns. Below her the shadows stirred. It would soon be dark. Already all was silence.

Then she heard the soft muffled tread of a horse being led. A shadow emerged from the shadows and the dying light fastened hungrily on the gold at his throat and wrists. Her heart contracted painfully. It was Thomas.

She watched him lurch drunkenly across the green. Once he staggered against his horse and stood for a moment, his head laid against the beast's neck. She heard him laughing softly, long after both horse and rider had disappeared into the darkness of the stable block. She waited impatiently to see him emerge. It was fully dark now and a thin crescent moon rode low in the sky. She watched it climb and still he did not come.

She found him sprawled drunkenly among the hay, a dim smoking lantern his only light. He was instantly awake, the wicked little knife he carried at his belt drawn and levelled at her heart the moment she entered. He thrust it back into its sheath. The blue eyes smiled sardonically.

'Well, well. 'Tis fair Eleanor. What brings you out into the chill night? Touting for custom among the guard?'

The insult struck her only a glancing blow. She was prepared for it and smiled back at him, trading sneer for sneer. 'So this is where you sleep it off.' She glanced disdainfully around her, then at him. 'I am not surprised you hide yourself here. You are in fit company, among the beasts.'

He rose languorously to his feet and focussed his half-closed eyes upon her face. He was unshaven and the day's growth of beard gave him a wild renegade look. His garments too were soiled and shabby, incongruous beside the barbaric gold collar that encircled his neck. Eleanor's gaze sharpened suspiciously.

'What have you done, Thomas, that you need to hide?'

'Alas, I am undone, discovered in all my wickedness. Was it my peasant's garb that betrayed me?' The blue eyes considered her for a moment. Then bluntly he said, 'I've been a-rieving, Eleanor.' He laughed at her incomprehension. 'Burning, looting, pillaging. Sadly there was no time for rape.'

Her eyes widened. 'Raiding? You've been raiding? In God's name why?'

'Three questions in a row murders the art of conversation, Eleanor. The answer to the first two is yes. To the third, well, I see that you have already concluded that penury has not so far over-whelmed me that I need to steal another's goods and chattels. So why, then? You have wit enough to fathom the answer for yourself. Why should I burn and harry another man's lands, except out of pure spite and enmity?'

'Salisbury,' she breathed. 'You've been raiding Salisbury's lands.'

'Admirable. I knew there was more in that lovely head than treachery and blind lust. So now you can run along and inform your Yorkist paramour of my misdeeds.'

Eleanor's eyes blazed ferociously. 'Warwick is nothing to me, as well you know, Thomas. In heaven's name, I've not laid eyes on the man for over a year.'

'As long as that?' He came and stood close to her. 'A long time, then, since a man has touched you, since you have touched a man.' He laid his long sensitive fingers on the curve of her throat and slid them down towards her breasts. 'Do you want me, Eleanor?' he whispered close to her mouth. 'Do you still want me?' His hand gently cupped her breast and she opened her eyes and saw his indifferent amused gaze upon her. 'Me? Or will any man do?'

His mouth smothered her exclamation of rage but the kiss was only another weapon to demean her; hard, passionless, empty of all feeling. His teeth fastened cruelly in her lip as she tried to pull away, his body pinioned her helplessly against the wall and despite the pain, despite the shame and rage, her mouth opened to his and the longing of ten years flowed out of her.

He lifted his head and released her then. She saw her own blood wet and red upon his mouth. He smiled. 'Forgive me. I do not think I could do justice to such passion tonight. And besides, I did not come prepared. I have not a single coin upon me and I could not presume to ask for credit.' Then he drew the little sapphire ring from his finger. 'Take this, my sweet.' He dropped it contemptuously down the front of her gown. 'It's worth a great deal more than you are.'

He left her shivering and robbed of her wits as he always did. She put up a trembling hand and touched her bruised and bleeding mouth. It was the least of her pain. Her eyes were dry and hard as the little sapphire stone. This time he'd not even left her with the tears for weeping.

She kept to her chamber all of the next day and nursed both her wounded mouth and her wounded pride. Lying inert upon her bed, she dulled the worst with wine. The coward's cure, Elizabeth had always called it, but cowardly or not it was effective. With half a pitcher of malmsey inside her she could achieve something very near self-respect.

She dragged herself up from the bed and stared at herself in the long glass. The wine had brought a becoming flush to her cheeks and even her swollen mouth could not detract from the fire and brilliance of her eyes. Where then was the fault? Why was she spurned and unloved? Because she had broken a few of their petty artificial rules? Because she did not shrink and simper but stared a man boldly in the eye? Her mouth drooped in self pity. That was Elizabeth's fault. She had schooled her too well in self-awareness, in self-love. What she had forgotten to teach her was that self must be all; complete, unneedful, sustaining itself always from within. Elizabeth had been able to look inside herself and see no lack. *She* looked and saw only emptiness. She needed love, tenderness, the touch of a man's hand . . . She closed her eyes and emptied the goblet in one greedy gulp. She thought of Thomas, his mouth on hers, his body so warm and so close. Even in the pain there had been pleasure. She dwelt longingly on the pleasure. Again she filled the goblet and the wine suffused her senses with its amber glow.

Dreams whirled her upwards on a spiral of muddled optimism and euphoric hope. All would be different. Tomorrow the world would change; she would change. There would be love and warmth and compassion and she would stand on the pinnacle of her ambition and reach up into the heaven she had made. The soft white clouds brushed insubstantially against her face. Through their chilly haze she saw the world as she would have it. Harry gone – she did not quite know where. And Thomas. *Thomas.* The clouds swirled drunkenly about her head and parted for one awful moment of clarity. She stared down at the ring that she had not been able to resist the temptation to wear. 'Take this, my sweet. It's worth far more than you are.'

She refilled her goblet for the tenth time and began the slow agonising descent from the clouds. She stared blankly into the brimming cup and slopped it uncaringly onto her hand. Was this all her future mirrored here? This drunken bleary hag? Where was Eleanor? Where was lithe beautiful Eleanor? Crushed by Thomas's angry mouth? Ground to dust beneath his disdainful heel? Imprisoned here in the dark indigo depths of a jewel? How Elizabeth would have wept to see her, reduced to this snivelling pitiful wretch seeking comfort from a wine jar. Elizabeth had really loved her.

She rushed headlong to the bottom of the pit. Had she? Had Elizabeth ever loved any but herself? Had she only seen Eleanor as an extension of that self? She began to weep, great empty racking sobs that brought nausea burning into her throat. Had anyone ever really loved her? Not Harry, not her three fair daughters and her ugly incubus son. Not Thomas. Most decidedly not Thomas. She clutched frantically at the bedpost for support, then of her own will let it go. The ground and darkness came blissfully up to meet her.

The next day Eleanor roused herself and bade Rene prepare her a bath. Her head throbbed unmercifully but the few hours of oblivion had cleared her mind and amazingly, the optimism persisted. She vowed a new beginning. She would emerge from this bloated chrysalis of a life, she would shed her old serpent skin; like the phoenix she would rise again. She smiled wryly.

Why must she always scale the heights or plumb the depths? There must be somewhere more comfortable in between.

She knelt by the fire while Rene combed her dripping hair into sleek glittering waves. Her mind ran on trivial things: the choice of a gown, a jewel, whether the high horned hennin or the demure venetian cap. She would call her daughters to her; together they would go down to the hall and stir them from their complacency. She was not some drab who could be banished to the shadows. She was Eleanor Percy, Lady Poynings, Baroness Brian and FitzPayn. She was the future Countess of Northumberland and the mother of their heir.

Then at the last moment her courage failed her. Sumptuously jewelled and gowned as she was she could not face Thomas, she could not face any of them. So she sent Rene away and refused the dish of fruit and figs that was sent up for her. She looked longingly at the pitcher of wine that promised blessed oblivion again.

She rose from her chair and paced awhile then took up the book of Italian verse that had been Elizabeth's. Elizabeth had loved Cavalcanti.

She read aloud to banish the silence:

'You have in you the flowers and the verdure,
And all that's light or beautiful to sight
So far outshining sun, that nurture
No man who knows not your delight
In this world live no other creatures
So full of beauty or of countless pleasures . . .'

A voice from the door took up the refrain softly and finished it.

'Whoever fears love needs but view your features
To rest assured of his many treasures.'

Eleanor looked up, startled. Thomas stood with his back against the door; clean, sober, immaculate in dark blue silk. 'Get out,' she snapped. 'I am in no mood for humiliation tonight.'

'Nor I, Eleanor.' Thomas smiled uncertainly. 'I am contrite, penitent, remorseful. I have come for absolution.'

'And you think you deserve it?'

He advanced a little further into the room. 'Not yet. I have not abased myself sufficiently yet.'

She turned away from him. 'Leave me be, Thomas,' she said wearily. 'Let your penance be that. It's time you found another whetstone on which to sharpen your tongue. I fear I am blunted with overuse.'

He smiled ruefully. 'I wish I did not deserve that so well.'

She looked at him then. His eyes for once were grave and a darker blue without their perpetual mockery. 'Why, Thomas?' she asked with equal gravity. 'Why must you persecute me so?'

'If I offered something as trivial as jealousy, would you believe me?'

'And if I said that you had no cause, that I had allowed no man but Harry into my bed and him only grudgingly – would you believe me?'

'I should want to.'

'Then ask, Thomas. Ask it and be done with it. I shall not lie to you.'

The blue eyes were uncertain. 'Perhaps that is what I am so mortally afraid of. I might not like the truth.'

'Nevertheless you must hear it. Perhaps I need absolution too. Warwick then,' she said quietly, 'who has loomed so large between us and with so little cause.' He had looked away from her and it was easier to talk without his eyes upon her. She kept nothing back: the little there had been between herself and Warwick, the more that at the time she had wanted and finally that foolish pathetic little betrayal.

His fingers laid themselves gently against her mouth. 'It doesn't matter,' he said. 'We are beyond blame and justification now, beyond reproach. I have shot all my arrows against you, Eleanor. My quiver is empty. I am disarmed and freely admit my defeat. If you were the whore of Satan herself I should still love you.'

He took her hand and drew it slowly to his mouth. 'And we will touch and once we have touched we must consummate that touching. Then we shall be lost beyond recall.' He raised his beautiful brilliant eyes to her face. 'Lock the door, Eleanor,' he whispered. 'I am already lost.'

For all their long waiting there was no haste. His touch was slow and unhurried. His mouth lingered with long pleasurable deliberation on every hollow and curve as with infinite patience he drew her down and took her effortlessly through the forbidden gate outside which she had waited so long. They came together like age-old lovers, the dream fulfilled so often in their minds that they came to it almost prepared, yet it was more than either had ever dreamt of, a supreme ecstasy of all the senses that took them beyond recall, beyond shame and conscience, beyond speech and thought. Then they lay close together in the frightening aftermath of silence. Thomas sighed and shuddered as if with extreme cold. 'Oh, Eleanor,' he said softly. 'I fear, I very much fear we have destroyed ourselves.'

It was like the brief blazing splendour of summer. All was warmth and shining light. Concealment was impossible. One look at her lovely radiant face told all. Strangely, they were let alone as if all knew how short-lived a thing this must be and had not the heart to grudge them these few happy hours. Only Alianore fought against it and was doubly stricken to see how far Thomas had passed from her influence. It was done, he said, for good or ill. He would pay the price when the time came and be glad of it.

Discreetly, Eleanor had moved to Elizabeth's old apartments in the Postern Tower. Thomas did not come to her nightly. It was not such a light and trivial thing that it needed constant affirmation. The magnitude of each consummation could stay with them for days. For the rest they were content to stay within sight and sound of each other; to look, to smile, to touch and then to consummate that touching. And so the summer burnt itself out into sombre bronze days.

It was in the autumn that Harry came home. Thomas brought the news to her himself and within the space of a minute her world was drained and colourless again. She moved and spoke with careful restraint, her breathing was measured and shallow as if the slightest sudden movement would snap the tenuous thread of calm on which she hung and plunge her forever into madness.

Carefully, like a child, she said, 'Does Harry know?'

'Yes. He will know. All the world knows, so why not Harry? As well to try and hide the sun, my love.' His voice was hard and flippant and he smiled his old tired smile of contempt.

'What will he do?' Stupid, inane questions the answers to which didn't even matter. It was all that she felt herself capable of.

'Harry? Do? What he has done all his life, I expect. Little or nothing. Harry has this wonderful facility for self-deception. As long as we do not make him drain his cup of bitterness to the very dregs, I daresay he'll eventually convince himself that it never happened. Poor Harry has never shone at anything of consequence but I must admit he makes an admirable cuckold; a perfect Hephaistos to your Aphrodite. I cannot remember, was I to be Hermes or Mars?' He was sneering again, defending himself with the weapon of his tongue.

Eleanor looked hard into his eyes, beyond the scorn. 'And what shall we do?'

'What can we do, save go our own ways sweetly rejoicing? I shall bow and scrape and fiddle and gracefully withdraw like the courtly knight I am. And you, my sweet, will sigh and spin and resume your duties like the good and loving wife you are.' Then he turned and looked at her. His face was pale, his eyes terrible in their agony. 'Then both of us will slowly and surely die.'

They stared at each other in silent longing, afraid to speak, afraid to touch. Then Eleanor said fiercely, 'I won't. I can't. I cannot give you up.'

He caught her to him and held her close. 'Can't? Won't? We are not children, Eleanor. We knew the risk. We knew that inevitably there must be an end to it.'

'That doesn't make it any easier to bear.'

'No. It doesn't,' Thomas admitted. 'Nevertheless, we must face it. Harry has his release. Tomorrow or the next day he will be home.'

She moved away from him. Each word sounded like a death knell in her ears. Tomorrow or the next day Harry would be home. She thought with loathing of his cold damp hands, of his foul drunken breath upon her. Sweet Mother of God, how could she suffer it after Thomas? 'We could fight it,' she said. 'We could go away . . .'

'And live in an ivory tower with a dragon to guard the door and each day I would climb down the rope of your hair and fetch ambrosia for our dinner.' Thomas smiled. 'I think even Harry would balk at that.'

'Damn Harry,' she screamed. 'Damn Harry and Northumberland and all of the world. I will not let it end.'

He came and laid his arms around her. 'In our minds and hearts it will never end, not till one or the other of us is dead. But to the rest of the world it must be seen to be finished. Do you think they would ever let us alone? Where would we go? Where would we hide from the pack that my father would set on our tail? He would not see Harry spurned lightly.' He chafed her cold hands and kissed them and struggled to maintain his precarious calm. It would be the hardest thing he had ever done to relinquish her – especially to Harry. 'Do you know,' he said mildly, 'I hate him. Harry, I mean. I always despised him for being weak and insipid. I've always envied him being the eldest son. I've envied him Northumberland and hated him because he did not care for it as I did.' He smiled with the gentleness he kept only for her. 'I love this place almost as much as I love you. I love the hills and the wildness and the freedom. Harry is more at home at Court. He likes a quiet ordered life where his greatest decision is the choice of a book. That's perhaps not his fault. He was raised at Court and I can well believe that an excess of our saintly monarch could turn any man. At any rate, he lost his love for the north if he ever had one. It's merely a possession to him.' He stroked the hair tenderly from her face. 'And then I envied him you. Dull, dispassionate Harry and lovely lustful Eleanor. It was almost laughable, like Venus and Cyclops. But do you see the impossible irony of it? There are only two things I have ever really wanted in all my life. One is Northumberland; the other is you. Is it not a cruel travesty that Harry possesses both?'

She did not answer him. There was nothing to say and they stood close together for a little while longer and he kissed her for the last time. Outside the wind screeched round the high tower room and mocked them.

Thomas was drunk as he had been to a greater or lesser degree ever since his brother's homecoming. He lay in the dim shuttered room, slipping quietly and gracefully into oblivion. The room swam hazily, the bed swayed like a ship on a running sea and lurched terrifyingly as he tried to sit up. He fell back, nausea clawing at his throat. His head spun sickeningly in a vortex of red and yellow light and out of it came the round hateful face of his brother Harry.

He still wondered how he had survived the charade of last night – the prodigal returned and everyone all but choking on the fatted calf. He remembered the hot and crowded hall, the pungent sickly-sweet odour of rich and heavily spiced food; his father pretending a heartiness that was as incongruous on him as silks on a beggar, his mother taut as a bowstring. He had not dared look at Eleanor beyond that first agonised glance. She had been so pale and resigned, like Eurydice descending into Hell. He, like Orpheus, had stood by helplessly and watched her burn. And Harry, dear well-beloved Harry, bland, oblivious, his round vapid face tinged with uncertain pleasure at this apparently heartfelt welcome. Harry did not know – yet.

He himself had drunk enough to fell ten men that night but not enough to keep his thoughts from Eleanor. His imagination had become a subtle inescapable weapon of torture. Was Harry touching her? Did he kiss her? Did he hold her close? He had slept eventually but not for long. At dawn he had begun the whole wearisome process again. Happily, by noon he could hardly stand.

Then Harry had come, heralded by a loud discordant knocking that had sent his nerves screaming. He had been prepared for a confrontation but Harry had presented his usual imperturbable front. The very look of him was sobering.

Harry's eyes had swept disdainfully over his rumpled clothes and wild unshaven face. Thomas's own had been hot and dangerous.

'Forgive the squalor, Harry,' he had said. 'I have slept in the arms of Bacchus all night. My usual bedfellow was occupied elsewhere.'

The remark provoked nothing but a patronising smile. Was Harry really so obtuse?

His brother said woodenly, 'I came for the key of the wine cellar. The Constable said you had it.'

Thomas began to laugh, wave after wave of drunken uncontrollable laughter that slowly turned the corners of Harry's mouth down in a look of formidable disapproval. 'Is that all, Harry?' Thomas said eventually. He detached the key from his belt and held it out. 'I dare say you'll find it half empty by now.'

Harry tapped the key solemnly against his thigh and his look of pious disapproval brought a fresh wave of laughter from Thomas. 'For God's sake, Harry, don't pout. You look like an outraged virgin. So, I think, must St Agatha have looked after they burned off her breast.'

Harry's pursed mouth stretched into a faint supercilious smile. 'Still sneering, Tom?' He shook his head. 'You'll never change, will you? I had hoped this last year might teach you something.'

Thomas leaned back in his chair and regarded his brother through narrowed eyes. I wonder, he thought, if he knows how near I am to fratricide. He said in his slow, languorous voice, 'Such as, Harry? Instruct me in the folly of my ways, I pray you.'

'Such as that life is not one long drunken rout. It has responsibilities, duties.'

'Which you have successfully shirked for the past year, I notice.'

'That was hardly my fault,' Harry threw back. 'I was a prisoner.'

'And I can see how rigorous your captivity was by your healthy cherubic glow. Did they put you to the question, Harry? The rack, the lash, the screw? Or did you yield to no more than a quelling look as you did with Salisbury?'

Harry flushed scarlet with mortification. 'I wondered when you'd bring that up. I suppose you could have done better.'

'Infinitely so. And there are three thousand corpses buried in Lauderdale to prove it.'

The scarlet crept to the roots of Harry's fair hair but he stood his ground. 'I think I have more than paid for my error, if error there was. I have been more than a year in captivity.'

'Ah, yes.' Thomas heaved a long and elaborate sigh. 'Your captivity. We are harking back to that again, are we? The highlight of your dull and dreary life; your enslavement in the bottomless pit? On the contrary, I hear that you were quite feted, Harry. Treated as a prized and valued guest, as indeed you were – to the tune of eight thousand pounds, part of which came from my own revenues. So let us hear no more of your captivity, Harry, lest I am too well reminded of the cost and what a poor bargain it was.'

Harry held his look for less than a moment before the ruthless blue eyes bore his down. 'I am well aware of your opinion of me, Thomas,' he said stiffly. 'You've made it more than plain many a time.' He raised his eyes and attempted a crafty, knowledgeable look. 'And I know why. You've always grudged me Northumberland, haven't you, Tom?' He thought that by his brother's silence he had won a point and went on with foolish confidence. 'Oh, yes. I know you've always envied me. It must have been a blow to you when little Harry was born, crushing your hopes for good and all.' He smiled. 'Accept it, Tom. You'll never have Northumberland now.'

Thomas had smiled, all his hatred and malice shining blindingly from his eyes. 'Will I not, Harry?' he said softly. 'I've had your wife, why not all else?'

Thomas turned his face into the pillow. Oh, the joy of it. To have wiped that sanctimonious smile from his face, to see him stumbling and falling like a drunkard toward the door. He had laughed till he had wept. Only now had the implications dawned upon him. Now his tears were real. *Eleanor.* Oh, dear Jesus, what had he done to Eleanor? What would Harry do to Eleanor?

Harry stared unseeingly into the dead fire. He had been cold for a long time, his fingers cramped and rigid round the full cup of wine yet he was unaware of heat or cold, unaware of feeling of any kind. Eleanor and Thomas. Stupidly he repeated it over and over again. He supposed he should have felt rage, shame, grief even. *Eleanor and Thomas.* If he had not heard it from his brother's own foul mouth he would not have believed it. It was not Eleanor's unfaithfulness that shocked him. But with his own brother! It was almost like incest.

No wonder she had turned from him in disgust last night. No wonder she had wept, wild, demented tears that had rendered him more incapable than her sneering ever had. He felt the first pricking of anger in his frozen mind. He thought of Eleanor in his brother's arms, of her vile, unhealthy lust that Thomas obviously catered for so well. It emphasised the lack in him and his anger grew, fed by the image of a naked Eleanor. How they must have laughed at him, dull, stupid Harry who'd never have seen unless it had been thrust beneath his nose. Who else was laughing? Who else knew? Suddenly it dawned on him. They all knew, down to the last and meanest scullion. Only he had been oblivious.

He closed his eyes and tears forced themselves from beneath his heavy lids. Dear God, how he wished that he had never come back. He thought almost longingly of Scotland. He had been almost happy there, with time to read and think. And there had been women there who had not looked at him with contempt in their eyes. With the corner of his sleeve he wiped away the unmanly tears. Thomas would have loved that, to see him crying like a maid. There was still little Harry, his beloved son. Little Harry was all the consolation and comfort he needed. Then the thought came, so slowly and insidiously that he was totally unprepared for it. It struck him like a hard and painful blow. His son? Could he be sure? The dark, alien little face rose before him and he searched it frantically for some likeness to himself and found none. But then there was none of Eleanor either, he argued, and surely he could not have felt such a strong and possessive love for any but his own? But the seed was sown and had already taken deep and tenacious root. He would never really know. That was the cruellest thing. It was just another uncertainty to add to the multitude he already suffered.

He pushed himself wearily to his feet. His shoulders sagged with despair and defeat but his face had a dangerous grimness. Whether Harry was his son or not he would make sure that it was a long time before he looked on his mother's face again.

Like all the calamities of Eleanor's life it came upon her unprepared. Perhaps if she had been less numbed by her own unhappiness she might have read a portent into Harry's grim order that she be confined to her chamber. Even Rene and the children had been denied to her. She had not particularly cared then, she did not particularly care now on this bright September day with its mocking golden warmth. The year was dying and so was she.

Her departure was furtive and ignominious, with only Harry and a handful of discreet retainers to accompany her. She was grateful for that at least. She would not have wished Thomas to see her brought so low.

She mounted the horse with difficulty. She had refused the litter despite the bruises of Harry's half-hearted beating. She smiled as the dull ache settled again in her back. Poor Harry. He could not even do that well. Not that she blamed him for it. She'd heard by now of Thomas's blatant confession and laughed for the first time in a week and full in Harry's face at that. If Thomas was not afraid of him knowing then neither was she.

It was more than twenty miles to Holystone, a long and tortuous road through thickly wooded fells and hills. Never once did she slacken her pace or complain, never once did she look at Harry though she was aware that his eyes rarely left her. If he sought for some sign of despair he was disappointed or perhaps he thought that even at this last pass she might scream and rail against her fate. She would not give him even that small satisfaction and rode almost eagerly as if she welcomed the prospect of a long separation. And in her heart she did. Her surroundings were of little consequence, her company less. There was no one she grieved to leave behind except Thomas and he was as inaccessible to her now as the moon. She might even enjoy the respite for she was sure enough of her own power and position to know that Harry could not keep her here for long. At least she would be free of him, free of all pretence and worldly cares. The idea became almost pleasurable. She had forgotten how supremely adaptable she was. She smiled almost happily to herself. It would take a better man than Harry to bring her down.

They came to the last bend in the road and she saw the priory, solid and secure behind high walls. The gates were thrown wide and a tall sombre figure waited to greet them.

She dismounted slowly and only now did her courage threaten to fail her.

Then she heard Harry's strangled exclamation. 'Eleanor!'

She turned to look at him. Her face, softly swathed in pale silk, looked almost virginal and the smile that she gave him was radiant. You see, her eyes said cruelly. I'd rather this than life without him. Then she turned and walked away from him and crossed the dark forbidding threshold. Slowly the great doors swung shut behind her and sealed her from the world.

1454–1461

Let us walk in a new vineyard, let us make a gay new garden in the month of March with this fair white rose and herb, the Earl of March.

– William Gregory

Leconfield

Hal looked down at the parchment beneath his hand and York's great seal riven like the two halves of a coin. It was signed with his new flaunting title: *Richard, by the Grace of God, Duke of York and Lord Protector of the Realm.* Hal's mouth curved in faint disdain. He was almost there, only a hair's breadth away from the crown itself, a giant step from that ignominious time two years before when he had vainly tried to bring Somerset down. Then the quarrel between the two men had been at its height. York's constant submissions to have his rival removed from office had been met with the usual evasions and rebuffs and it soon became clear that fair words would gain him nothing. His alternative strategy of force had met with as little success. He had not only badly misjudged his moment but had also underestimated Somerset's influence with the king. The presence of his army outside London had been a strong enough threat to force the king and queen to a parley and reluctantly Henry had agreed to yield Somerset up if York would disband. Triumphantly York had entered the city with a bare dozen men at his back, expecting to find Somerset under close arrest. Instead it was himself who was swiftly committed to the Tower.

Hal had not been surprised at Richard of York's arrest but he had been at his almost immediate release. Trickery had won the day for Somerset and the queen that time. Hal doubted if York would be quite so gullible again.

Since then, as if in retribution, the tide had flowed swiftly against the queen: first came the final and humiliating loss of Gascony; and then last year at the end of July the shattering blow of the king's collapse. Margaret had rallied as best she could and for a while the king's condition had remained unknown to all but the intimates of her Council, but the wall of secrecy could not stand up to York's battering for long. By September there was no help for it but to reveal the mindless dribbling idiot that was Henry the King.

To York it must have seemed like a gift from the gods and if his triumph was a little dimmed by the birth of a son, Edward, to the queen in October, it had made him all the more determined to leave no vestige of power in her hands. In the spring of this following year, Somerset had been confined to the Tower to await trial and Margaret had openly wept as York was named Protector. The same thought was in all their minds. What was there to stop him now?

Hal pushed himself from the narrow constricting chair. He was growing old, much to his surprise. He had never thought he would live so long. He moved leisurely across the room and stretched himself to ease the stiffness that had settled in his limbs. He had never relished the prospect of growing old; the inevitable decay of his faculties, the gradual process of ceasing to be a participant in life and becoming merely a spectator. He would happily forego that. He smiled grimly. How much longer then? He sensed that the time was not far off now, that his life was moving slowly and inevitably to its climax. He felt Elizabeth's presence more often now, more strongly. That was portent enough. He knew that she would not let him come to it unprepared.

Broodingly he stared from the window. It all looked so peaceful and still, the soft languorous curve of the moor and hardly a breeze to stir the heavy summer heads of the trees. It was hard to believe that a few miles away men were tearing each other to pieces and were not even sure of the reason why. At this moment his son Thomas terrorised the city of York. He glanced again toward the letter. The wording was curt and imperious – that the Earl of Northumberland present himself with all speed before the Council at Westminster to answer for the gross misconduct of Thomas, the Lord Egremont, and Sir Richard Percy.

Gross misconduct! A mild epithet for the burning and killing that had been carried out in his name this last year. Once his conscience would never have permitted it but he had no conscience now. His emotions were of a harder and baser kind and if his last act on earth was to do Salisbury hurt then he would die well content. They might fence with fine words and policy at Westminster but here in the north they were more direct. For over a year now it had been open aggression between himself and Salisbury. Not a day passed without some confrontation and it was such a trivial thing that had sparked it all off. The bone of contention had been Wressel, one of the few of his grandfather's possessions that he had not won back. That Chancellor Cromwell had held it was affront enough but that it should pass to Salisbury, through the marriage of one of his sons to Cromwell's niece! He would have felt almost dishonoured if he had let it pass without comment. There was nothing he could do about the marriage but at least he had provided them with a fitting reception, and had added the satisfaction of seeing Salisbury running like a frightened rabbit to that of his forcible possession of Wressel. Inevitably retribution had followed retribution. Now it was outright war. Thomas was the main aggressor, persecuting their adversaries with a ferocity that sometimes bordered on madness – the courtier turned renegade, though Hal thought privately that it was more some secret inner war he fought than for any one cause. He wondered if he still thought of Eleanor. It was nearly four years now, time perhaps to forgive and forget but Harry stubbornly refused even to consider her release. He blamed himself in part, that it should ever have happened at all. He had been too preoccupied with Harry's release, terrified lest he should be condemned to the same dreary life that Hal had once known. If he had been more aware, if he had seen what everyone else had seen only too clearly. Harry had not been the only one in happy and total ignorance. They had all been changed by it, Thomas especially. It was hard to recognise his courteous and cultured son in the bitter and ruthless man he had become. Harry wore his resentment like a badge, always stiff and sullen whenever Thomas was there. He had become a lonely, almost sad, figure with affection for none except his motherless little son. And between them all was Alianore, so thin and worn and anxious of late, exhausted with the effort of keeping her warring sons apart. He sighed deeply. War within, war without, and the promise of worse to come, for his quarrel with Salisbury was only a symptom of the greater disease which had men all over England taking the same precautionary moves. Quietly and unobtrusively castles were being victualled and provisioned, men were being recruited to swell the retinues of the lords into miniature armies. He himself had recruited another five hundred men. No man was taking the risk of being unprepared when the time came – as it surely would, and soon now. York's peremptory summons was proof of that.

He went back to the table and picked it up. How then should he answer the Lord Protector? Should he go or not? He smiled and slowly tore the parchment across. If York wanted speech with him, then let him come and seek him.

And come he did, with such speed and force that he sent Exeter scurrying southwards in a sweat of fear. Even Thomas, who would exploit a gamble to the limit withdrew from York and contented himself with keeping the Protector pinned down while he burnt and harried a path around him. For five days York was a virtual prisoner in his own city; on the sixth he broke out and came looking for Hal.

The confrontation lacked York's usual finesse. He had obviously weighed his chances of winning Northumberland over and dismissed them out of hand.

'So,' he said loudly. 'What excuse do you offer for this gross affront?'

'None,' Hal answered him mildly. 'What indeed could I say that you would want to hear?'

'Northumberland!' Menacingly York crossed the room toward him. 'For nigh on a week I have been all but held to ransom by your reprobate sons. At this very moment Egremont and his rabble are harrying my brother-in-law Salisbury's lands.'

Hal raised his brows. '*Our* brother-in-law,' he corrected him. 'Or have you forgotten that we are one big happy family?'

'Don't play at words with me, Northumberland. We've known each other too long and too well for that. Salisbury has laid complaint against you in Council. You have been summoned to Council. Unless you can give me a good explanation of your refusal to attend I shall have no option but to endorse Salisbury's complaint.'

Coldly Hal said, 'No doubt Salisbury has omitted to mention the damage his son Thomas Neville did to my own castle at Topcliffe or the fact that my hunting lodge at Cockermouth is a total ruin. Besides these, the burning of a few fields and the mild affront to your dignity seem to be of small moment.'

'I do not consider the calculated and consistent destruction of half of York to be of small moment,' York argued grimly.

'Nor I, my lord. If it were true. I think perhaps that our illustrious kinsman is prone to exaggerate his injury. And if I were you, my lord, I would abandon this fruitless argument now, for I'll guarantee that there is no complaint Salisbury can bring against me where I cannot bring a better one.'

York's smile was suddenly conciliatory. 'I appreciate that this is a private quarrel and that there are faults on both sides. But there is the wider concept to be thought of. Kinsman against kinsman, brother against brother. These things have a way of spreading. Before we know what we are about . . .' He spread his hands expressively.

'Shall I say the offending words for you?' Hal's eyes rested disdainfully on York's face. 'Is it civil war that you speak of? I cannot believe that your Grace can find that so disagreeable after all your efforts these past five years to bring about just that.'

York's face was impassive but his eyes gleamed with suppressed anger. 'Well, my lord. Seeing as you speak so plainly then so shall I, and tell you that these squabbles are not confined to the North. There is unrest and disquiet all over England and with good cause. The king is a virtual madman, the queen an adulterous foreigner who tries to foist her bastard upon us as Prince of Wales . . .'

'Plain speech indeed,' Hal cut him off icily. 'Have you proof of this slander against the queen?'

'One look at Henry would be proof enough for most men,' said York. 'Or are we to believe this child conceived by the Holy Ghost? God, man! This is Somerset's bastard, clear enough. If you doubt it then you are the only man in England who does.'

'A man's opinion is his own,' Hal answered equably. 'But the law of England takes no account of opinion or personal preference and the law says that the child is Edward, Prince of Wales and England's lawful heir. Fortunately most men are in the habit of obeying the law.'

'Only you it seems are exempt,' York commented acidly.

'It would appear that we are about to embark on our fruitless argument again. So let us speak plainer still, my lord. If I appear to be above the law then it is because here in the north there is no law save that which we make ourselves. Normally, Westminster pays us no heed save to gather its tithes and taxes. I suggest that it remains so. If Salisbury and I began this quarrel single-handed then let us finish it in a like manner, unless, of course, Salisbury feels he cannot win without aid from yourself. I have never felt the need to go snivelling with my grievances to Westminster, so why should he? Or is that part and parcel of the bargain struck between you? Your help in defeating me in return for his in defeating the king?'

York's fair skin flamed with anger. 'My loyalty to the king himself has never been in question. My sole objective . . .'

'That is not strictly true,' Hal interrupted him again. 'I have questioned it many a time and on each occasion you have been found sadly lacking. Oh, I have heard all your eloquent vindications for that which, in all honesty, I can only call outright rebellion; that all is done for England's good, to protect the king from evil and perverted council. I seem to have heard it all before, or perhaps you have forgotten that we Percys are old hands at the making and breaking of kings. All you have said, Henry Bolingbroke said before he took the crown from King Richard.' He stared hard into York's crafty eyes. 'Does it still rankle so much? I suppose no more than it does with me that my family lost all because they were swayed from their true loyalty by such plausible reasoning as you yourself now put forth. England was ruled by a madman then, my lord.' He paused and turned the heavy seal upon his thumb. 'I shall tell you something that was told to me by a man who had forgotten more about the ways of kings than you will ever know. It was said of King Richard but applies equally well to Henry. "A king is a king, crowned, hallowed and annointed. No man has the right to take that from him."' Hal smiled thinly. 'I shall not deviate from that, my lord. I advise you to do the same.'

York raised his downcast eyes and suddenly looked old and anxious far beyond his years. 'I am sorry, Northumberland,' he said stiffly. 'For all our differences, I had hoped there might be some common ground on which we could meet and avoid open hostility. I see sadly that there is none.'

'None, my lord,' Hal said gravely. 'Not here, nor in heaven or in hell.'

Westminster

The queen descended with regal grace from the dais, her small bejewelled hand resting lightly on her husband's arm. She bestowed a look of almost martial triumph on the packed and joyful throng. She had won, the look said. York was down and out of power. The king was king again in more than just name. Her eyes went anxiously to the thin stooped figure beside her. Henry was well again, well enough at least to have ousted York and his upstart crew. It had been the miracle she had prayed for and fittingly it had occurred at the holy season of Christmas. As Christ had come among them, so Henry had been reborn; returned from his divine mission, for so he named the lapse of nearly five months that had brought them close to ruin. He'd had converse with the saints themselves and had added sadly that he feared he had not been pure enough in spirit yet to be vouchsafed a word with God. It made Margaret agonisingly aware of how precarious his sanity still was. Though she cossetted him like a child, she knew at the heart of her that his malady had no cure. That blank and distant look would only have to settle on his face for an instant and she would be filled with terror at the thought of him slipping back into the shadows. Time was so precious. She had so little left to make all safe for her son and her dynasty. She must preserve Henry and his fragile reason till then. She glanced with fierce pride to where the infant prince was born aloft by James of Wiltshire. Edward was all of her life now, beyond Henry and well-beloved Somerset, even beyond herself. He was her hope, her salvation, her entire future. She looked again at the king. Already he was tiring, the waxen lids drooping listlessly over the melancholy eyes. She beckoned Somerset to attend him. 'Cherish him,' she whispered fervently. 'He is all our hope till our little prince is grown.'

Hal watched her thoughtfully. She was so small, so slight that she could have drifted on the wind yet she walked among them like an Amazon, nodding and smiling at her staunchest supporters, pausing to exchange a rousing word where she thought there was apathy or doubt. She had extravagant praise for him and Clifford in their efforts against Salisbury; then she moved swiftly on to kiss the sallow and unattractive child that was Somerset's niece and held her hands out lovingly to the tall man who was the Lady Margaret Beaufort's betrothed – Edmund Tudor, the bastard of Queen Katherine and her Welsh squire, as he was called, and also a new and valuable recruit from the Yorkist camp. Hal turned his eyes from the queen's avid face. He was suddenly reminded of a whore touting for trade. Poor Henry, he thought. Poor, sick, deluded Henry who was the only innocent among them. How cruelly life had treated that gentle and simple man; first Gloucester, now York. No wonder he retreated into a world of his own.

Then the queen began to address them, her pale fanatical face lit with the vehemence of her words. She spoke of the necessity for the swift and total destruction of York and his malcontents. Had not the last year proved how base his motives were? They must strike before they were struck at, destroy before they were destroyed. The words fell emptily into Hal's mind. He was sick of lost and dying causes, sick of war and the prospect of war. Even the exhilaration of his conflict with Salisbury had begun to pall. His mouth tightened. There was no doubt that Salisbury had got the better of him this time: two of his sons in Newgate and a king's ransom to get them out. He blamed Thomas, stupid, reckless ungovernable fool that he was. He could not lay his tongue to a word that described the madness that had sent Thomas and Richard against a Neville force ten times their number. They were lucky even to be alive. Yet possibly this was the more subtle punishment; at least it was for him. They had been captured, tried and convicted of riot at a court specially convened by Salisbury. He wondered how much that had cost him though no doubt he regarded it as a fair investment to be recouped a thousandfold from the fine and damages the court had imposed. Eleven thousand pounds. The sum was staggering and so obvious a ploy to keep Thomas and Richard in ward. He had no intention of paying even the half of it as Salisbury well knew, and whilst York had been in power there had been no other way to free them. Besides, a short spell in confinement would have done Thomas no harm. Now the king was well again, it would not be hard to persuade him to intervene.

Then Margaret's strident voice intruded over his thoughts. 'Array yourselves, my lords. In the name of your gracious king and the most puissant Prince Edward, prepare for war and the glorious triumph of Lancaster.'

The words rang hollowly in his ears all the way to Newgate, above the rattle of harness and hoofbeats, above the pounding of his own heart. He knew that there would be no triumph for Lancaster, glorious or otherwise. There would be only death and destruction and the end of his own small and insignificant life.

Within the confines of Newgate death was not so feared. To most of the poor wretches crammed inside its walls death came almost as a positive relief from the pungent, malodorous stench of life that permeated even to the upper rooms of the more privileged.

Hal's wealth and position had bought his sons a single cell above ground but even here the walls were slimed with damp and there was a whisper of rats in the darkness. Hal held his sleeve across his mouth against the appalling stench and kept his eyes fixed on the sweat-stained jerkin of the turnkey. Another short fat man trailed in his wake bearing a resinous torch aloft. It was all the light there was. All else was dark and grim as the bowels of hell. Christ's passion, Hal thought. I keep my hounds in better kennels than this.

The turnkey inserted the key in the lock and closed his hand round the expected coin. He touched the greasy lip of his Paris cap. 'I'm obliged, m'lord.' He indicated a frayed loop of rope set inside the door. 'Ring that when you're ready. I'll come and let you out.' The door swung shut behind him, again the key grated in the lock and for the first time in six months Hal viewed his errant sons.

Thomas rose unhurriedly from the low bed. 'His name is Wat,' he said, jerking his thumb after the departed turnkey. 'Though I prefer to think of him as Abaddon, the angel of the Bottomless Pit. The short fat one is his *âme damnée*. I have dubbed him Cerberus because he barks like a dog and guards the gates of this particular hell. I'm afraid they both reek a mite but then I suppose so do we by now.' The blue eyes narrowed in a brief smile as he poured wine into a tarnished cup. '*Abaddon* is a procurer *par excellence*,' he went on lightly. 'There is nothing he cannot obtain at a price. The finest wines, a capon swimming in pepper sauce, even a clean whore if that's what takes your fancy. You'll be glad to hear that it doesn't mine or Richard's. Our palates override our lust these days.'

Hal smiled. Thomas always talked to cover emotion. Only his eyes betrayed how pleased he was to see him. Then he looked at Richard who was still lying on the other of the two beds. Apart from a rickety table and a chair they were all the furniture the narrow cell boasted.

'You look pale, Richard,' he said gently. 'Are you well?'

Thomas answered for him as he always did. Richard merely smiled. 'Of course he's pale.' Thomas pointed to the small barred square of daylight high up on the wall. 'Behold our window on the world and our total supply of air.' He sat down beside his younger brother and fondly ruffled his hair. 'Besides, the damp's no good for his leg. It's stiff as a branding iron today.'

Hal moved the single chair to face his sons and started as a rat scurried from one dark corner to another.

Thomas laughed. 'Don't look so outraged, father. Rats, like the stench, emanate from the straw on which our fellow unfortunates below stairs sleep, eat and defecate in turn. Though rats prefer to live and breed in filth they are more particular where they eat. It is well known, even among the rats, that Richard and I keep the best table in Newgate.'

Hal winced. 'So there is nothing that you lack then?'

'Nothing that your money can buy. Though I'd give a good deal for a long clean draught of air.' Thomas's voice suddenly lost its bantering tone. 'How much longer, father? Another six months of this and I shall be witless.'

'Not long. You must know that the king has recovered. York is vanquished and Salisbury with him. It will be simple enough now to move the king to have the fine set aside.'

Thomas's brilliant eyes were suddenly fixed accusingly on his face. 'You never thought of paying it then?'

'No,' said Hal slowly. 'I would not have given Salisbury the satisfaction.'

'I see. It was worth it for Harry, but not for us. I would have thought that pound for pound Richard and I were the better buy. There are two of us.'

'Is that remark supposed to shame me? Because I can tell you now, Thomas, it does not. Harry's ransom, however overpriced you may think it, was an honourable bargain between honourable men. Your price is sheer extortion and I am not open to either bribes or blackmail. Besides,' he smiled disarmingly, 'I thought it might teach you a lesson, namely that you are neither indestructible nor immortal.'

Thomas smiled back at him. 'I'm afraid I'm feeling abandoned and unloved and consequently peeved. Tell us the news. We are as starved for that as we are for air. Where is the dog York? Gone back to his kennel at Fotheringay and his rabid pack with him?'

Hal nodded. 'Though I doubt he'll be there for long. There are definite rumours that he is gathering an army. The queen is doing the same.'

'Then there is to be war,' Richard said solemnly.

'I cannot see how it can be avoided now,' Hal answered him. 'York has shown his hand too clearly.'

'Then get us out of this hell-hole,' Thomas said fiercely. 'I swear I'll die of pique if you strike a blow without me.'

'I cannot see how York can overcome the obstacle of King Henry,' Richard objected. 'If he still professes loyalty to Henry himself, then how can he take the crown whilst Henry lives?'

'Child,' Thomas said, 'you have it in a nutshell. He cannot, *ergo* Henry must die. It's a tried and tested formula. Poor Henry will disappear behind the walls of the Tower and emerge a corpse. There will be much wailing and wringing of hands. The Yorkists will say, well of course Henry always *was* sickly. York will reluctantly assume the crown if he has not already done so. *Et voilà*. It is accomplished.'

'And what about Prince Edward.'

'A babe, Richard, merely a babe and prey to a multitude of diseases yet. One of which I'm sure York will see to it that he's smitten with.' Thomas looked at his father. 'Am I not right, my lord?'

Hal nodded. The picture rose sharp and clear in his mind, the vague uneasiness that had haunted him all his life defined with awful clarity. 'Yes, Thomas. You are right. Frighteningly so.'

The royal army was camped five miles from St Albans, the little town sprung up like an impertinent weed at the foot of the great soaring abbey. In Somerset's gaudy silk-hung tent, Hal was part of the stunned and sickening silence that had fallen in the wake of York's departed messenger. Tom Clifford was the first to break it. 'Christ. If York is almost upon us, we've no time to wait for support to come up. We've no choice but to fight.'

'And lose without a shadow of a doubt,' Buckingham commented sourly. 'York's man made it abundantly clear that we were outnumbered three to one.'

'Bluff.' Somerset argued but he still chewed agitatedly at his lip. As always he had miscalculated. The last word they'd had was of York camped at Ware over twenty miles away. He had not expected York to advance so speedily. He thought he had allowed ample time for their own support to come up. How then to delay York? How to buy some time?

'I think we should consider the possibility of a parley,' Buckingham said. 'Why not carry on to St Albans and send envoys from there with regard to opening negotiations?'

'Parley! Negotiate!' Somerset shouted. 'You're a fool, Buckingham. Do you think York can be fobbed off with promises now?'

Buckingham regarded him coldly down the length of his thin nose. 'He was at Dartford,' he snapped. 'Why not now?'

'Because at Dartford he was deceived,' Hal intervened. 'I do not think he will be again.'

Somerset looked gratified, which was not Hal's intent. 'Our best chance lies in standing our ground here,' Somerset said. 'At least we are in open country and can deploy what forces we have to advantage.'

'And what forces are those?' Buckingham demanded aggressively. 'The few thousand that we brought from Westminster while the rest stroll toward us at their leisure because you didn't send out the summonses in time?' Buckingham's heavy face was flushed with anger. 'It's you the Yorkists are after, not the king. If it wasn't for you and your bungling incompetence there'd be no battle to be fought at all.'

'No doubt you further suggest that I give myself up to York's mercy and save you the trouble of unsheathing your sword?'

'My lords,' Hal's face was tight with strain. 'While we sit here squabbling York is bearing down upon us.' He glanced toward the curtained recess where the king still knelt in fervent prayer. 'I suggest that my lord Clifford lays both cases before his Grace and allows him to decide.'

'Then I shall await that decision in my tent,' Buckingham said loftily. 'I find the air here somewhat stifling.'

Hal followed in the Duke's outraged wake but went straight to his tent. He'd had a bellyful of Somerset himself and he was fast losing patience: with Somerset for his incompetence; with Buckingham for refusing to face the issue; with King Henry for merely being King Henry and no king at all. It had been a mistake to bring him in the first place. Margaret had protested fiercely that the king's person was too precious to be risked in combat. Somerset had argued that without the king there would be no royal army, that men would not fight wholeheartedly for a king who sat at his ease in Westminster. Henry would merely be a figurehead, he had assured her. What else had he ever been all his life? Hal thought. Only if prayers could win the coming encounter would Henry be of use.

Hal sat heavily on the long chest that contained his armour. His hands were shaking and beneath the heavy padded shirt his skin pricked with sweat. He was not afraid. He had long since abandoned fear and its accompanying emotions. It was more that he felt confused and uncertain, as if his actions were no longer his own. It was only a week since Margaret's vociferous call to arms. There had been no time for farewells, no time to broach the matter of Thomas and Richard's release. Events had moved so swiftly, yet it seemed that York had moved swifter still. He saw the fight as already lost. This foolish parody of an army was more like a courtly progress. All they needed was a fool in cap and bells and God help them, they had that in Henry. And Somerset, sweeping them along on the noisy breath of his self-opinionated policies as he had swept them out of Westminster, ill-prepared and more antagonistic toward each other than toward York. There were too many wavering loyalties. The king himself was not in question, but there were some who would think twice before plunging into battle on Somerset's account. Buckingham was one, and ridiculously, two of Salisbury's sons marched with them, knowing full well it was their father they would have to face at the end of the road. He doubted if they would stand by the king when the time came. He thought longingly of Alianore; of Harry and Ralph in blissful ignorance at Berwick; of Thomas and Richard fretting and discontented in Newgate – but safe, all blessedly safe. Whatever the outcome of the next few days for him, they would live beyond it.

Clifford's gruff and angry voice preceded him into the tent. 'We're to move on to St Albans,' he announced. 'The king decrees it.' Predictably, then, Henry had grasped at Buckingham's slender olive branch and gone against Somerset.

Clifford's face was an ill-tempered scowl. 'Talk, parley, negotiate. Anything but strike the blow that should have been struck years ago.'

Hal was forced to agree with him. They had settled for inaction too often. He said with more hope than he actually felt, 'It might

298

give us time to strengthen our forces. If we could hold York off even for a day or two.'

'I don't think so, Hal.' Clifford stroked his beard thoughtfully. 'You know, it's a long and unretraceable step to take up arms against your lawful king, and ridiculous as this may sound with ten thousand of his men marching toward us, I don't think York is ready to take it yet. I think this is more in the nature of a witch-hunt. Somerset is the main target and perhaps one or two others who would not stand lightly by and watch him take full power.'

Hal smiled. 'Meaning you and I, Tom?'

Clifford grinned. 'Well, you must admit that both York and Salisbury's path would run that bit smoother if you and I were out of the way.'

'Yes. I can see the logic in that.' A fleeting smile of pure amusement touched his mouth. 'So what then? Are we to be the sacrificial lambs on the altar of York's ambition?'

'Not without a fight we're not,' Clifford said grimly. 'We'll give them hell, won't we, Hal?' He laughed almost joyously. 'I've faced better men than York and survived.'

Hal nodded. 'Aye. We'll give them hell, Tom — or die in the attempt.'

When Clifford had gone he opened the chest and lifted out the sword still wrapped in its velvet as it had been since the day Ralph Neville had given it him. He was not so tall as the old man had been and it felt heavy and cumbersome in his hands. Lovingly he touched the still keen blade and traced the fine pattern etched into the steel. *Espérance:* the old man's war cry and now his. Yet what was there to hope for now? Perhaps only that he would die as well and as bravely as the old man had.

When they reached St Albans the next day they found that York had already beaten them to it and lay camped in the fields outside the town. Surprisingly they were allowed to enter peaceably enough and found the monks of the Abbey better prepared than they were with ready-made barricades to set at the entrance to each street. The king retired immediately behind the cloister walls and left his uncertain and uneasy army to fend for themselves. Buckingham was in sole command, a pacifist at heart who was going to put off the moment of confrontation for as long as he possibly could. The day passed without incident and they were lulled into a half-hearted complacency as York remained inactive. The next day the inevitable messenger came with the usual protestation of loyalty but insistent that York's grievances be given redress. It was quite clear that it was Somerset York was after.

Buckingham smiled archly. He would gladly have given Somerset up, bound and trussed if need be, but the ultimate decision rested with the king and after much meditation and private prayer it seemed he was still enough of a king to feel insult in York's peremptory demand. He announced primly that if Somerset had indeed erred, which he did not admit, then he would be tried and punished accordingly because he, the king, decreed it, not because York demanded it. Then as if that little defiance had sapped all of his courage, he added timorously that he would be more than pleased to discuss any other of his cousin of York's grievances that he cared to place before him.

By this time Buckingham thought the danger well and truly past. York had armed and disarmed so often in the past that even the vast numbers of his following ceased to trouble him. They would talk themselves out of this extremity as they had done before. The king vigorously endorsed the delusion, and so confident were they that by the third day they were lounging at their ease when the attack came.

There was not time even to arm themselves and only the barricades saved them from total and immediate annihilation. Frantically Buckingham attempted to deploy his scattered panic-stricken men but even before they were half formed up, his orders were drowned by howling Yorkists attacking their defenceless rear.

Hal emerged from his tent with only a mail shirt and his sword for protection. Clifford was waiting for him. 'It's Warwick,' he yelled. 'He's broken through the houses at the back of us.'

There was not time to answer, no time even to draw breath before the hordes of screaming Yorkists were upon them. He fought side by side with Clifford but his arms felt like lead and the great sword seemed to weigh him down. His mind was dull and stagnant as if he had emerged from sleep. He had no heart for a fight he knew could never be won.

Then suddenly he and Clifford were alone and ringed by a score of the enemy, faceless in their helms with no badge but York's falcon to name them. Yet instinctively Hal knew that one of them was Salisbury. So this was how it was to end. He had lost. It was finished and the bitterness of defeat already numbed his mind. Clifford was the first to fall and whether it was the sight of his friend and nephew lying broken and bleeding at his feet that roused him or only that perverse and unpredictable part of him that he had never dared let out of its cage, he rallied. He felled three men with a single stroke of the great two-handed sword before he was struck himself. He screamed his war cry aloud and the sound of it froze the blood of the men around him. Then he stared down in surprise at the blood spurting from the great gaping wound in his chest. There was no pain, only a spreading of warmth that filled all of his heart and mind. He saw Elizabeth's pale, smiling face and felt her presence envelop and shield him so that when the final blow came he felt nothing.

Black silk brushed soft as a raven's wing against Alianore's cheek as she turned to speak to her youngest son. William carefully avoided her glance; like his brothers he could not bear the awful unspoken grief in her eyes. She had borne it well. The shocked and death-like silence had stayed with her only a day. The next she had returned calmly to her monotonous, unchanging duties and had even taken the steward to task for a discrepancy in the tally of casks. Only, she had changed. She had aged a thousand bitter years.

She surveyed the remnants of her once great and happy family. The continued absence of Thomas and Richard was the greatest loss. George and William were there, as if to compensate. George was a prebend at Beverley now and William, Bishop of Carlisle: two prim and distant strangers to her. It seemed years since she had seen them, years since life had had any meaning above the commonplace. Was it possible that Hal had only been dead a month?

She looked to the head of the table where Harry sat, stiffly conscious of his new dignity as Northumberland. Poor Harry, she thought. Such an unloved and unlovable man and likely to remain so, for he still refused to contemplate Eleanor's return. She might have forgiven him for that but not for his obvious reluctance to plead the cause of Thomas and Richard's release. He'd pleaded a thousand excuses, none of them convincing enough to allay the suspicion that perhaps he was more than happy to see Thomas behind bars. Though, of course, she thought in mitigation, the king was indeed powerless and trembling on the verge of madness again. He'd escaped the battle of St Albans with only a graze from a chance arrow but had been led like a captive back to London and a demented Margaret. The other losses had been negligible; only a hundred dead all told and significantly, only three of the lords: Somerset, Clifford and her beloved Hal. The battle, it seemed, had abruptly ceased when it was known that they had fallen. Cold-blooded murder, or so Harry had named it, and if there was grief and bitterness in it for him there was infinitely more for her. She knew without doubt that it had been her own brother who had struck the killing blow. Perhaps if any lasting peace had come out of it, it might have lessened her sense of loss. But nothing had been resolved. Margaret writhed impotently beneath her defeat, for York was Protector again and Constable in Somerset's place. Salisbury held the Treasury and Warwick was Captain of Calais. There were still brief spasmodic outbursts on the queen's behalf but none that ever came to anything. Margaret, for the moment, was truly powerless. Not that Alianore cared. At least Margaret had her husband by her, and her sons did not burn with a hot unhealthy desire for vengeance that threatened to plunge them back into the horror of war as soon as the right moment came. Yet was she any better? When such a love was torn from your heart there had to be something to fill its place.

Then she saw how her presence discomfited them all. George was almost scarlet in the face with the effort of continued discretion. Harry drummed his fingers on the table in open impatience, while William fiddled with his robes and looked more like a pilfering clerk than a bishop. Ralph merely looked sad. She would have laughed if she could have remembered how.

All so afraid to speak his name, yet if they had but known it, it was the one thing she wanted to hear. Above all she needed to keep his memory alive.

She rose and saw the relief on their faces as she announced her intention to retire. Then clearly and without tremor she said, 'I know that it would be pointless to expect you not to want to avenge your father's death. He was too well loved by all of us to let his murder pass, for that is what it was as I understand it. Cold, cruel murder for no better reason than that he stood in the way of a lesser man's ambition. And as I name your father as victim so shall I name his murderer. My brother, your uncle; Richard, Earl of Salisbury.' She glanced round at their astounded faces. 'You see? I can speak his name without tears or swoons. My heart cries out for vengeance as loudly as yours and though perhaps I can be with you in nothing more than thought, I would not be shut out of all your councils, and lay no restraint upon you save that what you do is worthy of his name.'

She left them then, a tall sad figure in her mourning black yet a faint colour was beginning to bloom beneath her pallor. Hate, like love, made one feel so terribly alive.

In her chamber she surveyed her reflection briefly and decided that black most definitely did not suit her. It drained what little colour she had and aged her by ten years. She smiled faintly at herself. She would not be like Elizabeth and wear it to the grave. The smile faded abruptly. Elizabeth. How she had misjudged her and thought her mad. Yet perhaps this cold emptiness was a kind of madness and to fill it with hatred was the only sanity. What other course was there for her? None that did not offer a living death; the cloister, the veil, a life of good and pious works. How could she settle for peace when there was only war in her heart? She had tried to force that upon Hal because Salisbury was her brother, because she had loved him even when he was beyond all love. And how had Richard rewarded her? By taking her life and her love, almost her very sanity. Her eyes grew hard and black as polished jet. Whatever victory Richard thought he had gained from this, she would see that he did not profit from it. She might be a frail woman but she had six strong sons to do her bidding and if Richard prided himself on his Neville ruthlessness, she could match it. Once, a long time ago, she had been a Neville too.

Then she dragged the jewel chest from beneath the bed. They would need money. Their resources were low and God knew when Harry could expect his stipend for the Wardenship. They had fifty or more worthless tallies as it was. Briskly she tipped the contents on to the bed. Such a wealth of ornament, though she rarely wore more than the emerald betrothal ring and the collar of pearls Hal had given her after Harry was born. Only one thing more would she keep, the long heavy chain of white gold with its tear shaped diamond – to compensate for any that he might ever have caused her to shed. Oh Hal, she thought in sudden anguish. There were not enough diamonds beneath the earth for that. Ruthlessly she thrust it back among the rest. She was not strong enough to remember tendernesses like that. One moment of weakness could break her resolve and she'd become the useless grief-stricken woman they all feared she was. Besides, she did not need a bauble for remembrance when every hour was full of her need for him, every day there was some reminder of her loss.

She moved away from the glittering hoard. It was a fine calm evening and what wind there was had lost itself in the barricade of trees behind the house. She threw the casement wide and looked down into the shadowy court. It was a joy in itself to be at Leconfield. The great rambling house had saved her reason once before; it would do so again. There was peace of a different kind here, in the warmth of carefully polished oak, in the gleam of brass and silver, in the far-stretching demesne lands that were lush and green and rich with game. She'd left a part of herself here that was young and brave. She'd come back to see if she could find it again. She had far greater need of it now.

A soft apologetic knock at the door disturbed her. It was Harry, flushed and well fortified with wine. It occurred to her that she rarely saw Harry sober these days.

'I hope I did not disturb you. I know it is late but I thought – you said you did not want to be shut out. It can wait till the morning if you are tired.'

'There is no need to apologise, Harry,' she said gently. 'I am not tired. I'm afraid that sleep and I are passing strangers of late.'

He advanced slowly into the room. His eyes darted to the heap of jewels and back to her face again.

Alianore answered his unspoken question. 'We shall need money, Harry. You cannot wage war with empty pockets and that I believe must be your intent: to continue your father's fight against Salisbury.'

Harry's mouth was suddenly sulky and she thought with amazement, he dislikes women, even me. She could see from the look in his eyes the way his thoughts ran. She should be weeping and wailing and tearing her hair, not poking her fingers into his pie. On second thoughts though, he would not care for such unseemly display; quietly stitching with an occasional sob into her sleeve, that was more his idea of her. Dear God. No wonder Eleanor had tired of him.

She said, more out of irritation than expecting a response, 'Harry. Is it not time that you gave serious thought to Eleanor? You cannot keep her at Holystone indefinitely. She is Countess of Northumberland now.'

'I see no reason to think on it,' he said stiffly. 'Eleanor is better where she is.'

'As Thomas and Richard are better where they are?' Alianore gave a faint derisive smile. 'Sometimes I think that you would be happier if we were all under lock and key.'

At least she had provoked him from that dreary impassivity. He said in his thick voice, 'Thomas deserves no better. Even Father thought that.'

'But not indefinitely,' Alianore answered him coldly. 'Six months to cool his heels was well enough but it has been twice that now and I know it was your father's wish that they be released. He was on the point of approaching the king before he was killed.'

'There's no point in approaching the king now, even if I'd a mind to, which I have not.'

'Ah. There we have it then, Harry. No more lame excuses then. Is it your intention to keep your brothers in a debtors' gaol forever? I can understand your spleen against Thomas. But what of Richard? He is surely innocent of any crime against you?'

'Not as far as Thomas is concerned, he is not. He'd aid and abet him into Hell if Thomas asked it.'

'That is an emotion commonly recognised as loyalty, Harry. I doubt if you have ever felt it. You seem to exist as separate from the rest of us, but I can tell you this, you'll not survive without us or win your fight against Salisbury. The Nevilles' strength is their family tie. I was part of that family once and whatever shame or crime or corruption was within, it was kept within. The more the corruption, the more solid it made us. That is their strength. It has spread their power and influence the length and breadth of England – the aggrandisement of family, Harry, not of self.' She paused and laid her hand gently upon his sleeve. 'If we are to survive it must be together, as a family. You cannot cut out your heart, Harry. The whole body dies then.'

Still he resisted her. 'There's nothing I can do about Thomas or Richard,' he said stubbornly. 'The king has hardly wits enough to dress himself these days. And I can't see York setting them free without payment of the fine.'

'All right then,' Alianore said patiently. 'Set Thomas and Richard aside for the moment. What about Eleanor? You can do something about her.'

Harry's face was mutinous. 'I have already expressed my views on that subject. I see no point in repeating myself.'

Alianore viewed her son with something very near to distaste. He had changed so much from the quiet but happy child she remembered. Had the change been entirely of Eleanor's making, or were they all not in some part to blame? It had been so easy to overlook Harry when Thomas had been there. She said gently, 'Was it all Eleanor's fault, Harry? Can you not look into your own heart and find some fault, however small? A woman rarely strays beyond her husband if she is content, if her dreams and desires are fulfilled.'

Harry's mouth drew down with disdain. 'I fear that all Eleanor's desires are of the bodily kind.'

'And you find that strange, Harry? That a woman should have such desires? I desired your father for all of his life. Even now there are nights when I long for him.'

If she had been a younger woman and not his mother she

would have been insulted by his look. He turned away from her, his mouth womanly and prim. 'It is not a subject I care for overmuch,' he said. 'And anyway, there is no comparison. One thing Eleanor always managed to convey was that she did not desire me.'

'I think you will find her much changed,' Alianore said carefully. 'At least I thought so. Five years is a long time.'

Harry swung round. 'You've seen her?'

'Well? Did you think I could totally abandon her?'

'You had no right. I gave no permission . . .'

'I had every right,' Alianore snapped. 'Eleanor is part of this family whether you like it or not. She is your wife. She is the mother of your daughters and that son you dote so well upon.'

Harry's face suffused with ugly colour. 'They have no need of her and neither have I. Let her rot and pine and waste away for lack of love and a man. Why do you think I put her there?'

Alianore stared at him for a moment in utter loathing. Then she walked to the door and held it open. 'I am not surprised that she preferred Thomas,' she said cruelly. 'I must admit that at this moment, so do I.'

Even when she had closed it on his bitter and angry face she felt no remorse. Harry must learn – they must all learn – to accept what could not be changed.

She sat at the little dressing chest and martialled the crystal vials of scent into battle order. Now to the matter of Thomas and Richard. If Harry would not do aught about it then she must. She pursed her lips thoughtfully. Ralph must be her only ally in this. Harry she certainly could not trust and George and William would think it scandalous and a slight on their calling. Her eyes travelled to the shining jewels. The diamond pendant alone should be enough. She did not think that turnkeys were vastly overpaid.

Thomas sat with his spine pressed hard against the damp wall and watched the fat brown speck that had just dined off his wrist make its bloated laborious way up his forearm. He smiled. Tomorrow, with luck, he would feast as well. Without disturbing the flea's progress he felt for the cold steel of the knife tucked inside his filthy shirt. He ran his thumb lovingly along the blade and caressed its needle point. Exactly the weapon to slit that dog Cerberus's throat. The thought gave him almost as much pleasure as that of freedom.

He frowned and glanced in concern at his brother. Richard was pale and weak, for the rich sustaining food had ceased abruptly with their father's death. They had existed on bread and slops for the last six months although the occasional feast that Ralph managed to smuggle in had helped. If anything, Thomas was the leaner of the two, for discreetly he'd made sure that Richard had the lion's share. It had not stopped the pitiful wasting of his body and spirit. Richard had neither the stamina nor the heart for long confinement. His own suffering was of a less physical kind. His father's death; the rise of York that had been the death knell to their hopes of freedom; the fact that Eleanor still suffered: all these had worn him down and killed all that was clean and decent in him. Another year of this and their mother's brave attempt to free them would have been of no avail. He would have used the knife upon himself.

Then he heard the distant sound of a key being turned. He glanced down at the flea nestling snugly in the crook of his arm. 'Journey's end, little friend,' he murmured and crushed it ruthlessly with his thumb.

He rose and went to stand in the dark corner where the torchlight did not reach, straining his ears to the slow approaching footsteps. He recognised instantly the slow shuffling tread of the little fat man: he was alone. Abaddon then, bless him, had kept to his bed as he had been very well paid to do. Stealthily he drew the knife from his shirt and motioned Richard to the chair that stood in direct view of the door. It seemed a long time before the key eventually ground in the lock and the noise of it when it came was like cannon fire in their ears. Swiftly Thomas clamped his arm round the warder's greasy neck. The knife was laid coldly at his throat. 'Cerberus, dear heart,' he said softly. 'Now isn't this cosy? One whine from you and you'll bark for your dinner in Hades.'

Richard unfastened the keys from the terrified man's belt; then together they thrust him down on the rough plank bed. Thomas's knife caressed the soft fat coils of his throat and pricked a fine droplet of blood. Richard tugged at his arm. 'Come on, Tom. We've no time for that. Let's get away.'

Thomas reluctantly withdrew the blade. 'A pity,' he said like a disappointed child. 'I was so looking forward to it.'

Then they ran, Thomas loosing the prisoners in the adjoining cells before they plunged down the narrow stair. On the lower floor the stench almost felled them and a warder rose ponderously from his stool to sit again abruptly as Thomas's fist cracked into his jaw. They paused only to relieve him of his keys, which they threw to the ragged screaming mob that rampaged in their wake and spilled out into the courtyard behind them. The two brothers made straight for the deserted gatehouse, gulping like drunkards at the air. Thomas almost wept with relief. Only one more door, one more lock.

Then Ralph emerged from the shadows leading their mounts. He grinned down into his brother's filthy face. 'So there you are, Thomas,' he said. 'I had thought you'd decided to stay.'

Thomas said nothing. He leant his head against the horse's neck and cried like a child.

The king nibbled at a split and broken nail and fixed his vague disinterested gaze on a point far beyond the speaker's head. The words droned on unintelligibly like the hum of a gathering bee. Henry heard nothing, but that was by choice. There was nothing that the Earl of Warwick could say that he would want to hear, though it was one of his good days when his mind was sharp and clear. He kept that to himself. Better that they all think him a fool. The more power to his elbow when they discovered he was not and he denounced them for the knaves and charlatans that they were. And when would that be? Henry blinked and Warwick's dark intense face came into focus. He closed his eyes as he felt his new clarity of mind waning. It only needed the slightest distraction, the minutest deviation from the path on which he had so strenuously set his thoughts. With an effort he dragged his mind back from the shadows and soothed it with happy thoughts. His new foundations at Eton and Cambridge were flourishing; he'd received commendation from the Pope. He admonished himself severely there: pride, the deadliest of sins. All was done through God, and the mortification of the flesh and spirit was the only true path. He leant back in the high-backed chair of state so that the hair shirt tortured his flesh anew. Pride, the deadliest of sins, and these creatures who strutted and preened before him were eaten up with it. It would be God's work to bring them to proper humility. His thoughts slipped into confusion again. Yet what of forgiveness? Did not our Blessed Lord hold it the highest of virtues? And truly he had tried to love York and Warwick, to forgive them for their human fault. Or was it he who was at fault? He looked distractedly toward the queen. She was his sole prop now. His dear Beaufort was gone, Northumberland too. Murdered? Cut down by Warwick and gentle York? The shadows loomed frighteningly close. Then Margaret moved into the periphery of his vision. Her brilliant eyes dragged him from his gloomy thoughts, her smile soothed his agony of doubt. He gave a little scream as the door of the chamber burst open. A wild unkempt figure staggered toward him, long black curls writhing like serpents about his face. Forsooth, Henry thought irrelevantly, was it the Blessed St John?

The man knelt and laid his brow on the king's scuffed leather boot. 'Most gracious king. I throw myself on your mercy. Do with me as you will.'

Henry dared to look down on the supplicant head. The sight of vermin crawling in the dark hair did not disturb him, he was plagued oft times himself. He struggled with his memory. The face meant nothing, but the voice, he remembered the voice. Then his muddled thoughts resolved themselves and when Warwick yelled for the guard he held up his hand. The immediate silence pleased him and he said, 'Forsooth, Thomas. What have we here? I thought you were the Blessed St John.'

The king felt the ripple of shock that passed through the assembly at the sound of his voice without its usual tremor of weakness. 'Tell me, Thomas. What calamity has befallen you that you appear before me thus?'

The queen moved lovingly to his side and he basked in the approval of her eyes. He also saw York and Warwick turn pale. Pride, my lords, he thought, it will be your undoing.

'Go on, my lord Egremont,' Margaret said in a hushed and eager voice. 'Tell his Grace what evil has befallen you, what manner of men have brought you to this state.'

Henry listened patiently and intelligently, his eyes widening in horror and pity and once or twice he threw a glance of pious censure at Warwick. When he had heard all he held out his hands to Thomas who by now was almost too weak to stand. 'By God and all His saints, it's a sorry tale.' Again his eyes travelled boldly to Warwick. 'The fine and the punishment are to be set aside, by virtue of the great and noble service that your father did us before he was so cruelly slain.' Henry smiled, a child's smile of pure pleasure. 'You are free, my lord Egremont. Both you and your brother. Your king so decrees it.'

'He was as sane as you or me that day,' Thomas told his mother jubilantly. 'He must have been, to have recognised me beneath my fleas and crusting of filth. Poor Henry. He thought I was John the Baptist.' He sighed. 'I wish Father had been there to see the look on York's face. The king so decreed it, Henry said. And York vanished like the demon in a puff of green smoke.'

Alianore smiled, content to listen for as long as he wanted to talk. How she had missed the sound of him, like cool mountain water sluicing over her. It was almost like having Hal by her again. 'And how long before Warwick and Salisbury conjure him up again?'

Thomas looked thoughtful. 'That depends how long the king can stay this side of reason. For the moment they have retired quietly to their estates.'

Alianore nodded. So they had a breathing space at least. Time to gather strength before the next assault. She knew her brother well enough to know that he would not be content with obscurity for long. 'Meanwhile,' she said, 'we have our own house to set in order. Have you spoken with Harry?'

Thomas laughed. 'Well, we've not actually conversed, but we have progressed to nodding acquaintance. I'm not sure if it is you or me he is most angry with.' He smiled lovingly at her. 'It'll be a long time before he forgives you for plotting my release behind his back.'

'I dare say. But I think he needs to examine his own conscience first. His treatment of Eleanor is little short of inhuman.'

Thomas was silent for a moment then he said quietly, 'To give Harry his due, he can bear a grudge better than any man I know. How long is it now – five years?'

'Almost,' Alianore hesitated, knowing that she trod on dangerous ground. 'Did you know that I went to see her a year ago?'

'I didn't know. But I thought you might.'

'Am I so predictable then?'

'Yes. Emotionally you are. I knew you would have gone for my sake.' He fell silent and his eyes begged what he could not ask.

'She was well enough,' Alianore answered him without hesitation. 'A little pale and thin but it suited her. She asked after you and I told her the truth. I think she would rather have known than think that you had ceased to care for her. She said she had not heard from you for some time.' She paused, watching his handsome expressive face. 'Was that wise, Thomas. Was it wise to maintain the link?'

Thomas shrugged. 'Was it wise ever to have begun it at all? Was it wise to have rubbed Harry's nose in it, as I did?' He stared down at his hands. 'I fear the heart is not governed by wisdom.'

Alianore did not pursue it. 'Well. What's done is done,' she said with rather unfeeling briskness. 'It is today and tomorrow that we must consider. We must convince Harry that this was no more than a passing fancy. You were bored. Eleanor was piqued from his lack of attention. No. Better perhaps that she was lonely, distraught from his long captivity . . .'

'How picturesquely you put it,' Thomas interrupted her. 'With just a few sharp words you have reduced my feelings for Eleanor to the commonplace and I fancy too that you have almost given it an air of the ridiculous. I resent that, you know. There was never anything ridiculous or commonplace about Eleanor and me.' His eyes gleamed dangerously. 'Now, if you are trying to say that we should let well alone, that we should stay away from each other whenever we can and keep our distance when we can't, then I would prefer that you said so plainly.'

'I'm sorry, Thomas.' His eyes brought a faint flush to her cheeks. 'It's only that it is such an awkward . . .'

'Delicate is the word. Delicate like fragrant blossom. Once bruised the petals wither and die and lose all of their sweetness.' He turned his face away, but his voice was heavy with sadness. 'I shall always love her but not so obviously that I shall cause either you or Harry embarrassment. Will that do? I can promise you nothing more.'

'Yes. It will do very well, Thomas,' Alianore said gently. 'I should not have needed to ask.' She rose to her feet and laid a concerned hand on his shoulder. 'And Harry?'

'Harry must learn to live with his pain, as I have, as you have. I dare say we shall all survive.'

She nodded, heavy with the burden of his sadness that was a faint echo of her own. Impulsively she stooped and kissed his thin cheek. Would they? she thought bleakly; could they survive with so much hatred and discord within, let alone that which waited for them outside? Perhaps Harry was right and Eleanor was better where she was.

Harry stood shivering in the shadow of the trees. He had been there an hour already and the sharp east wind was beginning to penetrate his heavy cloak. It was not the first time he had come, to watch, to stare. Even now he did not know why he came. But he did, no further than this though. Here his courage always failed him and he turned back and rode home, as cold and miserable and alone as ever.

He edged his horse forward to the brow of the hill. The priory glittered like a sepulchre beneath its dusting of fine snow; Eleanor's tomb – and he had walled her in alive. He moved back into the shadows of the great barren oak. It was guilt more than anything that held him back. Five years – when he had only meant to keep her there a few months. He had wanted her to ask, to beg, him for her freedom. But she never had and each month that had passed he had grown more stubborn, more determined to live without her. And he had, if you could call this bleak desolate existence of his, life. Now he wondered desperately what in heaven's name he had gained from it all except the disgust and contempt of his family. Even Alianore had turned against him and his son had not been the comfort that he had hoped – there was always that nagging doubt each time that dark little satyr's face was turned toward him.

He shuddered as a gust of wind rocked him in the saddle. And then to have lost his one comfort, the only one who had looked at him with compassion and understanding. He still mourned his father passionately and for a while his grief had driven even Eleanor from his mind. His revenge against his murderers had been slow and methodical like all else about him. With his brother George and Clifford's son, John, he had witnessed York and Salisbury being stripped of office and a month later the king had decreed that the Nevilles pay compensation for Northumberland's death. That had angered him. What compensation could there be for the loss of such a man? Then the scales had tipped fractionally in York's favour again. The French had attacked Sandwich and massacred the inhabitants. Margaret had lost in a day the credibility it had taken her years to achieve, and worse, it had gained York a voice in Council again. Only a small foothold perhaps, but enough to set him on the scaling ladder again, especially as the king babbled continually of peace and had insisted on that sickening parody of an armistice at St Paul's with Yorkist and Lancastrian walking hand in hand like brothers. It had almost been laughable: the queen and York, Warwick and Exeter, himself and Salisbury. So an uneasy peace prevailing everywhere and he was unwillingly part of it. Thomas and Richard were free – his face flooded with angry colour at the thought of his younger brother. He had known his mistake the minute he had set eyes on that arrogant face again. He had been wrong to punish Eleanor. It was Thomas who should have borne the blame, it was Thomas who should have suffered, as he had suffered, as Eleanor still suffered.

He wiped his brow with the back of his hand, for in spite of the cold he was sweating. Then he spurred his horse recklessly down the hill. He wanted her, he needed her. He only prayed that she did not send him away.

He was admitted without question and led by a tall, moustached nun through rooms as cold as charity. The thin treble of female voices came faintly through the walls. There was a smell of coarse soap and vinegar mingled with the dry nauseous odour of sweat. The nun halted him with a heavy hand. 'Wait here. I will prepare the countess. She may be at her devotions.'

Harry's eyes widened and he felt a sudden desire to laugh. Eleanor – praying! He had not thought that she knew how.

The nun emerged from a narrow door and viewed him with her inbred distaste for his species. 'The countess will see you,' she said and left him.

He approached the open door nervously. His heart was hammering like a boy's. His face burned with colour. He stared from the doorway at the small nunly figure who sat on the bare planks of her bed. 'Eleanor,' he said in disbelief. 'Eleanor?'

She looked up at him then. Her face, framed in a severe barbette, was serene. 'Come in, my lord,' she said quietly. 'I am happy to see you after so long.'

He moved awkwardly into the cramped little cell. There was nowhere else for him to sit except upon the bed. He did so self-consciously, rubbing his hands upon his thighs in the manner he knew irritated her so. He stared at her novice's habit. 'Eleanor, you haven't . . .'

'No,' she forestalled him, smiling. 'I have not taken the veil,' she said, though she'd thought of it more than once in a shallow meaningless way; when her hopes had been at their lowest, when even this poor imitation of life had been better than no life at all. She had compromised by wearing their habit. It made her feel less of an outsider and besides all the gowns that she had brought were practically in rags. 'Would it trouble you if I did, Harry?'

Harry swallowed, all his defences crumbling before that sweet reproachful gaze. 'Yes, it would, Eleanor. It would trouble me very much.'

She did not reply but her eyes remained thoughtfully on his face. She was careful to keep her own impassive. If she had learned nothing else here she had acquired an iron control of her emotions. Though her whole body was stiff with loathing for him she smiled her virgin's smile.

'How are the children?' she enquired lightly. 'Elizabeth must be quite grown by now.'

Harry smiled eagerly. The commonplace always relaxed him.

'And little Harry?' Eleanor took up the elaborate stitching she had laid aside to greet him.

'Not so little now. He's quite tall for his age, a proud and winsome child though a little shy. He has great charm of manner, though.' Like Thomas, a voice at the back of his mind reminded him. He thrust the thought away, plunging into an inane and pointless tale of little Harry's prowess to cover his emotion.

Eleanor listened demurely, her eyes cast down to her work. You fool, she thought. You stupid ridiculous fool. As if I care. As if I care about anything but escaping from this pious sickening place. The sudden intensity of feeling almost shattered her calm and she frowned at a misplaced stitch. She had loathed every hour of every dreary day; the same repetitive tasks, the continual abasement of self, the repression of all vanity and pride. She had not looked upon her own reflection once in five years. That she had endured it at all was a miracle and she wondered vaguely how many times she had drawn pen and parchment toward her, willing to suffer any debasement if only he would let her come home. It had never quite come to that for there was a harder and more practical side to her now that knew that for life to be bearable after her release, it must be on her own terms. It must be Harry who begged, not she. She laid her work aside and looked at him. He hadn't changed. His face was heavier perhaps, his colour higher, but the staid unimaginative set of his mouth was the same. She noticed too with revulsion that a white nervous spittle flecked his lips.

'Harry,' she said with just the right amount of hesitation in her voice. 'The children. Could I . . . Could I perhaps see them?'

She saw from his eyes the battle already won. Clumsily he reached for her hand. 'Eleanor,' he said hoarsely. 'Come home. I beg you to come home.'

She smiled and slid adroitly from his grasp. 'Oh, Harry,' she whispered. 'Once I thought of nothing else, but now . . . Harry, it's been a long time. I'm afraid that . . .' She flushed becomingly, the douce maidenly wife that he had always desired. 'I don't know that I could be a wife to you again – in the physical sense.'

He coloured himself then and dried his damp palms on his plum-coloured hose. Not that it mattered. He was not a man of inordinate lust. If he had of been, well, he might not be here now and the knowledge that Eleanor was cured of it would compensate for any lack he felt. Perhaps in time he could bring her to it again, gently, tenderly as he had always imagined it, with love.

Eleanor turned and looked at him, disturbed by his silence. Had she broached the matter too soon? Yet even as she thought it she saw the frown ease from his brow.

'I am glad that you have been honest with me,' he said gravely. 'That in itself is a good beginning and I can promise you that I shall not force you to anything against your will.' He looked at her with tender eyes. 'A new beginning, Eleanor. Is it too much to hope for?'

She shook her head. 'I don't know, Harry. There's so much to forgive and forget.' She turned her wide innocent eyes full upon his face. 'I must say it, Harry. Thomas. What of Thomas? Will I be suspect merely because we are in the same room together? Will you read volumes from every word exchanged between us? I have lived in peace and solitude for so long now, I could not bear to be persecuted by your unfounded jealousy.'

He rose like a hungry fish to the bait. 'Eleanor. Oh, Eleanor.' He snatched her hand from where she had laid it tentatively on his arm. 'I know now that you were not to blame.' He lifted it to his mouth and kissed it reverently. 'Whatever there was between you and Thomas, I promise you'll suffer no more for it.'

She looked up into his face. It had been easier than she thought, and he was so desperate for love and comfort that he would have taken her with only half the persuasion. She inclined her cheek for his respectful kiss. 'Then I'll come, Harry.' It was harder than ever to keep the triumph from her voice.

The first sight of her was like a blow to his heart. Thomas watched her descend the staircase holding her son by the hand. Sycorax the witch and her son Caliban, he thought, for he was not deceived by her douce facade. If anything he thought her

317

more deadly than ever. And more beautiful too. It suddenly struck him that she was no longer young but she maintained the illusion to perfection. Her hair was coiled in shining braids about her head, her long neck was roped with pearls. Her skin glowed like alabaster against the vivid blue gown, but she had lost that soft wanton warmth he had loved so well. She was cold and aloof and so dreadfully controlled. He looked away, knowing the very moment that her head would turn toward him. He was not ready for her yet.

Alianore watched them both, filled with unease. Not a word had been spoken, not a look exchanged yet she felt the intensity of feeling between them. It was almost a physical thing. She glanced discreetly at Harry, smug and foolish at Eleanor's side. No, she thought sadly, Harry would not feel it. His emotions were of a far more basic kind. It was Eleanor who particularly disturbed her, a vastly different Eleanor from the one who had swayed her to plead her cause a year ago. She remembered that Eleanor vividly, penitent, remorseful, her eyes shining with perpetually unshed tears. A foolish, broken woman pining for her children. Alianore raised her brows cynically. She wondered if Harry had been similarly fooled. She's laughing at us, she thought angrily. At Harry with his clumsy attempts to court her, at her and her obvious need for family warmth, perhaps even at Thomas for trying to resist her. Alianore sipped her wine thoughtfully. Thank God, she thought, that she was to accompany Harry to Berwick at the end of the week.

She gave her attention back to the family that she had so strenuously gathered together; all her sons, her daughter Catherine and her husband Edmund Grey, even Anne, widowed for the second time and betrothed for a third to Sir Hugh Vaughan. Only Joan was absent, content in her cloister at Whitby. She surveyed them proudly and saw in each of them a little part of herself and Hal. They were bound by one blood, one cause – and the cause at this moment was triumphant. This time the Yorkists were well and truly vanquished; York and his son Rutland banished to Ireland, Edward of March, her brother Salisbury and Warwick to Calais. As she had predicted, Richard had not kept to obscurity for long. There had been a move to dislodge Warwick from the

Captaincy of Calais that he had still held only by virtue of his popularity with his men. Salisbury had come out in support of his son and York had naturally backed him. It had been the prelude to St Albans all over again save that this time it was the Yorkists who were outnumbered and had needed to buy time. There was none to be had at the price they had offered and the rout and sack of York's stronghold at Ludlow had been his Armageddon. Four of her sons had been present and Harry spoke of it now, his thick heavy voice making the savage destruction of the town seem even uglier than it was.

Then Thomas interrupted him quietly. 'I can see nothing glorious in the rape of a beautiful and peaceful town by drunken soldiery, even if they were our own.'

Alianore's heart missed a beat as Harry swung round belligerently. 'And what would you have done then?' Harry demanded loudly. 'Allowed them time to reach for their swords so that all was fair and chivalrous? This is war, not some fancy jousting match.'

'Even in war there can be honour,' Thomas said mildly. 'These were simple people; weavers, tanners, shopkeepers, who were guilty of nothing except the misfortune of living in York's town. I see nothing honourable in the savage despoilation of women and children.'

'I agree with you there, Egremont,' Edmund Grey said. 'Exeter's men were despicable. I was ashamed that we fought for the same cause.'

'God's passion,' Harry cried, instinctively going against what Thomas had said merely because Thomas had said it. 'We are squeamish. You fight dogs like dogs.'

'But you do not become one, Harry,' Thomas said.

Harry grew redder still and slopped wine on the sleeve of his new saffron doublet. 'You can talk. What of all Salisbury's manors that you laid waste?'

'Property, Harry. Only property. I have never killed just for the love of it.'

To Alianore's relief Edmund Grey intervened and Harry subsided sulkily. He was drinking too much, at least for him. Wine made him doubly aggressive, doubly obtuse. She saw his eyes rest hungrily on his wife but Eleanor's painted smile remained fixed and condescending. He's like a dog waiting to be stroked, Alianore thought pitifully.

'I fear that the queen must learn to take countenance of more than the wishes of her immediate following,' Grey said heavily. 'Exeter tells me that the Treasury is empty. What the king does not foolishly give away in alms, Wiltshire appropriates for himself. The king is in debt to the tune of one hundred thousand marks.' He rapped the table smartly with his hand. 'Who's to pay, then? Not I for one. I've enough to do provisioning my own men.'

'My, my. Such disloyalty to our fair Marguerite.' Harry sniggered over the rim of his cup. 'I could almost think you a Yorkist, my lord.'

Grey regarded him with distaste. 'Loyalty does not necessarily mean blind obedience, Northumberland. I am loyal to the king because he is the king. A mild criticism of his policies does not make me less so.'

'The queen would think so. She insists on blind obedience, blind loyalty. It is the best kind. It never does to question too deeply.' Harry's glazed eyes flickered hotly over Thomas's face. 'One is not always well rewarded by what one finds.'

Alianore's mouth tightened and covertly she signalled to the steward that Harry was to be offered no more wine. He was bent on argument, she could see that, and again she thanked God that he would be gone soon to Berwick. There was trouble expected on the Border as the young king of Scotland was out of tutelage and following the well-worn policy of alliance with France. There were rumours of a simultaneous attack on Berwick and Calais, no doubt abetted by her exiled brother and nephew. She looked again at her eldest son and marked his weak and flaccid mouth. He seemed even less of a man since his father's death. Hal had been both his idol and his protector and Hal's loss had been a bitter blow. But no more to him than to her, than to any of them. She thought he might have rallied, that the dignity of earldom and headship of their house might have bolstered his confidence. But in reality it was she who ruled here now. Through her sons she kept her finger on the pulse of events. George was at Beverley and well placed to bring her the tidings from York; William was similarly placed at Carlisle. Ralph was her chief emissary to the Court and Thomas – she smiled indulgently – Thomas went where he pleased and took his faithful Richard with him. Perhaps her obvious bias in his favour should have troubled her. It had always been Thomas. Harry had always irritated her and he had grown no more endearing over the years. He was past change now. She would have to endure him as he was, both she and Eleanor.

Then his loud and drunken voice drew every eye toward him as he yelled at the steward for more wine. The old man pretended deafness, then threw a questioning glance at her. Alianore sighed and nodded. Hopefully he would drink himself to sleep and once more she comforted herself with the thought of Berwick, though how long he could stay there was conjecture. Already the war drums were beating softly again. The queen was openly recruiting levies under the Privy Seal and distributing her son's badge of the swan to any who would wear it. There were rumours of men slipping quietly across the Channel to join Warwick. Even some ships sent against him had sailed unobtrusively into Calais harbour and were not heard of again. She had thought St Albans the end. She saw now it had only been the beginning.

She smiled, distracted by Catherine's high infectious laugh. She was bickering fondly with Ralph, poking fun at the brevity of his doublet which was the height of fashion at court. She called laughingly to her mother. 'I think it is time that Ralph was wed,' she said prettily. 'Thomas and Richard too. You allow these brothers of mine too much licence for wenching. It's time that they took a wife.'

Alianore turned pale. Of course. Poor Catherine did not know.

Harry's head came up off his chest like a dog scenting blood. 'Yes,' he said thickly. 'I think it's time that Thomas took a wife. It would be a great comfort to me to know that he had one of his own.'

'Harry!' Alianore called to him sharply, more to divert the attack onto herself than to reprove him.

'And what's the matter with that? You're always harping on

about how the Nevilles gained all their power through marrying it and I was betrothed to Eleanor when I was twelve. How is Thomas exempt? What is so bloody special about Thomas?'

'Not only Thomas,' she corrected him. 'Ralph and Richard also. It was always your father's policy that his sons should marry where they would. You were the exception Harry, because you were the heir and the responsibility was yours to provide for the continuance of our house.'

If she had thought to mollify him with that little speech she was disappointed. 'Well, they've had long enough to choose for themselves.' Like a terrier with a rat Harry sought his brother's eyes again. 'You especially, Thomas, seem hard to please. Is there nothing we can offer to suit your taste? Nothing that is not already spoken for, I mean. Perhaps you set your sights too high though I understand that outside marriage you are not so particular. I have heard tell that the innkeeper's daughter at Egremont has a son that bears a remarkable likeness to you.' He sniggered loudly, unaware of the awful silence around him, of Eleanor, stiff and pale as an effigy beside him, unaware of anything but seven years of pain and rage. Now his emotions were loosed they had gone far beyond his control.

Then Thomas raised his head and smiled and what Harry saw in his eyes struck more terror into him than if he had held his blade at his throat. 'Quite a speech, Harry,' he said pleasantly. 'Almost effusive for you, though purely Bacchanalian, I realise that.' He smiled at the stiff and silent assembly. 'You must forgive poor Harry. He is quite a child in his cups. I've said time and time again that he should be kept to milk and thin gruel. Anything stronger brings the tears to his eyes and he clacks like a Berwick eelwife.'

There were indeed tears in Harry's eyes as fear and anger swept over him in swift and confusing succession. Under that killing blue gaze his tongue swelled up and filled his mouth. He felt his hands and feet to be grotesquely large. He might have backed off then as he always did, if Thomas had not laughed.

'You're such a clod, Harry,' he said with amusement. 'I fear that bright conversation never was your strong point, was it, dear heart? You should stick to something you are good at, Harry,

322

like . . .' He spread his long eloquent hands. 'Now there you have me at a disadvantage for once. What are you good at, Harry? Except making a cock of yourself.'

And still the longed-for outburst did not come. Words seethed and bubbled in the cauldron of his mind only to choke him and stick fast behind his thickened tongue. At last he said, stuttering and stumbling like a halfwit, 'You think you're bloody clever, don't you, eh? With your bloody Latin and bloody Greek and fine fancy words. You think me a clod, eh? Well, clod or not, I've got what you want. I know, I know.' He giggled and hiccoughed and what he knew was drowned by a loud vulgar belch but the words were coming too thick and fast now for him to care. He stabbed his finger at Thomas. 'Fornicator, seducer, thief! You said you'd steal anything, Thomas. Does that still include my wife? Well, think on this then. She doesn't want you any more, nor any of the grief and misery you trail in your wake.' He grabbed Eleanor's arm, his fingers tearing the fine tissue of silk. 'Tell him, Eleanor. Tell him to go to hell.'

Eleanor winced as his fingers dug viciously into her flesh. 'Tell him,' Harry screamed but still she did not raise her eyes. Neither did she speak.

Then Thomas spoke, so softly that it was barely heard despite the deep and trembling silence. 'Let her go, Harry, or I'll kill you.'

His brother froze, fixed by the terrible basilisk eyes. Then his hand slowly unclenched itself from Eleanor's arm and he pushed himself unsteadily to his feet, swaying back and forth whilst the ground steadied itself. Then with a roar he launched himself across the space between them.

Thomas leisurely stepped from his brother's path and watched with incredulous amusement as Harry brought down a laden trestle and wrestled noisily with a dismembered fowl. Then so swiftly that none could discern the movement his knife was drawn and poised over the frantic throbbing pulse in Harry's throat.

'Thomas,' Alianore's voice came to him faintly. 'For pity's sake, Thomas.'

'It's all right,' Thomas said without moving his eyes from his brother's face. 'I merely gloat.' He thrust the knife tenderly into the half-eaten fowl that perched on Harry's chest. Then he rose gracefully and gave his brother a last disdainful look. 'I would not harm him,' he said. 'Eagles do not hawk at flies.'

He walked away from all of them without a backward glance and the door closed softly behind him. Alianore stared after him, dry eyed and angry. She did not know then that she would never see him again.

Thomas saddled the horse with steady and competent hands, for the aftermath of his deadly rage had not yet come upon him. That would be later, when the wine had ceased to warm him, perhaps in the morning when he woke and found himself a virtual exile from all he loved and cared for. It did not matter now, nothing mattered now except putting as many miles as possible between himself and Harry. He would never see Eleanor again, he knew that; never touch her or hold her again, never melt the ice that had turned her so cold. It was as well perhaps, for once begun it could never be ended again. It would destroy them both, if it had not done so already. He wondered what havoc he had left behind him this time, what more grief and misery he had trailed in his wake as Harry had put it. He smiled grudgingly. That was quite well said for Harry. Perhaps there was hope for him yet.

He set his foot in the stirrup and was half in the saddle before he heard the familiar limping step. 'Richard,' he called softly. 'Don't lurk in the shadows like a goblin. I do not weep or do anything unmanly. Come out and show yourself.'

Richard stared at him accusingly. 'You're leaving,' he said. 'For good?'

'Or bad or worse,' said Thomas flippantly. 'Yes. I'm leaving.'

'Without me?'

'Is that a question or an answer? If it's an answer, then it is polite to wait to be asked first; if it's a question then it is I who should have asked it. Do you want to come? I'm not even sure where I'm going yet. Egremont, Wressel, perhaps off to some foreign war to die a Trojan death. It's not very much to offer, is it, Richard? You'd leave more behind you here.'

'It's enough,' Richard said bluntly.

'Child, that fair brings a tear to my jaded wordly eye. Youth and innocence are always so refreshingly foolish.' Then he held out his hand and his eyes were grave and tender as Richard clasped it. 'Come then, my little *fidus Achates*. Find yourself a horse and we'll see what this wild and wicked world has to offer us.'

It was years since she had been to Warkworth, not since that dreadful summer when Alnwick was burnt. Hal had never cared for it particularly though he had never told her why. Alianore thought perhaps it was because it was from here that he had begun his exile's life. She felt rather like an exile herself, having been moved by her cautious sons, first from Leconfield, then from the house at York. Both, it seemed, were unsafe, surrounded as they were by Yorkist lands.

She walked from empty room to empty room. Her servants trailed after her laden with boxes and chests and mountains of linen and she watched anxiously as a priceless tapestry was hoisted in the chamber she had chosen for herself. A feather mattress appeared, surmounting two pairs of thin legs, and she frowned in irritation at the small rectangular tear in its cover. Then she sighed and looked at the gilded bed on which it was reverently laid. The tear was suddenly unimportant. She remembered that the last time she had lain in it had been with Hal.

Then a small hand touched hers and she looked distractedly into the solemn face of Eleanor's son. She wondered vaguely why she always thought of him as that; never Harry's son, as if he had had no part in his making at all. She forced a smile and felt guilty that she did not care for him more. He was not an easy child to like. He rarely laughed and smiled less and then it was always a secret smile as if it was himself that amused him instead of what he saw. If she was honest, it was his dark sinister little face that she disliked. He was not an ugly child. His bones were small and sharp, his mouth perhaps too thin and pointed, like a woman's. His eyes were rather beautiful in fact, Hal's eyes, the greenish gold of a summer sea. They were long and narrow and heavily lashed beneath dark slanting brows that gave him a mildly quizzical look. His hair was a dead heavy black cropped short and unflatteringly straight to his ears. His voice was exquisite, soft, mellifluous, liquid, like water running over mossed stones. It was not a child's voice, but then Harry had never been a child in the true sense of the word. Children laughed and cried and screamed out of temper. Harry had never done any of these to her knowledge, but he *was* a child, she told herself firmly, and needed love and care as they all did. She held out her hand and tried harder with the smile as he clasped it with his own. She was surprised at its warmth and softness. She did not know why, but she had expected it to be cold.

They walked back through the cluttered and chaotic rooms. 'When will my father be home?' the boy asked gravely.

'I don't know, Harry,' she answered him truthfully. 'So many things are uncertain at the moment. It depends on what the king decides.'

'Don't you mean the queen?' he asked innocently. 'I heard my lord of Exeter say that it was the queen who gave the orders. The king just gives alms.'

Alianore repressed a smile. 'Well,' she said and suddenly felt more light-hearted than she had for years, 'sometimes the king is unwell and the cares of state are beyond him. He is a pious and saintly man and does not care for war.'

Harry considered this for a moment, then said, 'He should not be king then. He should be a saint. I should not let a man build my house unless I thought he knew how to lay bricks.'

Alianore halted, torn between exasperation and laughter. She knelt so that her face was on a level with his. 'Harry,' she said seriously, 'you must not say such things.'

'Why not, if they are true?'

'Because sometimes the truth is better kept to oneself. Henry is king as you are Northumberland's son. It does not matter whether you are a good or a bad son, nothing can change the fact that you *are* his son. So it is with the king.'

Harry nodded with understanding though she could see his agile mind searching for an argument against what seemed to him a weakling philosophy. 'Is that why we are fighting against the Duke of York, because *he* wants to be king?'

'Yes. It is, Harry.'

'It does not matter then that he might be a better king?'

'No, it does not matter. The man who tends your father's horses might make a better king but that does not give him the right. A man is born a king. He is not made so.'

'My great-grandfather made a king. Father told me so. Was it wrong for him to make a king?'

Alianore smiled sadly. 'I think he thought so, Harry. In the end.' She changed the subject briskly as they emerged into the sun. 'There. We have set the world to rights and put kings in their places. What do you want to do now?'

'I don't know,' he said. 'Perhaps we could go down to the river.' He looked at her doubtfully. 'I could pick some flowers for my mother. Would she be pleased, do you think?'

She was surprised at the sudden emotion in his voice as he spoke of Eleanor. Poor mite, she thought compassionately, and though she had not meant to venture as far as the river she said. 'Yes. I think she would like that.'

They walked together in silence and he helped her with great courtesy down the steep and rocky path. She sat with her back against a rock and watched him roam by the water's edge. She was glad she had come. The sun and the cool ripple of the water were soothing and she had not realised how tired she was until now.

Harry came and deposited a smooth green stone in her lap. 'What is it?' he asked solemnly.

She regarded him sleepily through half-closed eyes. 'It's a green pebble, Harry,' she said simply. 'What did you think it was?'

He looked mildly disappointed. 'I thought it might be an emerald.'

She opened her eyes. It was the first childish thing she had ever heard him say. 'Emeralds are clearer and brighter, Harry.' She held out her hand and the ring shot green fire into his eyes. 'That is an emerald.'

He examined it carefully. 'It's very beautiful,' he said. 'I think you also must have been very beautiful once.'

Ridiculously she blushed. 'Go and gather your flowers, Harry.' She ruffled his thick hair playfully. 'It will be time to go soon.'

She watched him as he plucked the long-stemmed marguerites that grew in profusion along the river banks. He moved through the long grass with a fluid natural grace that reminded her of Thomas. She blinked the sudden foolish tears from her eyes. Still no word in all these months. Could he so finally have turned his back on her after the way she had loved him? She had been furious with him for a week, more so with Harry. To have their affairs so publicly displayed, for Harry to have shamed Eleanor so dreadfully. He was paying daily for that and his life had become one long grovelling apology. From Thomas there had been nothing, though she knew quite well where he was and all that he did; the queen's lieutenant and forever in council with Somerset and Exeter as the threat of war grew stronger. The rumours came thick and fast: that York had landed; that Warwick had taken London and the Tower; that poor Daft Harry had exchanged his crown for the foot of St Thomas. Only one thing was certain, that York was planning to invade before the summer was out and accordingly the royal army was camped at Northampton awaiting the first news of his landing. Ralph was with them, as were Thomas and Richard. Perhaps now they were to be idle for a while. Thomas would send word.

She smiled with a brightness she did not feel as little Harry approached laden with flowers. He laid them carefully at her feet and divided them into two equal piles. 'Those are for you, *grandmère*,' he said. 'The rest are for my lady mother.'

Again she caught the faint note of distress in his voice. 'Do you miss your father very much, Harry?' she asked him.

'Usually. Not so much today as I have been with you.'

'And your mother? Are you happier now that she is with you again?'

The boy raised solemn eyes to her face. 'Not really. I would be if I thought she was happy to be with me.' He looked down at the marguerites. 'I don't think she likes me very much.'

Alianore did not humour him with empty reassurances. Eleanor's antipathy toward her son was well known, not that her daughters had fared much better. They would be packed off to their marriage beds as soon as decency allowed. Eleanor was already betrothed to Lord de la Warr, even though she was barely twelve.

Henry held out a white starred flower. 'This is the queen's device, isn't it? I have seen Uncle Ralph with one tucked in his sleeve. Is it called a marguerite?'

'Some call it the daisy flower,' Alianore said. 'All these were planted here a long time ago in memory of another Margaret – Margaret Neville. She was your great-grandmother and my great-aunt. Her husband was the first Earl of Northumberland.' She rose to her feet and brushed the wisps of grass from her skirt. 'A little way down river is the hermitage where she is buried. It was built as a shrine for her. A priest lives there to say a mass for her every day.'

Harry looked impressed. 'He must have loved her very much.'

Alianore took his free hand. 'Yes,' she said. 'He did.'

They walked a little way without speaking. The boy seemed reluctant to go back and his footsteps began to drag as soon as the castle came into sight. Alianore paused pretending to rest.

Harry sat on a mound of rock and looked back toward the river. 'Is it true that the Earl of Salisbury is your brother?' he said suddenly.

'Yes. It is true.'

'Your true brother, as I am Elizabeth's and Eleanor's and Margaret's?'

'Yes.' She forestalled his next question. 'That makes him your uncle, and the Earl of Warwick is your cousin as is half the world, Harry if you've a drop of Neville blood in you.'

He looked up at her perceptively. 'Am I being a nuisance? Father says I am when I ask too many questions.'

She laughed and walked on. 'That is how you learn, Harry, by questioning. Perhaps it's just that you want to learn too quickly.'

He caught up with her and shyly took her hand. She sensed that physical contact was important to him. No doubt he was rarely kissed or caressed. She had never thought of him before as needing such. Then she felt him stiffen; she could almost feel the blood drain from his hand and leave it cold and limp within hers. Eleanor had emerged from the tower and stood watching them as they watched her. She came slowly toward them, her hair loosely netted, her damask skirts fluttering in the light breeze. She smiled mechanically at Alianore; her son she totally ignored.

'Dear God, Alianore. This is a tower of Babel indeed. One of my chests has gone missing containing three of my best gowns. Margaret is wailing like a mad thing over that stupid little dog of hers which she says is dying. That clod Musgrave trod on it and then tramped mud all over my green Turkey rug.'

Alianore stared at her coldly as the child beside her visibly shrank and diminished. His face was suddenly totally inanimate. It bore that faintly bovine look that reminded her of Harry. She tightened her grip on his limp hand as they mounted the steps of the keep. Eleanor followed complaining loudly and administered a resounding slap to a harassed page who had dared tread on her hem.

'I want that chest found immediately. There's a fortune in pearls sewn into the bodice of the blue velvet alone,' she said.

Alianore raised her eyes from the deep bronze bowl where she had placed the marguerites. 'We have been down by the river,' she said brightly. 'Harry has picked you a posy.'

Eleanor stared vaguely at the limp flowers. Their heads drooped in unison with the child's, their petals curled inward in shame. 'How nice,' she said and immediately deposited them in the arms of a passing page. 'Now about the chest. What shall I do about my gowns?'

Alianore's eyes blazed with sudden anger as little Harry pulled himself from her grasp and ran back the way they had come. 'Quite honestly, Eleanor, I could not care if you never set eyes on them again. I think that lonely neglected child is more important than your gowns.'

Eleanor's face grew ugly with spite. 'If you think so, my lady, then you look for the child. I shall look for my gowns.'

Alianore smiled disdainfully after her narrow retreating back. Now there was the Eleanor she knew and loathed.

She found the boy huddled in a corner of the ramparts. She thought for a moment he had been weeping but the eyes he turned toward her were quite dry and terrifying in their loathing; but not for her, not even for Eleanor. It was himself he found so despicable.

Alianore sat beside him tucking the skirts of her serviceable fustian gown beneath her feet. 'So this is where you are hiding, Harry? You *are* hiding, aren't you?'

The boy nodded miserably.

'Who from, Harry? Not from yourself, I hope, because that you can never do.' She did not press him for an answer. At that age he would have none to give. She took his hand. It was cold and lifeless as she had first imagined it would be. She could feel the misery in him as a tangible thing. His hand drew a little warmth from hers. Poor, sad, unloved little creature, she thought. His mother was an unfriendly stranger and his father was no better, with his overwhelming spasmodic love that was more to comfort himself than the child. She said gently, 'Once when I was young I was alone for a long time. I tried to hide myself away because another person had hurt me. I tried to pretend that I didn't care and because I pretended, so did he. For a while we were both unhappy. Then I stopped pretending. I came out of hiding and found that he was just as frightened of being sent away as I was.' She stroked his small well-shaped fingers. 'Sometimes it is necessary to give love first in order to get some back. And you must also have love and respect for yourself. If you do not, how then can you expect them from others?' She pulled him to his feet and took him to the ramparts. The view was breathtaking. From sky to sky the moor ran wildly like a verdant colourful sea, erupting into the broken crag of Great Tosson, falling away to the deep lush valley where the Coquet ran like a silver thread. At their backs the distant hills were soft and blue as a cushat's breast, the Cheviot crowned with fleecy cloud. Once, as a child, she had believed the world ended there.

'All this will be yours some day, Harry. A wild lonely place full of wild lonely men. If you learn to love it well it will reward you better than any of us can. The land is solid, unchanging, not given to caprice as we mortals are. Love it, cherish it, protect it and it will never betray you. And with such beauty and constancy as you have here what does it matter if some poor frail human fails you now and again?' She smiled down into his dark little face. 'You must never be afraid of love. All misery is based on fear, all fear on misery.' She pointed down into the bailey where her household crawled like fleas on a giant's brow. 'You see how small and insignificant we are when viewed from a height. You must climb to that height, Harry. Wherever you are, whatever you do, you must climb to the highest point no matter how small and unimportant the task. That makes for pride, Harry. Pride and self-esteem. Have you never felt inordinately proud of yourself, Harry?'

He frowned. 'I don't think so, unless it was when I killed a rabbit with the bow that father gave me. He was proud of me. He said I had a fine eye.'

Alianore sighed in exasperation. 'You know, Harry,' she said, 'I don't think I have ever heard you laugh. Tell me what pleases you, what makes you feel happy inside.'

His expression did not change from its perpetual gravity. He looked up at her unsmilingly, his long narrow eyes filled with sun. 'To be with you,' he said simply.

She knelt and kissed his sallow high-boned cheek. Oh what joy it was to be needed again.

She woke long before it was light, disturbed by the sound of voices. For a while she lay still with her eyes closed. The voices waned and then waxed strong again. There were footsteps, the clatter and screech of iron-shod hooves, the unmistakable sound of bolts being drawn.

She sat up and felt for her robe in the darkness. Then the door opened and Eleanor stood on the threshold, a guttering candle held aloft. 'There's a messenger,' she said. 'Come quickly.'

Alianore thrust her arms numbly into the robe and followed her out onto the landing. She looked down into the hall. The Constable's massive width hid the courier's face but she knew from his livery that he came from her son William. The Constable came to meet her and delivered the news without preamble. 'Warwick, Edward of March and the Earl of Salisbury landed at Sandwich five days ago. They advanced immediately on London and have successfully taken the Tower. Yesterday morning they left for Northampton. His Grace the bishop of Carlisle advises that all precautions be taken here and that the Earl be summoned from Berwick immediately.'

Alianore nodded. 'Of course. Yes, of course. See that a man is sent.' She drew her robe closer, for though it was high summer the stones of the hall still harboured a winter's cold and the long expectancy of war had still not prepared her for the sick feeling that crept from her stomach to her throat. She looked at Eleanor and though her face was quiet and watchful her eyes gleamed with a queer little flame. There was still that wild barbaric streak in her that was excited by conflict.

Alianore drew the Constable aside. 'Was there any other news?' she asked anxiously. 'My other sons, are they with the king at Northampton still?'

The Constable shook his head. 'All the news the bishop sent I repeated to you, my lady. I have no certain news, but I think it more than likely.'

Alianore smiled faintly and thanked him. As always she must wait and hope and surmise. She shivered. The hall was vast and oppressive despite the hastily rekindled fire. The flames leapt grudgingly in the yawning hearth and flung her shadow grotesquely on the far wall.

Eleanor touched her arm. 'Come away,' she said. 'There's nothing to be done yet.'

It was soothing for once to be cossetted herself and meekly she allowed herself to be led back to her chamber. The bed was cold, the sheets already sheened with damp. Eleanor brought a fur and laid it round her shoulders. 'It will be well,' she said confidently. 'I know it.'

Alianore did not answer. She was long past being comforted by words. She watched with dull unseeing eyes as Eleanor prodded the inert fire back to life and set a pan of wine to warm. 'I will fetch you a draught to sooth you,' she said, and smiled. 'To make time fly on silken wings. It will make the waiting less.'

Alianore moved nearer the fire. Her limbs were cramped and cold and she could not seem to drag her mind from the mesh of doubt and fear that the Constable's heavy voice had laid upon it. She must rouse herself, for what earthly good would she be to any if they lost the day – there, she had said it. If they lost the day, if all her sons were slaughtered like sheep. The acknowledgement of the worst made it seem less likely and she felt a little of the numbness ease from her. It was the uncertainty that was so killing; so much to be construed from so little. She thought again of William's brief message. Her brother, then, had landed almost a week ago with York's son and her nephew Warwick. Where then was York? Still in Ireland? Or perhaps already embarked, thinking to fall upon the Lancastrians from the west? It was useless to conjecture. She must stick to what little she knew: that the Yorkists had taken London, seemingly with ease. That was the greatest shock. She had thought the Tower so strongly held. Then yesterday they had left for Northampton. She calculated swiftly. With a forced march they could reach Northampton by – tomorrow. Again her blood froze and she looked quickly toward the window. The solid square of darkness was comforting and suddenly she did not want the night to end. In darkness there was safety and refuge for her sons.

The door opened softly and Eleanor drifted in on an icy draught. 'There,' she said with an incongruously matronly smile that made Alianore want to laugh. 'This will ease you.'

'What is it?' Alianore enquired suspiciously.

Eleanor knelt by the hearth and bound her hand in her skirts to lift the bowl from the fire. The liquid steamed and spat and filled the air with a strange sickly odour. She handed her the steaming cup. 'Valerian, the herb of Ephesus, and mandragora drawn screaming from the earth shall make all silence and softness,' she quoted softly.

Alianore held the scalding cup between her chilled hands. 'Did Elizabeth teach you that?'

'Yes, and all manner of other weird and wonderful things,' Eleanor added mockingly.

'But not love or charity or kindness,' said Alianore, thinking of little Harry.

'Possibly not,' Eleanor responded quickly. 'I do not think she'd had enough experience of that to pass it on. You certainly showed her none while she lived.'

The criticism was justified and Alianore said, 'I know that and am repentant of it now, but as you can see Elizabeth's lack so clearly, can't you see that of your own son?'

'I would have thought his father made up for any lack in me,' Eleanor said with spite. 'The boy has been well schooled to think of me as only a little less than a common whore. I can see it in his eyes, that sick reproachful look.'

'That is not true. I do not think it is your morals he reproaches you for. The child is desperate for affection, Eleanor.'

'Are not we all?' Eleanor said. Then she laughed softly. 'What a strange and muddled world. There's such a wealth of love and yet it is all wrongly dispersed. We are all left wanting. I want Thomas and cannot have him; Harry wants me and is denied. You want your husband back; little Harry wants love where there is none. We all carry our pitcher to the well and find it dry.'

The blatant confession should have angered her but the other woman's eyes were so poignantly sad that Alianore said. 'Yet we must all make the best of what we *do* have. I know Harry is not all that a woman could wish for in a husband but he is . . .' She paused and Eleanor pounced eagerly on the hesitation.

'Yes. I have always found it difficult to find the exact word to describe him. Harry is like the chameleon, changing with the sun, or in his case, according to the amount of wine he has consumed. His mood can range from pleasantly mellow to maudlin, right through to outright violence.' She smiled up into Alianore's pale shocked face. 'Harry is an animal, and therefore I treat him as such. You would not think him vain, would you? Well, he is. He's always looking for love, for comfort, for praise yet he gives none. When Harry walks into a room it is always empty for him. He never sees the need of others, only his own reflected in their eyes. He never sees their lack of love, he's too afraid they might see his.'

'That is not vanity, Eleanor. That is lack of self-esteem.'

'But self is the important word. It is never, does Harry love? It is always, is Harry loved?' Eleanor's mouth grew thin and angry. 'Well, not by me he isn't, not ever by me. Not him nor that changeling he fathered on me.' Her eyes burned so hotly with loathing that Alianore flinched from their look. 'Shall I tell you how that child was conceived? On the night that Elizabeth died, while I was sick and weeping with grief. Harry was drunk and while I wept he grunted and belched and slobbered like a rabid dog. Little Harry was the result of that. Do you wonder that I cannot look at him without shuddering?'

Alianore said nothing. She wished she didn't believe it. She wished she could say with conviction that her son was not capable of such an act. But he was; when he was drunk he was. 'I'm sorry for you, Eleanor,' she said at last. 'I'm sorry for you, and little Harry, for both of my sons.' She sighed. What sorrow there was in loving. She cared so deeply for them all, even for Eleanor in a vague compassionate way. She sipped a little of the cooling wine. Perhaps it was better not to care. Richard had always thought so. She drank again of the strangely pungent brew and felt the strong narcotic warming her. It was a long time since she had thought of her brother with love. How strange to think that the man who was advancing so ruthlessly toward her sons, bent on their destruction, had once laid beside her and snivelled his childish grievances onto her breast; that the man who had slain Hal had once lifted her laughingly from the mud of a fall and kissed her tears away. She could see him now, his fair curls blown by the wind, carefully dividing the apple he had so boldly stolen for their feast. Richard, George, William, Thomas, her brothers; Richard, George, William, Thomas, her sons. Their names and faces ran together in her mind and became one, one indivisible love, one longing.

She felt Eleanor's hands wrap her more warmly in the fur. Her face was a blur haloed by the fire. *Elizabeth.* Suddenly she was afraid. She remembered a long time ago, before even Harry was born. 'Look upon me well, Alianore, and see yourself forty years hence. Old and alone with all you loved beneath cold, barren earth.' She moaned softly and tried to rise from the chair but her limbs were heavy and weighted with iron. Her eyelids fluttered briefly then closed on the diffused circle of light that was Eleanor's face. She sighed and the world slipped quietly away into darkness.

Eleanor stayed motionless at her feet, staring blindly into the fire's warmth. Oh, Thomas, she thought, Thomas, my heart. God keep you safe for me.

Three days had passed and Alianore had abandoned any pretence of keeping herself occupied. She sat for hours staring from the turret room that overlooked the gatehouse. She watched the road, she watched the river, she watched the guards who paced the wall, alert for any quickening of their slow ambling gait. She watched the sky and played a silly childish game to pass the time, seeing which of the racing clouds touched the tip of the postern tower first. She saw them darken as the day wore on. By evening it had begun to rain.

The sound was soothing, for the wind had dropped to the merest stirring of the air and the rain fell, soft and sibilant, gathering in clear scented pools on the leads of the chapel roof. She stirred reluctantly, blinking her dry tired eyes, dragging herself down the worn concave steps. She halted in the doorway, aware of the deep penetrating silence. Even the noise of the garrison was stilled. Suspense and tension hung over them like a storm cloud, growing blacker by the minute as another day ended and still no news came. She had sent scurriers out that very morning, west to Carlisle and William, south to Beverley and George. She'd been more than hopeful of hearing something today.

Lifting her face to the rain that was now little more than a sheening of the air, she walked slowly toward the hall. She dreaded the moment of entrance when every eye would turn expectantly toward her and then dispiritedly away. At the door she stumbled on the hem of her robe and fell heavily to her knees. The sharp pain soon passed but she stayed crouched like a dog, too weary to make the effort to rise. She began to cry. Great racking sobs tore from her lungs and echoed back from the high walls. Her breath rasped noisily in her throat. Then slowly she became aware of other sounds; horsemen, voices. The guard-house erupted into sudden, violent life. The winch groaned and rattled as the chains engaged and with a long rushing screech of air the drawbridge fell.

She ran, stumbling, falling, slithering on the wet mossy stones. The long torchlit tunnel swarmed with men and horses and her face flamed with gladness as she saw Ralph. His own was grim and terrible as he lowered Richard gently from his horse. Alianore grew pale and sick as she saw the gaping wound beneath his heart.

The Constable swept him up like a child and carried him into the guardroom. Tenderly Alianore knelt beside him and saw all of his left side soaked in blood. She rose unsteadily to her feet and looked at Ralph. 'Dear God in heaven,' she said. 'What has happened?'

'Grey of Ruthin betrayed us,' he said harshly. 'At Northampton. He deserted to Salisbury at the height of the battle.'

Alianore was stunned. Edmund Grey, Catherine's husband? She looked down at Richard, moaning softly as the Constable staunched his wound. Then her heart began to beat with slow sickening strokes. Where was Thomas?

She sank down weakly onto the hard bench. Ralph was speaking, his voice heavy and inarticulate with loss. Grey's defection had cost them the battle. Buckingham, Shrewsbury and Beaumont were slain, the king wounded and captured. Alianore raised her eyes to his face. He was talking more to prepare himself than her. She knew long before the words left his lips that Thomas was dead.

'Tell me,' she whispered faintly.

'He was struck down in the king's tent trying to save Henry from capture. We thought at first he was only badly wounded. Clifford and I managed to get him from the field and we hid him in his tent. He died an hour later.' Ralph's voice broke on tears and he fumbled inside his torn and bloodstained tunic. 'He asked that I should give you this.'

She unfolded the letter with strenuous calm. Strangely it was written on the back of a torn and discarded Yorkist pamphlet. A little of the scurrilous verse was still legible beneath the stains of blood and sweat:

> 'Daft Harry, Daft Harry,
> pawned his crown for a cross.
> Daft Harry, Daft Harry,
> no one mourns its loss.'

She turned it over carefully and began to read:

My dear and well beloved lady mother; Alas, sweet Nel, I fear I am about to disappoint you again by an untimely and intemperate death. I confess, I had not thought dying such a tedious thing. I had envisaged a so much more spectacular end like Hector on the field of Troy; in fact, to be truthful, until this last minute, I had not envisaged it at all. Now like Isocrates after Choeronea, I die of grief at a battle lost.

My dispositions are few, having dissipated my meagre wealth in a happy and riotous youth. I should like Ralph to have the ten couple of hounds that I bred at Egremont. To Richard I bequeth the chestnut mare and my sapphire clasp, to George and William the care of my reprobate soul. To Harry I leave nothing but pure dislike, I dare say he'll be content enough with my death. To you, my sweet mother, I leave a contrite and loving heart. Look after the sibling Richard for me, he's too gentle and sweet for this world. No doubt he'll be led into all manner of disaster without me.

I am tired now and have to rely on Clifford's illiterate scrawl for this last. Nemesis calls in a most raucous and unseemly voice. Tell Aphrodite I loved her well. Let her remember poor Hermes.

Your devoted and dutiful son, Thomas, Lord Egremont.

He had managed to scrawl his own signature and she could read his pain and the agony of effort in the tortured strokes, so unlike his rounded flamboyant hand. She laid the letter against her heart and looked up at the harsh and broken sound of a man weeping. Richard struggled up from the straw of his bed. The tears coursed hot and vengeful down his face.

'It was Warwick that killed him,' he sobbed. 'Richard Neville, Earl of Warwick, struck him down.' He tried to rise and fell heavily with a scream of pain. From his knees he looked up at his mother. 'By God, madam,' he said bitterly, 'your blood has much to answer for.'

The leech book lay open on the little desk, its heavy grained pages weighted with a knife. Beside it lay the letter which Eleanor took up and read for the hundredth time. 'Tell Aphrodite I loved her well. Let her remember poor Hermes.' Her full mouth curved bitterly. Sometimes she would have given anything to forget. She was free now from the terrible agony of those first few days but the grief had diminished and hardened like fine steel. It was lodged like a knife somewhere below her heart.

She folded the letter with infinite care till it was small enough to be inserted in the gold reliquary she wore around her neck – a companion for the sapphire ring. She glanced round the bare walls of the old tower room. They'd seen all the joy and happiness that she'd ever had; now let them see her grief and vengeance. Instinctively, she looked across at the dismantled bed. If she closed her eyes she could see him there, his warm naked body beside hers, his mouth teasing the soft hollows of her throat till she turned and kissed him. She had kissed him once more when they had brought his body back from Northampton but his mouth had been cold and dead then, his body haggled with vicious unhealed wounds. It was the fine scar that she herself had healed that had finally made her weep. And once begun it seemed that the tears would never stop. For two days she'd wept insanely and uncontrollably. Harry had battered furiously upon the door, weeping himself with rage. When she had finally emerged, his had been the first face she had seen and even then he'd not had the wit to keep his triumph from his eyes. 'Don't crow, my lord,' she'd said. 'He'll still possess me more in death than you ever have in all your life.'

Harry didn't matter now. Thomas's death had freed her from any lip service she had been obliged to pay him. She did not care if he sent her back to Holystone. She could do her work as well from there.

She went to the window. The queen's army was camped in sprawling disorder along the banks of the Aln. Overnight, tents had sprung up like fairy rings and from their pinnacled roofs banners and standards hung stiff with frost. It was November, three months and twelve days since Thomas had been killed and time enough for Margaret to have gathered together more men than Eleanor had ever seen. An army of retribution, the queen called it, to wield the sword of vengeance against the traitor York who had at last decided to show his face after Salisbury and Warwick had marched the witless Henry back to London. To the queen's immense satisfaction he had been all but shown the door by a cautious and still loyal Parliament. His outright bid to supplant Henry had been dismissed out of hand, but they had granted him the Protectorate again and to Margaret's fury and disbelief had persuaded the King to disinherit the Prince Edward and name York as his heir. Yet it was the Nevilles who wielded the real power. Warwick had charge of the hapless king and his father and brothers monopolised the government. Every man in England knew, except perhaps York himself, that it was only Warwick's forceful strategy that had brought him this far. Eleanor still vividly remembered that day in the gardens at York. He had been sure of his triumph even then. She wondered if he had thought of her since. Had she perhaps fleetingly crossed his mind as he had struck Thomas down? She had thought of him, every hour of every day since. Once more she looked at the queen's vast renegade army and she smiled disdainfully. Not even they had the power to bring Warwick down. But she had. And she would.

She turned back into the room and picked up the small grey book. She turned the stiff pages till she came to the last. She began to recite in a clear hard voice, 'In the name of Satan, Asmodeus and all the lords of darkness, I curse thee . . .'

In the hall below her, her husband scowled his discontent at the page who brought his supper. He stared down dismally at his plate: half a fowl, a lump of cheese and a dish of eels swimming in a thin greasy sauce. He supposed he was lucky to get that, after Margaret and her court of vultures had picked his town clean. He pushed the food away untasted and fed the fowl to the dogs. He began to pace indecisively, thinking of the raggle-taggle army camped outside his walls getting noisily and aggressively drunk. The knowledge that the queen had beggared both herself and her supporters to raise it turned him doubly sick. She had her army, but at what a cost to English pride. Berwick had gone, the price of the five thousand Scots who marched with them. There were some French too, mercenaries who fought purely for reward. The irony of it was borne strongly upon him. All the king's ancient enemies now turned out in his defence. The disloyal thought crossed his mind: was it worth it? All the money and lives that would be lost – and for what? A foreign queen and an heir more than likely born on the sinister side. Then he would think of Henry, poor gentle Henry who had been almost a brother to him once. He would remember the happy, carefree days: hunting in the park at Windsor and Shene; discoursing fiercely on God and the world while they roasted chestnuts on a winter fire. There had been a gentleness in himself then, before Eleanor and life had driven it out. He sank down dejectedly on the steps of the dais. All motives of vengeance and hatred apart, he knew he could not desert Henry.

He was on his feet again almost immediately. But nothing could be achieved like this. He might be a bad husband and a worse lover but he was a damn fine soldier and this was all wrong. Henry himself would have wept if he could see the damage done already by the foreign soldiery, even to his own lands, and as far as the Scots were concerned, especially to his own lands. Reprimand was useless. The queen considered no sacrifice too great if York's defeat were the end result. 'When the wolves enter my house I have no compunction about turning the dogs on them.' And that is exactly what they were: dogs, curs, hell hounds. And he would run with the pack because he had to. Did that make him one of them? He was suddenly reminded of Thomas that night at Leconfield and of his own inane remarks. Had he not said that you fight dogs with dogs? The ridiculous thing was that if he had been sober he would have heartily agreed with his brother's condemnation of Exeter's excesses at Ludlow. But because Thomas had said it . . . Well, Thomas was dead now, in theory at least. A smile twisted his mouth. He was not sure now that he did not prefer him alive. Thomas was far beyond criticism and reproach now, entombed in shining valour, or so all the world seemed to see him.

He mounted the spiral of narrow turnpike stairs that led to his mother's apartments. How ironic and unfair life was, he thought.

He had longed so much to be rid of Thomas, yet now he was a greater rival dead than he had ever been alive. He wondered if they would mourn him so well.

He knocked respectfully and waited till her voice bade him enter. He felt like an inadequate steward come to explain a shortage in the accounts.

Alianore looked up at him with vague disinterest, frowning as if she tried to recollect who he was. He felt like screaming at her, 'I am Harry. Harry, your son. I am alive.' Instead he smiled nervously and said, 'I'm sorry if I disturb you. I thought I would make my farewells now. There may not be time in the morning.'

Alianore nodded and wondered why everything Harry said was preceded by an apology. 'Yes, of course.' She glanced unhappily to the window where the noise of the revelling soldiers beat faintly against the glass. 'I shall not be sorry to see them leave.'

Or me, Harry thought, as her heavy black gown shrieked reproach at him for still being alive.

Her voice too tolled like a mourning bell. 'All is prepared then?' she asked, anxious to bring this stilted encounter to a close.

'Yes. Devon and Somerset are making their way from the west. We hope to rendezvous at York within the week.'

'And then?'

'And then press on to London. The queen is anxious to regain possession of the king, though I doubt if we will get that far without encounter. York must be well aware of our movements.'

Alianore looked at him in mild surprise. 'You sound almost eager, Harry.'

'Perhaps I am.' He could not have told her just how eager. War was something he particularly excelled at, despite his ethical distaste for it. The defeat at Northampton and his brother's death had overshadowed his own small triumph when he had successfully held off a Scots attack at Wark for nearly three weeks with only a handful of men. That the enemy had eventually taken Wark was no reflection on him. He had inflicted heavy losses with the hundred men that he'd had and then there had been the added bonus of the young King James blowing himself to bits with a faulty cannon. It was an advantage he could have exploited to the limit if the queen had been prepared to give him the time and the men. All that was over now. The enemy were suddenly allies though it went strongly against his better judgement to fight alongside a man you'd had at swordpoint barely a month before.

'Yes, perhaps I am,' he said again. 'It will be good to be in the field again. There is still much to be avenged.'

Alianore winced. Richard's voice echoed harshly in her ears. 'Dear God, madam, your blood has much to answer for.' She said worriedly, 'Keep a watch on Richard. His wound is barely healed. I am not really sure that he is well enough to ride with you.' She looked up into his face and caught a glimpse of his own pain before he covered it with his habitual expressionless stare. Poor Harry, she thought. Always last when by rights he should have been first. Eleanor thought him an animal, but what were any of them except what others had made them? She could still remember when he had been a shy and thoughtful child. She laid her hand gently on his arm. 'Have a care yourself too, Harry. I have not such a surfeit of sons that I can afford to lose any more.'

He smiled his grave uncertain smile and she was reminded for an instant of his own son. Impulsively she reached up and kissed him. 'Come home soon, Harry, and send word when you can. Perhaps then the waiting will not be so long.'

The tender moment stayed with him all through the next day when the queen's massive army began to make its devastating way south. It created a small impregnable island of sanity in the madness of the war, a breath of clean untainted air in the smoking desert they left in their wake, for Margaret had given instructions for all York and Neville estates to be destroyed en route. She rode at their head, small and frail, yet her ferocity exceeded any of theirs. She both fascinated and repelled, like a brilliant and deadly serpent. Even her own men had dubbed her the She-wolf of France.

They reached York on the first of December and were met by Somerset and the news that York and Salisbury were marching north to intercept them. Warwick, it seemed, was charged with holding London and keeping the king safe. Margaret was jubilant. Let them come, she cried, the further north the better. And true to temperament, York came, the fly being drawn into the queen's inextricable web. Three days before Christmas he had penetrated as far as his castle at Sandal, a few miles from York. Accordingly the queen moved her forces south to Pontefract. By Christmas Eve the two armies were only twenty miles apart.

It was a cheerless time for the Yorkists. Snow had begun intermittently to fall and the Lancastrians' iron control of the surrounding countryside saw them miserably short of food. Even though the royal army was well provisioned, the prospect of a siege was grim. Their own supplies would dwindle and there was always the risk that Warwick would arrive with a relieving force. In the cold dank hall at Pontefract, Margaret castigated herself and her captains for allowing the Yorkists to become so well entrenched. She had sent various insulting messages and challenges to York, though none really believed that he would be drawn by so obvious a ploy. Harry sat between his brothers Richard and Ralph and watched as her wrath fell upon young Somerset and Clifford in turn. He would be next, and boldly for him, he rose to his feet and said, 'Your Grace. I can see no point in all this wrangling. Our sole object is to draw York into the open. Let us set our minds to that.'

'Well then, set your mind to it, Northumberland,' the queen snapped. 'What do you suggest?'

The initial discomfort of bearing all eyes upon him soon passed, and Harry said with mounting authority, 'We must assume that York's inactivity is based on the hope that support will arrive from Warwick in the south or his son, Edward of March, in the west. Perhaps if we gave that hope a semblance of reality . . .'

'I do not follow you, my lord,' Margaret said irritably.

'I do,' John Clifford said. 'Though I am not sure how he means to achieve it.'

'By sending him his reinforcements,' Harry explained forcibly. 'A single messenger at first in Warwick's livery – there are enough dead men in the vicinity wearing it. Once York thinks relief is on its way he might relax his guard.'

Clifford took up the idea eagerly. 'Yes. And then perhaps a feigned skirmish at a distance. A hundred men, say, in Warwick's livery fighting off a supposed royalist attack. York would be duty bound to aid them.'

The queen smiled. '*Et voilà*. The snail is drawn from his shell.'

Harry returned the smile hesitantly. 'We must hope so, your Grace. We must truly hope so.'

It was well and meticulously planned, for it was not so much York who needed to be deceived as Salisbury. He was the one who would question such a conveniently timed deliverance. That night they roamed the desolate towns like grave-robbers, stripping the dead and rotting corpses of their scarlet livery, scouring every field and ditch for the bear and ragged staff. They even found a soiled and bloodstained banner and restored it tenderly to its former glory. It shone gaudily in the queen's tent, its bestial emblem disturbing among the marguerites and swans. The Queen ordered that it be turned to the wall. Of all her enemies, Margaret feared Warwick the most.

At dawn the next day a young anonymous squire was arrayed in his renegade livery and schooled to perfection by Andrew Trollope. Margaret inspected him critically before he left, averting her gaze from the badge upon his sleeve. He looked dusty and dishevelled enough to have ridden through the night. His face was pale and his voice hoarse with strain but it could well have passed for exhaustion. Margaret clasped his trembling hand. 'God speed,' she cried in her passionate voice. 'For this day's work you earn the eternal gratitude of your queen. I shall pray for your safe and speedy return to us.'

They all prayed, Harry most fervently of all. The worst thing was there was no way of gauging the success or failure of his plan. All through the day he half expected to hear that the body of the messenger had been cast from the walls of Sandal. By nightfall there was still no news, good or bad, and he went ahead with his preparations. Trollope was to lead the pseudo-Yorkist force, himself and Ralph the attacking Lancastrians. Somerset and Clifford would have command of the main body and remain concealed in the trees above the road till he gave the command to attack. For the rest they must trust to luck. That was when he began to doubt. Luck had never been particularly kind to him that he could remember.

At least the weather favoured them, a fine drifting sleet that masked the movement of the main army away from Pontefract and saw them safe in the woods above Sandal long before it was light. At dawn he and Trollope advanced to within a mile of Wakefield and waited. It was York's custom to send out foraging parties and he thought it prudent to let them get as far afield as time allowed. Besides, the fewer men in Sandal the better.

He gave Trollope a mile start, watching the scarlet-clad column strung out like droplets of blood in the snow. When the last had disappeared from sight, he ordered the pursuit.

He had timed it to perfection and fell noisily on Trollope's rear within sight and sound of Sandal, but not so close that faces could be recognised, actions observed. So desperate was he for it to succeed that he fought with unaccustomed ferocity and wounded at least two of Trollope's men and received a graze himself. It was enough to convince the watching Yorkists. Within minutes of the encounter the gates of Sandal opened and York himself led his men out.

There was never any doubt of victory. Harry fell back and his apparent retreat drew the Yorkists on. They hardly noticed the men emerging silently from the trees and spreading out like long welcoming arms. Harry drew them further into the deadly embrace and Salisbury's wild cry of alarm came too late. The arms enfolded them and held them fast. The massacre had begun.

It lasted barely an hour and at the end the very air reeked of blood. The snow was thick and liquid with it and in the midst of the two thousand men he had led to their deaths lay the broken and bloodstained body of Richard of York. John Clifford advanced purposefully through the slain and dragged it up by its long fair hair. Then with one hard vicious stroke of his sword he severed the ambitious head forever.

Like Salome, the queen had the head mounted on a platter before her. She smiled fondly at Clifford whose gift it was and who had further endeared himself to her by despatching York's young son Rutland as he had made a vain bid to escape. She looked again at the severed head. The stump of the neck congealed blackly and trailed yellow sinew upon the plate. The eyes were wide and fixed and mirrored York's last earthly emotion: a mingling of horror and faint disbelief. Margaret could hardly believe it herself. She needed this grotesque affirmation that at last the traitor York was dead.

Then she turned smilingly to the man beside her, badly wounded but still very much alive. 'Well then, my lord of Salisbury, what shall we do with you?'

Richard Neville raised his eyes full of the same horror and disbelief. He had led such a charmed and protected life that he could not believe its end. Even an hour ago he had still hoped: imprisonment and eventual ransom; perhaps an exchange for the king himself. That hope had been quickly extinguished by the look on the queen's face. His eyes went painfully to the violated head. At least York was beyond pain and humiliation. He almost envied him that.

'So.' The queen rose slowly from her chair. 'Is your tongue stilled then, my lord? Where has all that wonderful eloquence gone? You had much to say when you named me whore and laid the taint of bastardy on my son; when you denounced noble Henry as a madman; when you rode into Council and waxed long and loud on the virtue of York.' She smiled cruelly. 'York's only virtue now is that he is dead, as is your son Thomas Neville, as your son Warwick soon will be.' She came closer, her heavy velvet skirts dabbling in the pool of blood that seeped from his wound. 'Fill that grandiloquent mouth now with the taste of defeat, for tomorrow you will die, unshriven and a traitor. You have but one night longer and I suggest that you spend it praying for your soul. Let your catechism be the names of those you have brutally used, the dead, the maimed, the disinherited whom you sacrificed in order to make this man king.' She smiled again, that small rapacious feminine smile that froze his blood. 'Well, he shall be king perhaps, after all; master of all he surveys from the walls of York. He shall be crowned with parchment and hallowed with urine and you shall reign beside him as he promised you. In the meantime I shall leave you in the care of Northumberland and Clifford and his Grace of Somerset. You should have much to talk of. I understand you knew their fathers well.'

She went gracefully and regally from the room and the sense of horror she left in her wake maintained the long and bitter silence.

It was Salisbury himself who broke it. He looked at Harry and said with an attempt at bravado, 'Well then, nephew. With what shall we pass the time?'

Harry regarded him bleakly. His body ached with slaughter and he'd taken no joy in the queen's cruel speech. His need for vengeance did not extend to the subtlety of mental torture. He would be content with Salisbury dead. He forced himself to continue the charade; both Clifford and Somerset would expect it. He had also noted Salisbury's meaningful 'nephew'. Was that an appeal to their kinship, a reminder that his mother was Salisbury's sister? He answered him with equal amity. 'A good point, uncle,' he said. 'I must consider carefully. I would not want to squander it fruitlessly as you have so little of it left.'

'A game of chance, perhaps,' suggested Clifford dryly. 'We'll give you fair odds. Better odds than you ever gave his father or mine.'

'Perhaps he is best left alone,' Somerset said. 'A man should have time with his thoughts when he is about to die.' He rose and smiled into Salisbury's ashen face. 'Do not fear, my lord. We shall not abandon you. We will see you safely to the scaffold in the morning and see it done. We would not have you die without kin or a known face by you.'

Harry paused for a moment before he left. 'I must confess,' he said quietly, 'I had not thought vengeance such a sweet and desirable thing.'

Salisbury raised his head and for a moment some of his old venom showed in his eyes. 'Aye, Northumberland. And no doubt my sons will think it too.'

'Of course,' Harry agreed smilingly. 'I had not thought for it to end there.'

At the door Clifford turned back. 'I would not leave you lonely, my lord. You shall have his Grace of York for company.'

When the door had closed and been barred behind them Salisbury buried his face in his hands. For the first time in thirty years he wept.

At dawn on the last day of December, Richard Neville, Earl of Salisbury, was led between Northumberland and Clifford to lay his head on a makeshift block. Exeter's bastard was his executioner and as Salisbury had desired, struck off his head in three competent strokes in honour of the Trinity. It was a far different trinity that was in the minds of the men who stood and watched it done. As the sword rose and fell thrice Somerset murmured, 'For Somerset; for Northumberland; for Clifford.'

As Margaret had promised, his head was set beside York's, flaunting its derisive paper crown. On their left was the pale tear-stained face of fifteen year-old Rutland; on their right the mangled head of Salisbury's second son. Two spaces had been left between them: one for York's son, Edward of March; the other for the Earl of Warwick.

The two women sat close together on the low couch, Alianore pale and sickly as she heard of her brother's death. Eleanor smiling quietly with triumph, savouring every detail of Harry's bloody tale. Then she raised her head and looked coldly into her husband's face. 'Yet Warwick's head is still firmly attached to his shoulders, though I hear he fled like a thief from the second encounter at St Albans. How so, Harry?'

Harry looked away from her predatory gaze. It had cost him enough to relive that day, yet he thought it had cost his mother more. He knelt by her in concern. 'If you would rather I . . .'

'No. No. Go on.' Alianore patted his hand and forced a smile. 'Tell all, Harry. I trust that I have heard the worst.'

Harry moved away to where the light shone less brightly. The worst for her, perhaps but not for the queen and the Lancastrian cause. It was this which had brought them so speedily north. A Yorkist king reigned now, proclaimed at Westminster a week ago to the very day. Critically he looked back on the weeks and months of Lancastrian victory that had led to this staggering bloodless defeat. He still asked himself how could it have happened. Then he began to speak, slowly and clearly, reaching among the words for the fault if there was one in his own careful strategy.

After Wakefield the royal army had swept triumphantly south consuming everything in its path like a swarm of starving locusts. Control of such a horde was becoming impossible, though Harry had tried his utmost, even quarrelling openly with the queen when a church was violated. Some of the privation could not be helped. They were a large unwieldy force needing to be fed and housed and victuals were not the most abundant of commodities at this time of year. It was among the mercenaries that the element of lawlessness was worst. They looted and raped and pillaged at will as if they were on enemy soil. He supposed that to them they were, for the Scots and French were the greatest offenders. He had fumed impotently. This would cost them dearer than Berwick at the end of the day.

The queen was beyond all reasoning. She had lived in a triumphant euphoric dream as if York's death were the ultimate victory. She had not even been moved by the disturbing news of James of Wiltshire's defeat at Mortimer's Cross. Granted it was only a small victory for Edward of March but they had lost some good men, Owen Tudor amongst them. James of Wiltshire, as always, had managed to escape. Harry and the other lords had seen it as a warning against complacency. There was still much to be done. London and the king had still to be wrested from Warwick's grasp and it was here that Harry feared that the reputation of the royalist army might go against them. The Londoners were still very much in the Earl of Warwick's pocket.

Yet it was Warwick himself who made the first fatal blunder. As they neared St Albans, the Lancastrian scouts came back with chilling reports of the Yorkist numbers and their superior weaponry. Burgundy, it seemed, had sent a troop of hand gunners that could fire both lead pellets and arrows of steel; they had caltraps and pavises as well as cannon and the estimates of their total strength would have stopped any but Margaret in his tracks. Margaret was too near to her goal to be diverted and against all advice she pressed on. Warwick had moved with unusual caution and had remained within hailing distance of London, a strategy that Harry could only grudgingly approve. That way he had reinforcements and supplies to hand and it was the Lancastrians who would have to make the running. It was with disbelief and joy that he had later heard that Warwick had ordered his army to remove to Barnet Heath.

The queen had accepted this change in their fortunes as no more than her due. Immediately she had roused her army, just fallen into their beds. In darkness and rain they had moved down Watling Street toward St Albans and as on that occasion five years before they found the Yorkists there before them. But this time it was Lancaster who had won the day. The handful of men who occupied the town were only a hundredth of the force they had been led to expect. The main Yorkist army under Warwick was still moving toward Barnet, blissfully ignorant of their proximity. Harry himself had led the first attack and fallen joyfully on the unprepared Yorkist vanguard. What had prompted Warwick to withhold the main body of his troops from their defence, Harry would never know. It was a mistake and a bad one, for defeat was contagious and as darkness fell it was seen that what was left of the Yorkist army was dwindling; in twos and threes at first, then in bands of twenty or thirty, riding stealthily away. By dawn Warwick himself was spurring furiously westward. That had been *their* first mistake, Harry thought bitterly. If they could have captured him then, the war would have been as good as won.

But they had other cause to celebrate. Warwick in his panic had abandoned his precious hostage, and the king was joyfully reunited with his wife and son after a separation of nearly a year. Perhaps it was then that they had become complacent; it was certainly then that his prediction regarding the army's past excesses was fulfilled. Their savage reputation had preceded them and had been vastly exaggerated by Yorkist propaganda. When they had arrived triumphant before London they had found the gates closed against them. After two days of delicate negotiation, Margaret had been persuaded to order her army back to St Albans despite the protests of her lords. That had been their second mistake, for no sooner were they dispersed than the news came that Edward of March and Warwick were approaching from the west. There was nothing for it but to retreat in their army's wake, for the gates of London were still firmly closed against them. Three days later they had opened to welcome Edward of March. Within a week he'd had himself proclaimed king.

It had been a disastrous blow for Margaret, for all of them, and one that even now he was not sure they could overcome. He said wearily, his voice hoarse and cracking with strain, 'Then we returned to York. The king and queen are there still, waiting to see which way the wind blows.'

Eleanor rose bemusedly. Edward of March – king? So Elizabeth had been right.

Then Alianore said, 'Poor Henry. After all he has been through. To have it all begin again.'

'It's the queen that needs your pity,' Eleanor said sneeringly. 'As does any woman married to a weak ineffectual man.'

Harry turned and looked into eyes that implied that she herself was one such. He smiled faintly. 'And you include yourself in their number, do you, Eleanor? I shall not argue with that. It is only your use of the word *woman* that I object to. The word I take to mean something of softness and warmth and femininity, none of which you have ever possessed. A pretty face alone does not qualify you for their ranks.'

Eleanor's eyes widened as if he had slapped her and for once she could think of no fitting reply. She stared at him for a long hard moment then went wordlessly from the room.

'Well said, Harry,' Alianore smiled at her son approvingly. 'I did not think you had it in you.'

'Neither did I,' Harry admitted ruefully. 'Perhaps it's because I have given up. I don't honestly think I care any more.'

Alianore could understand that. She had rather given up with Eleanor herself, as yet another facet of her complex personality had emerged these past few months. The list of Eleanor's roles was endless: whore; courtesan; virgin; nun; wife and mother – though these last two only sparingly when all else palled; and since Thomas's death, mystic and recluse. She spent all her time shut in Elizabeth's tower room, emerging only to exercise her complaining tongue. She was beginning to believe that Eleanor was a little touched, whether by God or the Devil she was not sure.

'Will you pour me a little of the hippocras, Harry?' she said.

353

'Or there's some burgundy there if you'd prefer it.'

He brought her a measure of the sweetly spiced wine but took nothing himself. 'I've seen enough men drunk these past six months to make me abstemious for life,' he told her when she commented on it. He sat down beside her and she marvelled again how he had changed. He was thinner, the planes of his face harsher and better defined, but it was the new confidence in his voice that amazed her. He seemed so self-assured.

She said so and he smiled shyly. 'Perhaps success has gone to my head, or perhaps it suddenly came to me how fallible we all are. I spent all those years fretting about such trivial things. I was not prepared for the enormity of death when I saw it. You know that I watched Salisbury die; all his great achievement, his wealth, his lands, all dissipated by one swift stroke of Exeter's sword. He bled no worse or better than I would have done, yet once he could reduce me to a shivering wreck with a few well-chosen words. Thomas had the same effect on me. I was always slower of thought and speech. I had to have time to think, to choose my words, and found that by the time I had, the need for them was long past. I was always struggling to keep up, trying so hard to find the right words that I forgot to listen. I have listened more of late and found that few people have anything of real importance to say. For all his marvellous eloquence, Salisbury could not talk himself free. He died with only a simple prayer on his lips.'

He felt her stiffen. 'Jesu, how thoughtless of me. I did not mean to distress you. Salisbury has been our enemy for so long, I forgot that he was not always so to you.' He looked anxiously into her pale face. 'Do you grieve for him very much?'

'No,' she answered him gravely. 'Not in the true sense of the word. I fear I am one of those foolish creatures who grieve for all unfortunates. I grieve for Richard in that sense. I suppose I should have hated him, but I do not think one can ever truly hate where once one has loved.'

'No,' he said, thinking of Eleanor. 'One just ceases to care and becomes indifferent.'

Alianore smiled sadly. 'I suppose life is less painful that way.'

'King Henry once told me that pain and suffering were a

necessity of life. They moulded and shaped us to acceptability in God's eyes.'

'Henry certainly has had his share of both.' Alianore looked gravely at her son. 'What will happen now?'

'I'm not sure. King Henry is still well venerated. It is only in the south that Edward of March and Warwick hold sway. For Edward to hold his advantage he must pursue it. While Henry lives he is nothing more than a usurper.'

'As Henry Bolingbroke was in your grandfather's time.' Alianore sighed. 'So the wheel comes full circle.' She laid a hand against his pale cheek. 'Do you return to York immediately?'

'In the morning. There are rumours that Edward of March gathers an army. We must be prepared.'

'Yes, of course.' She rose and clasped her thin hands together. 'Are you sure that Richard and Ralph are well?'

'And will remain so,' he assured her. She kissed him and blinked back the foolish tears. Another farewell, another season of waiting. It seemed she had spent all her life passing from one to the other.

The vociferous sounds of York rose from the street and pulsed against her ears like a labouring heart. Alianore had forgotten how noisy the city could be, especially with three thousand of the queen's army billetted within the walls. The rest were camped outside on Micklegate Stray, spread like a carpet of gaudy flowers on the white snowy fields. She moved quietly about the long low hall, sprinkling rosemary and thyme in the corners of the room. The decision to remove to York had been made on impulse, and despite the discomfort and overcrowding she had not regretted it. She had been bored with Alnwick, bored with herself and she'd felt a sudden and necessary urge to be with her sons. Even little Harry had failed to exercise his usual charm. She glanced to where he sat, arranging the pieces on the board for their daily game. How ridiculous to call him *little* Harry still, when he was almost as tall as her. He raised his eyes and smiled at her and she thought how that smile had been worth waiting for. It changed his face from the ordinary to the spectacular, lifting his eyes from green to gold. He was almost handsome when he smiled, and he did so quite often now. He rose and came toward her, still painfully thin but not in the dreadful angular way he had once been. His voice was still his greatest charm, soft and liquid as honey. It never rose above a certain pitch, his words always caressed, never bludgeoned. It was incredible to think that next year he would be sixteen. She crushed the last sprig of rosemary and breathed its dry pungent scent. He had only been a child of nine when Hal had died. Had she been without him so long?

Harry laid a long thoughtful finger against her cheek. 'I think you will make a poor adversary today,' he said lightly. 'What are you thinking of?'

'Of your grandfather,' she answered truthfully. One never lied or dissembled with Harry. 'And you. I was thinking you are almost a man now.'

'In years perhaps.' His face took on the brooding look she knew so well. He longed to be with his father, to be part of that monstrous war machine that crawled and seethed outside the walls. It was true enough that there were boys younger than he out there but somehow that part of his education had been neglected. He had not even been sent away on livery service as his father had. He had always seemed so weak and sickly, especially in those early years when the mildest of humours could bring him within an inch of death. They had all been faintly surprised that he had survived at all. Accordingly he had been raised more like a priest than a soldier.

She stroked his thick and heavy hair. 'It'll come, Harry,' she promised him. 'When the time is right. Besides, I have more need of you now.'

He smiled and like a cat blatantly enjoyed the caress. It still gave him pleasure to be touched. Then his mother's sharp voice called from the doorway and he turned his head disinterestedly and viewed her with the same indifference that his father did. He was past being hurt by her now.

Eleanor came excitedly into the room, her eyes blazing with their queer fanatical light. 'A messenger from the queen,' she announced triumphantly. 'We are to dine with the king tonight.'

The *king*. What a mockery the word was for this poor stooped black-gowned figure who shuffled like an old man though he was barely forty years old. It was little Harry's involuntary exclamation of disappointment that brought it home and Alianore's eyes dwelt sadly on Henry's halting progress. She supposed that pity and compassion were hardly fitting sentiments toward a king.

The queen swept ahead in borrowed jewels, the little Prince of Wales strutting arrogantly by her side. The penury of the Court was reflected in the skimpy repast and Alianore picked idly at dry and stringy pheasant and noticed that there was a skin of mould upon the cheese. The wine too was sour and vinegary. She sighed but not with discontent. She was happy just to be near her sons and her eyes dwelt tenderly upon them. Richard was still pale but fully recovered from his wound, less so from Thomas's death. Though Ralph had tried, he could never take Thomas's place. Again she marvelled at Harry's quiet confidence and thought how unkind fate was to have brought it to him so late. He had lost so much. They had all lost so much, especially Eleanor. She seemed to have aged a great deal this last year. The fine lines around her eyes were ingrained with lead paste and two bright spots of cochineal bloomed feverishly upon her cheeks. She was drinking heavily of the thin sour wine and her fingers twined constantly in the chain around her neck. She had lost that serenity and stillness that had once been so unnerving. Now she seemed consumed by some inner fire that only showed itself in the burning heat of her eyes. What new madness had she taken for comfort this time? Alianore wondered and pitied her.

Then young Harry touched her arm. 'Who is the tall man immediately behind the queen?'

'Henry Holland, Duke of Exeter,' she answered. 'And the man in the crimson is Devon.' The chief drones courting the queen bee while the king sat smiling benignly at everybody and nobody.

'And the woman?' said Harry. 'The young woman?'

There was no doubt who he meant. She was incredibly beautiful, a strange ethereal beauty that seemed of another world. Alianore frowned. The face was completely unknown to her till an older woman came to stand by her side. Of course, Jacquetta of Bedford, and this was her daughter Elizabeth. 'Her name is

Elizabeth Woodville,' she said slowly. 'Her father is the tall fair man speaking to your Uncle William.'

'She is very beautiful,' Harry said.

Alianore nodded. Dangerously so. It was the same destructive beauty that another Elizabeth had had. Then she smiled in greeting at her nephew Westmorland. He was the only Neville present beside herself and his younger brother John. She thought suddenly of her sister Cecily, York's widow and mother of a king, mother too of young Rutland that Clifford had so brutally slain. She must be all but demented: husband, brother and son taken from her all in a day. Yet Cecily had lost no more than she. Was grief any less because it was spread over years? She looked almost resentfully to the cause of this blood sacrifice: gentle saintly Henry who would have wept if he had crushed a fly beneath his heel. Or was Margaret to blame for fighting like a vixen for the rights of her husband and son? Was the fault indeed York's because the blood of kings had run too strongly in his veins? Her father had said once of his feud with Hal that there was no right or wrong to it. And neither was there here; no right, no wrong, no victory or defeat. She would suffer, Cecily would suffer, the only victor would be death. She roused herself from her morbid thoughts. There was a little scuffle by the door and the queen had risen slowly to her feet. A dark young man, was it Lord Willough-by or Roos?, advanced down the hall, his face grim and pale from the news he carried.

'Your Grace.' He knelt and looked up into the queen's avid face and his voice in the silence was loud. 'Your Grace, the usurper Edward of March has reached Pontefract, an army of some fifty thousand with him.'

The house was deathly quiet, though York still trembled from the tumult of the army's departure. It had begun to snow again, heavy white flakes that froze as soon as they touched the tram-pled ground as if to cleanse it from the stench of war. The angelus bell rang shrilly from St Denys though none would answer its plaintive call. The city lay wrapped in its own fearful silence. The streets were deserted, the merchants' houses shuttered and bar-red against the looters that would surely come whoever had the

358

victory. It was as if death and grief and privation already stalked the night.

Alianore held out idle hands to the roaring fire. All the others in the hall were feverishly and determinedly occupied. Eleanor's little daughter Margaret laid dried fronds of southernwood between the clean linen; the steward's wife scoured a brass pot to a mirror sheen; the dowager Lady Clifford plied both needle and tongue at a furious rate. 'Well, I've no doubt that Warwick and March will get their just desserts this time. My son John says the lords are determined to make an end to it. Three months we've been under arms already and all our manors going to rack and ruin in the meantime, I shouldn't be surprised.' She broke off to reprimand Margaret who now plucked tunelessly at a harp. 'Of course, I don't know how the Yorkists have the gall to venture so far north, and in winter too. They must be desperate for a confrontation to take such a risk.' She smoothed out the square of fine linen on her knees. 'Clifford says they haven't a prayer of victory.'

'Fifty thousand is quite a number of men,' said young Harry from his corner.

Alianore looked up, thankful that at last he had stopped sulking. Not that she blamed him. To have been abandoned with the womenfolk must have hurt his tender pride.

Lady Clifford glared at him balefully and plunged her needle into the linen as if she impaled his heart. 'What have numbers got to do with it? It's right that counts, and we have the right. God is surely with us as he is with Henry the king.'

Harry did not deign to reply to such an illogical argument. He came and sat beside Alianore and stared gloomily at the floor. 'When will we know?' he asked.

'Soon enough, Harry. The queen is keeping herself well in-formed. She has scurriers out even now.' The waiting was just as hard for her. Five hours now since they'd had any news and that had told them little except that the armies had clashed eight or nine miles out of York on the Pontefract road. She clasped his hand. 'Soon, Harry. We'll hear soon.'

Yet nothing had come by nightfall and the house buried itself deeper in silence and snow. That earlier frenzy of activity had exhausted itself and was replaced by strained boredom. Harry played a slow and brooding game of chess with the steward; Margaret slyly tormented her dog; and Lady Clifford muttered to herself between bouts of nasal snoring. Alianore merely enjoyed the peace.

They ate a cheerless meal in near silence. Lady Clifford complained that the fish was cold and underdone; the steward retorted that she was lucky to have it at all. Alianore glared at them both, wondering how they could eat when every mouthful choked her. Tempers became progressively frayed as the night wore on. Lady Clifford screamed at a page for spilling wax on her gown and Margaret whined out of boredom. Alianore waspishly ordered her to her bed and slapped her when she protested. Remorsefully, she crept in to see her before she retired. Only when she surveyed the pale golden head did it occur to her: where on earth was Eleanor?

She found her in the round turret room that looked out over the river. She was crouched on her knees, staring glassily at the single flame that was the room's only light. She remained motionless for a full minute after Alianore spoke to her. Then slowly she turned.

'What are you doing, Eleanor?'

Eleanor smiled. 'Praying.'

'For what?'

Eleanor's eyes widened into that look of childish innocence that looked so out of place on her ageing raddled face. 'For victory,' she said. 'What else?'

Alianore lifted the empty goblet that lay overturned on the floor. The pitcher beside it was almost empty, and she said incredulously, 'You're drunk.'

'And what if I am?' Eleanor threw back aggressively. 'We all take our comfort where we can and if I take mine here, what is it to you?'

'It's everything to me,' Alianore shouted. 'You are my son's wife.'

'So you insist on reminding me from time to time,' Eleanor said. 'But this time I think it's Harry's memory that is at fault. I think it's he who has forgotten.'

'Do you blame him, Eleanor?'

'I neither blame nor excuse him. That would necessitate thinking about him, something I would rather not do.' She drained the last of the wine into the goblet and held it out to Alianore. 'Herein lie all dreams and destinies. No grief or death or disappointment. Liquid happiness, the fountain of youth and beauty.' She drank the contents in a single gulp. 'Thomas taught me that,' she said and smiled. 'He said that Bacchus was the only god worthy of eternal worship.'

Alianore held out her hands as pity overwhelmed disgust. 'Come away, Eleanor,' she said gently. 'You should not be alone.'

'Oh, I am not alone.' Eleanor flung out her hand to the dark corner. 'Elizabeth and Thomas are with me. They've come to gloat. Did you not know that this is Elizabeth's great moment, the fulfilling of Merlin's prophecy? "And there shall come a giant, snow white in colour and he shall beget a people that is radiant." Edward of March is the giant, of the snow white rose, and he shall beget a dynasty that is radiant, as is his emblem the sun in splendour. You see how it fits?' Eleanor smiled triumphantly. 'You all laughed at her, didn't you? You all thought she was mad. But it's true. There is a king of Mortimer blood, of Elizabeth's blood.'

Alianore stared at her in dread. 'And Thomas?' she asked quietly. 'Why has he come?'

Eleanor looked up and smiled wickedly. 'Oh, Thomas. Why, he has come to see Harry die.'

Alianore fled from the room pursued by Eleanor's hysterical laughter, running like a mad thing herself till she was safe behind her own locked door. She's mad, she thought. Crazed by wine or grief or both. She laid her cold hands against her burning cheeks. Fool. Fool. She cursed herself for her own stupidity, for allowing Eleanor to get the better of her like that. It was just what she had wanted. Eleanor had always loved to shock, to try and imitate Elizabeth who had been as far removed from her as the sun from the moon. Now if Elizabeth had said it, she might have believed it. But not Eleanor, not silly, vain, drunken Eleanor.

She went and flung the shutters of the room wide and stood in the icy draught. The city still hung suspended in its petrified silence. Snow moulded the dark roofs and sheathed the church's spire. Walmgate stretched away from her, a carpet of untrodden virgin snow. She shivered uncontrollably and summoned up all the force of her will to lay the curse of Eleanor's words. They were only words, she reminded herself, foolish empty words spoken by a foolish empty woman.

She pulled the tight-fitting cap from her head and unfastened her hair from its braids. She remembered sadly how Thomas had loved to see it loosed. Jesu Mary, who would have thought . . . She stood quite still, forcing down the choking grief. She would not think of Thomas. He was not the one who had need of her now.

She lay down fully clothed upon the bed. Her body was limp with exhaustion but her mind churned inexorably on: Harry, Eleanor, Ralph, Richard, her brother Salisbury's severed head on York gate . . . Her eyes flew wide, then closed again. Poor Richard, poor Eleanor, poor wretched Henry. The pity flowed out of her and encompassed all the world. She wondered who there was to say poor Alianore.

She was the first to hear him, though the flying hooves were muffled and she drifted at last on the edge of sleep. She was instantly awake and listening. A mailed fist hammered urgently on the door and she flew to the window and saw only shadows and the glint of steel below her. She looked back down Walmgate to where the riders had trampled the snow. Was it Harry? To come so furtively and with so few?

At the head of the stairs she waited, transfixed by dread. She heard the steward's shuffling gait and his muttered curse as he fumbled with the bolts. Then Harry's voice came on a rush of freezing air. She let out her breath in a long sigh of relief. He was safe.

Joyfully she embraced him and was chilled by the snow upon his cloak. She drew him into the still warm hall and bade the steward fetch a page to rouse the fire. She looked at him anxiously. He looked so tired and worn and his eyes had their old look of uncertainty.

'They're safe and well,' he answered the unspoken question in her eyes. 'Sleeping like babes, the last I saw of them.' He took her hand and chafed it between his own as if it were she who was cold, not he. 'I cannot stay long. I have orders for Somerset. The queen chivvies us to better deeds tomorrow.'

'Tomorrow?' Alianore's eyes widened. 'Is it not over then?'

Harry looked away. 'It's only just begun,' he said wretchedly. 'We've fought like devils since dawn, in and around Towton. We've killed more men than we did at Wakefield but still they come. They seem undaunted by death or disaster.'

'Harry, you speak as if the battle were already lost.'

He shook his head. 'I'm tired and dispirited, that's all. We'd hoped to see the end of it today, one way or the other.' He looked up at her bleakly. 'The king should be with us,' he said passionately. 'We'd all fight better if we could see the man we were fighting for.' He rose awkwardly to his feet, already ashamed of the mild disloyalty. 'I must go,' he said abruptly. 'Exeter will be waiting.'

Alianore still stared at him mutely, not knowing what to say or how to comfort him. She walked with him to the door and lifted her face for his kiss. She said faintly as it closed behind him, 'God go with you, Harry.'

Then he was gone and her heart kept pace with the soft drumming of hooves till only its slow anguished beat remained, so loud in the awful silence.

The next day dawned fresh and clear and pale sunshine struck a hard and garish brilliance from the snow. The trampled fields were pure and innocent again, a white shining desert merging with a bright uncertain sky. The city remained inert, the houses dwarfed by the spires of church and abbey and above them all the Minster soared heavenward, crowned and pinnacled in ice. Softly the muted tongue of its bell called out. It was Sunday, a week before the Passion of Our Lord.

In the small private chapel at the rear of the house, a priest in Lenten purple intoned the Mass. Alianore knelt cramped and cold and found no comfort in the sterile words. All her prayers had been said, all her supplications made; it had been a long and sleepless night. She lifted her face for the sacrament; the wafer melted swiftly on her tongue. She thought of Eleanor still plunged into oblivion in that dim little room. 'Herein lie all dreams and destinies.' She wanted to smile. If only it were true.

She left the chapel feeling none of the promised uplift and quiet joy. Her eyes pricked from lack of sleep, her lungs ached for a breath of air. It seemed that she had been confined to these four walls for months instead of days.

Quietly she slipped out into the pleasaunce. The snow was crisp and packed hard as ice, a white unbroken swathe veined with the fine blue shadow of skeletal trees. The trident print of a bird's claw led to an apple tree where a blackbird trilled its virile song among the sheathed green buds. She felt some of the tension ease from her. She had forgotten it would soon be spring.

'Would you rather be alone?' Young Harry's voice put the blackbird to shame and Alianore smiled.

'No. Not alone. Just quiet for a while,' she said.

Obediently he walked beside her in silence and it was she who eventually broke it. 'Your father came last night. Just for a short while.'

'I know,' he said. 'I could not sleep either.'

'He seemed very tired, very disheartened. I do not think that yesterday went so well for him.'

Harry was silent for a while. Then he said, 'You once told me that Henry is king as I am Northumberland's son. That it is a right of birth, not a title. How then can Edward of March be king?'

'He cannot in theory, unless he manages to depose Henry first. In practice he has been crowned and annointed, but that doesn't necessarily make him king.' She smiled. 'A man cannot take another wife till he has decently disposed of the first one.'

'But if Edward were the better king?' persisted Harry.

Alianore paused. 'Sometimes I am confused by your reasoning, Harry,' she said. 'Are you perhaps a Yorkist at heart yourself?'

He answered her quite honestly. 'No. I don't think I am anything in particular. I was just looking at the situation logically. I would not keep a dog that bit me merely because it *was* my dog.'

'Well, I suppose if there were any true answer to that then there would be no war,' Alianore said, and thought blissfully, no war, no grief, no agony of waiting always expecting the worst. She held out her hand to him. 'Let us forget the war, Harry.' She laughed suddenly. 'We'll eat the last of the trout today and let tomorrow take care of itself.'

The morning passed, long hours of *ennui* punctuated by petty annoyances. Lady Clifford retired purging to her room and blamed yesterday's uncooked fish. Margaret's little dog fouled the floor and whimpered for the rest of the day from the dark corner where the steward had kicked it. Eleanor deigned at last to appear, wearing what Alianore termed her cloistered look. Her face was scrubbed free of paint and in consequence she looked ten years younger. Her hair was drawn back so tightly beneath her cap that it lifted her brows a full inch. She wore a plain gown with long wide sleeves in which she hid her trembling hands. She spoke to none and sat crouched by the fire, her face a white empty mask. By noon, Alianore heartily wished her back in her chamber.

A fresh fall of snow had shortened the day. By four o'clock it was dark. Alianore lit the candles, then stood, taper poised, listening. It sounded at first like thunder, a dull and distant roaring sound, the merest vibration of the air. Then the ground quite clearly shifted beneath her feet, the candles guttered in their sconces. The sound grew, rolling toward her like a great clamorous wave: an army on the move, an army running, fleeing for its very life.

She ran in blind panic to the door and knocked the steward's fumbling hands from the bolts. The wind rushed in and held her pinned against the wall, then released her to fall limply against Harry's arm. The horrific avalanche bore down on them. Men limped and stumbled by in bloody rags, ghostly disembodied horsemen on foaming steeds rode them blindly down. A boy no more than Harry's age fell weeping against the door. His blood dripped and bloomed on the snow like a scarlet summer flower, his breath bubbled noisily in his pierced lungs. 'All lost. All lost.' He fell weakly into Harry's arms and coughed blood onto his sleeve. 'All lost,' he said again. 'Lancaster is fallen.'

Alianore stood paralysed with shock. An old man was running toward her, his face twisted with pain and horror. There was blood on his cheek, dried to hard black reptilian scales. She stared at him blankly for a moment, then behind her Harry gave a strangled cry. 'Ralph.'

'Ralph?' Her own voice was a foolish echo. Ralph? Could this ancient hag-ridden creature be her brave happy son? She began to weep loudly. It was. Oh, dear God, it was. She clawed dementedly at his sleeve. 'Where is Harry? Where is Richard?'

His eyes gave her a bare second's warning. 'Richard is dead,' he said harshly. 'Harry is wounded. We've laid him in the church for safety. Warwick is not far behind us.'

The words struck only a glancing blow to the iron cage in which she had swiftly enclosed her mind. She followed him blindly, stumbling on trembling limbs, slithering on the blood that soaked her skirts a foot above the hem. Little Harry's hand sought hers in the darkness and she clung to it as if it were all that held her to life. She did not release it even when they stood within the cold portals of the church.

They had laid Harry on the altar, wrapped in a cloak so that she would not see his wounds, yet she saw the scarlet stain that spread from his back and trickled in rivulets down the white embroidered cloth. 'Harry,' she whispered. 'Harry, my son.'

He opened his eyes and she thought how blue and clear they were. He smiled weakly and dragged the thin thread of his voice up through his broken body. 'Stay with me.' He turned his eyes painfully toward his son. 'And Harry. I should like yours to be the last face I see.'

'Harry, Harry,' she soothed herself more than him, 'you'll mend.' She smiled at him bravely but his face was blurred by her tears. 'Worse hurts than this have mended, my son.'

Then he looked past her to the woman framed in the doorway. 'Eleanor,' he cried hoarsely. 'Eleanor.'

His wife stared at him in vague surprise, laid like a blood sacrifice upon the altar. She walked slowly toward him, her loosened hair lifting like a cloak at her back. Her cheeks were becomingly flushed and her eyes burned with a cold blue flame. She looked down on him and her mouth turned in a thin gloating smile.

Harry slid a white bloodless hand from beneath the cloak and grasped her wrist. 'Eleanor.' His voice was so faint that she had to stoop to catch his words. 'Free at last then, my love,' he whispered. 'But before you celebrate, one question. I must know.' His eyes held hers in the only honest moment either had known. 'Harry. Is he my son?'

Her eyes widened with genuine surprise. She had not dreamed that he had doubted it. The ultimate cruelty hovered on her tongue but his eyes and the tall cross at his back forbade it. 'Yes,' she breathed spitefully. 'He is all yours, Harry, every sickly bone of him.' She leant forward so that her mouth almost touched his. 'Thomas would never have sired such a weak and puling thing.'

Harry smiled and a long deep sigh shuddered through him. 'Oh, Eleanor,' he whispered. 'My poor unhappy Eleanor.'

He was still smiling, his eyes resting sadly on her face. 'Harry,' she said sharply and shook him as if he had had the ill grace to fall asleep whilst she still spoke. His head rolled away from her and his unseeing eyes looked blindly at the cross. 'Harry?' Her high womanly scream suddenly filled all of the church.

Alianore knelt on the hard polished tiles that floored the great hall at York. She had been kept thus an hour or more and her flesh had shrunk and frozen within the damp bloody gown. Her legs had long ago ceased to belong to her. Then the paralysis of grief had spread slowly through her. Now all of her body was as numbed as her mind. Beside her Eleanor crouched shivering, her head hanging like a beaten dog. Between them Harry stood, ramrod straight. Even though the guard had struck him twice he still refused to kneel. She turned to look at him as he stared unflinchingly ahead, the last candle in the growing darkness. Ralph was gone, fled north with Somerset and Exeter and the king and queen. She should have let him take Harry as he had wanted to; she should have gone herself, but then she had never dreamed that the nightmare of loss would extend so far. They had not even found Richard's body. He lay nameless and forgotten, a broken bloody corpse among thirty thousand broken bloody corpses. Such an anonymous toll was impossible to conceive. The named dead struck harder, men she had known, who had been part of her life. Clifford, Dacre, her nephew John Neville, two of her beloved sons. She banished the thought and fixed her mind on the tracing of frost etched on the high lattice window. Then the trumpets shrilled and shattered the calm. Every eye, willing or not, went to the man who had entered the room. A giant indeed, he topped the man who flanked him by a clear foot. Then his image blurred and the man beside him swung into sharp painful focus: it was her brother Thomas.

She averted her eyes to the cold floor till the point of an elegant jewelled shoe prodded disdainfully at her skirts. She raised them carefully and slowly, travelling the entire six foot four inches of blue silk to meet the coldly sensual eyes of Edward Plantagenet. They rested briefly on her, a fraction longer on Eleanor, then fixed icily on Harry's mutinous face. 'Well, insolent pup? Do you yelp as well as yap?'

Then to Alianore's shame and grief her brother Thomas stepped forward and struck him. 'Kneel,' he shouted. 'Kneel before your king.'

Harry's eyes were liquid fire as they rested insolently on Edward's face. Quietly and clearly he said, 'I see no king.'

Edward's mouth thinned with anger. He jerked his head to the burly guard. 'Take him,' he said thickly.

'Your Grace,' Alianore laid her hand plaintively on Edward's jewelled shoe. 'For pity's sake, my lord. He is only a boy.'

Edward stared at her stonily. 'So was Rutland, my brother. You did not spare him.'

Alianore dropped her eyes from his cruel face. On his breast white roses bloomed, sprung from the ground of rich blue silk in a sheen of pearls. Elizabeth's own emblem, the badge of all her illustrious house. She thought perhaps she heard the mirthless sound of her laughter, her soft ageless voice, old as time, young as spring. 'Look upon me well, Alianore, for you see yourself forty years hence with all you loved beneath cold barren earth.' Elizabeth indeed had reason to gloat.

1464

There is no fruit within my bower
No flower except for a single rose
All the rest have been devoured.

— Guillaume de Machant

It was the first day of July, 1464. Alianore reckoned it to be nine years since Hal had died, four since Thomas, three since Harry and Richard, less than half a year since Ralph had perished fighting at Hedgely Moor. So the calendar of her life had run, punctuated by death and loss. Like Elizabeth she wore perpetual mourning now for no sooner had she shed it for one than she donned it for another. William had been the latest, the youngest of her sons, dying such a tame and passive death in his bed that she had hardly mourned him. Only George was left, ironically the most timid and sickly of all her great brood. Only George was left. Amazingly, her own empty useless life dragged on. She was sixty-four years old.

She rose stiffly, the damp of the walls impregnated forever in her bones. The thin black gown hung on her like a shroud, its hem frayed from constant pacing. She had one other of rubbed shiny velvet but that was all. There were no gowns or jewels now. Even the treasured betrothal ring had gone to buy food. After all, she could not let poor Eleanor starve. And it had almost come to that many a time, when Warwick's army had stood without the walls, when they had fled in the wake of Margaret's beaten army, after Hedgely Moor, after Hexham.

Poor Eleanor, how she grieved. Not for Harry or her son but at the loss of some inner battle that she had waged these past few years. It was only recently that Alianore had discovered the enemy to be Warwick. She had heard the whole pathetic tale. Who would have thought, looking at Eleanor now, that she could ever have charmed him. Her hair was bundled carelessly into a net, faded and coarse as sun-bleached straw. She was thin and sharp and ferocious as a drawn sword and when her face was not contorted with hatred it was as empty and void as glass. Alianore smiled. They had grown close this past year, out of necessity rather than choice. She was the rock that kept Eleanor anchored to sanity and the younger woman's need of her was reason enough for her to go on. Each other was all they had now.

She went and stood by her and together they watched Alnwick being stripped to the bone. Not that there was much left now. The best had gone long ago to support the hopeless Lancastrian cause. And besides, this was no new thing to Alianore. Three years ago she had watched whilst Warwick and his minions had ravaged and plundered Leconfield: the plate, the books, the rare and precious ornaments, tapestries rolled like cannon and piled on the back of carts, even the priceless Venetian glass from the windows. If he was nothing else, her nephew Warwick was thorough right down to the disposal of her grand-daughter Margaret in marriage and of herself and Eleanor to some obscure convent. Dear William had rescued them from that. Within a month of Towton both she and Eleanor were with the vanquished queen in the north. And then had begun the long and futile struggle to resurrect the king's cause. The queen had run with her begging bowl between France and Scotland in turn. And in turn each had used her to their own advantage. In desperation Margaret had bartered away England's possessions and damned herself further in her supporters' eyes. Carlisle was pledged to the Scots; Calais to sly ruthless Louis of France. And all to no avail. Margaret had lost all credence and was regarded both at home and abroad as a scrounging impecunious relative that courtesy insisted be invited to table but was afterward quickly shown the door. And Henry – well, who could help but contrast that faded witless old man with the glorious scion of York? The waverers had quickly drifted to Edward and those he could not win over with his charm he had bought or bribed. Some were above that, those whose lives were inextricably bound to King Henry or for whom the toll of bitterness and vengeance was too great to be laid aside with fine words and treaties. Her son Ralph had been one, fighting for Henry to a bloody and inevitable end on Hedgely Moor, his last comfort the fact that he had not deserted the king when so many others had. It had been of less comfort to her. Others seemed to survive well enough without honour. Somerset had turned his coat a dozen times, yet Edward was always quick to forgive and forget. Only a few, it seemed, were beyond the pale. They included Alianore and what was left of her family. Warwick's brother Montagu was Earl of Northumberland now.

Sadly she thought of young Harry. A year in the Fleet, two years now in the Tower. What manner of man would he be now? How would that unhappy and sensitive nature have dealt with such long confinement? How would he be twisted and warped? She had not seen him since that day at York and there had never been answers to the few brief letters she had sent. She knew he was alive and while he lived there was hope. She smiled faintly to herself and marvelled at her own spirit. All pride and hope should have been crushed from her long ago, yet amazingly a little spark remained, inviolate, unquenchable, despite the deprivation and humiliation that Warwick had inflicted on her with such inordinate pleasure, for his had been the task of reducing the north. She had starved but she had never been hungry, she had shivered but she had never been cold. Her body might be frail and broken but her mind was still strong as steel.

She moved away from the window. The distant pounding of the great brass guns against Bamburgh came faintly on the air. Bamburgh, the last defiance, the last of the great Lancastrian fortresses to fall, as inevitably it would, as had Alnwick and Dunstanburgh and Warkworth before it. But not so easily, nor whole. This was the last token resistance by men who had nothing more to lose. They would die and the Yorkists would take Bamburgh or what was left of it. The great broken and useless edifice would be their monument and tomb. Such loss, such waste, and all so that one man could be king in place of another. She wondered, without really caring, where poor daft Harry was now. The last she'd heard he had been spirited away to

Harlech whilst Margaret ate humble pie in Paris, trying to wheedle another loan from stingy Louis. Now there was a shining example of vain persistent hope. It would need a miracle for Lancaster to rise from the ashes of that last defeat at Hexham. There vacillating Somerset had lost his head and thirty loyal Lancastrian lords with him. It had been so obviously the end. Only Margaret failed to see it. The thought struck her: were her own hopes so vain? At least now for her there was a light in the darkness. She had Leconfield again and a pension of a meagre fifty marks a year to go with it, both prised from a reluctant Edward by the entreaties of his mother. Alianore had felt a mild cynical surprise that her sister should have exerted herself on her behalf. Cecily was not renowned for her compassion, yet as Dowager Duchess of York and mother of the king she could afford to be generous. Perhaps she even foresaw a time when she herself would be in like need.

She laid their few possessions in the small camphor-wood chest: the darned and patched shifts; the faded threadbare gowns, the length of tawdry veiling that Eleanor prized like a child. It was as a child that she spoke to her now, her voice high and bright and chivvying. 'Come, Eleanor. It will soon be time.'

Eleanor continued to stare from the window. Strangely she was reluctant to leave. Her eyes travelled the green sward of the bailey and were halted by the high curtain wall, then on again over the cluttered sloping roofs to the high crenellation that ringed the town. She remembered when it had been built and as it had imprisoned and suffocated her then, now it caged and held her safe. She had grown used to walls; Holystone, Alnwick, the walls of this grim cold room or others like it. It was the world outside which frightened her. What further loss, what further humiliation awaited her there? She strained her ears to the far sound of the guns, an echo of her own thundering heart. She thought bleakly of Harry and her son. Not that she missed either. It was the loss that she resented so much. They had both been taken from her before she had been ready to yield them up, like her gowns and her furs and her jewels. All lost, swallowed by the greedy multiple mouths of the Yorkist hydra. So the toll mounted, a colossal debit to be laid to the account of the man upon whom she heaped all calumny and blame. *Warwick*. The name was a distorted animal growl in her throat. Her mind went no further, her eyes saw nothing else – that dark arrogant head and in her dreams, the neck cleaved to the yellow of sinew, the white of bone. She heard the steady drip of his blood onto the cold dark earth, and beneath it the worm, the snail. The dream remained unfulfilled, the dreadful curse invoked daily like a Paternoster had failed. The force of her hatred was not yet strong enough to bring the demons to her, and yet some days she could hardly breathe for it. It choked and burned her throat like acid, it misted her eyes with hot unshed tears. But still he lived, still he breathed . . . She felt Alianore's steadying hand upon her shoulder as the door resounded with a brief discourteous knock that did not wait upon their answer. The scarlet livery of the Earl of Warwick filled the room.

The two women smiled at each other for comfort. Together they walked down the narrow stair, two ancient forgotten women. Alianore's steps were painful and laborious, slowed more by memory than by years. She caught a blurred tearful glimpse of a young girl, dark hair streaming, running to meet the tall fair man who rode in at the gate. Oh, Hal, she thought, my dearest, dearest love. Thank God he had been spared the pain of this.

Hand in hand they emerged from the dark cavernous doorway and stood for a moment blinded by sunlight. Eleanor stared bleakly at the ancient litter that was to take them to Leconfield. 'Well,' she said forlornly. 'What now?'

Alianore lifted her softly wrinkled face to the sun and smiled. 'Now, Eleanor. Now we begin again.'

All Futura Books are available at your bookshop or newsagent, or can be ordered from the following address:
Futura Books, Cash Sales Department,
P.O. Box 11, Falmouth, Cornwall TR10 9EN.

Please send cheque or postal order (no currency), and allow 60p for postage and packing for the first book plus 25p for the second book and 15p for each additional book ordered up to a maximum charge of £1.90 in U.K.

B.F.P.O. customers please allow 60p for the first book, 25p for the second book plus 15p per copy for the next 7 books, thereafter 9p per book.

Overseas customers, including Eire, please allow £1.25 for postage and packing for the first book, 75p for the second book and 28p for each subsequent title ordered.